Don't go back in that car, the voice snarled.

*W*hat do you want with a seinji, a shallow playboy, a neurotic inventor, and a Sensitive anyway? You're better off on your own, like it was before you met that cowardly vampire.

I closed my eyes. Like all my mental voices, this one felt like an extension of me. But I didn't have the ability to silence it like I could the others. It had begun quietly near the end of our last mission and grown like a tumor ever since. The only time it voluntarily muted was when Vayl showed.

I scratched at an itch that threaded from wrist to elbow. Hell, maybe I'd still be standing there today, sinking nails into skin, if not for Jack, who let out a series of his rare, throaty woofs. They snapped the hold that voice had woven over me. As I forced my feet to carry me back to the hearse, it suddenly felt like I was attending my own funeral. Because I knew it was time to face the facts. Either I really despised everybody in that car. Or my psyche had picked up a passenger.

Praise for the Jaz Parks series:

"The humor really shines as Rardin's kick-ass heroine guides readers through her insane life."

—*Romantic Times* on *One More Bite*

BITE
MARKS

A JAZ PARKS NOVEL

Jennifer Rardin

www.orbitbooks.net

NEW YORK • LONDON

Orbit
Hachette Book Group
237 Park Avenue, New York, NY 10017
www.HachetteBookGroup.com

First Edition: October 2009

Orbit is an imprint of Hachette Book Group, Inc. The Orbit name and logo are
trademarks of Little, Brown Book Group Limited.

The characters and events in this book are fictitious. Any similarity to real persons,
living or dead, is coincidental and not intended by the author.

Library of Congress Cataloging-in-Publication Data
Rardin, Jennifer.
    Bite marks / Jennifer Rardin. — 1st ed.
        p. cm.
    ISBN 978-0-316-04382-3
    1. Parks, Jaz (Fictitious character)—Fiction. 2. Assassins—Fiction.
    3. Vampires—Fiction. 4. Murder for hire—Fiction.
    I. Title.
    PS3618.A74B57 2009
    813'.6—dc22

                                                              2009015618

                    10 9 8 7 6 5 4 3 2 1

              Printed in the United States of America

This book is for my brothers—I love you all!

Bite Marks

Hear, O Israel: The LORD our God is one LORD:
And thou shalt love the LORD thy God with all thine heart, and
with all thy soul, and with all thy might.
And these words, which I command thee this day, shall be in thine
heart:
And thou shalt teach them diligently unto thy children, and shalt
talk of them when thou sittest in thine house, and when thou
walkest by the way, and when thou liest down, and when thou
risest up.
And thou shalt bind them for a sign upon thine hand, and they
shall be as frontlets between thine eyes.
And thou shalt write them upon the posts of thy house, and on thy
gates.

—Deuteronomy 6:4–9

Chapter One

My ass felt like a slab of dead flesh, too nerveless to even quiver as the butcher slaps it onto his cutting table. Twelve hours of flying from Manila to Sydney with another sixty minutes' hop after that is hell on the hindquarters, even when they've been cushioned by the most expensive seats available.

I stifled the urge to massage my butt cheeks as I descended the stairs of Vayl's chartered jet onto the tarmac of Canberra International Airport, its serviceable hangars and practical block terminal hardly preparing visitors for Australia's capital, which from the air had reminded me of a set from *Shrek III*. Tall white buildings sprouting from masses of evergreens set in a precise plan; fairy-tale perfection from a distance but up close slanting just left of happily ever after.

Shrek was always having issues with his butt, I recalled, wondering if anyone would notice if I paused to rub mine against the stair railing. Nope, bad plan. I hadn't seen Bergman and Cassandra in over two months, and I didn't want my crew's first look at me to remind them we'd begun a shithole of an assignment that, if botched, could severely cripple the U.S. space program, not to mention vital parts of our anatomies. Plus, with Cole as my third greeter, I figured our hey-how-are-yous probably shouldn't start with a lot of ass-grabbing.

I didn't sense that Cole itched to get his hands on me as he stood at the bottom of the stairs. But his ear-to-ear grin, framed by the usual mop of sun-bleached hair, warned me that flexibility might be required. Because Something was Cooking. I eyed my former recruit, trying to get a sense of how bad it might be by the size of the gum wad rolling around his tongue. Then the music began.

"What have you done now?" I asked as my foot hit the fourth step and I realized he'd rented himself a black tuxedo, though he'd traded the bridal shop's shoes for his red high-tops. "And should I be better dressed?"

I frowned at my Jaded Unicorns T-shirt, which showed my fave new band galloping across a meadow wearing fake horns on their foreheads. At least I'd worn black jeans.

Cole's answer drowned in a sudden wail of funereal blues. Which made me double-check the landscape. Nope, not even close to New Orleans. In fact, the airport, surrounded by the brownish green grasses of Australia's autumn, reminded me a lot of the farmlands of Illinois. Except today was May 22, so back in the Midwest everything would be shooting out of the ground, green as a tree frog and bursting into bloom. Here, winter had crept to the country's edge, and I could feel it sinking its claws into my neck along with the chill breeze that swept down the hills into Canberra's valley.

I flipped up the collar of my new leather jacket, the mournful tone of the music reminding me of the bullet wound that had killed my last one. Below me, keeping time to my slow descent, two trumpeters, a trombonist, and a sax-man wearing black suits and matching shades slow-marched from behind a baggage van, belting out a song fit for a head of state. If he'd just been assassinated.

I turned back and whistled. Jack had been cooped up so long I couldn't believe he still stood at the cabin door, sniffing, as if he didn't approve of this sudden change of season. He stared at me, his white face setting off deep brown eyes that looked somewhat mournful as his gray ears twitched as if to ask, *Where did the tropics go?* But we both knew he was really thinking, *You put me on another fat metal bird when you* know *my paws belong on the ground. How* could *you?*

"We're here," I told him.

He nodded (no, I'm not kidding; the dog is, like, one step away from hosting his own talk show) and bounded down the steps, racing toward the plane's landing gear so he could make sure the pilot had settled it firmly into place. Satisfied, he lifted a leg. There. Now the gut-churning ear-popper belonged to him. And if it tried to lift him back into the clouds he'd show it who was boss.

Cassandra laughed. She stood opposite Cole, her hand on the rail as if waiting to help me down. But I wouldn't be touching her if I could help it. I preferred a little mystery in my future, and our psychic had a way of spoiling the fun.

Which wasn't quite fair. The first time she'd touched me, in the Reading Room above her health food store, she'd had a vision that saved my brother's life. It was just, you know, now that the two of them were an item, I didn't want her next conversation with Dave to include the words, "Oh, honey, your twin sister is such a freak in the bedroom! You'll never guess what I picked up on her today!"

As our eyes met, she gave me her regal smile and flipped her heavy black braids over her shoulder, revealing a tangerine stole, which she'd thrown over a navy blue turtleneck and white, rhinestone-studded jeans. An enormous bag made from the same orange furball as her wrap hung over one elbow, its mysterious bulges suggesting that it had been a marsupial on its home planet before space commandos had trapped it, shaved it, and shipped the clippings to her favorite retail outlet. Only the former oracle of a North African god could've pulled off that ensemble.

I jerked my head toward the band and raised my eyebrows.

"It wasn't me," she mouthed, her six pairs of earrings waving a double negative as she shook her head and rolled her eyes toward Bergman.

I felt a rush of affection as I glanced at my old roomie and current sci-guy. In some ways he hadn't changed at all since college. He stood at her shoulder, hands stuffed deep in his pockets, looking so worried about the rip in the knee of his jeans you'd have thought he'd just been mugged and was trying to decide if his insurance would cover the replacement cost. His beige sweater hung limply from shoulders that were bowed under the weight of an army-green backpack. Its bulk helped provide balance for his head, which seemed extra large today, maybe because he wore a brown ball cap fronting the Atlanta Braves logo. His lack of glasses encouraged the look too. I'd forgotten that he'd had Lasik surgery and didn't need them anymore.

Genius that he was, Bergman caught my gaze, flipped his own to Cassandra, and figured out in milliseconds what I was thinking. "Oh no!" he yelled over the dirge. "It was all *his* idea!" He pointed a bony finger in Cole's direction.

Before I could snap his head off, Cole clasped his hands over his heart and sank to one knee. "We are all so sorry for your loss!" he cried. He threw a dramatic gesture toward the hold of the plane, where six frowning pallbearers were taking a casket from the hands of the jet's flight crew. But it wasn't just any old deathbox. Some company with a sense of style but zero restraint had built this sucker to resemble a golf bag. An umbrella, a black towel, and even a couple of irons had been tacked to the side, while the heads of the rest of the clubs jutted from the coffin's end.

I glared down at Cole, so pissed I wouldn't have been surprised if smoke had poofed from my nostrils.

Control your temper, Jaz, I told myself. *You know what happens when you lose it.*

I'd love to see you lose it. I frowned as I pushed the unwelcome voice to the back of my brain and said, "Cole, you *shouldn't* have."

He rose to his feet and dusted off his pants. The moment I reached his side he snaked an arm around my shoulders. "We all know how difficult this must be for you." He put a hand to his chest. "As your *former* boyfriend—"

"We were never—!"

"—I realized it was on me to make sure your *dead* boyfriend arrived in Australia in the style to which he has—uh, had—become accustomed."

Cole pulled me toward the casket with Bergman, Cassandra, and the sad-band following as he crooked his finger at the hearse I'd asked him to order. Except I hadn't told him to request a white Mercedes stretch with enough room for an NBA player and all his devastated relatives.

It pulled up beside us, its driver stepping out and promptly disappearing. At first I thought he'd fallen. Jack, also interested in his welfare, raced over to check him out. When the dog didn't immediately surface, I leaned over to get a better view. Then I grabbed Cole's arm and squeezed.

"If that's a gnome whose crotch Jack is nosing, I'm going to tie your hair in a bun and sell you to the pirates who operate off this coast. I hear they're always looking for fresh young girlfriends."

Our boss, Pete, wanted to brief us personally on the details of this assignment, but we both already knew it involved gnomes attacking the Canberra Deep Space Complex, one of NASA's three eyes to the cosmos. Not every gnome wanted to stomp Canberra's eye to jelly. Just the Ufranites, a fanatical sect that'd transformed half their farmers to soldiers in less than a decade.

Cole sighed. "Would you chill? I know Ruvin's got the long forehead and chin of a gnome, but look at him! He's over three and a half feet tall, there's no tail in sight, and if his nose was blue you'd have seen it from inside the plane. He's a seinji."

Okay, seinji I could deal with. They were distant relatives of gnomes. But nearly all of them had, like Vayl, found a way to live among humans. To blend. "Still—"

He leaned his chin on my shoulder. "I checked him out. He's fine. Plus—and this is the part that's going to make you add at least twenty bucks to my Christmas gift—Ruvin's an independent contractor."

"He doesn't work for the funeral home full-time?"

"Nope. Only when they have to double or triple up. Or when guys like me request him"—he paused for dramatic effect— "because his next pickup is the Odeam Digital Security team."

"Really?" So Cole knew what Pete had told me and Vayl. That our target worked for the most trusted software security company in America.

He nodded. "I planted one of Bergman's new bugs on Ruvin. If we're lucky we'll know our target's name before the Odeam team has left the airport." He beamed at me. Like I was supposed to forgive him for conning Vayl into traveling to Australia via golf bag.

I narrowed my eyes at him. "You do understand the whole team is suspect, right? We may have to take them all out before this is over."

Cole swallowed. Nodded.

I checked my watch. Three thirty p.m. We might just have time. If we *hurried*.

"Let's get him loaded," I said.

Cole squeezed my shoulder. "But then you'll miss the best part."

I wrapped my arm around his waist so I could jerk him close enough to whisper in his ear, "You're about to lose *your* best part."

"Hey, this event is costing somebody a lot of money. You might as well enjoy it." He grinned down at me, his bright blue eyes daring me to loosen up and have some fun.

"This is not necessary."

Cole popped a huge green bubble in my face. "Picking up a casket-rider and the woman you're about to fall out of love with is boring. Arranging a funeral procession with a displaced band from the French Quarter and a quartet of professional mourners is one for the diary. You do keep a diary, don't you, Jaz?"

"No! And don't call me that. I'm here as Lucille Robinson, remember?"

Cole frowned. "But if you're Lucille, who am I?"

"Hell if I know. As I recall, your last text said you didn't like the name they'd picked for you and had demanded a new one."

"Damn straight! The CIA has no imagination, you know."

I'd have told him to pipe down, but between the band's latest number and the wails of the four women who'd emerged from the backseat of the hearse to drape themselves and a blanket of flowers over the casket's tee-time accessories, I could barely hear his whispers.

"Sure," I agreed, mainly because I thought I'd seen the coffin wobble. Had one of the pallbearers stumbled, or . . . I checked my watch again. Holy crap, we were cutting this close!

"Do you want to know my new name?" Cole asked as we led Cassandra and Bergman toward the country club casket. Would Tiger Woods be caught dead in one of those? I thought not.

I sighed and said, "Since we're going to be working together for the next few days, a clue to your fake ID might help."

"Thor Longfellow."

I stopped and stared, not even turning when I heard Cassandra stumble to a halt behind me. "No."

His hair bounced cheerfully as he nodded. I asked, "How did you get away with that?"

He shrugged. "The girl who assigns identities really likes Thai food, and I know this place on the East Side—"

"Say no more." I should've guessed he'd charmed that ridiculous cover out of a woman. I got moving again, picking up the pace when I realized the pallbearers had begun to look at the coffin, and each other, curiously.

"Oh, please, could you just put him in the car now?" I asked, attempting to make my voice quiver. Instead I sounded like I'd tried to squeeze myself into my old training bra. At least it got Jack's attention. He trotted over to inspect me for injuries, which gave me a chance to grab his leash.

Ruvin, duded up in a white uniform to match the hearse, with green buttons that complemented its future load, opened the back door. The pallbearers had just begun to slide the casket in when the ruby-luscious ring on my left hand shot a stream of warmth up my arm.

Oh, shit, he's awake!

Most vampires would've slept through the whole transfer. But Vayl had powers, baby, and one of those was the ability to draw in another vamp's *cantrantia*, his or her essential skill, and make it his own. Which meant the one time he'd been forced to stay awake through the entire day, he hadn't just slept it off at the next sunrise. He'd seen the dawn and another two hours of light before going down. Same deal, only reversed, that evening. And every day since. Nice for him—and me—until now.

I handed Jack off to Cassandra, flung my arms into the air, and began to wail, "I can't stand it! This is the worst thing that's ever happened to me! Life will never be the same again! He was so young! We never even had kids!" On and on I ranted, barely pausing to breathe between screeches.

"Oh, you're good!" Cole scrubbed at his day-old stubble to hide his smile, which quickly transformed into a jaw-dropper when a fist punched through the golf bag's lid. Luckily only the two of us noticed. The rest were distracted by the youngest mourner, who'd ripped her dress, maybe thinking she had to one-up me if she wanted a decent tip.

"Oh, God, why did this happen to me!" I flung myself across the hand, which began to work its way up my ribs like they were a ladder to the Promised Land. But I could feel Vayl's mood through Cirilai, the ring that bound us closer than a promise, and fun was the last thing on his mind. I sent him soothing thoughts, yanked a handful of roses from the bouquet decorating the lid, and shoved them into his fist.

The mourners, inspired by their colleague's wardrobe malfunction and my overacting, kicked it into high gear. Their screams bounced off the hearse and sank into the coffin, sending Vayl into a frenzy. Despite the tradition followed by most of his kind, he'd never spent his days in the spelunker's paradise he presently inhabited. Only Pete's promise of a hefty bonus and the help of a sedative known to work on vampires had convinced him to travel this way at all.

His other hand crashed through the lid, wrapped around my jacket, and forced me down, holding me so tight that I rode the casket into the hearse as Cole, Bergman, and Cassandra helped the pallbearers shove it the rest of the way home. Somebody slammed the door shut and, since the back of the car had no windows, I began to open the latches.

"I'm getting you out!" I called. I popped the last closure and Vayl shoved back the lid, rolling me into the narrow space between the coffin and the hearse's inner wall, raining roses on me like I was a parade float. Now it was my turn to grit my teeth and wriggle.

"I'm stuck!" I yelled.

The lid slammed and Vayl, moving so fast all my eyes caught was a blur of black leather and bloodred cashmere, grabbed my arms and pulled me into the backseat. We landed on our sides, tangled like teenagers, our mouths so close I could feel the steam of his heavy breaths washing over my cheeks.

I pulled my head back, inspecting him for damage. His short, dark curls practically stood on end. His winged eyebrows looked like they wanted to fly off his forehead, but his eyes, the orange of a tiger lily, were already fading to brown. "That was . . . unpleasant," he said, his expression still taut enough to show the bulge of his fangs under his upper lip.

"But this is nice," I said as I slipped my hand inside his coat. I made my next move quick, because company was coming and the CIA frowns on fraternization. Not that my crew would've gossiped about me grabbing my boss's rear. They knew how to keep their mouths shut. So did we, for that matter. But people who risk death with you on a regular basis just seem to figure things out. And if the Oversight Committee questioned them I didn't want them to have to lie any more than necessary.

"Jasmine!" Vayl's breath caught. "You pick the worst moments!" Which was true, because people had begun to pile into the hearse. I could hear the delight in his voice though. Damn near three hundred years old and he still loved to be groped.

"I think my necklace is tangled in your sweater," I said. Since the line my shark's tooth, shells, and beads were strung on had been tested to six hundred pounds, one guess which would give first.

"I do not care what is wound where as long as I am rid of that box."

"That bag was lined with real silk!" Cole announced as he bounced into the seat beside Ruvin.

I covered Vayl's mouth before he could reply, because absolutely nothing he said could've helped. I gasped when he licked my palm. "What're you doing?"

"Your hand is bleeding," he whispered.

Oh, great, the roses. I hadn't even felt their thorns dig in when I'd ripped them out of the bunch. But now that I knew, my wounds began to throb, along with a vein in my temple as Bergman and Cassandra got comfy in the seat opposite us. Jack, bummed to be stuck in yet another enclosed space, hopped up on the seat beside us and stuck his nose against the window.

"Somebody needs to pay the mourners," Bergman said to Vayl. "They say they won't cry another tear until—"

"What mourners?" he growled.

I dropped my fist to his chest, thought better of patting it. Hell, his sweater no doubt cost more than my entire wardrobe. "It's a long story. One you probably shouldn't hear until you've had some nourishment and Cole's a couple of miles away. Hang on."

I freed my necklace and, taking Jack with me, slipped out the door, making sure the light didn't hit Vayl's position. Though he'd applied Bergman's skin lotion and brought his fedora and sunglasses, the UV still hurt when it struck him. It just didn't make him burst into flame anymore.

Pulling a wad of bills from an inner pocket of my jacket, I headed toward the oldest, and loudest, mourner. "How much?" I asked.

She named a number that made me bite my tongue. I nearly bartered, but realized as a widow wallowing in grief, I probably wouldn't have the emotional stability to go there. Which made me wonder how many bereaved families got screwed the world over.

I gave her the dough and passed an even larger amount to the band. They, at least, made a pretty noise for their pay. I headed back to the hearse.

Stop.

Like competitors in a game of Simon Says, my feet obeyed. That the order came from a voice inside my head shouldn't have been disturbing. I talk to myself all the time, and my imaginary people come in all shapes and sizes. Except this one had risen recently, without welcome or permission, or a face to make it familiar.

Don't go back in that car, it snarled. *What do you want with a seinji, a shallow playboy, a neurotic inventor, and a See-it-all anyway? You're better off on your own, like it was before you met that cowardly vampire.*

I closed my eyes. Like all my mental voices, this one felt like an extension of me. But I didn't have the ability to silence it like I could the others. It had begun quietly near the end of our last mission and grown like a tumor ever since. The only time it voluntarily muted was when Vayl showed.

I scratched at an itch that threaded from wrist to elbow. Hell, maybe I'd still be standing there today, sinking nails into skin, if not for Jack, who let out a series of his rare, throaty woofs. They snapped the hold that voice had woven over me. As I forced my feet to carry me back to the hearse, it suddenly felt like I was attending my own funeral. Because I knew it was time to face the facts. Either I really despised everybody in that car. Or my psyche had picked up a passenger.

Chapter Two

If Vayl and I were asked to teach a class, and I'm kinda surprised it hasn't happened already, we'd probably begin by saying, "Welcome to Assassination for Beginners, boys and girls. You in the back! Put that knife away! We don't kill anybody until the final! Geez!"

"Anyway, one of the reasons we've never yet failed a mission is because we're terrific liars. We're not talking mundane, slip-a-speeding-ticket fibs. No. We mean world-class shit. For instance, if you can't make your targets believe you're smitten to the point where you'd like to birth two or three evil spawn with them, you might as well go back to Analysis."

I'd lied to all kinds of lowlifes in my time with the Agency. It sucked that, once again, I was using that finely honed ability against my own people. Still, I made sure Lucille Robinson's smile was pasted to my face when I got back into the hearse. Because my crew had to think I wanted them close. And Vayl could never know he'd hooked up with another head case. After his ordeal with Liliana he could have sworn off relationships for good. And the fact that he'd never married again showed how deeply she'd wounded him. I didn't want to be the one to reopen those scars.

But our team's like a tight family. Hard to fool, especially when you're trying. So when Bergman sat forward, slipped off his backpack, and gave me his you're-about-to-be-a-happy-girl look, I could've kissed him.

"What've you got in there?" I asked, so glad for the distraction I didn't care if it was a bomb and he was about to teach me which wire I should cut if the Daring Defusers got stuck in traffic.

He looked over his shoulder. "Thor?" he said, barely managing not to snicker. "We need a little privacy here."

"No problem." Cole raised the limo's mirrored window between himself, Ruvin, and us. I spared a thought for the mourners we'd abandoned, but apparently they'd carpooled with the pallbearers since they all had another gig in an hour. For their sakes, I hoped the guy in the coffin was fully dead this time.

When Bergman felt we were secure he said, "I promised you an extra-special invention."

I sucked in my breath. "Already?"

He nodded. "I've been working on it for a while. I *was* going to sell it. But . . . well, that client doesn't deserve it nearly as much as you."

I didn't have to fake the Christmas-morning anticipation on my face when he put the bag on the floor between us. Jack gave it a sniff, pronounced it inedible, and stuck his nose back on the window.

I glanced at Vayl. "Go on; open it," he said. "It is bound to amaze us." Under his breath he added, "And perhaps it will take my mind off the humiliation of having to crawl inside a golf bag at two thirty this morning."

I reached out to touch him, but a major itch on my thigh detoured my hand. I said, "I'm sorry. I had no idea that's what the company sent. I won't leave the arrangements to Cole again." Now the other thigh itched. What the hell?

"Did you forget to wash your blue jeans before you put them on today?" asked Cassandra as she ran her hand down Jack's furry gray back.

"No."

And why do you give a fuck, Miss High-and-Mighty with your name-brand outfits and effortless elegance? All you have to do is lift your little finger and you have me outclassed.

Without looking I grabbed Vayl's hand and squeezed. His strong fingers, wrapping around mine like a lifeline, pulled me away from the voice in my head, which faded into a slimy gray mist as I smiled at Cassandra, reminding myself firmly that my brother had recently told me she made him feel like a king. "Guess I'm just anxious to see what Bergman's brought me."

She nodded eagerly. "Me too. So open your present already, will you?"

After a moment's hesitation, Vayl released my hand so I could unzip the backpack. Movement inside made me jump back.

"Jaz Parks," Bergman said formally, "meet RAFS."

Out of the bag poked a head with inky black ears set wide apart and two golden eyes whose vertical irises betrayed the inspiration of Bergman's schematic. A soft whir of hidden machinery accompanied its smooth leap onto the floor at my feet.

"It's a cat!" I said. Oops. Jack turned around, his tongue dropping as he spied the new creature sharing his temporary confinement. I swear he smiled as he realized the potential for play that had just appeared. "Don't you dare!" I warned, lunging for his collar. Too late.

He jumped at RAFS, who sprang onto the seat between Bergman and Cassandra.

"This is not a toy, you gigantic slobberbag!" Bergman shouted. He shielded the cat with his body while Jack tried to stick his nose into the crack between our consultant's elbow and knee. It must've been a ticklish spot because, even as I snagged Jack's leash, Bergman began to giggle. Which caused the mechanical cat to feel its shelter had experienced an earthquake of an unsafe magnitude.

It squirted out of Bergman's clutches onto the top of the seat and, from there, jumped onto the casket. When it stared, unblinking, at us I could've sworn I saw—

"Bergman? Did you actually program in cat-snooty?" I asked as I struggled to keep Jack from joining his new buddy on its smooth, wooden perch.

As I glanced from the inventor to his prize I saw him nod happily. "I did. But that was just for fun. The serious attributes will make you wish you had a whole fleet of them."

"What's it do?"

He reached into his back pocket and handed me a container that held fake eyelashes. "Go ahead," he said eagerly. "Put them on."

Cassandra dipped her hand into her bag, did a couple of mixing bowl motions, and came out with a compact. "Here, this should help," she said as she snapped it open and offered me the mirror.

"Thanks." I stuck the lashes onto my own, reassuring myself that I didn't suddenly resemble my dad's sister, Candy, who'd danced her way across the States before the poles got too slick and she decided marrying a rich old coot who could buy her bigger boobs and a cushy retirement home in Orlando might be a better plan.

Vayl asked, "How will the cat help us, Miles?"

"RAFS is a mobile surveillance system with offensive capabilities, in that I gave her claws and teeth. And grenades. But those haven't been sufficiently tested yet, so . . ."

I looked at the kittybot, trying and failing to figure out just how she would launch a minibomb. "You said . . . her?"

Bergman shrugged. "RAFS seems female to me."

I pointed to my lashes. "What are these for?"

Vayl leaned forward, his lips twitching. "They make you look . . . sooty." I could tell he wasn't talking about chimney sweeping. Especially when his eyes dropped first to my neck, then to my chest.

I was glad nobody could hear my heart speed up, although Cassandra's smirk showed she wasn't unaware. Still, I tried to keep the conversation on the right track.

"Are they like our party line?" I asked. We hadn't yet shared out the earpieces and fake moles that would allow us all to talk with each other at a distance of at least two miles, because Bergman had promised an upgrade. Who knew that he'd also bring a cat that somehow connected with me through my blinkers?

Bergman didn't even try to hide the smug. "Somewhat. You should see them at night. Point a light at them and they glow."

I threw up my arms. "Great, now I'm gonna *look* like a freak too!"

"I like freaks," said Vayl. His eyes, shining the emerald green he saved just for me, demanded some sort of response. I wished we were still vacationing on his island so I could show him how much his comment meant to me. Instead I scratched a new itch on my shoulder and turned back to Bergman.

"Come on, spill. What do the eye gadgets do?"

He grinned. "RAFS, you are now under Jasmine Parks's voice command." He whispered, "Tell her to switch to video mode."

I looked at the cat, its smooth shell made less foreign by the jet-black color Bergman had chosen for it. "RAFS, switch to video mode."

A holographic image of Bergman and Cassandra, as seen through the cat's eyes, appeared before mine.

"Is it operating?" asked Bergman.

I nodded. "How does it work?" I asked.

"RAFS beams the message to receivers in the lashes, which project an image just far enough from your eyes for you to get a clear view." I gaped at Bergman. "What?" he asked.

"Dude! You never explain your inventions!" I studied his face. "You didn't send a clone of yourself or something?"

"No!" He chuckled. "Maybe I'm just trying to impress you with my engineering genius."

"I've known you since I was eighteen. You had me the second you rigged our refrigerator to dispense Diet Coke out the water spigot."

His smile widened. "Okay, well, maybe I do have ulterior motives. But those can wait until you've gotten to know RAFS better." He nodded at the cat. "She records audio too. And when you're outfitted with the party line, she can receive that signal. You can also access all of the CIA's databases through her, as well as Cassandra's *Enkyklios*."

"No!" Cassandra's portable library was such a fascinating blend of cinema, history, and magic that I couldn't imagine an alternative.

Our Seer nodded. "We needed another backup, so when Bergman offered RAFS and said she'd belong to you, it seemed like the perfect plan. Especially when he explained that one of her abilities was inspired by the *Enkyklios* to begin with."

"Wait a minute. You're basically handing me the chance to research any *other* I come across, plus enter the new events I experience, all on my own? Without one of you Sisters of the Second Sight looking over my shoulder?"

She nodded. "We're making you an honorary member of the Guild."

"But I'm not psychic."

"Your Spirit Eye qualifies you in most of the Sisters' minds. The rest are willing to welcome you as long as the title remains honorary. That means you won't have any voting privileges."

Why was it nobody wanted to give me a say? The Greek werewolves who'd accepted me as a low-level pack member hadn't forked over any power in their elections either. But to be fair, if I was anybody else, I wouldn't let an assassin influence my policy either.

"Wow." I glanced up at Vayl, wondering what he thought of this new development. *Well, he definitely approves of my boobs.* "Would you pay attention?"

"I am fully aware." He leaned over to whisper, "I have never made love to a Sister of the Second Sight. Find out if they have a catalog, would you? Perhaps you could order something in the way of a bustier and high heels?"

I stared into those bright green eyes and couldn't find a shred of humor. *Son of a bitch! He's serious!*

"Oh, for chrissake." I didn't know if I was pissed at him for totally veering off subject or at myself for the blush that burned my cheeks. I pinned my attention on Bergman, who would never mix business with pleasure. Or pleasure with pleasure, for that matter. "So, besides the information it's toting, how is the cat like the *Enkyklios?*"

Bergman leaned forward, rubbing his hands on his knees with excitement. "Remember the first time Cassandra showed us one of the stories from it? How all the glass balls kept rearranging themselves, changing shape as they searched for the information she wanted?"

How could I forget? That story had played out the personal tragedy that still sometimes woke me up screaming. I cleared my throat. "I remember."

"Considering the tight spaces you might need RAFS to slip into, I thought it would be helpful if she could change shapes the way the *Enkyklios* does. So I asked Cassandra to help me imbue her with some special qualities—"

I held up my hand. "Wait a second. You mean she's a *magical* robot?"

He winced. "It's not like she's going to pull out a wand and start zapping mice into oblivion. But, yeah, she can rearrange her anatomy in . . . Here, let me demonstrate. Call her."

I whistled. Jack wheeled around, put his front paws up on my legs, and shoved his face into mine. "Dude, what have you been eating? No, don't tell me." I reached into my jacket pocket and found a Milk-Bone. "Here. Pretend you're brushing your teeth." As if I needed further evidence that he deserved lapdog privileges, he jumped into the seat beside me, curled into the smallest ball he could manage (mega-beach), and began chomping at his treat.

Bergman waited until Jack was settled before saying, "Obviously RAFS doesn't respond to whistling. She's a *cat*. Try calling her name."

"Come here, RAFS."

"You could be sweeter."

"She's made of metal."

"And other stuff!"

"Look, she came when I called," I said, motioning to the robokitty, who'd climbed onto Vayl's shoulder right next to me.

"Jaz!" Bergman wasn't whining. Quite.

I rolled my eyes at Vayl. *Seriously? I have to make nice with Bergman's walking camera?*

Since we'd been working together long enough to read every nuance of each other's expressions, he got the message instantly. His response? *Yes.*

And I thought the neurotic in him wouldn't piss me off until we'd at least gotten to the rental house.

Vayl's lips rose a couple of millimeters. In anyone else it would've been a grin.

I said, "Fine, I'll pretend she's going to stalk off in a huff if I give her any sass." I leaned back to get a better view, making sure I gave Jack a good petting as I did so he wouldn't feel left out if he noticed me paying attention to another "animal."

The sound her innards made tried to be a purr, though it reminded me more of computer fans than contented cat. Up close, her eyes seemed the most real, even when her pupils expanded and contracted to fine-tune her video feed. I reached out to touch her, poised to pull back in case she swiped at my hand, but she allowed me to run a finger down her front leg. It felt metallic but yielding, reminding me of the alien costumes on a bad Sci Fi Channel movie.

"RAFS doesn't fit you," I murmured. "It's probably an acronym for some impossibly long and hard to pronounce gearhead title."

"Hey!" objected Bergman, but weakly, because it was true.

Ignoring him, I went on. "You need a space-age name. One I wouldn't be surprised to hear if Captain Kirk landed on your planet and found you rubbing up against his leg right before you disintegrated the henchmen he'd brought along just in case. Let's see . . ."

"How about Pluto?" suggested Cassandra.

"You're not naming my best-yet invention after a demoted planet!" Bergman objected.

"I had a great deal to do with the success of your invention!" Cassandra reminded him.

"I never said you didn't!"

"Stop!" I yelled. "You two are giving me flashbacks to when I had to give you time-outs. Show me you've matured so I don't have to call a nanny!" I turned to Vayl. "Tell your kids to behave."

"Need I remind you that these are the good ones?" He reached up and pulled the cat down onto his lap. "What if we call her Astral?"

"That I like. All in favor—I don't care because she's mine." I leaned forward and patted Bergman on the knee. "Thanks, Miles. She's amazing."

"But you haven't seen the best part."

"Oh yeah, the shape-changing thing." I was about to say, "Have at it." But the beach ball beside me had been eyeing Astral and realized he might have a chance to give her a big welcome-to-the-family kiss now that Vayl held her quiet in one place.

Without warning he lobbed himself over my lap and landed on Vayl's, reaching under his own forelegs to lick Astral's smooth back. He yelped when his slobbers melted her, leaving a quarter-inch-thick blob to roll its eyes at Jack as he yanked his tail between his legs, jumped to the floor, and took refuge next to Cassandra.

"Bergman!" snapped Vayl.

At the same time I said, "What the hell?"

And Bergman held out both hands like he'd just introduced us to his favorite new girlfriend. "See?"

The black blob in Vayl's lap wiggled over his thigh onto the seat between us. She slithered up to the headrest before quietly re-forming. The only extra noises she made were a series of clicks when her claws emerged, evidently as part of a test cycle, because they pulled back into her paws shortly afterward.

"That's freaking cool," I breathed. Bergman smiled.

"How is she powered?" asked Vayl.

He shrugged, back to his old share-no-secrets self. "No need to worry about that for another five years anyway," he assured us.

I watched her lick the dog spit off her back. "Where does the waste go that she collects along the way?" I asked.

"I've designed an outlet. The capsule looks a lot like cat poop, so when she needs to release one, there's never a problem. She just goes into the bathroom—"

Vayl raised an eyebrow. "The cat is toilet trained?"

"I thought that would be easiest. So you don't have to deal with litter boxes when you're traveling."

I sat back, eyeing my dog. His eyes were half closed, his tongue drooped in ecstasy under Cassandra's head-scratchings. So watching his new friend turn to goo hadn't traumatized him. I wondered what he'd do if she exploded.

I said, "Bergman, you're a genius."

Chapter Three

B etween the city of Canberra and the Space Complex that uses its name lies a depressed little burg called Wirdilling. We meant to reach it via Tourist Drive 5, which runs in a huge curvy loop past all kinds of camera-clicking stops. While taking photos would've been great for our cover—we didn't. Because it was nearly four thirty in the afternoon, and if we wanted to make Wirdilling before midnight we all needed to preserve our energy on the excellent chance that we might have to shove our feet through the floorboards of the wreck Cole had rented and walk it there.

I guess I shouldn't have been surprised to find myself and Vayl squeezed into a 1980 powder-blue Leyland Mini Clubman with a dog, a robot, two irritated crew members and a bubble-blowing comedian. A shrunken station wagon that might've been made to seat five, but only if they were anorexic starlets, the Clubman was a four-speed brake-eater that tended to wheeze when we hit any grade steeper than two degrees. The rest of the time the engine rattled so loudly we had to shout to be heard. Which meant the car spent the majority of the drive through the tree-dotted hills that rolled down to Murrumbidgee River and up to the Tidbinbilla mountain range either gasping like a badly medicated asthmatic or roaring like a mean drunk.

Normally I'd have babied the poor girl. After all, a car isn't responsible for its renter. But ever since I'd given blood to save the life of a werewolf named Trayton, fires tended to break out when I got pissed. And if I didn't find some outlet for the emotion making the skin around my eyes redden like stove burners, there was a good chance Cole's gum would transform into lava. So I rode the gearshift like a crashing pilot, shoving it from third to fourth and back again way more than I needed to, and shaking the steering wheel when I thought the Wheezer needed an extra push to make it up the next slope.

"Jasmine?" Vayl murmured from the seat next to me, balancing his mug o' packaged vamp-juice out in front of him to prevent spillage. "Are you going to be all right?"

"I'll be fine." I glanced at him, allowing myself a second to appreciate his fedora. No man of this age can pull off the look the way an original can. Under the shadow of its brim his chemically darkened skin resisted the few waning rays of sun the Clubman's tinted windows allowed in. I guess I could give Cole some credit for at least trying to protect Vayl that far. But geez!

For the third time this trip I mentally replayed the scene in the funeral home's plain, gray-walled garage. We'd stepped out of the hearse in the first of four bays, all of which led to a closed black door the size of a home-theater screen. I'd nodded appreciatively at the Jeep Patriot parked next to us. Painted a dark orange, it also glowed with flecks of gold and red to my extra-sensitized eyes.

"Now, that is a machine," I'd said, licking my lips to keep the drool from spilling over.

"Isn't she a beaut?" said Ruvin, running his hand along the side panel like it was a woman's hip. "Sometimes I dream we're walking on the beach together, just her and me. And she's kinda wobbling 'cause she's on her back tires. Then she looks at me. And squeezes my hand. And says, 'Ruvin, only amateurs use the automatic wash.' And I promise never to wipe her with an old rag."

We stared. Even me, and I've been known to dream about my Corvette from time to time. Ruvin pointed to a steel rod welded across the front of the grille. "Look here! Can you guess what this is?"

I said, "If I didn't know better, I'd guess you were planning on busting through some fairly high snowdrifts."

"It's a bull bar," Ruvin told me. "Protects my ute in case I hit a roo."

"Roo? As in the kanga kind?" asked Cole.

"Yeah," I replied. "Ruvin, here, says we don't have to worry while we're driving the Jeep because—"

"Oh no." Cole shook his head while Ruvin clutched at his heart, like maybe I'd just suggested we borrow his kids for a couple of days. "Ruvin's not renting us his wheels. Our ride is parked in the third bay."

"Oh. Okay." Mentally kissing the Jeep goodbye, I grabbed my trunk and weapons bag from the hearse's storage compartment and skirted the Jeep. Where I stood gaping until Bergman bumped into me.

"Is he serious?" Bergman whispered.

"Where are we supposed to put all the extra equipment?" Cassandra asked.

Since Wirdilling was a village of six hundred, we couldn't just melt into the crowd. Especially when we were renting one of the local's houses. So we'd decided to use a cover that always got us eager cooperation. It also required a few more bags.

"Strap them to the top," said Cole. He opened the trunk *(no wonder they call it a boot here, it's about the size of my foot!)* and pulled out some tie-downs. "See? We're prepared."

I didn't realize I'd dropped my stuff and raised my hands to strangle him until Vayl pulled me aside. "Perhaps not in front of our driver?" he suggested.

I turned to Ruvin, who'd helped Vayl bring over the last of the luggage. "So what do you think of all this?" I asked him brightly. My smile was faked, but not my interest. I couldn't wait to hear what kind of bullshit story Cole had fed him.

The little man grinned up at me, the gap between his front teeth so wide I could see what he'd eaten for lunch through it. "Aw, your boy Thor is brilliant, that's all!" he said, his accent almost as thick as his ear hair. "How else're you gonna get Gerard Butler into the country without tipping off the crazies, eh, mate?" He reached out and shook Vayl's hand. "Loved you in *300*. What a performance! You need anything at all, I'm your bloke. Don't just drive the dead around all day, ya know. I've got my hand in lotsa kettles. Here, lemme give you my card."

While Cassandra and I traded Vayl-looks-nothing-like-Gerard eye rolls, Ruvin and my boss were playing tug-of-war with the dog-eared ID. "You can reach my wife, Tabitha, at the same number," Ruvin was saying as he banged his blunt finger against it. "You should call her when you're hiring, mate. She's a genius with hair and makeup. Got her own shop in back of our house. You wouldn't believe what she can do with the old cows who come in there!"

Having been briefed on Ruvin's connections to our target, Vayl dropped his arm to the man's shoulder. "We will put her name at the top of the list. In the meantime, we have a project with which you could be very helpful." He started to talk. But with me opening the hood, slamming it, and doing the same to all the doors as my rage began to build, he decided the deal might be made more smoothly if they moved to the other side of the hearse.

"Hey, Lucille!" called Cole. "I think your dog needs to take a leak!"

Since I'd failed to force any of the doors to fall off, I rounded the front of the car and snatched the keys from his hand on my way to the driver's seat.

"What?" he asked, his eyes showing more white than usual

when he caught my expression. He and Jack exchanged wary glances.

I said, "I'm driving. And I suggest you fasten your seat belt. Otherwise I'll be tempted to roll this puppy just for the joy of seeing your head hit the ceiling."

"Lucille—"

Cassandra pulled Bergman away from his attempt to stuff one last trunk into the back of the Clubman, and strode forward to yank Jack's leash from Cole's hand. "Miles and I will take him outside," she said, giving us both her don't-kill-each-other look.

Cole came over to stand beside me. "Damn, woman, what's gotten your panties in a bunch?"

I waited until they'd cleared the garage. Then I lowered my voice anyway. Nobody, not even my boss, needed to hear what I was about to say. "You fucked with Vayl, you fucked with me, okay, we get it. You're pissed that we're a couple. This is your hilarious way of getting us back. Mission accomplished. But you know what? Nothing's changed. We're still together and you've taken it so far that now you just look like an ass. I tried to be gentle with you, because you're one of the greatest guys I've ever met. But I swear, if you screw with me again I will take you down. Permanently."

I stopped. Ground my teeth together. Because behind my words I could hear another voice. Feeding me lines. *Goddammit, this is worse than I thought!*

Cole shoved his hands in his pockets, his mouth twisted so oddly that it took me a second to realize he was frowning. "You and Vayl ended up with each other and didn't even have the decency to buy me a stupid T-shirt. So I figured you'd at least see the humor—" He stopped. Shot his eyes to mine.

"What?"

He grabbed me by both shoulders. "Who's in there with you?"

Aargh! "I have no idea what you're—"

Cole's eyes hardened, the flint in them so unexpected I forgot what I meant to say. "Don't try to con me, *Lucille*. You may be the DeWALT of Sensitives, but I can smell *other* just like anybody else who's died once already. And there's *two* scents coming from you when I should only be getting that adrenaline punch that lifts me up on my toes every time I get a whiff of you."

Kill him! Now! Before he ruins everything! I'd actually slid my hand into my right pocket, wrapped it around the hilt of the knife my seamstress had cleverly hidden along the length of my thigh, before I realized what I was considering. I shoved my left hand into the opposite pocket and squeezed my fingers around the ring I carried there. It had always brought me comfort before. Now I wanted more.

Matt, talk to me. Tell me what to do!

But my fiancé's voice had never joined the chorus in my head. When he'd died, he'd gone silent for good.

The other voice knew exactly what to say. *Tell him to back off! Your business is none of his! We're doing fine all on our own.* It felt like a fog, settling over my synapses, numbing them into immobility while it ate away at my independence.

I grabbed Cole's wrist. The contact helped me think a little more clearly. I forced the words past a sudden blockage in my throat. "I'm pretty sure I've been possessed. I don't know how it happened. Maybe one of those Scidairan bitches hexed me during that big battle before we killed Samos last week. Don't tell Vayl."

"You can't seriously think you're going to hide this from him?"

I nodded, gritting my teeth at the thought of how mad he'd be if he ever found out. I said, "He wants a strong woman. Not some wimp who can't even keep her own mind clear."

Do I really believe that? Vayl could be such a help in this—pain speared through the back of my right eyeball. Just as quickly it was gone, along with my train of thought.

Cole glanced over his shoulder to make sure Vayl and Ruvin were still talking. They'd opened the passenger door of his Jeep, and Ruvin was sitting in the seat, showing off the interior while they chatted.

Cole murmured, "I don't think you have any idea what he wants from a woman or why he picked you. You're just making stuff up as you go instead of checking the source."

"I don't want to lose him!"

"And you think this is a deal breaker?"

My eye began to throb again. I rubbed at it. "Yes." The ache vanished.

He shook his head and sighed. "How are you going to keep him from figuring it out? I mean, it helped that I'm a Sensitive. But what tipped me off to start with was the fact that you were acting weird."

"Sex."

"Seriously?"

I shrugged. "He can't suspect much if every time we're alone instead of talking I have my way with him." Cole shook his head. "You don't think it'll work?" I asked.

He rolled his eyes. "Vayl might be a vampire, but he's also a guy. Who's about to be deliriously happy. Good God, if you work this right, he won't even be mad if he finds out because of the way you decided to hide it from him."

I nodded. And reached around to scratch my back.

It itched even more after I'd driven a glorified golf cart through the bewildering maze of roundabouts that makes Canberra almost as famous as its massive termite mounds (er, I mean public buildings) full of politicians. By the time we left the city's shrubbery-choked streets and hit the hills, I was rubbing my back against the seat like a bear scratching against her favorite tree. And in Australia, that had to be eucalyptus.

In the distance they joined other species in covering the mountains like lush green hair. Up close, they towered among the rocks, their lower branches practically nonexistent. Which didn't seem to be a problem for the koalas. Or the parrots. Still, what dominated the landscape was the closely grazed succession of hills. You could play golf on those suckers if you didn't mind going vertical.

The Wheezer did.

"Dammit, Cole, couldn't you have at least rented something with an engine?" I barked. "If I lifted the hood on this sucker I'll bet I'd see the skeleton of Tigger, because this car hasn't had any bounce since Reagan was president."

Vayl stared at his mug, decided the contents were finally warm enough, and took a sip. He said, "Perhaps we should move on to a subject that does not make any of us feel the need to kill our sniper."

Bergman snorted. "I guess that means you don't want to discuss your spectacular airport entrance?"

"Why do you do that?" Cassandra demanded. "The subject was closed. Everybody was ready to let it drop. And then you stirred it up again. You're like a drama junkie, you know that?"

Jack stuck his nose in her chin, as if agreeing. Continuing with his I'm-a-Pomeranian fantasy, my dog had chosen, not floorboards, but laps as his preferred method of travel. He lay across all three of them, like a raja who must be kept dirt free in case of spontaneous parades.

Bergman said, "I'm no—" but he couldn't see Cassandra over Cole's mop of hair. His struggle to meet her eyes forced a complete backseat resettlement, not easy when you're sharing a 140-pound load, but everybody finally found new locations for their butts and elbows. After which he said, "I just like closure, that's all."

She said, "Vayl didn't strangle Cole back at the airport. The end."

But it wasn't. Vayl sent a dark look over his shoulder. "Believe me, I was exercising phenomenal restraint."

Through the rearview mirror I could see Cole's fingers, which had been scratching Jack's back, freeze. "Aw, come on, Vayl. How many vamps have slept inside a golf coffin? Your buddies will be so impressed."

Noting that Vayl's knees were nearly at the level of his shoulders, I said, "Not if he can't stand upright anymore after riding in your rental from Dollhouse Accessories, Inc. Did you forget that we might need to jump out of this vehicle and run at some point? The way this muther rides, we're all going to have to do twenty minutes of yoga before we can even think of walking again!"

Astral chose that moment to stand. Since she'd settled on the ledge below the rear window, my view was now completely obscured by stretching kitty, whose accompanying mechanical clicks caught everyone's attention.

"She's just recalibrating," Bergman explained. "She does it every hour or so to make sure her internal compass is still accurate."

"Ow!" Cole grabbed the back of his head. "She kicked me! What are her legs made of, tire irons?"

When no one replied he met my eyes in the mirror.

"Okay," he admitted. "It may be a little tighter in here than I'd anticipated. But think of it as a team-building experience. This way nobody has to fall off a wall and hope the rest of us catch him."

Vayl turned in his seat. "I believe Cassandra was right after all. Perhaps we should talk about the assignment before visions of you thudding to the ground inspire me to make a reservation with Adventures R Us."

Bergman reached up, adjusted his ball cap, and dropped his hands back to his lap, which was when I knew something was up with it. Would he ever reveal its true purpose to us, or was this some kind of test run we weren't supposed to acknowledge?

I tried to pick up any oddities in its design while Cole said, "Pete said he was going to brief us. How's that going to work?"

Bergman looked over his shoulder. "Astral? Please play Pete's briefing."

Astral yawned and a hologram of my supervisor unfolded on

the hood of the Wheezer, startling me so much I pulled my foot off the accelerator. He sat behind his old metal desk, his brown suit nearly hidden behind three teetering piles of files.

Flicking his hand against a black spot-microphone on his lapel he said, "Is it on?" Unintelligible reply from the cameraman. "Jaz, I know you're mad at me for cutting your vacation three weeks short." I snorted. *Yeah, bub, so short I didn't even have time to make arrangements for my dog.*

He ran his hand across his last couple of hairs. Had they turned from blond to white in the past week? I couldn't tell. Uncanny, though, the way he turned his head as if he knew I was sitting behind the wheel. As I eased into the gas he said, "I wanted to make it up to you. So I returned your father's investment in your last mission. He said the senators stiffed him." Which could only mean he'd withheld the information they'd asked him to gather.

Vayl and I traded glances. He said, "I told you Albert was honorable."

Wow. My dad taking the high road? Even if it only pertained to buttoning his lip regarding the inner functionings of our team? And Pete, spending actual money to make us even? Maybe I could count on those two after all.

Pete picked up a sheaf of papers, banged them against the desk, and set them back down. He said, "As you know, the cult I've sent you after believes their god, Ufran, lives on one of the rings of Saturn. And they're furious that NASA is, to quote their Web page, 'invading the sanctity of his celestial home by peeping through his curtains.'"

"Wait," said Cole. "There are curtains hanging from Saturn's rings?"

"It's a metaphor," I said.

Pete, just a recording who didn't expect commentary from the crowd, had moved on. "—Ufranites had convinced Bob Green, a software engineer for Odeam Security, to carry their larvae into the Canberra Deep Space Complex, at which time they were supposed to wreak havoc on the Complex's vital systems. But while Green and his team were waiting for their plane yesterday, the larvae hatched prematurely."

Big silence as we all imagined that scene. Human carriers were a new phenomenon. Traditionally gnomes deposited their larvae in their castoffs. Those who were born tailless, or whose noses never turned blue, were either made to incubate the larvae, or worse, act as midwives during the "birth." But they hadn't yet formed a coalition, or called the cops, so word hadn't gotten around yet that Bob Green's experience was typical. Certain death, lying twitching on the concourse carpet while slimy red worms burst through your blood vessels and out of your skin, leaving you bleeding to death like an Ebola victim.

Bergman cleared his throat. "But we're still after the Odeam team. Which means what? That they had a backup carrier ready, just in case?"

Cole said, "They'd have to, because hatchings are notoriously unpredictable. Which you'd know if you didn't spend all day in the lab."

"I don't . . . okay, I do spend a lot of time inside. But look at the results!" He jerked a thumb toward Astral, who currently looked like she'd swallowed a high-quality flashlight.

"Pay attention," snapped Vayl, slanting his chin toward Pete, who'd paused to take a swig from his coffee cup. Aww. It was one I'd brought back for him from a mission to Nevada. It said KILLER CUPPA JOE on the side and had a picture of a cowboy shooting his six-guns at a snarling monster whose head was shaped like a gigantic coffee bean.

Pete said, "If the Ufranites just wanted to foul up the Complex's software, they could use the Odeam man himself. But our analysts say that isn't enough for them. They want to sever the connections between the satellite dishes and their computer controllers so absolutely that repair costs will force NASA to divert funds from all of their other projects, causing *them* to fail too. This would cause billions of dollars of damage that the American people won't want to pay to repair. In which case, NASA will be forced to close down the complex."

"What about the communication stations in California and Madrid?" asked Bergman.

As if he could read Bergman's mind, Pete said, "We've learned that NASA's other two complexes have been targeted as well. I've sent teams to each site. But yours is particularly important, because somewhere in the area the shaman who plotted this entire fiasco is pulling the strings. The name of his warren is N'Paltick. Find it, figure out how to discredit him, and we believe the Ufranites will abandon this plan for good."

"Discredit? Or destroy?" asked Bergman dryly.

Vayl and I traded glances. "We are not in the business of creating martyrs," he said. "If Jasmine and I find an opportunity to reveal this shaman's true colors to his followers, we will take it."

Pete seemed to look at me again. Kinda freaky. Like the Jesus picture in Granny May's pastor's home. We'd only gone once, to drop off a loaf of banana bread when his wife had died. Those eyes had followed me everywhere. And they hadn't been happy with me. Pete, at least, seemed halfway content. "The Oversight Committee has completely backed off, Jaz. Relax. Do your usual excellent job. You have nothing to worry about from here." He cleared his throat. "And as long as I'm around, you never will."

His image blinked out. I blinked a couple of times too. Wow. Did he have any idea how long I'd been hoping to hear those words?

I felt a smile lift my lips as I rounded another curve. I gave the Wheezer more gas, basking in job-security glow, enjoying the fact that I got to drive on the left side of the road again. *You know what would make this moment perfect? If the Clubman was a Maserati. And*

Vayl and I were alone on his island, rushing toward one of our who-can-get-naked-fastest evenings in his cool, shadowy bedroom, which always smelled like pine and fresh oranges.

Cole snapped me out of my daydream by asking, "Is there any way to kill the larvae while they're still in the carrier? You know, some kind of shot or something?"

I felt the corners of my mouth drop. What kind of friend pulls a chimp move like that and throws poop all over your fantasies? *One who sucks almost as bad as your life,* said that nasty new voice. I sawed at my shoulder as I said, "Doctors haven't found a way to dump the larvae from the bloodstream once they're ingested."

"Ugh! You mean the computer guy ate them?" asked Cassandra. She looked down at Jack. "You wouldn't do that, would you?" He nodded, his expression assuring her his tastes definitely ran to gnome slugs.

Vayl said, "More likely he drank them. The eggs are tiny after all. It is only after they reach the bloodstream that they experience their first metamorphosis."

Bergman said, "So there's no way we could save these guys?" I caught his drift. Anybody who'd made the Odeam team had to be popping the lid off the IQ container. So he kinda connected.

Vayl took off his sunglasses, his icy blue eyes pinning Bergman in place. "Bob Green was carrying the seeds of a space complex's destruction. He died because he cared more about buying an in-ground pool than he did about his country. After a day's delay to regroup, the team is back on track, due to arrive in Wirdilling later this evening. We do not know if Green's replacement will be carrying the larvae, or if an original team member had already agreed to act as backup. Our sources are only certain that another has taken his place, and NASA is deeply worried that he will succeed where his predecessor failed."

Cole spoke up. "Hopefully the bug I planted on Ruvin will clear up the situation for us right away. Maybe we'll be able to take this guy out tonight and spend the next couple of days exploring the bush."

"Why would we want to do that?" asked Bergman.

Cole blew a bubble, and for a second the scent of cinnamon filled the car. As soon as it popped and he'd licked up the mess he said, "Besides my professional goals, I have a couple of private ones, my man. One of those is to pet a kangaroo before I leave Australia. I understand there's lots of Eastern Grays around this area. What do you say? Are you in?"

Bergman looked at him like he'd just made the worst financial investment of his life. "Kangaroos are wild animals. I've heard they claw like girl fighters and kick like jackhammers. You're going to get your skull crushed."

Cole held up a finger. "Or I'm going to pet a kangaroo. How cool would that be?"

Deciding not to waste any more time on the crazy man, Bergman turned back to Vayl. "What happens if we can't stop the carrier?"

Vayl pulled in a breath. "America faces catastrophe, and not just the sort Pete mentioned. Because NASA administrators fear if their communications facilities are crippled, their program could be halted just when they have begun to receive signals from deep space."

Though I'd heard this before, I still couldn't quite believe it. Pete had left it up to Vayl whether or not to share this morsel, so the kids in the back were hearing it for the first time. They received the news with varying reactions.

Cassandra nodded, as if unsurprised by the fact that somebody way the hell out there might want to give us a call.

Cole slammed his hand against the roof of the car. "I *knew* it! I'll bet they have gigantic pear-shaped heads and goggle eyes too!"

Bergman cocked his head sideways in the show-me-proof gesture that had started many of our college debates. He said, "Assuming I believe that last part, which could be all kinds of noise having nothing to do with alien language, I still don't quite buy the gnomes wanting to destroy NASA. That seems like a lot of work to protect Ufran's privacy."

"Maybe they've heard about the alien contact," said Cole, his eyes still shining at the idea. "Maybe they're so freaked they're trying to shut it down before the rest of the world finds out."

Cassandra shook her head. "No matter why they've put this plan in motion, you have to agree they're a proactive bunch."

I nodded. "Luckily, so are we."

Chapter Four

We'd decided to spend the first hour of our wait for the Odeam team stuffing our faces at Wirdilling's one and only eatery. But as I stood beside Vayl at the end of a row of connected gray-faced shops, contemplating what might be the scariest little pub in the southern hemisphere, I told myself I wasn't that hungry. Because apparently somewhere nearby lurked a kickass fishing lake that people liked to visit during the warmer seasons. They didn't always come prepared, so some bright businessman had decided to build a bait shop. And then stick a pub called Crindertab's on the end of it. At least I hoped it hadn't developed the other way.

The bait shop had a CLOSED sign hanging from its faded green door. We weren't so lucky with Crindertab's. Its entry, peeling paint so old it probably contained enough lead to line a bunker, had one small window that allowed enough dim light to emerge to convince us the place was inhabited. I looked over my shoulder, longing to join Jack and Astral in the Wheezer, where they regarded each other warily from opposite ends of the interior.

Vayl opened the door. A tsunami of country music burst out of the opening, reminding me of all the reasons that I hated eating out.

I spun around. "I'll have mine to go. Salad. Italian dressing. Lotsa crackers."

Vayl's hand on my arm stopped me, unaccountably made my ribs itch. "I refuse to endure these tortures alone."

His nod directed my attention to a setup to the left of the door. Which was when I realized the owner of the voice wailing Patsy Cline's "Walkin' After Midnight" sat behind a fold-out table, all but the top of her silver bangs hidden behind a bank of karaoke equipment.

Okay, this is just too weird to miss. But the ash-gray walls covered with framed pictures of old stamps (uniformed man and woman in a background of red, Pink Floydesque flowers about to eat each other, pissed-off Victoria holding her scepter in one hand and a Christmas ornament in the other) didn't increase my appetite as I followed Vayl to a long wooden table in the corner whose top looked like it had been hammered by the boot heels of thousands of drunken cowboys.

I dodged a little girl who was speeding toward the bathroom. Barefoot. A couple of sets of old folks laughed at her progress, and I thought she'd come to eat with them. Until a plump waitress with black roots glaring out of her bleached-blond hair slammed through the kitchen doors and yelled, "Alice! Gitchyer shoes on! Bloody hell, you'll have the health inspectors down my throat in a minute!

"Don't mind my daughter," she told me when she caught me gaping. "She doesn't bite. Much!"

She grinned and moved on, leaving me to scope out the rest of the clientele. Who were even older than Alice's ungrandfolks. Ah, but they loved those wail-and-woof songs. Much foot-tapping and head-bobbing after the microphone changed hands and a man's voice began to sing a George Jones classic. His face hid behind a speaker but his stick-legs, covered by faded jeans and scuffed boots, entertained by pulling a few Elvis moves under the table as he belted, "Son she was hotter than a two dollar pistol, she was the fastest thing around."

Vayl had taken his place at the head of the table. I sat to his left and Cole took the empty chair next to mine. He nodded toward the couples' gams, two-stepping joyously while their upper bodies played hide-and-seek with the electronics. "So, have we just seen the ultimate in performance anxiety?"

I shook my head. "That may be the most bizarre thing I've witnessed all day."

"Do you think they'll let me sing?" asked Cole.

"No!"

Before Cole could protest, Bergman dusted the crumbs off his seat and plonked his butt down opposite me. "Somebody's a collector," he said, nodding to the stamp prints.

"Or a pack rat," Cassandra suggested as she sank down beside him, pointing out a shelf running all the way around the room about twelve inches below the ceiling. It sagged so badly under its load of fake plants, old tins, and cracked china that I was glad I'd chosen a middle-of-the-room chair.

Cole pulled a napkin from the dispenser and wadded his gum up in it. "If you could collect anything, what would it be?" he asked. Raising his hand like he meant for the teacher to pick him next, he twirled it around in the air a few times before pointing it at Bergman.

He answered instantly. "Girls' phone numbers."

Cole grinned. "I might be able to help you there. How about you, Lucille?"

"I don't see the point," I said. "Whatever it was would sit there gathering dust I'd never have time to wipe off."

Alice's mum came to take our orders. Her round, cheery face lifted my spirits instantly. I searched her with the extra sense that had come after my first death. Nope. No powers on her. She was just naturally fun to be around.

"G'day!" she said joyfully in that broad accent so many Americans confused for British. "It's too bloody cold for camping. Tourists?" she guessed.

Vayl gave her his tight-lipped smile. *His* accent was so slight you hardly even noticed it unless he was upset. But as soon as he began talking I could see her trying to place his origin. "We are from Hollywood," he said. "Our company, Shoot-Yeah Productions, is planning to do a film here next summer. Perhaps you have heard of us?"

As she shook her head, her mouth ratcheting open in a suitable show of awe, Cole added, "We specialize in action films starring some of America's hottest new stars. And we're always looking for fresh new faces." His grin told her she might just be the freshest he'd seen yet. He stuck out his hand. "My name's Thor Longfellow."

"Well, isn't that exciting?" she said as she gave it a dainty shake. "I'm Polly Smythe. Are you looking for extras? I can scream like bloody murder. Wanna hear?"

"That won't be necessary," said Cassandra. "Unfortunately our casting director had to stay back in California. He's deathly afraid of wallabies. Oddly enough, he has no problem with crocodiles. But the wallabies make him crazy. Poor thing."

All during Cassandra's comment, delivered in a serious but angelic manner, Cole's face had brightened to Jonathan-apple red as he struggled to hold back his laughter.

"Crazy, huh?" said Polly, frowning at the eccentricities of western Americans.

Cassandra nodded her head gravely. "He saw one at the zoo last year and spent the next week in the hospital. 'Giant hopping rats!' he kept squealing, rather like a Tourette's patient. Only he doesn't have Tourette's, does he?" she asked Cole.

"No," Cole squeaked, shaking his head rapidly as little gasps of overripe giggles escaped his quivering lips.

"Oh. Well, that is too bad." Polly glanced down at the pad in her hand, remembered why she'd come to the table in the first place, and said, "What can I get for you today?"

A diaper for Cole, because he's not going to be able to hold it in much longer.

"You going to be all right there, dude?" I asked him.

He nodded.

"Do you want me to order for you?"

Another nod.

So I did. And after Polly left, Cole buried his face in a pile of napkins and leaned under the table, leaving the rest of us to pretend that our companion made a habit of howling into paper products before every meal.

The food sucked less than the music, though it left me with such a greasy-spoon aftertaste that Vayl suggested a walk might settle my stomach. Leaving a few bills on the table he told our desserting crew, "We will meet you at the rental house."

Within moments we'd left Crindertab's and he'd pulled me around the corner into an empty side street. He pressed me up against the stone wall. "It has been too long," he breathed as his lips grazed my nose, cheeks, chin. His cane began a slow slide up my leg.

I swallowed a burp. My breath tasted like fish and chips. Great. I didn't even know if he liked Murray cod. And I'd run out of mints somewhere between Sydney and Canberra. Also my chest itched like I'd dipped the girls in formaldehyde before strapping on a wool bra for the evening. I hadn't felt less sexy since I'd broken my ankle in ninth grade and watched them pull the cast off to reveal—ugh. I still shudder to remember that moment. Me, sitting on the patient's table hiding my face while Dave (who'd come for moral support) laughed like a wind-up clown and yelled, "Oh my God, it's outta control! Quick, somebody call Gillette!"

I directed my words into Vayl's chest, trying to ignore his roving hands, not to mention that tiger-carved treasure tickling my calf, as I said, "It's been less than twenty-four hours, you nympho." But I missed it like crazy. And I couldn't help comparing that setting to this one.

His island, which office gossip had branded as a working gold mine, was a private paradise in the Philippines with a white-sand beach, a redbrick house fit for a family of ten, and a series of orange groves, which Vayl laughingly said brought him a more preferable income than ore, since at least the fruit grew back. If I closed my eyes I could still feel the warm ocean breeze brushing over my skin and through my hair, following the path of Vayl's kisses.

We'd have been there still if Pete hadn't interrupted our bliss with his urgent, only-you-can-pull-this-off, mission and then dropped the bomb that he'd already sent our regular crew in ahead of us so no way could we refuse to go. The son of a bitch. I might've begun to get mad again, thinking of the danger he could've put my people in. But he had taken major steps to appease me. Plus, Vayl, close and real, made it tough to hold grudges.

I wrapped my arms around his shoulders and held him tight. Because it felt like floating to snuggle with someone who cared that much. And rubbing against his buttons was even better than scratching. He seemed to like it too.

"To the house," he said hoarsely, taking my hand.

"To the car first," I whispered. "I'm not going anywhere without my weapons bag." And once we got there, Jack did such a pathetic you-should-walk-me tail drag that we decided to take him and Astral too.

Night had fallen while we'd eaten. And enough streetlamps had been broken or left bulbless that it was easy for us to move through the shadows without being seen. Because of that, Wirdilling should've felt like a sheltering hand, hiding us from unwelcome eyes. Except its bones were shattered. And maybe its spirit too. Plastic bags and dented beer cans littered the street outside the single row of stores that passed for downtown.

To the left of Crindertab's sat a beauty shop called JoJo's with a sun-bleached picture of Hugh Jackman taped to the front window to encourage guys, as well as gals, to take advantage of their NO APPOINTMENTS NEEDED! policy. The organized client could stop into the library adjacent to JoJo's first to pick up a dust-covered book, or maybe an old issue of *New Idea* magazine from the stack I saw teetering by the front door.

Completing the set of businesses south of the main drag, or Wirdilling Drive as the city father had named it, was a mobile home with bright green siding and a six-foot sign that yelled KIPPINGS GENERAL MERCHANT to ignorant shoppers. Kippings sat just across from our side street, which allowed drivers access to its two white gas pumps. At one end of the building a red box with the word POST painted on it also reminded them where they could drop their letters if their schedules demanded a drive-by. Less stressed individuals could follow another sign inside to the actual post office.

A third marker, standing by the edge of the road like a wary hitchhiker, pointed proudly to the sky as it announced: *Historical Site! Wirdilling's oldest standing structure, the wooden water tower was built in 1811 and used continuously until it was replaced by the new tower in 1939.*

North of Wirdilling Drive, another stretch of storefronts advertised an insurance broker, antique dealer, Fooboo's Bar, and a hardware store. An alley separated this row of businesses from a small doctor's office whose window was so caked with dust it was clear no one had practiced there in years.

East of this stretch of capitalism, separated by several houses that all looked like they'd melted slightly during the hottest days of the previous summer, sat a school so nondescript it could've doubled as a warehouse. Two large signs nailed to the white picket fence that marked its border informed us that kids weren't allowed inside anymore. But the building looked better maintained than the rest of the town put together. Because it had been purchased by Canberra Deep Space Complex and converted into guest housing units. Not that big a deal. I'd seen churches at home done the same way. And yet I'd never witnessed anything as sad as a school that couldn't hold its kids anymore.

"Shouldn't we stop?" I asked, looking over my shoulder as the school disappeared behind a row of evergreens. NASA had informed us that they'd offered the Odeam team the chance to bunk at the school, and they'd jumped at it.

"Not until the entire crew is with us. And right now I am trying to beat them back to the house."

I felt a giggle spill out of my lips. "Vayl? Are you suggesting a quickie before the kids get home?"

The look he slanted me held just enough heat to make my boobs stop itching. "If I promised you satisfaction, would you be willing?"

I sighed, feeling my smile stretch toward my ears. "I have a feeling the answer to that one's always going to be a yes."

After that nothing could depress me. Not the tennis courts with their cracked surfaces and rotted nets. Not even the gray pole barn that sat next to them, a rectangular extension sticking out of its side like a malignant tumor. The sign on its door read WIRDILLING HALL, but it reminded me more of an illegal drug dump than a meeting place for clubs and social events. Especially since someone had used roofing paper to repair the spots where storms had torn off parts of the siding. It seemed appropriate for Jack to pause there to pee on an electric pole.

"I wish we were back on your island," I whispered as we continued into a residential area. "This place blows."

"I feel the same. But perhaps you will change your mind about Wirdilling once we have"—Vayl paused, gave me his spine-tingling smile—"*familiarized* ourselves with it."

"How is it that you can say a totally innocent word and seem to talk dirty?"

He shrugged. "I suppose it is one of the talents I learned living in the eighteenth century." He slid his hand around my back, leaving a trail of awareness that made me feel like I'd just stepped onto the battlement of an impossibly tall castle. I caught my breath as his palm moved down to my hip. It was actual work to distract myself from his touch when he pointed ahead of us with his free hand and said, "Look, we are approaching the house." He gazed down into my eyes, his own a sparkling green I began to lose myself in. "Shall we make a good memory out of a bad circumstance?"

I couldn't have spoken a clear word if I'd tried. So I just nodded and let him lead me past an open metal gate down a driveway that was more grass than gravel. The home, whose owner had happily vacated for five hundred bucks a week, hunched behind overgrown bushes that nearly hid its narrow front porch, which was supported by three thin beams. Two floor-to-ceiling windows might've given living room watchers a view if they hadn't been blocked by blinds and shrubbery, but the yard had turned bummer-brown, so I called the loss minimal. Bricks of various shades of red tried to provide some architectural interest, but they couldn't hide the fact that it was just a boring old ranch with a roof that needed replacing in a setting that had seen prettier days. Not much jumped into view at night, but I'd seen the Realtor's pictures attached to the rental agreement. They, along with satellite shots, had revealed a help-me-I'm-dying neighborhood on the edge of town with this house at its western tip. A thin stand of acacia surrounded it, and beyond that a series of roo-chomped hills led up to the tree-dotted slopes of Mount Tennent.

No surprise, I guess, that Vayl couldn't make the home's old lock cooperate. He jerked the key back and forth so violently I said, "You're about to snap that, you know."

"The door will not open."

"I noticed."

He jerked the key out, looked over his shoulder as if to see whether or not our crew had caught up to us. And then he kicked the door in.

"Vayl!"

"I will replace it before we leave." He handed me his cane and swept me into his arms, which would've been sooo romantic. Except I was also holding a leash and carrying a bag full of lethal over one shoulder. Plus, I *knew* my feet would make it through the doorway but my head would bang the frame like an oversized dresser. So, uh, I'll admit to some flailing on my part before I finally decided to drop the leash. At which point Jack chased Astral straight into the dining room, Vayl slid us into the house without braining me, and I readjusted my weapons bag. Except I miscalculated my allotted space and ended up hitting him in the jaw. Probably with my sawed off shotgun.

"Shit! I'm sorry! I was just—"

He shook his head. Worked his chin back and forth a couple of times. "It is fine. Just"—he glanced down at me—"do not move. All right?"

"Okay." I searched his face for bruises, thought I saw a line of purple rise, and just as quickly fall. "Good thing you're a quick healer," I said. "I mean, seeing as you're with me now. You probably didn't have to worry about bumps and scrapes with your other girlfriends, huh?"

He kicked the door shut, strode past the living room, turned left down the hall, and took another sharp left into the nearest bedroom. He didn't touch the light switch because we could both see fine in the dark.

"I once took up with a ballerina," he said as he sank onto the fringe-framed bedspread and pulled the bag off my arm. I heard the clunk as it landed in the big wicker basket at our feet that they probably used for dirty laundry. The cane went next. Smaller clink as he leaned it against the dresser that stood right next to the bed.

"Oh. Ballet. That's . . . artistic."

"She was very flexible."

"Ah."

"And incredibly devoted. To dancing. I prefer not to feel like anyone's plaything."

"How do I make you feel?"

He lowered his head, his lips so close to mine that his breath whispered into my mouth. "Like a man."

I wasn't sure how Vayl defined "quickie." But even with an agreed-upon slam-bam in our future, I was practically writhing in anticipation by the time he'd lifted my T-shirt. When his hands hovered over my abdomen instead of continuing their usual magic, I quit debating whether or not to rip his shirt open (damned buttons!) and said, "What is it?"

He rolled off the bed and turned on the light. "Have you eaten anything odd lately?"

"You mean besides that mysterious sea creature that might've been related to the Loch Ness monster in Crindertab's? No. Why?" I dropped my eyes. *Holy shit, I'm covered in bumps!* I jumped off the bed. Pointing to the bedcover I asked, "Have I been bitten by mites and fleas and crap?" As I asked, my midsection began to itch uncontrollably. I jerked my shirt down and scratched until the urge stopped.

Except it didn't disappear. It moved to my thighs. Then my back. Arms. Behind the neck . . .

"Jasmine," Vayl asked grimly, "is the first-aid kit still in your weapons bag?"

Half an hour later, fresh from the shower, covered in calamine and a ratty pink robe I'd found in the master-bedroom closet, I stared glumly at Vayl as he sat on one edge of the living room's plain brown sectional, spinning his cane between his fingers. Too keyed up to join him, I left my spot by the fireplace's narrow mantel and, followed faithfully by Jack, paced around a block of polished walnut that worked as the room's centerpiece and its coffee table. The only lovely item in the house, it threatened to scrape my shins every time I turned the corner. Astral stared at me from its center, having taken her place there as if so offended the homeowners hadn't provided some sort of decoration for it that she'd decided to temporarily volunteer her services.

Why is it that the things I find most beautiful are always the most dangerous?

The table, which would scar an awkward toddler or break an old woman's hip, was the perfect example. All the demons I'd dealt with were gorgeous. And Vayl, who'd benefited from one of God's better moods, only had to look at me with those wide, you-touch-my-soul eyes, and I totally forgot that he craved my blood like a junkie needs meth. Could take it too, whenever he wanted, if he ever decided to veer off the civilized track.

"And you have no idea when this began or why?" he asked.

I shrugged. Now that my whole sex-distraction-plan had caved like an old grave I could confess that I'd been possessed. That the rash had to be related. But he'd bolt, leaving me with a single week of heaven to cling to as I tried to keep my head above the massive whirlpool of sewage that was my life. Unacceptable.

Maybe he won't—

YES, he will!

Whose voice was in my head now? Mine? Or . . . "Maybe it's stress related," I said, rubbing a knuckle against the sudden pain in my eye. Geez, maybe I should see an optometrist when I got back to the States. "That vacation was doing me a lot of good. We don't just work, you know. We work our asses off. Lay our lives out there day after day . . ." Wow, no way could he be buying this bullshit. Could he?

I stared around the room. Two chairs sat at the walnut block's non-couch corners, extras from the dining table made comfy with tie-on red plaid cushions. Behind them, lining the wall like a mini-kitchen, a series of kiddie appliances in bright pink plastic invited the younger set to come in and play. And what a choice. The fridge, stove, sink, and table came complete with fake pots, pans, food and, quite possibly, dirty dishcloths laced with salmonella.

Good grief, brighten up, will you? You're not dead yet! Granny May chided me.

Sure thing. Say, I'll make with the cheery if you step off your porch. Because I've never seen you there before and I have to say it's kinda bugging me.

Silence.

I thought so.

I hunched my shoulders against the intensity of Vayl's gaze. "Say something," I demanded.

His eyes narrowed and did that color transformation that usually made my heart go *ka-wow!* This time it practically stopped. "Jasmine? What is—"

The front door slammed open and Cassandra rushed in, followed closely by Bergman and Cole.

"I'll build the circle!" Cassandra yelled. She pointed a double-edged short sword I hadn't realized she owned at Cole and said, "You secure all the entrances. Bergman!"

"Yeah!"

She yanked the chairs to the wall by the fireplace and shoved the walnut block beside them, leaving a clear spot in the center of the room. "Fill Jaz in so she can see if Astral has any ideas."

As Miles nodded and Cassandra dove for the bedroom, Cole paused long enough to say, "Nice getup, Jaz. What are you, the Ghost of Christmas Alcoholic?"

I looked down at the robe, which, okay, maybe it was a little on the Betty Ford Clinic side. But I couldn't help my lotion-covered legs. Could I?

"What is going on?" Vayl demanded, gripping his cane by the middle like he'd be banging heads with it if he didn't get some quick answers.

Bergman ticked off the facts on shaking fingers. "Jaz has an unexplained rash. You're angry about something. And I can't believe I let Pete convince me not to set up an alarm system." He began to mimic our supervisor—badly. "It's not that kind of mission, Miles. All you need to do is bring your phenomenal brain and a few—"

"Bergman!" Vayl's voice, deep as a roll of thunder, shoved him back on track.

He seesawed his hat until I thought he'd rubbed all the skin off his forehead. Then he said, "Okay. We were just driving away from Crindertab's when Cassandra's demon crossed the street behind us. Cole liked the looks of her and slowed down. That's how we saw. She grabbed one of the old men who'd left at the same time as us. Pulled him right out of his car. I don't know what she said to him, but when he shook his head she"—Bergman blinked really fast and practically twisted his mouth sideways to force back the tears—"she punched her fist up through the bottom of his jaw and ripped out his tongue."

Vayl let his cane ram the floor. "Evil bitch."

Bergman nodded, rubbing his hand across his mouth as if to confirm that all his parts were still there. "Cassandra screamed, and that's when the demon recognized her and tried to grab her. So Cole backed the Wheezer into her. She went flying and we booked."

"Wait," I said, holding up both hands. "You called her *Cassandra's* demon. You mean this is the same one she summoned to kill the scumbag farmer who raped her? The demon she broke the contract with over five hundred years ago and has been ducking ever since?"

We all looked at Cassandra, who'd stepped into the hall to listen. She gulped. Nodded.

And I thought *I* had problems.

CHAPTER FIVE

V ayl, an island of calm among three adults running around like they were about to be hit by an asteroid, asked the most pertinent question I'd heard yet. "Where is the demon now?"

Bergman said, "Hopefully she's still rolling on the road in front of the post office."

"Astral, I want to see that demon. Now." I snagged the kittybot and threw her into the yard.

Huh, she landed on her feet. Nice. Too bad we can't lock this door anymore though. We could be toast before that cat figures out what it's even chasing. Maybe we could block it with, say, a tank?

"You're sending RAFS into that kind of danger? Already?" I hadn't thought it possible, but Bergman had turned a paler shade of glue.

"She's mine now, and it's her job," I told him flatly.

I watched his Adam's apple bob a couple of times and gave him time to nod acceptance before I asked, "How is it possible for Cassandra's demon to be here? She wards herself against it every morning."

"You were supposed to ask Astral that question," Cassandra snapped as she ran back into the living room, trailing an armful of sheets, her sword held awkwardly out to one side. Since I'd spent some time studying demons I knew what she meant to do with the bedding. Jack suspected a game and grabbed a trailing end. Bergman just thought she'd lost it.

"This is no time to protect our deposit!" he shouted. "If blood gets all over the carpet, let it!"

She shook her head. "Start making knots. Rope would be better, but I don't want to waste time looking in the garage for something they probably don't have anyway. We need enough to make a circle around all five of us."

I yanked a knot into a yellow and green striped sheet. Cassandra had already finished one, which my malamute kept picking up and trying to transport into the dining room.

"Jack!" I yelled for the fifth time. "Drop it!"

"I know." Vayl disappeared into the bedroom. I couldn't even glance that way now. Not only did I dread seeing the suspicion settle over his face, but my eye hurt every time it wandered Vaylward.

When he came out he was holding a shoe, unfamiliar enough to have come from the same closet that had given up the boozer robe. "Here, Jack. Chew on this for a while."

Jack willingly switched gears, and I smiled my thanks at Vayl, though I glanced away quickly after. If he really began to suspect I was hiding something I'd have to do something crazy to distract him. And I wasn't sure the world was ready for Jaz's Sock Puppet Theater.

"Cole!" Cassandra yelled. "You'd better be praying over those locks!"

"I am, I am!" he replied. "Reverend Brendeen would be so proud to know something he taught me stuck!"

Vayl grimaced at the mention of prayers.

I asked, "This is going to hurt, isn't it? Being shut inside a blessed house, I mean?"

Vayl nodded so slightly I wouldn't have known he'd moved his head if I wasn't watching for it. "I cannot stay," he said. "Already my skin begins to scorch. I shall do my best to help from outside." He came close, his hands painfully gentle on my arms. "We are not finished," he murmured, his eyes slanting toward the bedroom, coming back to mine full of promises that made my toes curl.

I gave myself a second to catch my breath. But lost it again when he said, "And the next time we speak there will be no more secrets between us." He pulled me close, holding me so tight all the air left my lungs in an unladylike, "Oof." His lips came down on mine almost like an attack, as if he couldn't believe I'd dare do anything other than stand within his arms and accept the heat of his lips and tongue. Just before it began to burn he pulled away.

He snatched his cane from its resting place and slammed out the door, leaving me knuckling my eye, staring after him with the good one like I'd never seen a vampire's back before. Cole came in right after. He kept looking at me while he and Bergman moved the couch in front of the door, while they prayed, while they helped Cassandra and me finish the knots.

"What?" I finally demanded.

"I'm just trying to decide if I prefer your chest covered in goopy pink lotion or if white would work better. What do you think, Bergman? Is hydrocortisone cleavage more the look Paris would go for this season?"

I dropped my sheet and my eyes at the same time. Nope, I wasn't hanging out. Not enough there to do much wandering in the first place. But my girls had managed quite a show all the same.

Dammit, Vayl!

I yanked my robe closed and stomped into the bedroom. Jack assumed I'd elevated the level of entertainment and trotted along beside me, still carrying the shoe, his mouth stretching around its edges in what I'd come to call his let's-party grin.

"Jasmine! The demon could be here any second!" called Cassandra.

"If I'm going to hell, I'm doing it with my underwear on!" I snapped.

Forty-five seconds later we were back. Jack wore a leash. I'd chosen a pair of dark blue jeans, a black long-sleeved shirt, my leather coat, and boots. We stepped inside the loop Cassandra had designed using prints and solids and one sheet covered in cute little koalas. Of course, now all you could see was part of an ear or maybe a fuzzy nostril, because we'd placed our knots about every twelve inches. Cassandra walked around the inside of the ring's edge, murmuring under her breath while Cole and Bergman watched her.

"What's she saying?" asked Bergman.

"It's from Deuteronomy," I told him, wishing I'd brought a double-edged blade like hers. My bolo wasn't going to do me any good for the work that might be ahead of us. Did I have time to call Raoul? Naw, my Spirit Guide labored under some strict rules. Which meant he probably wouldn't be allowed to interfere in a mess like this. Not when Cassandra had willingly entered into the contract with the demon we were arming against to start with.

Not that I blamed her. If I'd been in her shoes, slave to a reeking sleaze like Anastas Ocacio, forced to submit to his perversions, I'd have asked the devil to drag his body over the sharpest rocks on his land too. The fact that she'd been clever enough to find a Haitian holy man to help her protect her soul before the demon could throw it into hell afterward just raised my respect for her.

Bergman's wide eyes said he was impressed with her as well. *He sure didn't know what to say when demons were coming.* "She's quoting the Bible? Which part exactly?"

"Chapter six, verses four through nine. Do you know them?"

"I'm Jewish. What do you think?"

"Good. You might need them later. They're a classic incantation against evil, specifically demonic aggression."

Cole said, "I thought Cassandra worshipped some African god."

"She might. But if your soul was at risk, wouldn't you use every tool you had available to save it?"

"Good point."

"Now listen, we're just trying to banish the thing because we can't kill it while it's on our plane. So, Cole, although I appreciate the sentiment with that Parker-Hale, a sniper rifle is just going to piss her off. If you can find a blade that slices *and* dices within the next fifteen seconds, you may have a chance."

"Shitsuckers!" He slung his rifle over his shoulder. "Bergman! Got anything sharp on both sides in that backpack?"

Bergman stepped away from him. "No."

"Why are you looking so nervous?"

"We're about to get soul-raped! Wouldn't you be?"

Cole lunged at him. "Gimme that pack!"

Bergman dodged to the left, nearly falling out of the circle before regaining his balance and sliding behind the nearest obstacle. Me.

I glanced over my shoulder. "What the hell, Miles?"

"Don't let him have my pack!" Bergman pleaded. "Natchez gave it to me. He said it was lucky. He had it blessed by a priest and everything!"

"Why would Natchez give you his lucky pack?" I asked.

They'd become pretty good buddies during our mission together in Iran. But no way would one of my brother's best men give up an edge, even if it was just a psychological one, unless he had a damn good reason.

"It's part of his down payment."

I felt my eyebrows hit maximum lift. "For what?"

Cole had reached around me to tug at one of the straps, which caused Bergman to keep hitting me in the back as he said, "His share of the business. When he retires next spring he wants to come in as a partner. Which was the main reason I took this mission. I figured if I was letting Natch come on board, I should offer you a partnership too. Plus—ow!"

Another couple of blows to the back and now I could feel a headache coming on. "Cole, would you stop it! He doesn't have a sword!"

"Fine! But if my soul gets eaten I'm haunting you!" He went to Cassandra to see if he could charm her out of her blade, giving me room to turn and face Bergman.

"You want me to be your partner?"

"You and Vayl, if he's interested," he said, readjusting his straps. "My four-leaf clover's inside," he whispered. "Also Myron Shlotsky's rabbit's foot, which he left me in his will."

"Myron's dead?"

"No. He just decided to give away all his worldly goods and join a cult."

"Oh. Well." We'd voted Myron *Most Likely to Marry a Dominatrix* in college, so I couldn't say I was surprised.

Bergman shoved his finger up the bridge of his nose, still in the old habit of adjusting his glasses. He messed with his ball cap to make the gesture look a little less idiotic and said, "Look, I know you probably think I'm a wimp because I said all that stuff about not being scared anymore and really having a life. And I'm trying. But fear is a hard habit to break. It helps to have props."

"Of course. Like actors."

"Exactly. And about the partnership? You don't have to decide right away. Take some time and think about it. I figured, you know, if we survive this whole demon thing, you'd still have to give notice. And then we could talk about how you'd want the business to expand. I'd still be doing research and development, plus some consulting. But you and Vayl and Natchez would obviously be bringing a whole new set of clients to the table."

What a nice way to say we'd be turning mercenary.

I said, "Okay, I'll consider it. And thanks. I'm really honored that you'd trust me and Vayl enough to bring us into your business like this."

Bergman shrugged. "I've learned a lot working with you. The main thing is that life's too short to go solo. And I'm never going to get a girl if I'm working all the time. If I had partners I could take a day off once in a while."

I nodded. "This is true." I put a hand out, grabbing on to his arm to steady myself. Geez, when Astral opened her lines it was like transporting into an IMAX movie. The dizzy spell passed as my eyes adjusted to her video feed.

"I can see the demon," I said. "She's walking past that pole barn, uh, Wirdilling Hall. And my lips are starting to buzz because this is so weird. It's like Cole and Cassandra are standing right beside her."

Cole swung a fist. "Did I get her?"

"Nope. She's about a foot to your right."

Cole started to set up a front kick, but Cassandra pushed him off balance. "Would you stop?" she hissed. "My *soul* is at stake!"

"This is all for you!" he insisted. "I'm practicing up so we can kick ass and take names. But without actually saying her name, right?"

I said, "Not unless we want to summon her here. Which we don't." I let my vision readjust to the hologram. "She's wearing a hat so it's kind of hard to make out her features. There, she's walking under a streetlamp. Aw, shit."

"What?" they all asked at once.

"She threw her hat at the lamp and busted it."

"Of all the things she could've done, you're upset about that?" asked Cole.

"Yeah. Because before the light exploded I saw her face. She's even prettier than the Magistrate."

CHAPTER SIX

People judge hell's hierarchy all kinds of ways. But I've found the most accurate measure to be by the looks of its inhabitants. You beautiful, you bad. Receive a promotion, get a face-lift. The Magistrate had been one luscious demon, temptation in a *Playgirl* wrapper. I hadn't wanted to fight him. That's a good way to get yourself rolled in flour and deep-fried. But my Spirit Guide, Raoul, had helped make sure the battle was less David-and-Goliath than is usual in those cases. I could still remember the Magistrate snapping his whip at me as I tried to bury my admiration for his sleek perfection. All that considered, Cassandra's demon scuzzed him out.

"If you didn't summon her, how'd she get here?" I asked.

She shook her head and shrugged. Demons can't just pop into our world like we run to the bank. As far as I knew, they had to be called. But then, the rules governing their movements were more intricate than the IRS tax code. Maybe this demon had found a loophole.

Cassandra said, "I anointed my eyes as usual this morning. I'm sure I chanted the prayer of protection correctly. I've only been repeating it for over half a millennia."

"But she's here," I murmured, watching the demon stalk around

Wirdilling Hall, trying to catch our scent. "You must have done something different."

"No, nothing."

I barely heard her. Something about the way the hellspawn moved, so fluid she seemed nearly boneless, so confident I wondered why any of us should even bother to resist her, reached through Astral's optics and dug in.

She reminds me of a cougar, I thought as I noted her tawny skin and dark blond braid. She'd dressed to hunt in low-heeled boots, skintight jeans, and a silk top the color of lava that she'd unbuttoned far enough to show the sweat beading between her breasts. The headgear, a brown suede bush hat she'd probably taken off some soul-mangled station owner, completed the look.

Crap. Her head had come up. A sun-bleached old van had pulled into the lot beside Wirdilling Hall's main entrance. I only recognized its driver by his skinny legs and cowboy boots. It was our entertainer from Crindertab's, a tanned old dude with a cigarette dangling from his lips and enough hair left on his head to share with three of his baldest buddies. He didn't see the demon when he went around to the back of the van and began to unload equipment into the hall's add-on. Didn't hear her pull his silver-haired partner from her seat and into the shadows. Didn't even startle when she strode up to him and said in a sex-kitten purr, "I am looking for a dark-skinned woman named Cassandra. Have you seen her?"

He looked the demon up and down, squinted as he blew smoke into her face. "Nope."

She smiled. "I could make your fantasies come true, you know."

"Doubt it."

The smile faltered, evened out again. "Anything you like. Anything you can dream of."

"For a price, right? I ain't got that kinda pay."

"I wasn't talking about money."

"Neither was I." He spit the cigarette at her, and she jumped back, giving him time to reach for his belt. But he was old and unprepared. The knife glinted in Wirdilling Hall's single streetlight, only half out of its scabbard when she lunged. She grabbed him by both shoulders and tossed him like a scarecrow. He hit an electric post on the opposite side of the street, his back breaking around it like an accordion straw.

She dusted off her hands, straightened her clothes, and began sniffing around the hall again. Within two minutes she was moving toward the house. Astral followed, her padded feet silent on the rain-starved ground.

"Jaz?"

I forced my eyes to Cassandra. "What?"

"You're shaking."

I wiped the perspiration off my upper lip. *Shit, I just watched her murder two civilians and I still can't get over how gorgeous she is! How am I gonna function when she's in the same room?*

"Think!" I demanded. "She's got to be here for a reason. What's changed in your life since yesterday?"

Cassandra started to shake her head; then she pulled back, as if the realization had slapped her. "Oh."

"What?"

"David asked me to marry him."

CHAPTER SEVEN

My eardrums started to vibrate, like somebody had just hit a gong right next to my head. I couldn't believe the curtains weren't waving like banners, this was so huge! After Dave had lost his wife, I'd given up hoping he'd ever find somebody he could love as much as her. And now? But wait, maybe . . .

"What did you tell him?" I put both hands behind my back so she wouldn't see the crossed fingers.

Her eyes wavered. "He wanted me to wait. He wanted to be the one to tell you—"

"Cassandra!"

"I said yes."

"Aahhh!" We both screamed at the same time and started dancing around like we weren't about to get our asses thoroughly kicked by high-level evil.

"Um, ladies?" Cole said, tapping me on the shoulder. "Could we act like sorority girls who've just made it into Barbie's Dream House some other time? Cassandra's got a double-bladed sword. Bergman's got a lucky pack. And, Jaz, you've got your Spirit Eye to protect you. All I have is a new piece of bubble gum, a useless rifle, an even more worthless handgun, and your word that these knotted sheets are going to keep me from falling straight into hell."

"It's less a fall than a sidestep. But he has a point," I told my future sister-in-law.

"Yes, he does," she agreed. We hugged. Twice.

"Okay," I said. "Have you been engaged or married anytime since you made the deal?"

"No." Cassandra winced. "I never remarried after Harith died. There were . . . other men. Some of them I stayed with their entire lives. But . . . no. That step always seemed like it would be a lie, somehow."

"That must be it, then. Something in the fine print of your contract gives her leeway in case you pull a fast one and escape like you did. So the second you enter into a relationship bound by a holy promise, she's got you."

Which sucked. Because I knew exactly how Cassandra felt. I'd never dreamed I could find anyone who'd bring out the domestic in me the way Matt had. Never wanted anyone to try. Then Vayl had snuck past my defenses, and now practically all I could think about was the next time I could see him, touch him. If he asked . . . what would I say? Could we even do marriage, considering the fact that stepping inside a church would set him *and* his tuxedo on fire?

He's no good for you, said that voice. I put my hand to my throat, like I could choke it into silence. The laughter behind its next words proved how useless the gesture was. *You know I'm right. All he wants is to drain you and leave you dangling from the edge of the bed like some neglected old rag doll.*

Keep talking, I whispered inside my own mind. *You're beginning to sound familiar. Not like the echo of my own thoughts after all. More like—*

The front door shuddered. Astral's feed showed me why. The demon had thrown her hat up into the air, giving it time to transform into a razor-edged boomerang before it fell back into her hand and she flung it, hard, at the entrance.

How does she not cut her fingers off?

Granny May, still rocking on her front porch, snapped, *You're wondering about a demon's digits when her weapon's on fire? Girl, you should be thanking your lucky stars those prayers are strong enough to keep her from burning the house down.*

In fact, the flames that had given the boomerang an eerie bluish orange glow had extinguished the second it had hit the door. Unfortunately, the prayers Cole had shielded it with would only work for so long against a siege, and this bimbo clearly had nowhere else to be. She winged that weapon of hers fifteen or twenty times. Each time she knocked a bigger hole in our defenses.

"She's going to get in," I warned my crew.

"But we have the circle," said Cassandra.

"And Vayl," Bergman reminded me.

"Yeah, we do." But the demon had a contract. And I was terrified that nothing we did could prevent her from taking Cassandra's soul tonight. Even if it meant we lost our own in the fight.

Faces began to dance before my eyes. My old crew, laughing it up after another successful raid. Brad and Olivia. Dellan and Thea. My late sister-in-law, Jessie. And Matt, whose eyes still broke my heart every time I remembered them smiling into mine.

I looked around at the new crew I'd unwillingly collected. Bergman, pale as a bone marrow donee, hugging the straps of his pack like he hoped they'd transform into a jet propulsion unit and fly him outta this mess. Cole, blowing bubbles in such quick succession he'd begun to leave a fine film on his upper lip, getting a better grip on the demon-sticker he'd made by duct-taping two kitchen knives together. Cassandra, trembling so hard her earrings jingled, but standing tall. *No. I'm not losing these people too.*

I turned to Cassandra. "Gimme that sword. If I can get her to another plane I can kill her."

Not without a special weapon, snarled that voice. Not mine after all. Not even female.

"Don't, Jaz!" Cole put both hands on my shoulders just as I

grabbed for the sword. "She'll snap your head off before you can even take two steps outside the circle."

As soon as I touched the weapon in Cassandra's hands her head fell back.

Shit!

Why couldn't she time her visions better? In fact, why couldn't she just go fuzzy where I was concerned like she had with Dave?

A second later she straightened, but her eyes had focused on places nobody else could See. "You are not alone," she said, dropping her hands from the hilt.

I looked at the sword. *Kill her!* howled the voice. So familiar. Where had I heard it before? And not long ago either! *Take off her head!*

I'll slit my own throat first!

You would never—

Try me. And while you're at it, tell me who the fuck you are! Silence. Cassandra, maybe tired of watching me struggle, had turned to face Cole.

"Stay away from her. Please. She's no good for you. Not at all."

Cole lifted his hands from me like he'd been burned. "I'm done with Jaz. That's my other goal for the mission. I'm definitely going to fall out of love with her this week. You know what? I may already have."

"No, no, not Jaz. *Kyphas.*" She kept shaking her head, her face twisted with such misery that Bergman, who regularly begged people to experience their emotions at least twenty feet away from him, stepped forward and pulled her into his arms. She turned to him and smiled. "Yes, that's better. That could work."

As he frowned down at her, Cole and I exchanged puzzled looks. "Who's Kyphas?" he whispered.

The front door blew across the room, slamming the couch into the wall, leaving a dent our security deposit wouldn't cover. Cassandra's demon stepped in, her hat tipped back at a jaunty angle. "That would be me."

Chapter Eight

U p close, Kyphas's aura hit me like a full night of Vayl's un-divided attention. Who knows how I'd have reacted if girls were my thing? Cole sure looked like he was about to drop. Bergman seemed woozy. The living room itself may have grown red lighting and a Barry White soundtrack. I think the three of us would've trotted right out of that circle but for two simultaneous events. Kyphas began to steam, the smoke literally lifting off her golden skin as the prayers Cole had murmured over the windows combined with those Cassandra had enforced around our circle began to take their toll. And Jack started to growl.

If my dog were reduced to a pie chart, fully half would be mush. Give him a treat and he'll consider following you home. Hell, he's pals with my dad, and *nobody* likes him. But the sound coming from his throat lifted the hairs on the back of my neck, his warning clear as science glass. *Mess with my mistress and I will rough you up.*

I shook my head, feeling the demon's influence fall away even as Kyphas whipped her hat off, flipped it into boomerang mode, and hefted it at Jack. I stepped in front of him, but there was no need. Cassandra's circle held, bouncing the weapon back toward its owner. She ducked, allowing it to hit the window. Another failure, another bounce back into our shield. But it kept flying, and every time it made contact I could See it chipping away at our defenses, black sparks and white shards combining to make a light show my Spirit Eye would never forget.

I said, "We need to destroy that weapon."

"How are we going to do that without leaving the circle?" asked Bergman.

What do you say when you have no clue? I was reaching back into my memory, trying to recall if everybody else would still be protected if I broke the loop, when another body hurtled through the gaping hole that had once been the front entry.

"Vayl!" I stepped forward, but Cole grabbed my arm, held me back as my *sverhamin* slammed into the demon. They hit the Fisher Price fridge with a crash that made the whole room shake. The sucker took the impact like a child's toy should, but the door popped open and rained fake takeout all over the combatants as they rolled away.

Vayl had armored himself in ice, one of the powers he'd lifted off a Chinese vampire who was now mostly vapor. It immediately began to melt, the blessings coating the room surrounding it and attacking like white blood cells on bacteria. He was still better protected than Kyphas, whose skin had begun to bubble while she scratched at his slick coating and screamed her frustration that the boomerang wasn't working faster.

Vayl swung, hitting her cheekbone so solidly that when her neck snapped sideways I was sure it had broken. But she carried some unseen protections of her own. With her face bruising and her eye swelling shut, she wound up and delivered, knocking a chunk of ice off Vayl's chin. She followed with a kick to his ribs that threw him to one side.

Jack began to bark. "He's fine," I whispered, my hand working nervously on Cassandra's sword hilt. "He's holding his own."

But the armor was melting fast. Already I could see bare shoulder and the tattered remnants of his pants glaring through at the calf.

Fog had begun to fill the room along with a thin layer of water, heat, and the faint stench of death. It felt like we'd stepped into a swamp. Inside the circle we bounced on the balls of our feet in readiness, though we didn't know for what. Then the boomerang hit a window and shattered it. Kyphas shouted with triumph as it flew back through the door and banged into our shield. The blisters on her skin began to heal.

"Cassandra, Bergman, start praying," I said.

As they began the familiar incantation, " 'Hear, O Israel: The LORD our God is one LORD: And thou shalt love the LORD thy God with all thine heart, and with all thy soul, and with all thy might,' " I gripped the sword with both hands.

Vayl's entire back was exposed now, wide red stripes appearing over his existing scars where the holy words had begun to burn him. But he kept fighting, clubbing Kyphas with his glacial fists, lifting her so far off the floor I could see chair legs behind her dangling feet.

She reached up, caught the boomerang, and bounced it off the floor. In the seconds it took to return to her hand it transformed again, into a flaming dagger that she sank deep into his side.

My scream, lost in his bellow of pain, worked like a starting gun on Jack. He leaped from the circle. I yanked my hand back, thinking his leash had slipped to my wrist when I'd taken a better grip on Cassandra's sword. It hadn't. It had dropped altogether.

Suddenly one of those bits of trivia rushed back to me. The detail you forget the second you answer question twenty-five correctly on your Fiend Lore final. Which is the fact that demons get a kick out of infecting animals. And their favorite critter to smack with the Wicked Crazies is the canine.

As Jack sprinted toward Kyphas, his growl so fierce it brought goose bumps on my arms, I saw her eyes flash a sunspot yellow.

"NO!" I yelled, jumping from the circle.

"Jaz!" Cole's protest sounded like distant thunder as I swung. She moved just as I hit, protecting her neck by exposing her shoulder. I buried the sword so deep that it lodged in bone.

At the same time Vayl shoved his fist into her sternum. She took the hit full in the chest, the ice melting on contact with a frying hamburger sizzle. Then Jack bit.

Kyphas squealed like a pig at the county fair scramble as the wounds opened and her blood flowed, making Vayl's pupils flash red.

Jack's teeth sank deeper in her thigh and he *shook*, his growls resonating through her skin so deeply I could feel them through the sword hilt.

Damage. Yeah, we could tear her up. Make her fry even. But none of it would pull off the ultimate deed. I felt my heart twist as I heard Cassandra's voice, high and shaky behind me, repeating the litany that ought to protect her and my guys.

"'And these words, which I command thee this day, shall be in thine heart: And thou shalt teach them diligently unto thy children, and shalt talk of them when thou sittest in thine house, and when thou walkest by the way, and when thou liest down, and when thou risest up.'"

Powerful binding, especially when combined with our weaponry. But still not enough. We needed more!

"Raoul!" I yelled. "Quit dicking around in happy land, get your ass down here, and *help* already!"

I know, not the language you should use when requesting assistance from the Eldhayr who's already done you a string of whopping favors. But if he wasn't in the direct business of forgiveness, I figured it must be a sideline. So I was slightly surprised when he strode through the door wearing the exact expression Albert once reserved for my grounded-for-eternity lectures.

"You do realize you have the mouth of an illiterate homeless thief? And your timing!" He sighed. "Can you even imagine how quiet the last week has been?" he demanded in his slight Spanish accent. "I got actual work done."

I couldn't imagine what kind. How do you perform any sort of labor and then gallop to your earthly charge's rescue without putting a dent in your immaculate black beret or laying a single scuff on the toes of your massive all-weather boots?

"What do you call this?" I demanded as Vayl delivered another skull-cracking blow to Kyphas, who countered with an attack that would've punctured a lung if his chest hadn't been well protected.

Jack, deciding pit bulls had gotten way too much press, had dug in, refusing to release his grip despite desperate shaking on the demon's part.

Raoul shook his head and raised his sword. I recognized it immediately as the glittering weapon he'd wielded in his fight against Brude, when we'd tried to escape the Domytr's territory. Raoul hadn't been so fortunate in that fight. Then again, Brude had stacked the deck. This time I had a feeling the odds were better balanced. Especially when Kyphas's yellow eyes widened with alarm. She looked around the room and finally her expression said she felt outnumbered.

"Pax," she said, dropping her dagger to her side as a sign of goodwill. "Get this slavering mongrel off of me."

Slavering mongrel? I stole a glance at Jack. *Okay, I'll buy the slavering. But—* "I'll have you know that is a purebred malamute gnawing on your thigh."

"I don't care! Make him stop!"

"Those aren't the magic words. But they'll do." I grabbed Jack's collar. "Time to back off the ham bone, buddy." When he resisted I pulled a little harder, saying, "No more demon for you. Trust me, it'll give you major indigestion." With a combination of coaxing and prying I pulled him off Kyphas and shoved him back inside the circle, where Cole made sure he stayed.

I went to Vayl, whose armor had completely melted and who was now quietly bleeding all over the sandy brown area rug. Grabbing a throw blanket off the couch I pressed it against his wound. "You going to be all right?" I murmured as I stared at our uninvited guest.

"As soon as I get out of this house," he said.

"I'm leaving as well; I think my ass is melting," said Kyphas as she backed toward the door, her eyes darting all over the room, but always coming back to Raoul. He followed her, stepping slowly, his sword held ready if she decided to make an offensive move.

Vayl didn't want help rising, but I lent him a hand anyway as Cole asked Kyphas, "What about Cassandra?"

"We have a contract," she said. "You can fight for her if you wish, but she's mine. I will always come back for her."

It was so similar to something Vayl might've said to me that I glanced at him. He was glaring at the demon, his teeth practically grinding, though part of that might've been from the pain of his wound. Funny how context changes everything. I could see her words made him want to bury her, deep and permanently.

His voice was cold as the icy shell that'd coated him as he said, "Kyphas, have you ever set yourself against a Vampere Trust before?" Her eyes widened as she shook her head, accidentally backing into one of the porch poles before her boot found the single step that took her onto the front lawn. He dropped his arm from my shoulder as he gestured back to the house. "This is *my* Trust." He seemed to grow as he stalked after her. To tower within a dark cloud, while she glowed like an ivory carving as he growled. "You will not take Cassandra from my Trust."

I'd been shopping with my sister, Evie, enough to recognize that weighing-her-options look on Kyphas's face. Clearly she thought Vayl had offered her a bargain. Get out before further beatings could occur. On the other hand . . . She shook her head. "I will be back. With allies. And when we come for her, we will be taking the rest of you with us." She grinned, the curves of her face so perfect that her image would've made sculptors weep. Then she turned and ran into the night, her demonic strength taking her out of our vision almost instantly.

Chapter Nine

B ecause the blessings still lingered inside the house, we sat in the backyard, which had been fenced for privacy. Not that anybody lived close enough to wonder about the havoc we'd just caused. We'd chosen Wirdilling's Hermit Special for a reason. But still, the tall wooden fence. Either the owners like to sunbathe in the nude—doubtful considering how stinking hot it got in the summer—or they figured the fence was a good way to pen their kids in. Considering the wide array of rec equipment dotted around the lawn, including a swing set, a play place with more ladders than slides, and a plastic barn sheltering a trough full of sand, I was voting for use number two.

It seemed ironic to me that the six of us sat around a glass table on comfy woven lawn chairs gazing out onto a patch of grass that Jack was spending equal time sniffing and chewing, while Astral reigned quietly from her perch atop the clothesline pole. We might've been preparing to enjoy some shrimp on the barbie. Except the freshly grilled scent was coming off our vamp.

He sat at one end of the table, a towel stuffed against his wound, listening tiredly to Cole, who lounged at the other end bitching about being shanghaied. "You could've at least asked us if we wanted to be in your Trust before you made some big public announcement! Now we're committed. My mom's going to be so pissed."

"Must you tell her?" Vayl inquired.

"I tell her everything."

Bergman, stuck in the middle next to Cassandra and opposite Raoul and me, gaped at him. "She knows you're a CIA assassin?"

"Well, I might've left that part out."

Vayl checked the towel, decided it wasn't necessary anymore, folded it neatly, and tucked it under his chain. "Then she need not know this small detail of your life either."

"Small! Dude, Pete made us all read Jaz's report on your mission to Greece. Trusts are freaking weird!"

"No, Disa's Trust was strange." Vayl paused to think. "All right, in all probability most Vampere Trusts are somewhat bizarre. They are populated by vampires and their human guardians after all. But ours need not be like that. In fact, it is more a technicality anyway. Something I arranged to protect you all within the world in which I walk."

We stared. Okay, most of us gaped. Because we kept forgetting he wasn't like us. He'd been around way before you could drive to the hospital to give birth in antiseptic surroundings, aided by a guy with more education than most of the people you knew. He'd been born in a time when women routinely died in childbirth, just like his mom had. And he'd lived to see a day when we'd be shocked to hear of anything close to that. But he'd had to give up the sun, and maybe his soul, to do it.

"Why do we need protection?" I asked. As his *avhar*, I was the one who'd always get the honest answer. But within a Trust I wasn't sure what he, as my *sverhamin*, might require of me. It would be nice to know.

He picked a spot beyond the fence and focused on it, like he could see whole universes moving between the trees. "You understand your own world is not singular. Simply from the perspective of culture, religion, work, hobbies, you move within several different spheres, some of which never touch. *Others* like me live in your world, but still we are citizens of the Whence, which operates next to your realm, but only sometimes within it. In the Whence, I am Vampere, therefore I am expected to either declare myself Rogue, or stake a territory and create a Trust."

"Wait a second." Cole held up his hand. "We've got nests all over America and none of them use those names."

"No," Vayl agreed, dropping his eyes to meet Cole's. "But then, they are not Vampere."

"You mean . . . there's another race of vampires?"

"Of course. As you are American and I am Romanian. Or, perhaps more technically correct, as Jasmine is of European descent and Cassandra places her roots in northern Africa. The Vampere hail from a single mother. The Flock from one father."

"Now I'm confused," I said. "Only a few of the biggest West Coast nests call themselves the Flock. The rest use other identifiers."

Vayl nodded. "The Flock is what you would call the central government for those who descend from the Father."

"So the loners and the smaller gangs . . ." said Cole.

"Most are still members of the Flock," Vayl confirmed. "Some maintain independence, of course, as do the Rogues across the ocean. It is, as with anything involving more than a few beings, rather complicated."

"What's the difference?" I asked. Looking at it from a purely professional point of view, I hadn't seen much. I'd killed vamps within the Flock and the Vampere. They all went smoky in the end.

Vayl said, "Beyond what I have outlined, the main distinction between our two cultures lies in the way we turn our chosen ones. As you know, the Vampere take approximately a year. If we rush the process, we risk our own doom. The Flock have found a way to fly over that obstacle. Their turnings nearly always occur the night of the first bite."

"Seems to me like there'd be a lot more of them than you with that kind of advantage," said Cole.

"You would think so." The glitter in Vayl's eyes said otherwise.

Cole licked his lips. "So what group do you fall into now?"

"I have been Rogue since I left the Trust in Greece. But once Jasmine became my *avhar* and I her *sverhamin*, both our status and her vulnerability within the Whence increased. So now I have declared us a Trust."

"Because Jaz is at risk," Bergman said, as usual cutting to the heart of the matter. "Why?"

Vayl stretched his legs forward until his calves brushed my shins. I kept my eyes on my clasped hands, but I knew he felt the heat rise in my chest as I recalled how he loved to tangle his legs with mine, how he said the smoothness of my skin against his felt better than silk.

I dug my nails into my hands, forcing my mind to follow his words as he said, "Such a partnership is rare for vampires. The bonds that are forged can never be fully broken. And as time passes, the couple begins to form a deep and complex relationship that becomes the envy of their peers. The last to do so successfully—" Vayl pressed his lips together in almost a full grimace.

"What?" I asked. "You can't just stop in the middle like that!"

His eyes, so dark they had no color, revealed thoughts I could only guess at. "Her name was Nylla, and she had been turned in the time of Napoleon. She found her *avhar* dying of starvation in a POW camp during the Civil War." He stopped again.

I was so proud I didn't kick him I promised myself ice cream at the next opportunity. Gritting my teeth I said, "Go on."

"Like me, she hoped for . . . something beyond mere experience. I suppose in Tobias she sought"—he shrugged and shook his head—"the missing piece. The bit that should have prevented her from letting her soul slip to begin with."

"Did she find it?" asked Cassandra.

He nodded. "They both discovered something . . . new. Something beyond humanity. And yet not Vampere. Because Tobias stopped aging, but he continued to walk in the light. And Nylla ceased hunting, but she did not wither. Eventually they disappeared, as have all successful pairs before them. But their story remains, giving the rest of us"—his eyes touched mine—"hope."

"That explains a lot," said Bergman. "But it still doesn't answer my question."

Vayl's upper lip lifted. In him it was nearly a snarl. His need to avoid the subject made me want to *know*. "Tell the man," I demanded.

He couldn't play politician now that I'd put in the request. His eyes bored into mine as he said, "If, for instance, an *avhar* were to be snatched out of her bed by enemies of her *sverhamin*. If they were to take her to a dark room, bleed her for days, and then call her *sverhamin* and make certain demands in return for her safe homecoming, they would have him at their mercy. Because they could be assured he would do anything to get her back. And I do mean anything. I could tell you stories. Perhaps I should. Once a vampire named Henri—"

I didn't want to hear. So I interrupted, saying, "Vayl. We don't negotiate with—"

He waved away my policy-book quote with an impatient hand. "Do you think I would give a rat's damn about procedure if I heard you screaming at the other end of the phone?"

I bit my bottom lip, not sure how to reply. It was Bergman who asked, "And a Trust protects Jaz from this? How?"

"It brings the power of the Whence onto our side. As a Rogue couple she and I had few rights. But as members of a Trust we are much better armored. Those who would not have hesitated to move against us before will seek easier prey now rather than risk the ire of the Prevailers." When he saw our puzzled expressions he explained, "The Prevailers are a group of thirteen Elders who rule the Whence."

Good to know.

He pulled his legs back, sat up straighter. "At any rate, Jasmine is safer within the Whence if she can call upon the protection of a Trust. So I began to consider creating one. With the advent of such an excellent circle of work partners, I made the decision to formalize the proceeding."

"You formalized—without asking any of us?" Cole demanded.

"Why would I do that?" Vayl asked mildly. "It was only a paper organization. Something never meant to touch your world."

Cole rolled his eyes toward me like, *Come on, Jaz, jump in! Why aren't you as pissed about this as I am?* And I *was*, kinda. Except I had a bigger secret than Vayl's, so the guilt was outweighing the outrage.

This is a bad way to begin a relationship, said Granny May. She'd dumped the rocker and decided to water the plants that lined her front porch rail. *Why don't you just insult all his relatives while you're at it?*

Reluctantly, I said, "Uh, so if we do have to take this off paper, you know, into the real world? This will be a democratic organization. Right?"

Vayl nodded slowly. "As long as you all understand that I would be the president."

I looked at Cole. "Can you deal with that? Theoretically?"

Cole blew a bubble, making me wonder where he'd found black gum and if it tasted like the same color jelly beans. After it popped and he retrieved it he said, "Only if I can be Secretary of Social Events."

Before I could point out that no cabinet in the world carried that position, Vayl said, "Done." Cole nodded with satisfaction.

Hey, maybe I should invent myself a cool new office too.

While I pondered the possibilities Raoul said, "As long as we are avoiding the subject we should really be discussing, I'd like to know why Jack keeps looking at me like that." He sent a curious glance at my dog, who'd trotted back to the table and commandeered a spot between Vayl and me. He panted as he pointed his ears toward my Spirit Guide.

I said, "He thinks you might have a T-bone hidden under that nifty camo jacket of yours. Which looks fresh as a sheltered young virgin, by the way. Don't you ever sweat?"

Raoul chose to ignore me as he leaned over to pet the dog. "Don't let her teach you bad words," he said.

"It's too late," I snapped. "He swears like a drunken sailor."

"How do you know how much drunken sailors swear?" asked Vayl, one brow lowering. Not in jealousy. He knew I wouldn't waste time with anybody who couldn't walk a straight line. Nope, that expression meant pain, and when I looked I could see his wound was still seeping.

His refusal to sustain himself on fresh blood usually increased my respect for him. Except for now, when his slow heal made me think it was the stupidest damn decision he'd ever made. Especially when all he had to do was put his name on a list and willing donors would line up at his door like Black Friday shoppers.

"Jasmine!" Vayl reached over to shake my arm.

"What?"

"Your focus seems to have shifted."

"Oh yeah, um, drunken sailors. Well, my dad *was* a Marine you know. He knew guys."

Cassandra scooted her chair back, causing it to screech along the patio's surface like a mom who's had just about enough of her kids' bratty behavior. We turned to her.

"Did you have something you wanted to say?" asked Vayl.

She nodded graciously. "Yes." She looked Raoul straight in the eye. "I know I couldn't have made a worse mistake. But I've spent the past five hundred years living the best life I knew how in hopes that it would be enough to save me." She gulped a little before asking, "Was it?"

He shrugged. "I've been allowed to come, so you could take that as a good sign. Or maybe someone with more clout than me just wants to make sure Jasmine doesn't die again."

"Why?" asked Vayl, his voice deepening. "What happens if she is killed?"

Raoul stopped petting Jack and sat up. He avoided my eyes when he spoke, choosing instead to stare straight into Vayl's. "The human body can only bear so much, even when it has been enhanced to recover from the terrible damage death deals, as I have done for Jasmine twice already. Which is why the next time she dies—she won't be able to come back."

Cole sat forward so fast his chest hit the table with a low thud that made us all stare at him. "So you're saying she'll be like you? Just spirit material?"

Raoul shrugged. "It's a little more complicated than that. Sometimes—like now—I can take physical form. But I'm limited by my own strength as to how long the form lasts." He looked at me then, so I stopped biting my lip, unclenched my fists, and made myself breathe. No sense in showing how deep his little info-bomb had just torn into me. He said, "In my penthouse, when I'm visiting with you, I can take on an even more solid body. But in the place where I fight other sorts of creatures, where I spend most of my time, in fact, physical form is a hindrance."

Silence, deep and shocked, like when people have really heard about a death. Bergman spoke first. "Will she live longer, though? With that enhancement you said you gave her?"

Raoul made that somebody's-just-kicked-me-under-the-table face. "I *would* say yes. She has the potential to live longer than Cassandra. But her chosen lifestyle deeply cuts her odds."

Vayl and I locked gazes. *Think of it!* his eyes told me. *What I have dreamed of! We could gain eternity together, and you would not even have to turn.*

I tried to send his hopes back to him. It would, after all, be amazing. But I could barely see past tonight. Not with Kyphas lusting after our souls and some asswipe entity already in possession of a chunk of mine.

When his brows dropped I looked away. *Goddammit,* I'm *supposed to be the Sensitive here!*

"That could be good," Bergman put in, drawing my eyes from Vayl's. "Think about it, Jaz. If you and Vayl joined up with me and Natch, you could pick your jobs. Less risk. More chance of that thousand-year mark."

"What is he talking about?" asked Vayl.

"Yeah, what's the—" Cole began.

"When did you become a salesman?" I interrupted, hoping to shut Cole down before the discussion got ugly. "I never should've introduced you to Dave's unit. Ever since you hung with those Spec Ops studs you've gotten way too big for your shoe box."

Leave it to the skinny sucker to grin while Vayl repeated his question. Bergman had just begun to explain his offer and the reason Cole wasn't included—"You just started a new job. No way have you got any money to invest"—when Cassandra stood.

"I have to use the bathroom." She raised her eyebrows at me. *What? Oh, are we doing that girls-gang-up-in-the-can thing?*

I rose. "Me too."

"Have fun, ladies!" Cole took my chair and scooted it right next to Raoul's. "So, I was wondering if we could make a deal," he began as we moved away from the table. "How do you feel about kangaroos?"

I looked back at Vayl, but he was immersed in Bergman's pitch. Jack thought I needed company, though. He got up and padded after me. Even Astral decided we must be up to something interesting. Avoiding the dog, she ran ahead of Cassandra, somehow guessing to turn down the hall and slide through the doorway opposite my bedroom. She was waiting on the window ledge of the white-tiled, chrome-accessorized bathroom when we finally stepped inside.

Cassandra slid open the navy-blue shower curtain, turned the tub and sink faucets on full blast before taking a seat on the toilet. It had a squishy white lid, so she slowly sank to its base while the animals rearranged. Astral jumped onto Cassandra's lap. Jack settled down beside me where I stood beside the tub, staring at the towels hanging from round silver rings mounted on the wall. The towels' multicolored bubbles looked so real, I wanted to poke them to see if they'd actually pop.

She said, "I don't think Vayl can hear us now, even if he's trying." She held up her hand, as if she knew I wanted to protest. Which, of course, I did. When our eyes met I realized we'd reached a new cut-the-bullshit level of understanding. Refreshing. Scary. And weird, because if she went on to join my family she'd be the first relation I ever felt I could really be honest with.

"When I touched you I sensed another presence." She shuddered. "I don't know how such malevolence found its way past your defenses, but we have to get it out of you. You can't imagine how much it's already controlling you."

But I could. The rowdy crowd that gave faces to all the facets of my personality had gone into hiding, driven out by its overbearing, I'm-the-king—*wait a second. I know that attitude. I know that voice! No wonder everybody left except Granny May, and she's afraid to move. Aw shit, I'm in big trouble.*

"I'm listening," I said.

She gripped her hands together so tightly I could see her rings digging into the skin of her fingers. "I know how hard this will be for you. In your mind, trust has to do with money rich people put away for their grandchildren. Or maybe it's the name of our new community. But now you will have to learn the best meaning of the word."

I felt myself nod. But already half of me had stopped listening.

Cassandra clapped her hands once, the way she usually does when she's delighted. I jumped, because this time her eyes were blazing.

"*Onkheinem!*" she shouted.

"What the f—!"

"Stay with me, Jaz!" she interrupted. "Don't let it play on your resistance."

"What are you saying?"

She leaned forward, gazing earnestly into my eyes. "If any of us tell you something you wouldn't have wanted to hear in the first place, your possessor uses your natural response to influence your choices, thus gaining it the behavior it wants to see out of you. You must teach yourself to listen, even though you wouldn't normally wish to. You have to consider what you would once have dismissed." She took a breath. "Eventually you may have to open your mind and let one of us in."

No! Never!

Like it had been in the beginning, I couldn't tell if that inner voice was mine or his. But I could tell he wanted me to shove Cassandra out the door, out of my life. *Busybody, bitch!* he shrilled. *Get rid of her! Now!*

I pressed my lips together, the way I sometimes had to so I wouldn't puke in the bed or the hallway. *Just keep it in until you reach a flushable appliance*, I'd tell myself. Only this time what I had couldn't be flushed. I had an awful feeling it would require something a lot more painful. Like a burning. And what would be left afterward? Would it matter if he'd already eaten the best part of me, the same way I'd seen his ghost-subjects cannibalize each other?

I said, "Brude."

"Who?"

"His name's King Brude." I sighed, feeling major muscle groups loosen as I shared the news with somebody who might be able to help. "I ran into him during my last mission. In life he ruled a big patch of Scotland, probably with a bloody sword and a full dungeon. Now he's a Domytr."

She shook her head. "I'm not familiar—"

"Yeah, I wasn't either. I'm not sure what all his duties are, but I do know that he chases down stray souls for Lucifer. When I met him he was moonlighting, building his own army of ghosts and his own version of hell in the Thin. One without the rules that make Satan's place so warm and cozy."

She held up her hand, like I was talking too fast. But it was so hard for me to get the words out I was surprised she wasn't pounding me on the back to make them come faster. She said, "But the Thin is just a wisp of a place. When I first learned of it I was surprised lost souls ever found themselves caught there it seemed so holey."

When my eyebrows shot up she added, "Not holy like paradise. You know, like a pair of net stockings. Really easy to slide a pencil, or a spirit, through."

"O-kay. Never heard it described that way, though I guess you have a point. Personally, I think they stay because they're addicted to chaos. And Brude's a steady supplier."

"So how did he get stuck on, I mean in, you?"

I shook my head. "Both really apply. He became obsessed pretty much the second we met. As for the 'in' part, I'm not so sure." I dredged up the memories of our confrontations. So few, and yet all of them laced with the greenish red memory of unuttered screams. Which led me to realize that if I ever did lose it, I mean hurtle off the deep end, I would probably never stop howling.

I said, "He brought me over to his territory once. Maybe I got infested with something while I was there."

"Just walking in his world wouldn't be enough," Cassandra said. "Think of the Domytr, himself, like a virus. He can't get inside you unless—"

"I bit him!" I said, my mind suddenly clearing of everything except the end of that bone-shattering fight between him and Raoul, when I'd finally become desperate enough to stoop to beasty means if that was what it took to get me and my Spirit Guide the hell out of Dodge. *Damn! How could I have forgotten?*

The big prick with the impenetrable accent, grumbled Granny May. She'd abandoned the porch and now seemed to be sending messages from the mail slot on her front door. Not good. That meant he was making headway again.

Cassandra grasped my sleeve and tugged it. "Pay attention, Jaz, or so help me I'll shake you, and then you know my visions will make us both sorry."

I glued my eyes to hers.

"What happened when you bit him?" she asked.

Brude, yanking me away from Raoul's side, his tattoos writhing against me like living things as our bodies clashed. My seduction, brazen enough to cause him to cast aside the shadow-cape that had been protecting him. And when his armor had cracked, my teeth tearing into his carotid.

"His blood went down my throat. But we were in the Thin. I mean the whole episode started as a dream and ended in Raoul's penthouse. Although . . ."

"Tell me."

"I did come back to myself with a really bad taste in my mouth. And it didn't go away until I brushed my teeth."

Cassandra sat back, shook her head like I was some misbehaving child. "You *had* to bite him."

"He'd already kicked Raoul's ass, and you know what a terrific fighter *he* is."

"You're kidding. Raoul?" She said his name with the reverence we all reserved for it. He'd been a ranger in life. And instead of choosing to spend his *after*life in well-deserved peace he'd decided to go on fighting. Was it any wonder I had to defend him?

I said, "Brude made himself invincible in that time and place." I thought about it. "Yeah, Raoul could never have slipped under that armor. No guy could've. But a girl with a friendly face and sharp teeth was a different story."

Cassandra dropped her hands to her chin. "All right, we know how he got in. So all we have to figure is how to get him out."

My lips went dry. "Are we talking . . . like an exorcism?"

"I don't know. We should discuss this with the others."

I began to scratch my forearm. Hard and fast. If I'd had a balloon in my hand it would've stuck to the wall by the time I was done. "I don't—"

"Neither does Brude."

I sighed. "Okay. Just tell me one thing before this all goes down."

"Anything," she promised.

"What's a bustier?"

Chapter Ten

Cassandra did everything but check the corners of the dank little bathroom for Candid Cameras. "Bustiers? Are you joking?"

"You know, if you want to pull off this trust deal, you can't be making fun of me the first time I try it out!"

"Okay, okay! I just thought, you know, since you were engaged once . . ."

I shrugged. "Matt and I sort of skipped the costumes. I can't remember if we never had the time or if we were just always in that big of a hurry. Maybe if we'd been together longer we'd have gotten around to it." Stab of regret. Even now, with Vayl such a presence in my life that all I had to do was think of him to make the ragged edges smooth again, sometimes I missed Matt so sharply it was a struggle not to clutch my stomach and double over.

I forced my mind back to the subject, said, "So I'm getting the feeling Vayl likes the dressing up. And I don't have much in the way of variety. What was he hinting at before?"

While Cassandra explained, I wished I'd brought a notebook and a pen. Because she didn't stop at that item. Oh, no. Somewhere along the line my girlfriend had amassed vast experience in the world of undergarmentry. And when she realized I particularly liked the types that would transform my up-top look from average to let's-do-video! she really got on a roll. By the time she was done we were giggling like a couple of co-eds planning our first road trip.

A rap at the door shut us down.

"Yes?" said Cassandra.

"If you ladies are finished, we are ready to discuss our strategy regarding the demon," said Vayl.

She shot off the toilet like someone had pulled the fire alarm. Throwing open the door, she said, "Is she back?"

His eyes, a troubled shade of blue, cut to mine. "No. Raoul feels that we have time to plan. Perhaps you and he should discuss . . ." He stepped forward, his cane clicking on the tile as he closed on me.

"All right, then," she said. "Come on, Jasmine."

I hesitated, my way blocked not just by Vayl's physical presence, but by the intensity in his expression.

"She needs me," he told Cassandra, though he kept his eyes on mine. "I feel it more deeply than this wound in my side. And yet you are the one huddled here with her."

"Jaz needs all of us." When she caught his expression, hers softened. "But you most of all. Remember that, because how you handle the next few minutes could make the difference in her soul's salvation."

"Oh geez, Cassandra, let's not put any pressure on him or anything," I said as I twisted Cirilai on my finger. His eyes shot to it, alarm widening them, making me drop my hands to reassure him that I wasn't about to take it off. I had once, and the wall that had dropped between us had nearly destroyed us both. Trust. Maybe I could work on that.

"What is Cassandra talking about?" he asked me.

I tried to pull in one of those bracing breaths that get you through tough situations, but my lungs wouldn't cooperate. Too busy considering a full collapse. "I think you've sensed that something was wrong with me ever since we hit Canberra. I'm—"

I tried. The word wouldn't move past my frozen tongue. Brude had put a block on communications, and while I struggled against him, Cassandra watched me with a sympathy that made me fight all the harder, because it was a reflection of how far I'd fallen.

She turned to Vayl. "Jaz has been possessed."

He looked deep into my eyes. I fought to keep mine open against the sudden pain that pierced them.

Brude, you son of a bitch! Now that I know you've been the one torturing me, you gotta know how bad you're going to bleed when I finally beat you!

I'd have piled on more ire, but Vayl was checking Cassandra for confirmation of what he'd seen moving behind my pupils. By the time he turned back to me his irises were already darkening to the black with red flecks that reflected his most disturbing emotions.

"Possessed by what?" he murmured, still talking to me like he thought I could respond.

Cassandra answered. "She says it's one of Lucifer's minions. A Domytr she encountered on your last assignment that goes by the name of Brude."

"Why is she not talking?"

Our psychic considered me. "May I touch you?"

I tilted my head sideways, then nodded. She leaned forward and took my free hand. Just a brief clasp was enough to make her look like she'd eaten something rancid. "His strength increases when she is feeling some extreme emotion. Right now she's deeply"— Cassandra smiled at me—"nervous. About how you'll react to this."

I wanted to snap off a witty comment. *Hey, let's all discuss Jaz like she's not even here, why don't we?* But now my throat had closed so tight I'd begun to feel dizzy. A lot of good can be said for honesty. But too big of a dose can kill you.

From a distance, like the wail of a train horn, I heard Cassandra tell Vayl, "She believes you'll be furious when you find that Cole and I both accidentally discovered her secret before she could tell you. She's worried that you'll see her as weak now, or perhaps mentally unfit like Liliana and, in either case, undeserving of your affections. She wanted to handle this on her own, so that your new romance could have time to cement itself before it was rocked by such an event."

Cassandra went on, but her words disappeared in the hum my ears put out as they tried to cope with my narrowing vision. *Brude, I swear to Jesus if you let me pass out I'll make it a personal goal to pry every one of those tattoos off your skin with a screwdriver and a pair of pliers.*

Vayl emptied his hands, just like that, dropping the cane on the floor as if it mattered less to him than a flyer you'd crumple up the moment after some poor schmuck handed it to you on the street. He came close and tipped up my chin, a gesture so familiar it nearly made me smile.

"Jasmine," he whispered. "My *pretera*."

Geez, I didn't much feel like a wildcat. But if he insisted—

"I am not your father, your mother, nor your grandmother. I am not one of your Helsingers, and definitely not Matt. Listen to me. Look into my eyes. I will not leave you. Not ever—"

"You can't promise—"

I stopped. More out of surprise that I'd gotten my voice back than that Vayl had held up his hand to prevent my argument. His smile had vanished. "I can make any vow I like. I am your *sverhamin*, which means what I promise you, I follow through upon."

"So . . . you're not leaving me?"

"Ridiculous."

"And you're not pissed?"

"Of course."

My shoulders dropped. Once I wouldn't have cared. I'd have said, "F-you. I'm too busy to worry about your petty little problems." But that was when I was one of the walking wounded and my own issues outweighed everyone else's. Plus, it had been so long since anyone gave a crap how Vayl felt about anything. He really appreciated it when I paid attention. His kiss, light as a raindrop on my forehead, made me look up.

"Later for that," he said. "Now is the time to give Brude the boot before he paralyzes more than your vocal cords."

"Do you know how to do that?" Cassandra asked.

He shook his head. "Raoul might. And I think we should ask Pete as well."

"NO!" I didn't realize I'd shouted until I saw Cassandra back up. But I still couldn't help the panic that kept me babbling. "For shit's sake, you guys, the last thing I need is for you to call head-quarters and inform them that their black sheep just put another blotch on her record. And Raoul . . . what if he decides I'm dam-aged goods? Not fit to do Eldhayr work around here anymore? Maybe he'll reverse everything he's done and just . . ."

Cassandra hugged Astral like she were a real, live kitty. "Surely Raoul wouldn't kill you? He's one of the good guys!"

"But they look at death differently, don't they? It's not such a bad thing to them, because they're still fighting. They don't have anybody left down here to hold them."

Vayl rested his chin on his knuckles. "All right, then. Do you have any ideas, Cassandra?"

She shook her head. "No, but I have her." She held up Berg-man's invention, reminding us of all the information they'd down-loaded into her. Centuries' worth. "I suspect it'll take some time to unearth information on a creature so rare. But if anyone has ever discovered the Domytr's weakness, it would be a Sister."

I said, "Okay, and for a backup plan, what about that guy Ruvin?" I asked. "The seinji have a couple of famous demon fight-ers in their history. Maybe he knows something we—"

Vayl's shaking head stopped me. "He is laboring under the assumption that we are part of a Hollywood film company scouting production locations for our next blockbuster."

"And that we brought along Gerard Butler, why, to carry our cameras?"

Vayl's brows lowered. "Cole's fabrication seems to have stuck because Ruvin is, ah, easily deceived. I am reluctant to follow suit. The man has agreed to drive us around for the next couple of days, not to locate an exorcist."

I held up my hand. "Okay, I want to go on the record in stating that I refuse to puke green shit and float up to the ceiling while channeling Naomi Campbell before she's assaulted at least one employee for the day."

"Then it's settled," said Cassandra. "I'll start researching immediately. And you"—she pointed at me with one perfectly manicured orange-painted nail—"will stay positive. Astral may have all the information we need right in here." She tapped the cat's head. The metallic clicking sound that resulted reminded me to keep robokitty in the shadows if any of the neighbors decided to pay us a visit. She'd even begun to fool me, but as soon as someone touched her, our cover would be blown.

Cassandra whispered in Astral's ear, probably using the very same words she'd said to mobilize her traditional *Enkyklios* the last time she'd used it to help me. Then it had conjured up an image of a soul-eating monster called a reaver, whose buddies had hounded me for weeks. Somehow I had a feeling whatever Astral dug up would be just as threatening.

"This may take a while," said Cassandra as we watched the cat's ears twitch in a regular circuit from left to right and back again, stopping every few centimeters almost like they'd become parts of a clock face. "When she does come up with helpful information, she'll relay it to you by video feed, possibly without warning. So, ah, don't drive off a cliff or anything like that when it happens."

"O-kay." I suddenly felt as grumpy as a kid who's just realized she still has to wait two more weeks to open her Christmas presents. "Now can we get back to the guys? Cole's probably convinced Raoul to set up a whole petting zoo for him by now."

"We still need to talk," Vayl murmured as he picked up his cane.

I scratched at a particularly annoying itch on my left shoulder as I said, "Don't we always?"

Usually smoothing Jack's soft gray fur into place calms me down. He gives me that tongue-drooping grin while I bury my fingers in his coat and we both just—chill. He's even tall enough that I can give his head a scratch on the go, as I was now, moving through the dining room with its plain wooden table, four ancient chairs, and its wall full of family portraits, all of which I avoided viewing by keeping my eyes on the white linoleum floor beneath my feet.

But some moods just won't bend to soothing, and mine was one of them. I felt the fiery ball-o'-whacked in my chest burn even brighter as I followed Vayl and Cassandra out the door, back onto the patio. As soon as we cleared the doorway Jack took off for the yard's lone tree, fearful that some fence-leaping hound had marked it in his absence. Astral jumped onto the table, where she curled into a ball, her ears still roving like lighthouse beams. Bergman stopped pacing to stare.

"What did you do?"

"Gave her some research," I said. Cassandra smiled at me as she took her original seat.

"What kind?"

"I'll spill if you tell me what's up with that hat you're wearing."

His hand flew to the brim and yanked it down. "Nothing! Can't a guy support his favorite baseball team without people getting all over his case?"

"Bergman?"

"Yeah?"

"What's an RBI?"

He stared at me for a full five seconds. Then he said, "Fine. Don't share," and went over to slump in the chair beside Cassandra's.

Raoul and Cole, still sitting at the table with their heads together over a rough sketch that looked like a plate of spaghetti, hadn't heard a single word.

"Are you sure about this?" Raoul was asking. "I mean, some people consider their model trains a family heirloom. You could give them to your kids someday."

Cole shrugged. "If I even have kids, which I doubt, they'll probably be into something you and I have never heard of like virtual Play-Doh or paintball Monopoly. Anyhow, they may be in sorry shape, because they've been in Mom's attic for ten years. But, yeah, you keep your end of the bargain and you can have my old trains."

So Raoul had decided to carry through on his plans to tear out the bar in his penthouse, which Vayl had accidentally broken the last time we'd visited, and replace it with a model railroad layout. He'd found, in Cole, an equipment supplier. And apparently the price was getting the dumbass close enough to a kangaroo to give it a scratch under the chin.

I sat down beside my Spirit Guide, trying to decide how to convince him that this whole scheme would probably end up with him mending Cole's bent and broken body. Then I decided it just might keep him from studying me too closely. Which would be good, since everybody else had pretty much figured out something was off with me after spending ten minutes in my company, and I wanted him to think I was coasting.

A spurt of warmth from Cirilai, sending tingles down my hand to my fingertips, turned my attention to Vayl, who was regarding me intently.

He knows how much this all freaks me out. Of course he does. He's had my blood. He can tune into my emotions now. And he's, what, reassuring me? How . . . nice. And yet. Goddammit. Shouldn't I be stronger than this? Why do I need a Vampere hug? Why is this getting to me?

Because Brude is in your head, where no one should come uninvited, said Granny May. She'd cracked open the door. Poked her head out. *You hate that almost as much as you despise the idea that you might need help to get rid of him. But really, Jaz, how many times do we have to go over this? Wonder Woman might've been a superhero, but I'm pretty sure she never got laid.*

Oh, come on, what about Steve Trevor?

I think she hired him from the local escort service. All laurel, no—

Grandmother!

My point is that you're surrounded by good people now. At some point, if you don't decide it's all right to become as much a part of their team as they are of yours, you're just a frozen-faced mannequin living in a store window designed by some color-blind shtoock who doesn't believe in Christmas.

Granny May, I think you forgot to take your meds this morning.

That's entirely possible.

Good talking to you.

I ran my eyes around the table, seeking distraction, and finding instead the faces of five of the people who most cared about me in the world. Maybe I *should* tell Raoul. Geez, he probably had some firsthand experience in exor—well, you know. And Bergman. If science could scoop out Brude's sorry ass, Miles would find a way. I flipped my eyes back to Raoul. Nah, he'd started to doodle on his paper again and talk ecstatically about cork and engines. I leaned toward my old roomie.

"Bergman?" He jumped. "Sorry, I didn't mean to scare you."

"No, it wasn't you." He pulled a thin metal box out of his pocket and gave it to me. It fit snugly in my hand, its only feature a screen that currently showed blank. "The timer went off," Bergman explained. "I mean"—he held up his wrist—"the one on my watch that tells me we need to start paying attention to this."

He nodded to the item, which led directly to my second question. "What's it do?"

"It monitors the bug Cole left on Ruvin. As soon as the screen lights up, that means he's at the airport, which is when I start recording. If we find out through the conversation which one of the team is the carrier, I can activate the minibot inside the bug. At which time it will crawl off Ruvin and move itself to the coordinates the satellite has sent to it."

"Won't they see it moving?" Cole asked.

"It won't matter if they do," Bergman said. "It looks like an ant."

I set the box on the table and we all stared at it in admiration. "I wish I had more money, Bergman," Cole said. "I'd join up with you in a second."

"Thanks." Only a braniac like Miles would sound surprised to be receiving such a compliment.

"Perhaps while you all wait for your mission to develop, we can discuss the demon," said Raoul.

Stone silence as we all realized we couldn't avoid the subject any longer. On top of the fear that shadowed us I saw frustration too. Our odds seemed so hopeless, nobody much appreciated Raoul rubbing our noses in the fact that we only had a few hours left to enjoy our lives. I looked into my friends' eyes and thought about how many people go to their deaths pretending everything's just fine while knowing how utterly wrong they are.

I slapped my hands on the arms of my chair. "How many allies do you figure she'll bring, Raoul?"

"One for each combatant she had to fight this evening and another to confront those who stood inside the circle," Raoul guessed.

"So if you count Jack"—which I kinda thought she would— "five altogether?"

"That would be my estimate."

"Why not more?" asked Bergman. "I figured she'd bring a whole army of demons to overwhelm us."

Raoul shook his head. "The Eldhayr would never allow that kind of massing to occur without reprisal. But they might overlook a movement of five."

"Would your people deal with her before she reaches us?" asked Vayl.

Raoul shook his head. "If Cassandra were an innocent I might say yes. But because a contract exists, the other Eldhayr are constrained. As I said before, it could be that the only reason I'm allowed here is to make sure Jaz survives the coming night."

"Well, that's comforting," said Bergman.

Cole spat his gum into the yard and plunked both elbows on the table. "We are so screwed."

Chapter Eleven

One of the greatest traits of any living creature is the desire to survive and the belief, somewhere in the most idealistic part of the mind, that we can take positive steps to ensure that whatever wants to stop us from living gets derailed. Repeatedly, if necessary. Which was why our mutual depression lasted for all of twelve seconds.

At which point Cole banged his fist against the patio table and said, "I know! We attach our souls to our bodies with duct tape. They'll never be able to take off with them then. Hey, don't look so skeptical. My dad uses it for everything. It's held the headboard of his bed together for fifteen years now."

"Even better," Bergman joined in. "Coat our souls with Vaseline. That way nothing can get a grip and you've pulled off a great gag at the same time."

And they were off. Even Cassandra had a suggestion, though how we were supposed to snag a hundred hand buzzers this late in the game I had no idea. In the end we sobered up enough to decide the only way we could win was by guerilla warfare, using weapons Raoul offered to provide.

The idea was to lure Kyphas and the other demons away from the house, into a plane where we could defeat them. It would take some time to set up, but my Spirit Guide agreed to set his other projects aside until we'd pulled this one off.

"I'll take Cole with me to help, if you don't mind," he said as he stood.

Vayl and I traded startled looks. We'd been expecting to use our third's sharpshooting skills in our primary mission. But considering Cassandra's straits, maybe we could adjust that plan as well. "Can he go everywhere you need to?" I asked Raoul.

"He is a Sensitive," Raoul reminded me. "That means he can travel on any plane without incurring permanent damage." He turned to me. "Have you seen the portal I came through? The one just south of the house?"

I nodded. The others gaped a little. I didn't tend to mention the gate that seemed to follow me wherever I went. Too *Twilight Zone* when I was striving more for *Bewitched*.

The flame-framed door that would take Raoul and Cole back to the Eldhayr's base stood just on the other side of the fence between it and a line of acacia, its center as black as a midnight sky. It would stay that way until Raoul chanted the right words; then it would clear, showing them their ultimate destination. I described its location to the others. And I told Cole that if someone watched them walk through it, they'd think they were just wandering behind the nearest cover for a quick pee.

Raoul folded up his drawing and said, "We'll be back as soon as—"

He stopped when Bergman's bug tracker lit up like the table-ready pager they give you at Red Lobster.

"What do I do?" I asked as I picked it up. Blue lights blinked in succession around the edge of the screen, which, itself, had offered me a menu of options and small boxes beside each one to check. "Oh, I see," I said. I touched the square beside the words *Initiate Audio Reception*.

Ruvin's voice, warped into the falsetto adopted by the Bee Gees for most of their disco career, screeched out of the box. "Feel the city breakin' and everybody shakin', And we're stayin' alive, stayin' alive."

As Ruvin grooved through the song, Cole jumped out of his seat and started dancing, his hip wiggle causing Cassandra to poke her pinkies into her lips for an ear-piercing wolf whistle.

I stared for a second before dropping my head into my arms. "We are all gonna die."

Vayl said, "He is actually quite good."

I turned my cheek and laid it on my elbow. "You can't be condoning this!"

He shrugged. "This is why I relish rubbing shoulders with humans. You *live*. You do it well and thoroughly. Not all of you," he said, his glance wandering to Bergman, who'd pulled the box from my hands and was poking it with multiple fingers like it had sprouted a keyboard. "But most of those who are loyal to you know how to squeeze every last drop from their experiences. I had nearly forgotten the intensity of emotion wound around that philosophy."

"Were you that way? When you were human?"

He closed his eyes, trying to remember past the centuries of vampirism to a time when he'd been a husband. A dad. He opened his eyes. "Life was hard then. I remember happy times as a child. And again after Hanzi and Badu were born, when we felt sure they would not die as our other babes had. But I never managed that."

He gestured to Cole, who'd grown a goofy smile that had lured Cassandra into his dance.

I sat up and reached for Vayl's leg under the table, ignoring the itch that fired across my back as my hand smoothed up and down his thigh. "I'm kinda glad you never had that in common with Cole. He can be such a doof."

"And that does not appeal to you?"

The blue in his eyes began to morph to aqua as his fingers trailed across the top of my hand, sending prickles of heat up my arm, my neck, to my cheeks. My reaction? I leaned forward and sawed at my back with fingernails that I wished were three inches longer.

"Allow me," murmured Vayl, the amusement in his voice making my jaws clench. I let him scratch at the rash and decided this moment had to be the least romantic ever, anywhere. But, damn, it felt good!

All movement in the backyard stopped as Ruvin's voice piped out of Bergman's doohickey again. "G'day, mates! Welcome to Canberra! Here, let me help with your baggage!"

Sounds of a hatch rising, suitcases being flung, doors opening and closing. And, after a time, Ruvin starting his Jeep.

Raoul got up. "Cole, this is shaping up to be a long, boring eavesdrop. I think we have better things to do?"

Cole nodded. But then his attention whipped to the box as Ruvin said, "Bugger me, what a fright you gave me there! I thought you were sitting in the back with the rest of the blokes!"

And the reply, quiet but firm, "The Ufranites have taken your family. If you want them back safe, get out of the car and go to the rear."

"It's our guy!" Cole said.

"Maybe," I said. "Nothing says he can't have accomplices on the team. Any group that put together one backup plan probably made room for a couple more. Still."

I nodded to Bergman and he activated the bug, giving it the signal to transfer from Ruvin to the mysterious man who'd threatened him.

Vayl held up a hand. "They are moving." Only he could've heard the slide of clothes on the Jeep's leather interior as Ruvin exited the vehicle. But even the humans in the group couldn't mistake the familiar grunt and smack of a body hitting the asphalt.

"Clumsy you, falling down on the job," said the guy, the silky concern in his voice making me shiver with rising rage. "Here, let me help you up." Another grunt and a moan as the guy yanked Ruvin to his feet.

I could hear tears in the little man's voice as he said, "Wotthehell? I haven't said I won't cooperate!"

"You'd better, or the gnomes will boil your kids and have them for appetizers while your wife slowly roasts in a hole they've already dug for her."

I swallowed, hoping Ruvin would realize the threat wasn't all bluster. Gnomes didn't regularly stoop to cannibalism. But on special occasions they'd been known to munch a little long pork, especially around planting and harvest time. They stayed away from humans, a move my old Underground Creatures professor had shrugged off to fear of our massive military might. Possibly. Or maybe the Whence delivered its own brand of justice, which tolerated the gnomes' inclinations as long as they didn't piss off the wrong people.

Ruvin began to breathe so heavily I wondered if he was going to hyperventilate. "Y-you! D-don't hurt my family! I'll do anything you want. Just leave them alone!"

His tormenter laughed. "You'd better make good on that promise," he said. "Because the gnomes have chosen you to be the midwife for their larvae's birth. So you're going into the Space Complex with me tomorrow. And after the larvae have arrived safely, your family will be released."

Ruvin moaned. Which told me he knew what many *others* didn't. That gnome midwives weren't the nominally respected birth-helpers Americans sometimes used in place of doctors. They were the death-row inmates who'd lost every last appeal. Because the larvae would burst from their carrier starving for living flesh. And unless someone saved him, Ruvin's would be the sustaining meat that gave them the energy they needed to destroy Canberra Deep Space Complex.

The gnomes would probably keep his family alive until the

larvae ate him. But after, who knew? Once I'd have bet my own life on their safety, but this new shaman had flipped all the old traditions sideways. Which was why we were here in the first place.

Who is this shaman? I wondered, wishing we at least had a picture to study. *And why do they follow him? Are they really that hard up for answers that they'll swallow any line a dude throws out there just because he swears it came from their deity?*

No comment from Granny May, which meant Brude must be stomping around my subconscious again. Before I could take inner stock Ruvin said, "Promise. Promise me they'll be okay."

"Of course. You cooperate and your family will be just fine."

Deep, ragged breath. "Then I'll help. But I have other jobs waiting. If I don't show, they'll call my dispatcher, who'll call the cops, because I never miss an appointment."

"Just make sure you're at my front door at two a.m. Or your family dies."

"I'll be there, Mr. Barnes."

Aha! Our hearse driver had just been accosted by the vice president of Odeam Digital Security.

I wished I knew what that signaled for the other four members of the Odeam team. Two of them were software engineers named Johnson and Tykes. One was a marketing exec they called Pit, and Barnes had brought his executive assistant/mistress, Bindy LaRule.

But Barnes didn't reveal any more details of his plan. All we heard were car doors opening and closing, the engine starting, and chilly silence for what would be at least a forty-minute journey.

"Now is the time," said Vayl. He glanced at his watch. "It is nearly eight p.m. We have the benefit of darkness and plenty of time in which to work. Shall we meet back here in an hour?"

Raoul nodded. "We'll be done by then. Here, this should help if the demon returns before us." He handed me his sword, which made my arm dip so fast I hoped he never asked me to spar with the thing. I'd last for maybe thirty seconds before my elbow joint would completely unhinge and I'd be left with a dangly appendage that would force me to jerk my whole body in a semicircle just to slap somebody in the face!

I made myself smile. "Gee, thanks. What would you say the chances are of me needing to use this thing before you get back?"

"Minuscule." He nodded once, confidence showing even in the way the shine of his boots reflected the patio light. "She won't want to face you a second time without assuring herself a massacre-style win. That requires planning. And, as I told you before, her kind can't rise without being called. So she'll have to partner with another demon who's fulfilling contractual obligations. Between that and the fact that her kind are notoriously bad teammates, an hour is the least amount of time we have to spare."

I nodded, glancing toward Cassandra. I'd seen her bear up to an awful lot of strain, including Dave's temporary demise. Which was why I wasn't surprised to find her shoulder deep in her fur-bag, mumbling to herself about that ancient tome she'd just been reading that might help. When she stuck her head in the purse too, I realized we should probably have a talk about accessories. It's fine to take the possible loss of your soul in stride. But when your pocketbook is big enough to hold all your necessities *and* half your torso, it may be time for an intervention.

Chapter Twelve

Our next order of business required a quick change and, as usual, I made it in and out of the closet first. Which meant I spent a good five minutes in the bland little living room trying to restore some order to a place that would not be the same without major remodeling. Because the floor where Vayl and Kyphas had battled felt like a freshly tilled field under my feet. It was still wet, but water hadn't caused all the warping. I crouched, running my fingers along furrows so deep I could almost hear the wood screaming in protest against the violent infusion of power that had curved it at such impossible angles.

"Pete is going to be so pissed," I whispered, trying to calculate the cost of a new floor and, oh yeah, a replacement door. I picked the old one up and muscled it into the opening, leaning it against the frame as I tried to see where all the glass from the broken window had gone. Nothing had crunched under my feet while I'd assessed damages, so I pulled a mop out of the utility room that sat just off the kitchen and gave the floor a once-over, only then realizing the glass must've melted from the heat of the boomerang attack fusing with our holy defenses. One good thing about the cleanup—I discovered I had full range of motion in my Lucille Robinson getup.

Usually I dig the costumes I get to wear in the line of duty. Okay, there was that belly-dancing outfit that had made me want to find a small room where I could scream without triggering a 911 call. But otherwise, no complaints. Not even now that I'd kicked it into Hollywood producer mode.

Most people don't logic it out that these types dress like regular folks. They want glitz right down to the caterers. So when we use this cover, we give it to them. I wore midnight-blue pants containing just enough spandex to make me feel like I should hop on a treadmill as soon as we'd completed this leg of the mission. The wide satin belt held in the tails of a white tuxedo shirt, the ruffles of which peeked out from under my leather jacket. Bowing to practicality, I still kept Grief strapped into its shoulder holster, and I'd slipped on a pair of low-heeled black boots conducive to running and kicking, not necessarily in that order. My concession to the cover had been to choose a pair with pointy toes that, had they curled, would've qualified me to work on the set of *The Wizard of Oz*.

Since wigs and I didn't always agree (can anybody say awkward seatmate with an umbrella?), I'd had my stylist, Magic Mikey, straighten my hair and dye it darker red. The white streak that framed the right side of my face drove him crazy because it wouldn't take color. That's what happens when Mommy touches you during your unplanned excursion to hell. But since I couldn't tell *him* that, I said I preferred it that way and even the chemicals knew better than to cross me. Which is why even my beautician thinks I'm badass.

Factor the hair in with my big green eyes, deceptively frail frame, the aforementioned ruffles, and Astral lashes, and you're walking the bimbo line. So I'd added a pair of black, rectangular glasses that, thankfully, didn't interfere with Astral's transmissions.

Robokitty had followed my order to stay in the room I was sharing with Vayl while he changed. And now, finally, the pictures were coming in clear and hot. (Shut up. If you had to operate this close to that much sexy while itching like a flea-bitten mongrel, you'd voyeur it up too!)

Vayl had, for the sake of his own self-control, spent my changing time in the bathroom. As he moved back into the bedroom and noted Astral perched on the pillow, one corner of his lip curled.

"So is that how you want it, my *pretera?*" he murmured, the glint in his eyes sending a shiver up my spine. I abandoned the mop, leaning it against the wall by the door while I nodded. Like I thought he could see me. He probably sensed my excitement as he threw open his suitcase and pulled out a pair of brown motocross leathers that I knew would fit him so well I'd probably spend the evening wishing we needed to do a second-story job so I could watch him go up and down a ladder.

Next came a white silk shirt that I knew he'd leave halfway unbuttoned because he already wore an undershirt, the sleeveless kind that cling like a fan who's snuck past the bodyguard's defenses. And to cover it all, not his usual calf-length duster, but a supple leather jacket that would ride his hips, giving me a full view of his tight little tush if my dreams came true and we did need to scale a wall. Or climb a tree. Or, hell, maybe if I could just find an excuse to tie somebody's shoes while he was looking the other way.

I dropped to the couch. Which hit me so hard in the back I realized the upholstery had probably squeezed itself into an I-surrender ball sometime before the end of the last World War.

I wiggled around, trying to find a comfortable spot while Vayl peeled off his duster, and dumped his boots and socks. He slowed down with his sweater, staring off into the distance with an increasingly smug smile on his face like he knew I was leaning forward, gripping my knees with my hands so they wouldn't dig their nails into the wall, possibly clawing right through in an effort to speed up the process.

"You're fast!"

I sat up, crossing my arms over my chest like Bergman had just caught me in my underwear. "Yeah, ha-ha. That's why they hired me. I'm like Superman in the phone booth. Except, you know, tightless." Under my breath I added, "Astral, get out of there. Mission aborted. Repeat, mission aborted."

When I saw the flattened form of the cat slide out from beneath the bedroom door behind Bergman, who stood at the point where the hall intersected both the living room and dining room, I felt some of the tension bleed from my muscles. Not all, though. Because before she'd shut down video Astral had sent me a shot of Vayl. Half naked. And laughing.

"So?" Bergman held out his hands. "They sent me this outfit and said it would make me look like a cameraman. Would you be convinced?"

He'd put on a tan work shirt topped by a quilted vest covered with pockets. Hopefully at least a couple actually held the equipment that identified us as something other than a killing crew from the States. His jeans, while still looking as if they'd accompanied Moses across the desert, at least held together okay. And he still carried the backpack Astral had arrived in.

I said, "Yeah, I think I'd buy the photographer angle."

"Out of the way, peon!" Cassandra called as she strode down the hallway. When Bergman spun around she smiled. "I'm working on my world-class bitchy. I believe one of us needs to go there. What do you think?"

He nodded because, well, it was just hard to disagree with our Seer no matter what she wore. For her, our costumers had chosen skintight blue jeans tucked into high-heeled boots and a red mock turtleneck woven with sparkly thread that reflected the gems in her jewelry. Other people might be fooled by the fact that she wore more bling than Flavor Flav, but I wasn't. I knew she could saw off those heels, shove her hands into a pair of gloves, and muck stalls like a homegrown farm girl. Which was why I wanted so badly to make Kyphas go away for good. I couldn't imagine another woman

I could love more as a sister-in-law. Except, maybe, for Dave's late wife, Jessie. Thinking of her and looking at Dave's new girl made me shiver.

I won't let anyone hurt you, Cassandra, I promise.

As if she'd heard my thoughts she smiled at me. But all she said was, "I have good news."

"Yeah? Do you See us coming out on top in this whole deal?"

She shrugged. "That hasn't been made clear to me yet. But I don't See you traveling around in the Wheezer much longer. Perhaps one or two more trips and then you'll be switching—"

"Hot damn! That's the kind of vision I like!"

She nodded as she followed Bergman into the living room. He pulled out one of the chairs, dropped into it, and crossed his heels onto the table, oblivious to the fact that he might be permanently scarring the surface. This was the problem with beaker-sniffers. Their sense of beauty had taken such a molecular turn that they'd developed a sort of aesthetic blindness that some people found jarring.

"Get your damn feet off the table," I snapped.

He dropped his boots to the floor. "Are you going to be like this when we're partners?" he asked.

"If you're tearing up other people's furniture? Yeah."

"But . . ." He motioned to the floor.

"That's different."

"Why?"

"It's not pretty."

"Oh."

Astral had snap-crackle-popped back to form and sidled up to Cassandra's boots, which she seemed to find cuddly.

"You programmed a lot of cat moves into this one," Cassandra said to Bergman as she picked up the robokitty and sat down next to him.

"I wanted her to blend in. That move is actually her signal that she has information she wants to share with you."

Cassandra nodded. "Well done on both fronts, then." She looked at me. "Do you think we have the time?"

"Go for it," I said, so she whispered a few words in the cat's ear, causing her feet to curl up underneath her belly. Astral opened her mouth wide, like she was gagging on a fish bone, and a beam of light winked on from the back of her throat, as if some industrious vet had figured out a way to test from the inside out. Since the video also came straight to my receivers, for a second the holograms blurred, twin images that made me wonder if this was how my parents had viewed Dave and I the day we were born.

I moved to stand behind Astral. I figured I could lean against the fireplace if the dizzies kicked in, but the repositioning worked. The images connected. In fact, Astral was projecting the clearest hologram I'd ever seen from an *Enkyklios*. It was like watching live actors walk through a movie scene right in the front entryway. Unfortunately she hadn't found anything on Brude. The guy she'd indexed wasn't even a Scot, unless they'd taken to wearing chaps and Stetsons like the frontiersmen this dude resembled.

His gear seemed even more out of place given his location, standing before an enormous gate the color of tar. It interrupted a seemingly infinite stretch of spiked fencing on which one or more of the inhabitants had set a series of freshly axed human heads. Behind the gate a river flowed sluggishly inside its broad banks as if it had been partially dammed by old tires and the gutted carcasses of washing machines.

Fog hovered over the river and obscured nearly everything on its far side. But once in a while we could see people running, their faces taut and pale, darting terrified glances over their shoulders before the mist swallowed them again. More constant was the screaming. Nearly every thirty seconds it came. Not always from the same throat. And sometimes several voices shrieked together, like a choir of murder victims harmonizing their last earthly sounds. Sometimes, even worse, we heard the laughter of someone who's left sanity behind for good.

These were the sounds that made the cowboy jerk and stare through the tiny cracks between the wide bars of the gate. But he didn't stop for long before continuing with the graffiti. Nope, not kidding. He was writing somebody's name on the bars of the gate. But this was no ordinary act of vandalism. Because his tools were a gleaming silver hammer and chisel.

Now it was the cowboy's turn to glance over his shoulder. Whatever he'd heard galvanized him. He bent to his work like a jeweler doing the most important engraving of his life. Sweat beaded on his forehead and upper lip. By now he had seven letters. THRAOLE.

New sound. Something enormous, snuffling, crushing the things it stepped on as it neared the cowboy's side of the gate. I expected him to spin around. Raise the hammer like a club. Or better yet draw his gun. Which was when I realized he carried no other weapons. None.

What the hell? Where's your goddamn revolver? And what respectable cowboy leaves his rifle strapped to the saddle, you—

Though his shoulders twitched like they were covered in tarantulas, the man never looked back. He glared at his work, chiseled a hyphen and four more letters onto the gate: THRAOLE-LULI. Which was when the creature shouldered its way out of the fog. Still I couldn't see. Wrong angle to catch anything more than a hint of bloodshot eyes, a flash of curved tusks. And then the cowboy notched in the final letter. THRAOLE-LULID.

One wild cry from the fog-monster as the man swung around. I still expected him to attack. Instead he held the hammer and chisel high over his head and slammed them against each other. A light, bright as a welding torch, came from the tools, bringing tears to the cowboy's eyes. Making the fog-monster bellow with pain. When it faded the monster was gone. And the cowboy held a single tool. At one end was the hammer head. The handles had melded seamlessly, and at the other end was the pointed edge of the chisel.

After that came a quick succession of images. People (usually men) of different races stood in different spaces holding that hammer. It moved from a hospital in Japan to a farm in Armenia to a boat dealership in Maine. Each time the holder tried to separate the hammer from the chisel. And each time he or she failed. Died screaming. Crushed and bleeding in the jaws of unspeakable creatures that should never have pulled breath, much less walked lands that still remembered love, generosity, and honor.

And then, finally, audio of the kind that didn't make you want to huddle under a quilt with your teddy bear. A flat, bored voice piped out of Astral's chin, saying, "This is all we know of the history of the Rocenz, a tool crafted by Torledge, the Demon Lord of Lessening. According to legend he forged the hammer from the leg bone of the dragon Cryrise and the chisel from the rib of Frempreyn, the rail who led a failed uprising against Lucifer just after the Fall.

"The Rocenz is a Reducer. The user can diminish anything to its simplest version by using the hammer to chisel its name into metal or stone. If the work is done at the source of the threat's power, it will be completely destroyed. So, for instance, in the case of those we saw who attempted to fight the *earthbane*, if any of them could have carved their enemy's names on the gates of hell, those evildoers would have been diminished into puddles of blood marked with bits of bone and sinew. As far as we know, only Zell Culver, the Hart Ranch cowhand, ever succeeded. But the trick to separating the chisel from the hammer's handle died with him. Because Zell was dragged back into hell the day after he escaped.

"For our purposes, this tool can also transform and make clear what has been muddy for centuries. This could be most helpful to our research. However, the tool has been lost since 1923 when its carrier, Sister Yalida Turkova, went missing from her hotel in Marrakech, Morocco. We have been unable to locate it since."

The hologram blanked. Astral yawned widely, giving the miniature projector ample room to reset itself within her jaw before she closed her mouth again.

"That was pretty amazing," I said.

Bergman snorted.

"You don't buy it?" I asked him.

"Well, for one thing, you can't *forge* bone; it's too brittle."

Cassandra put Astral down so carefully I realized she'd thought about throwing the cat at him. Through clenched teeth she asked, "Do you mean to tell me you're stuck on semantics when souls are at stake here?"

He shrugged. "I don't see how it'll help us with Ky—" She raised her hand to stop him. "Your demon," he finished.

"I'm not the only one with a problem here," she informed him. She jerked her head at me. I sighed. Might as well bring Miles into the loop too. Otherwise he'd be pretty stunned when I decided to take up the bagpipes.

"Don't freak out, okay?"

Bergman drew his knees together like I'd threatened to kick him in the crotch. *Aw crap, was that the worst thing I could've said? Yeah, probably.*

"What?" he murmured.

"I've . . . kinda got some company . . . mentally speaking."

"You mean . . . you're schizophrenic?" He studied me carefully. "You seem pretty pulled together about the whole thing. Shouldn't you be more paranoid than I am? You know"—he wiggled his fingers and rolled his eyes—"watchers in the woodwork and stuff like that?"

"I'm not— Bergman, I bit a Domytr during my last mission and now his spirit has possessed me. Not completely. But, uh, he's making some headway. So we have to figure out how to boot him before I start acting the submissive little queen he's been jonesing for since we met."

"Geez, Jaz, Domytr's are badass."

"You've heard of them?" I couldn't believe it. I had a pretty thorough education, Cassandra's knowledge put that to shame, and neither one of us had heard of Brude's kind before he'd shoved his tats in our faces.

"Well, you know, I'm signed with groups outside the CIA." His teeth clicked shut and his face got that lemony-squish look that told me he'd done the I-know-nothing ass-clench.

Still I tried. "Come on, Bergman. What can you tell me about Domytrs? Knowledge is power, man."

"They used to be human."

"I already know that."

"Like you."

"What . . . do you mean?"

"Sensitives. Saved for something better. Who knows, maybe they even rose to Raoul's status. That's what my clients thought anyway. That they turned traitor sometime in the afterlife. Not sure how the, uh, people I worked for came to that conclusion, but they had some pretty good sources."

Sure, that made sense. Temptation was one of evil's most effective weapons. And Brude struck me as a greedy creep.

"Bergman, were you able to fulfill your contract?" asked Vayl. None of us had even noticed my *sverhamin* slip into the room, we'd been so intent on the picture show and the talk that followed. Now I couldn't believe I'd missed him. Only the cold bite of his power lifting the hairs on the back of my neck let me know how he'd pulled it off.

"What do you mean?" For a smart guy Bergman played dumb pretty well.

"Your clients would never have given you those details unless they had hired you to build a weapon that could defeat such a creature. Did you succeed?"

Miles pulled down the brim of his cap. "Not yet."

Vayl nodded, unsurprised. He spun his cane, making the blue jewel on its tip glitter in the lamplight. "If we can find this Rocenz, separate the pieces, and carve Brude's name on the gates of hell, I believe it will reduce him to the dust to which his original body has already fallen."

Bergman shot me a look. Pure suspicion. He stared back at Vayl and said, "Are you sure we should be talking this way in front of—" He jerked his head at me. But he meant Brude, who'd be listening intently. Unless he was an idiot. Which he wasn't. Dammit.

"Of course," Vayl replied. "If he knows how great the odds are that he will end up as fodder, perhaps he will voluntarily release Jasmine."

More conversation followed. Details I really should've paid attention to. Brude was probably taking notes and making flashcards. But Vayl's costume kept distracting me. Because it made him look like a rock star. I hadn't expected the jacket to be so . . . *oh-baby!* It was the kind you wear when riding a Harley. That offset, silver-zipper style that makes a woman's mouth water when it's worn open to reveal the broad chest of a vampire at the height of his powers.

"Jasmine?" Vayl asked. "Were you going to say something?"

I realized my mouth was hanging open and cranked it shut. My head started to itch. Great. Not only had the rash spread, now I'd look like I had dandruff while I was relieving the irritation. "I'm covered in bumps," I said glumly.

"Some more interesting than others," he replied softly as he reached my side.

"Would you shut *up?* Bergman's, like, five feet away!" My eyes darted to our techie, but he'd opened his backpack and appeared to be rummaging through it as happily as a kid in a toy box.

"You look, how do you say?" He dropped that crooked smile on me that makes my knees unlock. "Hot." The last word, barely a whisper, lost itself in my hair as he pressed his lips to that spot just below my ear that can, apparently, flip the off switch in my brain. Before I realized it my hands were inside that jacket, stroking the hard planes of his chest and stomach. And then, as if moving without any prompting from me they reached down, undid his belt, pulled it loose, and . . .

"Ahhh, that feels great," I moaned.

"I am completely grossed out over here!" Cassandra informed us.

Vayl, who'd been peering down at me with an expression of utter disbelief, stared at Cassandra over the top of my head. "It is not what you think," he assured her.

"As if I'd do something that disgusting," I said, pulling away from him, but keeping the belt, because the buckle relieved the itching so much better than fingernails. I continued using it to scratch the inflamed skin across my stomach as I sat down by Cassandra.

"You are pathetic," she told me.

"I'd get all offended, but I'm pretty sure you're right."

I ignored Vayl's glare, after all he probably had a spare belt in his suitcase, and concentrated on Miles, who'd found his treasure. "Here it is!" he said triumphantly. "The new, improved party line!"

He'd invented the group-communications devices years ago, so the chances of them blowing out an eardrum or melting off parts of our faces had decreased over time. Still, the fact that he'd tinkered with what I saw as the perfect system worried me. He opened up the silver case and handed us each a smaller box containing the set of items we needed to send and receive messages.

"What's different about them?" I asked without opening mine. Who knew? Maybe they were rigged to explode when you said a code word. Like "different."

"They work on the same general principle," Bergman explained. "A transmitter that resembles a beauty mark, which you should place near your mouth. And a receiver, which, before, was wired into an earring and then tracked into your ear. Now we have this."

He pressed his finger into his own box and lifted it up. Stuck to the end was what looked like a narrow piece of tape, only slightly thicker. More like the What's-in-Our-Oceans? window peels my sister, Evie, thought her kid needed all over the house now that she was a whopping three months old.

"It sticks inside your ear like this," he said, demonstrating with his own piece. "It sends clearer sound and nobody can tell you have it on."

"Awesome!"

"That's not even the best part!" Bergman declared. "It'll magnify sounds for you if you scratch it enough times. So if you want to hear a conversation that's happening from across the room, you can. Just remember to scratch it the same number of times when you're done otherwise you'll be risking permanent hearing loss. And, of course, while you're eavesdropping you won't be able to hear anybody else on the party line until you're done. I like to call it my RAFS redundancy plan. Except now that her name's Astral that doesn't sound nearly as cool."

"Dude, you keep coming up with awesome gizmos like this and you can call them anything you want," I said.

Vayl banged his cane on the floor, reminding me of a judge gaveling everybody into recess. "It looks to me as if everyone is ready. Shall we repair to the Wheezer?"

I held back a smile. *Shall we repair to the Wheezer. Too cute.* Vayl was like a British butler's studly cousin.

"Just a sec," I said. "Jack's in the backyard." Returning Vayl's belt on the way, I ran to the glass doors and called my dog, who'd just left a giant deposit I reminded myself to clean up before bedtime. "Yo, poop-meister! We're leaving!"

Hearing his favorite phrase next to "dinnertime," Jack bounded through the brown grass and into the house, bringing a rush of cool night air with him. Despite the fact that I'd already thrown on my jacket, I shivered. Nights like these were made for killing. I could always smell it in the air. And tonight, the scent in my nostrils meant blood.

* * *

Wirdilling Primary School made up in whitewash what it lacked in charm. It practically glowed in the streetlights, its black roof making it seem to become a part of the night sky, as much a nocturnal creature as the four of us. A square building with its own water tank out front, it gave off the oddest vibe, the deserted swings and seesaws in the side yard seeming to shout, *School sucks when the kiddies can't come!*

I'd backed the Wheezer into a parking space on the street a few feet from the fence. "Nobody home," I said. Not surprising. Our sources had informed us the Space Complex was hosting no guests other than the Odeam team this week.

Vayl said, "All right, remember your roles, please. We are acting as the Shoot-Yeah Productions crew. So keep that in mind at all times, yes?" At a little after 9:15 in the evening we didn't figure on anyone strolling past. But it always pays to play your part. You never know when the curtain peepers are at their posts.

We piled out of the vehicle. Bergman and Cassandra pulled tripods and video cameras out of the trunk, chatting with each other like they actually knew crap about lighting and B-roll. Vayl disappeared around the building's far side, probably to check out roof access in a way passersby couldn't witness. The rest of us headed for the gate.

As soon as we crossed into the playground I stopped. Bergman went on through. But Cassandra halted beside me.

"Do you feel it?" I murmured.

"Yes. Like a thrum through the soles of my feet," she said. She crouched down and laid her palms flat against the dying grass. "I'm not getting anything clear, just a sense of connected life. I think something big lies under this school."

"Keep moving. Let's see how far it extends." Since we were fenced in, I unhooked Jack's leash and let him run while the two of us paced off an asterisk from one end of the playground to the other, discovering the extent of the labyrinth under the old school, and trying to figure out what kind of *others* we'd sensed.

"It's everywhere!" Cassandra finally announced.

"Yeah, but who does it belong to?" I murmured as I passed Bergman.

"No clue," he responded. He'd set up the video camera and was now taking a still shot of the building's main entrance with one of his pocket clickers. I doubted we'd use that door during our return visit, but you never knew. His orders were to get pictures of every visible form of entry so we could figure out the best way to sneak in later that night. He went on. "Hey, don't let Jack pee on the tripod, okay? Tell him it's my territory."

"If *you* peed on it he'd know without anyone having to say a word," I told him.

His face puckered like a rotten pumpkin's. "You know, your standards have really bottomed out since the mutt moved in! I want this clear from the start. If we become partners, *you're* handling all the dog poo."

"Works for me. But that's a big 'if.' I'm still pretty happy at the Agency." I grabbed Jack's collar and steered him toward a tree in the corner of the playground. Which kinda disappointed him, because I'd told Astral to stick with Vayl. And Jack badly wanted to find her.

After marking the corner of the property and nosing around the fence in a halfhearted attempt to smell up somebody friendlier than the mystery creature who'd recently entered his life, Jack caught a scent. Noting the rigidity of his ears and the tension in his haunches I reached down and slowly clicked his leash back onto his collar.

"What is it, boy?" I asked softly. He didn't even turn to look at me, just lowered his nose and began to walk, setting one paw carefully beside the other.

"Jasmine?" Vayl sounded like he was standing right next to me, though I knew he must be crouched on the roof by now. Good to know Bergman's gadgets performed above standard.

"Jack's onto something," I said. "Maybe it's just a rabbit. You know dogs." Okay, I assumed he did. But maybe not. Had Vayl ever owned one? I realized we'd never had that conversation. And we should've. I also didn't know his mother's name. Or if he liked lobster. A thread of panic wrapped around my lungs, making me suck in my breath. I should know these things! Why didn't I know these things?

Because you don't belong with him. You never did. The only man you were meant for died eighteen months ago and you will never, ever find another like him. Now that I'd outed Brude in my own mind his accent had thickened considerably. Too bad I could still translate his brogue.

I tucked my chin into my chest. *You're in forbidden territory. Go there again and I'll kill you.*

You cannot kill me without killing yourself.

Yup.

You would commit such an atrocity?

Not happily. But you're a menace. Better to get rid of you while you're trapped inside me than let you pull off whatever heinous plan you've devised that includes me.

I waited. Listened. The only voice I heard was Vayl's, smooth and sweet as hot fudge as he said, "Jasmine, what is wrong?"

"Brude," I said shortly. "Nothing I can't handle." For now. "If you're finished up there we might've found something interesting down here." I thought for a second. "Also, I need to know your mother's name."

Was it just my imagination or was Bergman's doohickey sensitive enough to pick up the catch in Vayl's voice as he asked, "Why?"

"You know all about mine. And yours was like, a thousand times better." *Because, even though she never knew you, she cared enough to demand that the family make Cirilai to protect you.* "Plus, we could use her name as a code word or something. For when one of us is about to do something the other should just take on faith."

"It was Viorica."

"And if you were going to pick between lobster and crab, which would you choose?"

"What?"

"These are things we should know. What if we have to take a quiz someday? I can tell you right now that Bergman is allergic to eggs, and Cassandra's all-time favorite place to visit is Monaco. Have you ever had a dog?"

"I prefer crab. And yes, I have owned several dogs. But I grew tired of burying them every decade or so. Thus, my only pets are the tigers carved into my cane."

"There, was that so hard?"

Jack had begun to tug at his leash hard enough to make my shoulder ache, so I stopped resisting and followed him toward the northwest corner of the schoolhouse. Concrete steps led down to a basement entrance that had been both boarded and padlocked shut. But that wasn't the part that interested him. His nose led him to the side of the steps, to a gray brick wall so ordinary I'd never have given it a second look if not for him. I took a knee.

"What's that on your nose, dude?" A smudge of powder, the same color as the wall. I reached out to rub the spot he'd sniffed it from. Yanked my hand back. Because my fingers hadn't touched the rock-hard surface my eyes had registered. It had felt more like membrane, giving like Jell-O at the contact.

"We've got something over here," I said.

"Be casual," Vayl reminded everyone.

I looked up as Bergman reached the top of the steps and clicked off a couple of shots. Cassandra joined him, exclaiming over the viability of using this spot in our movie's murder scene. And then Vayl split the two of them in the middle, Astral sitting at his feet like a real cat, which was when I realized that was exactly the kind of pet he needed. Battery-driven. Likely to outlast even him.

Now that I had my audience, I flicked the barrier with a finger. It wiggled, pulling an excited gasp out of Bergman. He ran down the steps, jumping the last two in his rush to get a closer look.

"What kind of technology are we talking about here?" he asked himself as he poked at the fakeness. He gasped when his finger went through. Sagged against me when it came out whole, if dusty.

"I doubt if it's mechanical so much as chemical mixed with magic," said Cassandra as she and Vayl descended the steps. "But as soon as I touch it I'll be able to tell you a great deal more."

Jack and I backed toward the boarded door to give her room to work while Bergman pulled Astral out of the way. Vayl leaned on his cane, watching with interest as she knelt, steadying herself with one hand on the bottom step. She gently pressed the other against the Jell-O wall, squeezing her eyes tight as images filled her mind. Her lips flattened, like she'd just taken a bite of bad potato salad but couldn't spit it out, because her auntie had made it special, just for her.

Finally she nodded and stood. "This is a new doorway into a gnome warren. It's the one Pete told us about. N'Paltick." Nobody said anything, but the silence was full of unspoken speculation. She went on, "It was built for ease of access to these apartments. I also See gnomes swarming out of this entrance. They are quite excited, but I can't tell why."

Though the answer seemed obvious, Vayl still had to ask, "Is this the same warren that took Ruvin's family?"

She nodded. "A woman and two boys are sitting in a candlelit room. They seem all right. They're looking at the door in surprise." She glanced up at him. "In my vision they believe they're about to be rescued."

His eyes, bright blue with the intensity of his thoughts, wandered to mine. As I read the question in them I shrugged. We both knew we'd never find a better chance to humiliate the shaman than this one. A people blinded to their leader's whacked ways had to start questioning how tight he and the almighty Ufran really were when their god let common kidnappers make off with the bargaining chips—er, I mean—the midwife's family.

You know I'm for it, I told him silently. *Especially considering how much safer Cassandra will be down there.*

Gnomes and demons entered into a blood feud right after Lucifer's Fall. By now the gnomes were so far ahead they'd stopped keeping score. Other creatures might push them around, but demons couldn't seem to solve the gnomes' code. A lot of people had studied their defenses and weaponry trying to figure out why, including yours truly. My theory—faith.

Gnomes *believed.* Even the fanatics—who performed appalling actions in the name of a god whose name translated as "peace"— even they remained demon-immune. I figured this had to be due to their unshakable convictions. And that makes for slim pickings when you have to fill a monthly quota. So the last place Kyphas would look for Cassandra would be in an Ufranite warren.

A thought hit me. I tucked it away before Brude could see it.

"Are we in agreement then?" Vayl asked.

I nodded. "Maybe the prisoners have heard something that could help us identify all the carriers," I said for Brude's benefit.

"We have other means," Vayl reminded me.

"Yeah, but this way we get to . . . you know." I smiled. So did he.

Bergman held up a finger. "Hang on, you just made a big leap there. What did I miss?"

I clapped him on the back. "Probably better for you just to find out as you go." I turned back to Vayl, who was studying the brilliantly disguised gnome door.

"You're not thinking of diving in or anything, are you?" Bergman asked. He gestured at the fake wall. "We don't even know what's on the other side."

Ignoring Bergman's observation, Vayl said, "Jasmine, tell me.

If you had built an access door, the better to reach Odeam's traitor, why would you choose this particular location?"

I shrugged. "Lots of fake concrete just going to waste in the corner?"

He blew his breath out his nose. "Hardly. Where is your mind today?"

"Seriously? After flying forever, fighting a demon, not to mention the Domytr snapping up my synapses, you have to ask?"

"You could at least try."

Shit. I looked around. "I don't know, okay? The basement door is the only way in where they wouldn't be seen, and it's obviously solid as a—" I kicked at the door as I said, "brick." But my heel didn't contact wood, sending a shiver up the bone of my leg as expected. Instead it shoved completely through.

Because the gnomes had pulled off another illusion.

The original door had been removed and replaced by Paint plants. Those wizards of horticulture had created this ivy sometime in the sixteenth century. And since then all they'd done was improve it to the point that it came in every known color, its needlelike leaves laying so flat they were easily confused with the grain of wood. As shown by the door, it could be grown quickly and trained into any position, so even up close it resembled whatever the gardener desired.

I pulled my foot out. Big, noticeable dent, though I could already see leaves unbending. Funky.

"You know, someday you're going to throw a kick like that and something's going to bite your foot off," Bergman said.

"Could be," I replied. "Or maybe I'll knock something out before it has a chance to eat my face off."

"Save the debate for later," Vayl said. "They should have left a panel for ingress and egress. Jasmine, please check."

"Sure." I let loose with another kick, this one at about knee height. A door big enough for Jack to jump through popped open. I looked over my shoulder at Vayl.

"You guard the rear," he said. "We must keep Cassandra and

Bergman between us at all times." *So that if one of us is wounded,* his eyes added, *they will at least stand a chance of escaping.*

I nodded and drew my Walther PPK. As always, Bergman smiled when he saw it. He was the one who'd engineered it to transform into a crossbow, so I understood the pride in his eyes. But when the quick grin disappeared, I knew he'd just realized why I might need it.

Our reconnaissance took ten minutes. The basement had been emptied when the school was closed, and the Space Station hadn't yet filled it. Up top, the building held eight former classrooms that had been remodeled into apartments, each with its own bath and kitchenette. We marked the access points for each room and developed at least three escape plans. Then we reconvened at the door to N'Paltick.

Vayl and I stood in silent contemplation while Cassandra and Bergman huddled in the corner with the animals.

Glancing at them I said, more for their benefit than ours, "We'll have to take them all with us. Too risky to leave them here with the demon due back anytime now."

Vayl eyed our companions. The crook of his right brow demonstrated his concern. It wasn't necessarily that they'd get in the way. Just that they might do something stupid without even realizing it and get us all killed. Or worse, made into hors d'oeuvres.

"Stay between us," he told them. "Follow our orders precisely as given. This is no time to think independently, despite your obvious qualities in that area."

They nodded like a couple of little kids who've just learned they get to go into the haunted house at the fair, and they can't figure out if they're thrilled or terrified.

"Astral," I said. "Jump up here." I clapped my hands and she leaped into my arms.

Cool! If I decide to try a second career, robokitty and I can develop a Vegas act.

I walked over to the doorway. "Scout ahead." I threw her through the portal, wondering how far she'd fall before landing, and if she'd plummet so long even her programming would fail and she'd splat into a thousand pieces.

Bergman must've been thinking along the same lines. Because his squeal of protest reminded me of that time in college when I'd accidentally eaten his ChemGen project. Luckily he hadn't been studying ways to make botulism more lethal. He'd just been trying to come up with a tastier, less fattening form of peanut butter.

After waiting half a minute for the dust to clear, I said, "She's in a tunnel the size of a large culvert. The picture's coming in green, so it's not lit."

Vayl nodded. He didn't seem surprised. Which disappointed me. In fact, I realized it had become a challenge to raise his eyebrow, even a tick. You gotta figure a guy who's been around nearly three centuries is going to be hard to jolt. So when you do . . . score!

He said, "Get ready to crawl. Bergman? Cassandra? Keep one hand on the leg of the person in front of you at all times. Speak only when necessary, and then in whispers."

"What if we need a quick getaway?" asked Bergman.

"I doubt that will be possible," said Vayl. "If violence is called for we must be swift and certain. We cannot afford wavering," he said sternly, staring at Cassandra.

"Why are you looking at me?" she asked. "I can fight."

"You are the sweetest soul among us."

"Which is probably why Kyphas wants you so bad," said Bergman. He meant to be generous, I know, but his reward was a slap on the arm from me and a hail of frowns and shushes from everyone else. Even Jack turned his back on him. "What did I say?"

"Her name, dude." I rubbed the back of my neck, like she was already out there, aiming some devilish weapon at us. Standing on tiptoe so I could see over the wall of the basement steps to make sure the coast was still clear, I said, "It's almost like you're summoning her when you say it out loud. She can hear it from anywhere. Right now she knows you've said it and, if she cares to look, she can see what spot you were standing in when you said it. So don't say it."

"Look? Into what? She's got a crystal ball?"

I sighed. Why hadn't our consultant taken just one Basic Paranormality class? "Do you give off heat?"

"Yeah."

"Then all she has to do is look into something else that gives off heat. And assuming she's scouting hell for allies, it shouldn't be too tough to find a lava pit to squint into, now, should it?"

"Oh."

Geniuses! They're so great for the go-boom and the wireless yapping. But ask them one question about others *and their brains turn to mud!* I was about to let Bergman know exactly what I thought about the gap in his education when a new picture rose in front of my eyes. And I decided his positives might just outweigh his negatives. Astral was turning out to be real helpful.

I turned to Vayl. "The cat found a crossroads guarded by a gnome. He's alert." *And wearing a spiffy blue uniform that includes a tail ribbon. Since when are gnomes into insignia and brass? And,* I felt myself frowning, *guns?*

"He's armed too," I said. "It looks like the same kind of air-powered rifle we've seen most of the other burrow dwellers opt for."

Vayl inclined his head. "Then it is time to prepare."

Chapter Thirteen

As if we stood on a table spun by the same gears, Vayl and I both swiveled toward Cassandra. She looked from me to Vayl and back again. "Was there something—" She motioned toward the notcrete wall. "Do you want me to go first or . . ."

"We just assumed you understood how gnomes function," I said.

She shook her head. "My area of expertise *is* in ancient languages and religions. And the gnomes have been around as long as my people, but they wrote nothing down about their god. And since their history is an oral one that they share only among themselves, I haven't studied them at all."

I nodded. "All we really know is what we get from the outcasts who manage to escape before the community finds a way to sacrifice them. The gnomes call them *kimfs* and blow snot out one side of their noses after they say the word."

"No."

"I shit you not."

Cassandra shook her head. "So hypocritical."

"Yuh-huh. Anyhow, what you also didn't realize is that gnomes only see a little better than moles. Some of our analysts think they've spent too much time belowground. Some suggest it's a genetic malformation of the eye that could be corrected with surgery, or maybe even glasses. What matters to *us* is that if our little project here is successful, they won't be able to retaliate if they see us, because we all pretty much look the same to them. Like we've all pulled stockings over our faces so the only details they pick up are eyeholes and nose bumps. But if they get a whiff of us they can follow us clear across the continent. Because their sense of smell is almost as good as a bloodhound's."

"So"—Vayl nodded at her bag—"what have you got in there to help us out?"

"Why do you assume I'm carrying scent around with me?" Cassandra asked, somewhat defensively.

Vayl's lip quirked. "Come now, Cassandra. I have seen you pull a tire patch kit from your purse. Anyone that prepared is bound to have thrown in a supply of her favorite perfume."

She did a little sideways head bob, the kind you see on people who hate to admit they've just been caught in their own little obsession. She unsnapped the furbag and began rummaging around. "There's nothing wrong with carrying backup supplies, you know. I can't tell you how many times I've saved myself a trip to the store . . . Oh, here we go."

She pulled out a bottle of Febreze.

Bergman took it from her hand and read the label. "Meadows & Rain." He glanced at her as he spun the sprayer to on and did an experimental squeeze-'n'-sniff. "Not bad. Not my Axe, but fresh."

Cassandra resettled her straps on her shoulders and threw up her hands. "I know it's strange, but right before David deployed, he asked me to bring him something that smelled like home, because he wanted to feel like he was with me while he was away. And this is what I use on my curtains between cleanings. So I gave him a bottle to keep, and then I have this one to remind me that he's smelling the same scent wherever he is." She touched the blue plastic with an affectionate finger. "It sounds stupid when I say it out loud."

"Yeah." Bergman nodded. "It does."

I gave him a little shove. "I can't wait until you fall in love. You are going to act like the biggest dork, and we're all going to make unmerciful fun of you."

To my surprise he grinned and said, "Okay."

We took turns spraying each other. By the time we were done, all of us, including Jack, smelled like a feminine-hygiene commercial.

"Hurry up and get in there," I told my boss, giving his cane a nudge with my toe to encourage forward movement. "Or else you're going to have to braid my hair while we watch Bergman and Cassandra cavort around in a field full of flowers."

"At least Jack is not trying to make love to your leg," Vayl said.

"I can't believe you brought that up." I glared at Bergman. "I still haven't forgiven you for drenching me in dog pheromones, by the way. So just watch your step inside. This could be the perfect setup for my revenge."

"Hey, it worked out great!" Bergman squeaked. "You got a new best friend out of the deal!"

I looked down at my dog, who smiled up at me, his days as the pet of an international criminal mastermind a distant memory. "You are pretty cool," I told him. "But we're about to go into a bad place. So behave yourself, all right?" He bumped his nose into my leg, his substitute for a reassuring pat.

I took a better grip on his leash as we watched Vayl squeeze past the wiggly gray tunnel cover. Bergman and Cassandra followed, with me and Jack bringing up the rear. No way could I crawl through the gently sloping passageway while holding a gun, so I reholstered Grief. Its weight didn't provide the usual reassurance. Because according to Astral's video, the path opened at the crossroads, so Vayl would have to deal with the guard alone.

He'll be fine.

My body, bent abnormally by the low ceiling, disagreed. It was like my aching back, my stiff neck, even my chafed knees, knew this setup sucked. But my mind kept fighting it.

He's a vampire. What could go wrong?

Shut up, Brude!

Now what? I am trying to comfort you! Is that not what every good king does for his—

Knock it off! I took a deep breath. Wiped the sweat off my upper lip. *Vayl's not going to get his head blown off. And I won't be buried under tons of earth. The ceiling's in great shape. It's probably held up for a hundred years.*

On the other hand . . . *Fuck you, Pete! My next job had better be in the great wide open or, I swear, I'm gonna pull out your two remaining hairs and staple them to your ears!*

I took another breath. Realized I wasn't going to panic, and felt myself relax. Slightly. Although I understood at some level that if I heard one sound that remotely reminded me of an earthquake I could well bolt, leaving all my friends to fend for themselves.

Wuss.

Deciding to deal with my neuroses later, I concentrated on Astral's video feed. Saw the guard sniff the air, and take a second snort. Just as I realized he'd interpreted our Febreze for the intrusion it was, he drew the weapon he'd kept holstered at his side. Though it looked a lot like a sawed-off shotgun, I knew it worked on totally different principles.

People who live underground don't like to make big bangs that could cause cave-ins. This gun, powered by air compressed and heated by the breath of his shaman, scattered polished granite shot in a broad pattern that allowed even the most myopic shooters to hit their targets.

"Vayl! He's onto us!"

"Take cover!" Vayl ordered.

Bergman and Cassandra went flat.

"Astral!" I called as I drew Grief. "Go for that guard's moving arm!"

As Vayl lunged forward, trying to clear the tunnel before the guard could squeeze one off, I struggled to advance over my friends without crushing vital organs. Not easy when most of your vision is concentrated on robokitty's attack. My eyes had such a hard time following her speed that my stomach lurched in protest.

Astral hit the guard just before he pulled the trigger. She snarled just like a real cat and sank every one of her claws through the cloth of his sleeve. He yelled in protest as his arm wavered, the shot went wide, and Vayl emerged from the tunnel, a visible cloud streaming from his shoulders as he dropped the room's temperature enough to make the guard's tail shiver and his teeth clack.

"Stay here or you're gonna get frostbite," I told my crew as I left the tunnel, Jack bounding after me. As a Sensitive I can take Vayl's hits without icicles encasing my curls. And my malamute was made for cold weather.

Vayl grabbed the guard by his lapels with one hand while he knocked the gun to the floor with the other. In a move even quicker than Astral's he jerked the guard's head to one side, baring his neck. One bite, one push of power, and his victim's blood froze.

Vayl let the body fall. His grin, full-fanged and bloody, pulled a similar response from me. He stepped toward me, his power so full I could feel it rubbing between us like cool satin on hot skin. The scrape of boots on the floor made me spin around. Bergman and Cassandra had crawled out of the tunnel. I turned back to Vayl.

In that moment he'd pulled it all back, his jaw clenched so hard I was surprised it didn't break. He pointed his thumb over his shoulder. "I will discover where this right-hand passage leads."

"Oh. That—yeah. We'll wait here." I watched him go while Astral circled the chamber, awaiting new orders.

"That was . . . scary," said Bergman, pointing to the guard's throat.

"He's an assassin. What did you expect?" I asked. I realized I was petting Jack, and not because *he* needed it. I stopped.

Bergman shrugged. "One shot through the forehead with a gun."

"You watch too much TV."

"Why do you keep looking after him?" he asked, jerking his thumb toward the tunnel Vayl had taken. "Is he about to get into more trouble?"

I sighed and met Bergman's gaze. "No, I was just wondering."

"Wondering what?"

Should I explain? This guy wanted to partner with me. Which meant maybe he should know. Especially if it would back him off of a deal that might not be that great for his health. I pointed at the corpse. "What do you see?"

"A dead guy."

"What else?"

He looked closer. So did Cassandra. It was like they thought I'd asked them to solve a puzzle. He said, "Nice, clean uniform that makes him seem like he's about to march in a parade. Shiny shoes. Well-maintained weapon. No rings, so I guess he was single." He shrugged. "I don't know what else."

I said, "He was alive a few seconds ago. Breathing. Thinking. Trying to make us dead. But we won. We put him down, for good. Vayl and I, we're not right, Bergman. After a kill we don't stand around and analyze the remains like you just did. We jubilate. You get it? Inside, we're freaking high. Because we took that evil spark and crushed it. Just like God."

When he began to look a little sick I realized he'd begun to understand. I said, "That's why he had to leave. So you wouldn't see us—like that. So he could remind himself he's not even close to God. More the opposite."

Which was why he needed me. And why I needed my old buddy Miles. Not to mention my new pal Cassandra.

Huh.

Funny what you discover after a kill.

While we waited for Vayl to come down from the rush, I went through the guard's pockets. Found some dice, a wad of bills to prove they were loaded, a dirty handkerchief—"Catch, Bergman!"

He dodged it. "Gross!"

Chuckling, I continued my search. Nothing else in the pockets. Around the neck an amulet with the image of Ufran on one side and a star on the other. I took it.

"That seems a little sacrilegious," Cassandra protested.

"It's because of their religion that we're here," I reminded her. "Besides, we know a lot of these are used as hides for important papers." I tossed it to Bergman. "See if you can find a latch."

The guard had nothing else of interest on him, unless you counted a tattoo that showed like a bruise on his sun-starved calf. "Another star," Cassandra said.

"It's their symbol for purity," I told her. "The star means he could trace his ancestry back at least ten generations and they were all small, squat, and blue-schnozzed. In other words, pure gnomes."

Cassandra cocked her head to the side. "I can only imagine what they think of Americans, most of you of such mixed blood."

"Let's put it this way. They picked at least two dudes to infect with their larvae, and both came from the States. I know what that says to me."

"Got it!" Bergman held the amulet in both hands now, its Ufran face flipped open to reveal a hidey-hole packed with folded white paper. I snatched it and unfolded it. Barely big enough to fit in my palm, it held a crudely drawn picture.

Some of it I got right away. I knew Ufran's symbol, the star with the smiley face in its center, so I recognized it hanging in the sky. The gnomes standing on a hill, bowing down to it, I recognized from the pinecone-shaped tufts at the ends of their tails. Though I didn't quite get why an arrow had been drawn pointing to one in particular. Then I realized he was wearing the distinctive asparagus-carved headdress of the shaman. But I didn't understand the word that had been written above his head. *Ylmi.*

The artist had also drawn another group of crowned figures standing in front of a closed gate at the foot of a second hill. They all pointed their scepters to a grass tree from which protruded the trunk of another tree, one that looked to have burned in a recent brushfire. Of everything, the crowns made the least sense to me. As far as I knew, gnomes governed by smackdown. Nobody dared to call themselves royalty, much less wear head jewelry, for fear they'd be drummed out of the tribe for putting on airs the next time they lost a battle.

Though I didn't understand the entire message, that's definitely what it was. And I suddenly knew that was how I could communicate my previous idea to Cassandra without letting Brude know! "Bergman, I need to borrow a pen."

He dug one out of his ever-present pocket guard and handed it over. I sat on the floor. *Granny May? I need you to tell Cassandra what I was thinking. You know, while I distract Brude.* It might've been the hardest mental exercise I'd ever tried. Writing a note with the wisest part of my mind while having a heated argument with the Domytr in possession of its major controlling unit. But in the end I'd managed to piss him off royally as I created a message to Cassandra that said, *I think you should hide out in this warren until we've killed the demon. I know it's scary, but you're smart. Find the deepest, darkest corner of the place and just be still. We'll come for you as soon as we can.*

She read it twice, nodded, and pocketed it. I signaled for Bergman to hang the amulet back around the guard's neck. I expected him to get all icky-poo on me. He did it without complaining, but he did wipe his hands down the sides of his pants several times after.

Vayl returned, explaining that he'd explored the tunnel far enough to discover it led to the industrial center of the warren, where they heated the water they used to power the warren, and where they'd built the artificially lit farms they called gnoves.

"Let us take the alternate route," he suggested. "I believe Ruvin's family waits at the end of it."

"Along with the rest of the town," I said.

"Just so," said Vayl. "Which is why you must all stay directly behind me. I will be able to camouflage our approach."

"Except for the scent of Febreze?" Cassandra suggested.

Vayl considered her comment. Then he said, "The guard was expecting trouble. These creatures will not be. You would be amazed at what busy, self-absorbed people never see or choose to ignore."

She watched us both for a second. "I suppose, knowing how successful you two have been at this kind of work, I'll have to take your word on that."

I sent Astral ahead to warn us if anyone was coming, and we continued into the second tunnel. This one had been built much taller. As they often did, the gnomes had probably squatted in tunnels built by bigger creatures, bringing in more and more families, steadfastly refusing to leave until the original owners were forced to find more peaceful lodgings elsewhere. Those *others* must've been our height, or even taller. Which was what got Vayl and me started playing our Who Was Here First? game.

"I like the Lofhs for this warren," I said from over Bergman and Cassandra's shoulders. Jack glanced up at my comment like he'd met a few of the tall, shy, wallpainters. "I read that a tribe immigrated to Sydney back in the 1800s. Maybe a few came south."

Vayl ran his fingers across the well-worked stone as we walked toward a dawning light. Astral had already shown me it belonged to a flickering set of wall lamps that gave the warren a haunted-house atmosphere. "My guess is that these tunnels were built by the Rikk'n. I remember hearing that they had built several under-

ground towns in the region before gnomes discovered they preferred talking to fighting and crowded them out."

Bergman said, "You know, if my mom knew these *others* shared
a name with the little red-hatted statues she sticks in her garden
every spring she'd throw a fit! Don't gnomes have any redeeming
qualities?"

Vayl thought for a second. "They generally die quietly."

"Astral's at the end of the tunnel," I said. "She's registering
some manufactured light. Enough, at least, to keep the Ufranites
from constantly bumping into each other."

Always the scientist, Bergman said, "I'm guessing the ones who
run the gnoves wouldn't appreciate going from pitch dark to fake
sun day after day. Same with those who venture outside."

"I agree," said Vayl. "Perhaps your theory will help us in the
future," he added tactfully. "But now we need to know what Astral
is seeing."

I said, "It looks like a town square. The floor is flat and the ceiling's so high it doesn't even register. Kiosks have been carved out of
the rock, one right after another, from the entrance right around
the curve of the room. Gnomes are lined up at them, trading coins
for food and stuff that glows and . . . yeah, I think I see a T-shirt
booth. Most of the Ufranites are gathered in the center of the area,
which is almost parklike. Hell, they even have a bandstand with
potted trees in the back. Anyway, I see blankets on the floor with
plates, silverware, and tubs of food set out on them. Families are
sitting, talking to each other and their neighbors. Lots of smiles
and giggles. I'd say maybe eighty gnomes have collected, including
fifteen to twenty kids." I bit my lip. "You don't suppose they're getting ready to eat Ruvin's family tonight?"

Vayl's pinched nostrils told me he'd considered it. "Do you see
any cooking implements? Perhaps a large fire or a cauldron?"

I stared hard into Astral's projection. "No. Just that overgrown
gazebo everybody's sitting around. It's holding a three-piece band
with a drum and a couple of stringed gourds. I wouldn't call what

they're doing to those instruments playing, though." Gnome music sounded like a constipated guy trying—and failing—to clear his obstruction.

Cassandra had been crouching beside Jack, petting him to keep him calm as she leaned against the tunnel wall. Now she held up a hand, her distant expression on the one I usually dreaded. But maybe this time her vision had nothing to do with the death of one of my relatives.

"The shaman is coming," she whispered. She glanced up at us, her focus still far away. "He's like a huge ball of black fire in my mind's eye." She paused. "Something is off about him." She put a hand to her forehead, dug her fingernails in. "He doesn't seem . . . quite real. Why? Why would—" She stopped, her wide eyes staring into mine, panic swimming so close to the surface that I grabbed both of her arms without thinking.

"What is it?"

"My vision flipped. I was trying to get a better view of the shaman and suddenly I was Seeing a man's face. He's dead." Tears spilled from her eyes.

"Do you recognize him?"

She shook her head. Went still. "Someone . . . is trying to speak to me." She ran her hands along the floor, staring off into the distance like she was blind.

"Cassandra!" She jerked her head toward me, frowning as her eyes refocused. "The man," I reminded her. "Describe him."

"Dirty-blond hair. His eyes are open. They're dark blue. He's still snarling, like he died fighting. There's a scar, like a half-moon, running from the side of his left eye down almost to the corner of his mouth."

Oh. Fuck. "Cassandra, this is important. Look at his neck. Is there a tattoo just under his ear? It would be—"

She finished my sentence with me. "—of a wolf's head."

Vayl and I nodded at each other. We didn't need our extra connection to discuss how the shock had blown holes in our concentration. How we wanted to kill something. Right. Now. Because the man in Cassandra's vision had been one of ours. An agent named Ethan Mreck, who'd spent the past few years infiltrating one of the biggest threats to peace left in Europe. A band of wolves called the Valencian Weres.

As a werewolf himself, Ethan had moved in circles no one else could even visualize. Which was why his undercover work had brought our department so much valuable information. In fact, his intel had sparked our last mission, leading us to destroy Edward "The Raptor" Samos, the worst enemy to U.S. National Security since Adolf Hitler. We'd also severely crippled his girl-friend, the Scidairan coven leader, Floraidh Halsey. After those successes, we'd hoped Ethan could help us find a way to pull the plug on the Valencian Weres, who'd definitely be making a power play now that they smelled the chance to gain territory. But Ethan was dead.

I watched our psychic's darting eyes, saw her mouth tighten, and knew she was trying to pin down wisps of images that wanted to be caught and categorized about as bad as a butterfly does. I tried to help. "The fact that you Saw Ethan here, in the warren—that means the gnomes have to be connected to the Weres he was investigating, don't you think?"

She shook her head. "I don't know," she said helplessly. "All I can sense now is this terrible calamity, looming like the dust of ten thousand horsemen on the horizon." She clasped her hands together, her fingers worrying among each other as she gazed up at us. "We have to succeed in this mission."

I shrugged. "We always do." I frowned when she grabbed the sleeve of my jacket.

"No! You don't understand! Doom is here, close to us, waiting for us to fail!"

I raised my eyes to Vayl, who nodded carefully. "We hear you, Cassandra. We understand."

I hesitated. When she had nothing else to add I said, "We have to get moving now. You understand?"

As she bowed her head Vayl nodded. "I agree, and even more quickly than we had anticipated. Jasmine, can you get a more specific sense of the chamber's layout?"

I said, "Astral, look around the edge of the room. Stealth-mode, girl." As obedient as any well-trained dog, my cat stalked around the crowd without once being noticed. Her vigilance paid off when I was able to report details like more tunnels leading out of the town square, probably toward residential areas. Barrels full of waxy white flowers marked the shops and tunnel openings. The one arch they'd failed to decorate was located on the other side of the picnicking crowd. A single barred gateway, it was guarded by a gnome who looked a lot more interested in the band than his work.

"Go find out what's behind that gate," I told Astral as we edged toward the tunnel's mouth. Everybody could hear the music now. Seeing—not so easy. Our path took a bend before it opened into the square, but when Vayl and I leaned forward far enough we got our first look at those who called themselves Ufran's Chosen. All of them primmed and propered just in case he looked down from reading his evening paper and needed a moment to remind himself how much they respected him. Because somewhere along the way they'd decided he was big into smiting.

Vayl caught my attention. Raised his eyebrows. His unuttered question, *Has your scout uncovered anything helpful?*

I nodded. Astral had found the family. The kids huddled on a bench under the single window of a tiny, candlelit cell, finishing off the crumbs of supper while Mom paced its length. Her black hair, liberally laced with platinum highlights, combined with a double-sided updo to make her resemble a pissed-off lynx. Especially when she slapped the wall with the palm of her hand every time she made her turn. Seeing the rage on her face, I wondered for a second how they'd managed to cage her.

My guess? Her dress was partly to blame. It fit so tight I wasn't sure how she walked more than three steps without falling. The other reasons sat behind her dressed in jeans, white T-shirts, and suspenders, legs swinging back and forth, heels thumping into the rock at their backs in time with their mother's movements.

When I finished describing the scene, Vayl motioned us into a huddle. "Bergman," he whispered, "I believe we are going to need a distraction. As we skirt the crowd, I want you to deduce the best means to cause one. And when I give you the signal, do it."

Miles visibly gulped. But he didn't drop down his old scaredy slide. He said, "What should I do afterward?"

"Get out. The rest of us will free the family. We will meet you at the car." He gave Bergman his keys. "If we do not beat you there, make sure it is running."

Bergman said, "Now I understand why Jasmine always backs in."

Vayl returned to the front of the line and we all followed him around the corner. Now we could be seen. Theoretically. But the tingle at the back of my neck signaled his power boost. Not that he could actually cloak us. That would've been too sweet. But Vayl's ability worked almost as well, turning the attention toward what it wanted to see anyway. The band. An attractive member of the opposite—or maybe the same—sex. Nobody even turned their heads as we sidled around the edge of the crowd, avoiding family groups and last-minute snackers lined up at the shops that surrounded the square.

Once Jack danced sideways, his nose pulling him toward some little rugrat's tray of fried tentacles, but he responded well when I pulled him in closer and gave him my like-hell-you-will! glare.

By the time we reached the cell-side of the town's square, Bergman's forehead looked like a surgeon's during the fourth hour of a complex operation. Cassandra and I shared a look. *Should we swab him off or just let him sweat into his eyes?* I asked her silently.

Her answer was to nod toward his sleeve, so I gently lifted his forearm and wiped it across his face. *Thanks*, he mouthed. I nodded.

Vayl had led us to a corner on the guard's left that held a trash can and a bench carved out of the wall. Bergman sank onto it. Vayl grabbed his arm and pulled him back upright. Even Miles couldn't mistake the question on the vampire's face. *Are you ready?*

Slight jerk of the head, more a spasm than an actual nod.

Vayl's gesture could almost be interpreted as, *Shoo, then.* But he really meant *Get into position.*

Bergman looked around, as if trying to figure out where to go next.

In front of us, the side of the bandstand rose about five feet off the floor, its base holding up a finely tooled railing punctuated every few feet by a post that held up the wood-shingled roof. No stairs here; they'd been set at the very front so the performers would have to walk through the middle of the crowd to get to them.

All of the trees behind the bandstand sat on watering trays with rollers, which made me wonder how often they rearranged their shrubbery down here. In front, the crowd seemed relaxed, happy. Not at all the types who'd boil kids and roast their mom. Which just goes to show, you should never trust your first impressions.

Bergman crouched and scuttled into the first line of trees, his movements reminding me somewhat hilariously of an anorexic crab. I had to gulp back laughter as I told him through the party line, "You're out of Vayl's influence now. So be discreet until you get the order."

"Will do."

I checked on Cassandra. She had Jack firmly in hand. *Shaman?* I mouthed.

Soon, came her silent reply. And then a shrug and shake of the head. She still didn't like her vision of our potential target.

I gave her a *stay close* gesture. Then I brushed my hand against Vayl's. Doing my best to ignore the tingle it caused, I nodded to him. "Now," I whispered.

His slight nod acknowledged our readiness as he slipped up behind the guard and we followed, staying clear to give him room to work. So fast. One hand to the throat to stifle sound and crush the airway. One to the back of the neck to support the blow. Vayl held the guard, assuring death while I searched him for the cell keys. I had other ways in, but they wouldn't be as quick or possibly as quiet. Yup, there they were, hanging from a leather strap around his neck. One for the gate door. Another for the cell that sat at the end of a short path. They both worked perfectly.

As Ruvin's family crowded toward us, I held my finger to my lips. At the same time Cassandra whispered, "You must be quiet. Practically the whole warren sits outside this cell."

"Well, you picked a fine time to break us out, didn't you?" demanded Ruvin's wife.

"What's your name?" I asked.

"Tabitha," she snapped. The boys had run to her side.

"I'm Laal," said the taller one, who might've been nine or ten, but still only reached my mid-thigh. He pointed to his brother, who stood a head shorter. "This is Pajo."

I stuck out my hand, which Laal and Pajo politely shook. "Lucille Robinson," I said. "Your dad's pretty worried about you. And since we were in the area we thought we'd drop in and see if you'd like to join us for dinner. I think we're having pizza."

"Anytime now, Jasmine," Vayl's deep voice rang in my ear.

The boys were nodding so hard their chins practically banged their shirt collars, but Tabitha held them back. "How do you know Ruvin?"

I wanted to shake her and scream, "How stupid are you, bitch? The door is fucking open! Let's go!"

But she knew that just outside milled a crowd of would-be cannibals and she hadn't seen our references yet.

I stepped back. "Cassandra?"

She smiled and let some slack out on Jack's leash. As soon as he stuck his nose into their hands, the boys fell in love. Much hugging and petting of the grinning malamute while our Seer spoke softly to their mom.

"I know you must be terrified. But we are your best chance at escaping this predicament unscathed. Let us help you free your sons before anything more traumatic happens to them. Please?"

Tabitha glanced at Laal and Pajo. I expected a rush of warmth to ease the harsh lines of her face. Instead they tightened, as if she was doing unpleasant math problems in her head. "All right. Boys?" She snapped her fingers and they immediately left Jack to run to her side. *Wow. No whining or anything? Either she runs a really well-disciplined household or—no. I'm not going to think the worst of anyone for once. That's something Brude would do.* I turned to lead them out.

I murmured, "We're on our way," to Vayl. Then I looked back over my shoulder and whispered, "Two things. Be quieter than you've ever been in your life." Special smile for the boys. "Übersneaky, got it?" They nodded solemnly. "And stay as close as you can to the big man we're meeting at the gate. His name is Jeremy, and he can make it so the crowd doesn't see us. But we've arranged a little distraction as well. Just ignore it when it happens and follow Jeremy and me out. Got it?"

Ruvin's family nodded again. I hoped that meant they understood. Hard to say how much was sinking in. You never knew with somebody who'd spent time as a prisoner and was now escaping. Sometimes the moment itself overwhelmed everything else, even the ability to process the instructions they needed to make it successful. I looked over them to Cassandra, gave her a *keep an eye on them* look.

We crept down the path toward the gate. "Astral," I whispered. "Go back to the tunnel exit. Don't get caught."

We rejoined Vayl at the gate door. He'd hidden the guard's body. My guess would've been inside the trash can. *Good call.* Laal and Pajo didn't need to see us handling corpses if we could help it.

Vayl took stock. Tender look for me. Approval toward Cassandra and Jack. Curiosity in Tabitha's direction. And for the boys, a moment of intensity, like the silence before a shout.

He pulled me aside. Spoke directly into my ear. "We have to get these boys out safely."

"Of course."

"Understand me. Whatever else happens, here, or with the mission, we cannot let these boys die."

I stared into his eyes, which had turned the purple of a boxer's ribs after a bad beating. And I knew something about Laal and Pajo had reminded him sharply of his own murdered sons. Or maybe it was just that he'd finally found a chance to prevent another father from feeling the anguish he'd endured now for over two hundred and fifty years. Didn't matter to me.

I said, "The boys live no matter what. Of course. There was never another option."

He put both hands to my shoulders like he meant to hug me; then he looked over my head, remembered our circumstances, and dropped his arms. Turning toward the crowd so that he blocked most of us at the gate with both his bulk and power, he murmured, "Now, Bergman."

Motioning us forward, he began to move at a slow but even pace back the way we'd come.

Which was when Bergman popped out from behind the trees and climbed up the back of the bandstand. He shoved his way to the front of the stage, a camera in each hand, grinning like a lunatic and blowing an enormous bubble from a spare piece of gum he must've borrowed from Cole.

The band faded out. Its inattentive audience quickly swung its focus away from itself and to the stage as this new phenomenon began to click off picture after picture. Finally Bergman grabbed a microphone. "Okay, that was excellent. Now, my guy in Hollywood tells me if this movie's going to work we're gonna need all of you to really get into your parts. Okay? And . . . smile!"

Chapter Fourteen

I was genuinely shocked when I froze. Paralysis is not what I do. I think. On my feet. As they move. Generally at my target. Or away from danger. Or, in this case, toward the exit while I figured out how to rescue my idiot consultant before he got himself killed and Pete demoted me to, oh, I don't know . . . resident flyswatter?

But I was stuck. This was my first clue that Brude had commandeered my limbs. Then he turned me toward the source of what he thought would soon be lurid entertainment. In other words, a bloodbath. Starring my best friend, who was clicking off shots of the crowd and talking fast about some fantasy film starring Angelina Jolie and Warwick Davies. Dumbass.

Granny May! I yelled, an SOS to my own psyche. I saw her head shoot up from the green beans she'd been snapping into a bowl on her lap. She still sat on the front porch. But she looked less fearful. And I noticed she'd brought some sort of club outside with her. I focused on the item that lay on the floor beside her rocking chair. Nearly giggled out loud when I recognized the leg of an old iron lamp Gramps Lew had kept promising to fix but never seemed to get to. She'd taken to carrying it with her from room to room as a reminder, which had evolved into a joke. And once he'd died, it had become a memento. Now, maybe, it would take another role.

I see him, she whispered, leaning down to get a good grip on the club. *Trust me, Jazzy, he won't get any closer. You get on with your job, now.*

Hoping my mind could war on itself without causing irreparable damage, I tried to take a step. *Yes!* A couple more. *Go, Granny May!* I hustled to get back into formation, which was a lot like before, only now Vayl and I had three extra civilians lining up between us.

We'd made it a quarter of the way around the back edge of the crowd. Nobody had a clue their prisoners were escaping. All eyes had glued themselves to the idiot human on the platform, who seemed to be delivering a message of fame and good fortune that even the most devout among them found hard to ignore.

"I'm gonna kill him," I whispered. "If they don't get to him first, that is." Remembering the party line I said, "Do you hear that, Bergman? You were supposed to pull some amazing gadget out of your bag and fill the place with stink bombs or locusts or something. Not risk your freaking neck on a dumb stunt that Cole might pull. Just let me get these kids safe and then I'll—"

"I know what I'm doing here!" Bergman announced to the crowd, though I knew he'd aimed his statement at me. "You might question my methods a little bit, but this is how blockbusters get made. I'm telling you, Hugh Jackman started out the same way. Now, could we have all the gentlemen just line up on either side of the stairs here?"

The gnomish men traded puzzled looks. A couple of them rose. And why wouldn't they? Bergman sounded so confident.

"That's right," he said. "Form a kind of hallway for the shaman to walk through when he comes onstage. That's the way the director is visualizing it, so he wants me to get some shots to send back to him."

More gnomes stood. A living tunnel began to form. Because the shaman must have approved this stickman's presence. How else would he know about their leader's impending appearance?

"Excellent. Great." Bergman worked himself to the corner of

the bandstand closest to our exit as he snapped picture after picture. "Ope! I think I see the shaman coming! Already." Bergman's voice tried to strangle itself. He murmured, "Something's wrong with this parade. The shaman's standing on some kind of raft carried by uniformed guards, but he's stiff and wobbly. Almost like a mannequin . . . Do they believe in freeze-drying their religious leaders?"

"We have no information that he has even been sick," Vayl replied. "Proceed as planned."

Bergman gulped so loudly my ears popped. Then he yelled, "Everybody stand up straight! Yep, that means you people in the middle too. On your feet! Stand and face the shaman!"

Even from our spot, a city block from freedom, I could hear the distant rumble of drums heralding the main man's approach.

"RAFS! I mean, Astral!" Bergman yelled.

"What do you need?" I asked, using all my self-control to keep my voice at a whisper.

Some of the gnomes were frowning at him now. Moving toward the steps. Reaching up as if to grab him.

"A grenade would be ideal!"

"Astral, show me your location!" She stood in the entrance to our escape tunnel awaiting orders. "Bergman, what's her range?" I asked.

"About fifty yards."

"Come to me, Astral. Run!"

Sooner than I'd expected a streak of black reached my feet and leaped into my arms, slamming into my chest like an oversized volleyball. I tucked her under my arm, feeling ridiculously Monty Pythonesque as I pointed her toward the front of the shaman's parade, which had just come into view, a long row of guards carrying between them a cooking pot the size of a bathtub.

"Okay, girl, hawk a grenade as far as you can."

I felt her entire body pulse, a repeated motion just like you'd expect a cat to make. Except her mouth didn't yawn, releasing a rocket-propelled minibomb as I'd expected. I heard a *thunk* and looked down. Astral had dumped a red metal sphere beside my right foot.

"Shit!" I dropped her, grabbed the grenade, and lofted it as hard and as far as I could. Fortunately my college track training hadn't completely failed me, and the missile exploded in the air, raining shrapnel on the Ufranite guards below.

The sound itself, a *whump* so deafening I immediately glanced up to see if the ceiling was falling, terrified the gnomes into a stampede. Add to that the gong of the falling cauldron, the screams of the wounded, the wails of terrified women and children, and you have what Pete likes to call "a situation."

"Bergman! Why didn't you tell me the grenades came out her ass!"

"Where else would they launch from?"

"Where—where are you?" *So I can show you exactly what I think you can do with your cat and her grenades?*

"Where do you think? Booking down the tunnel! How come you're still hanging around there?"

Hard to stay pissed at a guy who asked such good questions.

I'd had to stop to launch Astral's weapon, but I was pretty sure no one had seen me. Now I caught up to the line, still remarkably intact considering the smoke and noise. But disturbing in that Tabitha was hurrying ahead of her sons, not even glancing over her shoulder to make sure they were keeping up with her.

Only a few more steps and Vayl would be inside the tunnel. Which was a good thing, because our camo wouldn't hold for much longer. With panicked gnomes running in random directions, he couldn't direct their thoughts anymore. Which meant we could be spotted at—

"The prisoners are escaping!" shrilled one man, a pointy-headed, shaggy-haired example of why gnomes rarely marry outside their species. I stepped out of line to meet his rush, hoping Laal and Pajo were looking the other way as I drew my bolo.

While Vayl led the rest of our party into the tunnel, I confronted Pencil-head with a blade as long as his legs. Astral took her place next to me, arching her back and hissing as he drew his own weapon, a dagger that he spun in an intricate pattern designed to display his skill and intimidate me into making a mistake. I tossed my bolo into my left hand. Back into my right.

He snickered at my obvious lack of ability and lowered his arms. Just the mistake I was waiting for. I flung the blade just like I practiced every day on the range back in Ohio. It flew true, splitting his skull like a ripe cantaloupe. He dropped with the hilt of my great-great-granddad's war knife sticking out from between his eyes. Unfortunately a couple of his buddies had heard his warning. And a few more saw him go down.

"Vayl," I said as I sidled toward the exit, robokitty in tow. "I've got five, no make that six, gnomes in pursuit." I pulled Grief, switched it into crossbow mode because I didn't want to make another loud noise in a place where I could be buried alive. I paused to take a shot. "Make that five. They must not be able to afford to arm everybody the same because I don't see rifles. All these goons have are knives and handguns."

A shot pinged off the rock above my head.

"Are they sounding a general alarm?"

"Not yet. That last kill pissed them off too much. Plus, I think they know everybody else is too distracted with the explosion."

"Can you hold them off until I get the boys out safely?"

"Sure." Another shot slammed into the path behind me. *Nope. And he probably knows that. But I'd be so pissed if he put my life ahead of those kids. And he knows that too.*

"Bergman," I said, forcing myself to breathe evenly because if I lost it now, I'd die. "How many of those grenades did you load into Astral?"

"Two," he told me. "But, like I said before, they're experimental. I was hoping we could try them out in a more controlled situation after the mission was over. I was amazed that one worked."

I wouldn't go that far.

I squeezed off another bolt as the cat and I backed to the tunnel. One more down. The odds looked better, but these Ufranites weren't giving up easily. Maybe they didn't like the fact that we'd just tried to bury tiny bits of steel in their shaman's face.

My remaining pursuers fell back, taking themselves out of range, though that meant they couldn't hit me either. They fanned out, trying to surround me before I could reach my escape hatch. I could see the plan in their eyes. They knew how long Grief needed to reload now. The second I turned to run, the last three gnomes would rush me. As soon as they got into range, they'd open up with their overengineered handguns and pop me into the next world for good. With a sound only slightly louder than a Jack fart.

The two sides of me warred. I wanted so badly to escape the confines of the tunnels that my eyeballs were straining for natural light. If they could, they'd probably leap from their sockets and bounce down the path, leading the rest of my body to freedom. At the same time I felt insulted at the possibility of death by "poof." When you get taken out, you kinda want it to happen with such an epic blast that people wish they were sitting on their toilets during the final kaboom. That way there's less mess to clean up later on.

Okay, well, if this is it, I glanced down at the cat, *let's do it up right*.

I said, "Astral, as soon as I shoot, launch a grenade in the same direction. Let's think airtime this go-around, okay? Imagine it's burrito night at Crindertab's."

She responded with her accordion dance. I gave her to the count of three and shot at the gnome farthest from me. A beat later she raised her butt and heaved. This toss reminded me of a second-grader's softball pitch. One that bounces before it hits the plate.

"Really?" I spared her a disgusted glance. "I'm about to get wasted and you shit out another dud?"

She looked up at me, her eyes crossed slightly as if somewhere in her circuits the ghost of a Siamese kitten lurked. Her tail twitched. And the grenade began to smoke. Bright blue. In the shape of a fist with the middle finger raised.

"Oh, Bergman," I chuckled, "you didn't."

His voice came back to me, breathless from running. "You like the effect?" he asked. "I think I got the same shade as Ufran's nose. At least, that's what I was going for."

The smoke, thick as yogurt, allowed me to back down the tunnel to where it turned before one of the gnomes caught up to me. We shot at nearly the same time. Only I didn't jump when the adrenaline surged. Or tighten my major muscles and forget to breathe.

I won the showdown. Later I might puke in reaction to the close call. Now I said, "Come on, Astral." I turned and rammed full into Vayl. "Ow! Geez, you could've warned me!"

He'd wrapped an arm around my waist to keep me from falling. Now he pulled me in closer. "You are the most spectacular woman I have ever met."

My toes literally curled inside my boots as he dropped a light kiss on my lips. A breathless moment later he'd disappeared into the square, swallowed by the smoke. I heard a strangled scream. *Well, that takes care of my prob—*

Another cry. And another. It sounded like reinforcements had arrived. And not one of them had counted on confronting a vampire in the full rush of his power. We'd created exactly the kind of havoc a shaman couldn't just shrug off. But we had to survive to make it work. We needed to get our asses out of here. NOW!

I knew Vayl could feel my urgency. He'd come. But would it be too late?

I transformed Grief back into gun mode, hoping whoever built these caverns had shored them up California style. I went back into the cavern, stood with my back to the tunnel entrance, and stared hard into the smoke, straining to see my *sverhamin*. It was a role he took seriously if the next groan I heard was any clue. Well, he could protect me until cows crapped coal, I also had a part to play in this relationship. And as his *avhar* it was my duty not only to watch his back in the fight he was waging, but to get him out in as good a shape as he was when he went in.

There! A face swimming out of the mist. Long, knobby-ended nose. Skin the shade of stale marshmallows. A moment of recognition as we both realized we'd met the enemy. Blur of movement as he raised his gun. But I'd beat him before he knew we were competing. I blew him back into the smoke.

"Jasmine!"

"Vayl, stop playing! We gotta go!"

Rush of cold air as he came to my side. "I do not play," he said as he wiped a droplet of blood from his lips.

"You were *eating*? A religious fanatic? Damn, don't you have any taste?" Together we turned and ran down the tunnel. Moments later we heard the tromp of boots coming after us.

Still Vayl had the breath to say, "Your dinner before made me hungry. You should be thanking that little Ufranite. If not for him I might be asking you for a donation."

"On second thought, snack on all the gnomes you like." I didn't mean it. I'd just begun sharing sheets with the guy and already I'd have given him anything he asked for. God forbid he ever figured it out. I also wouldn't tell him that when he took my hand and his power jumped through me, giving me speed no human should master, I wanted to giggle like I had the first time I'd ridden the Rock-O-Plane at the county fair. I'd already embarrassed myself enough for one lifetime.

Vayl handed me my bolo. "I believe you dropped this."

I hadn't even realized how much I hated leaving it until my fingers tightened around the hilt.

"You cleaned it and everything! Vayl, this is . . . wow! Thanks!"

For once I could tell exactly what was going on behind those amber eyes. So strange to have found another man who'd do anything to see me smile. I vowed never to take this one for granted.

We burst out of the illusionary door so quickly I'd have cracked my skull on the opposite wall if Vayl hadn't pulled us to a sudden stop. Bergman, who'd been standing in the corner by the other door, moved forward. He held a bulging white sack whose writing I couldn't read. But as soon as he threw the contents at the doorway I smelled the powdery grit of quick-drying concrete.

The door shimmered, twisted, and turned a putrid shade of yellow as the crete interacted with it. "What did you just do?" I asked.

"It's a temporary blockade," Bergman said.

"But . . . how did you know what to do?"

"I'd have been able to figure it out myself if I'd had the time. And RAFS. I mean, Astral," he said defensively.

"Okay. I just wondered how—"

"I called the Agency's warlock," he finally admitted. "It was Vayl's idea." He frowned as he handed my boss his phone. "By the way, he doesn't appreciate being called at seven a.m. when he didn't get to bed until three. I thought he might frogify me through the receiver there for a minute."

Vayl shrugged. "As far as I know Sterling is not on assignment, which means his band probably had a gig last night. Do not worry. He is a decent sort, if somewhat moody."

"Oh." Bergman nodded, like that made sense. "Well, Sterling told me to get something that the wall would really be made of and throw it at the fake door while I said—huh. I can't remember the words now. Anyway, he says it's only a temporary stopper, but it'll hold them long enough for us to get away."

Which was when we heard a series of thumps on the other side of the wall. Followed by shouts and cursing. Followed by prayers to Ufran for forgiveness for the cursing.

"Shouldn't we go?" It was Tabitha, checking her watch and pacing at the top of the steps while Laal and Pajo showered big love on Jack, who withstood the hugs and tugs with his usual good humor.

I started to nod; then I noticed the celebration was missing a partier. "Where's Cassandra?" As if I didn't know.

My *sverhamin* came so close to me that I could feel his breath on my cheeks as he murmured, "I must confess I lied to you earlier. That second tunnel led to the basement of a church. She has taken refuge there until we return for her."

"WHAT?"

Granny May grinned. *Nice acting, Jazzy. Brude is totally convinced.*

Vayl kept his voice level, calm, and low enough that only Bergman, he, and I could hear. "She thought it best. And I agreed."

I shrugged. "Sounds like a plan." When I felt Brude step back from the conversation I smiled and nodded, said, "Guess we'll have some good stories to trade next time we get together."

"Indeed." Vayl glanced at the door, still blocked despite the loud and continuous onslaught on its opposite side. "We should go."

"Fine." I took the stairs two at a time, Astral keeping up nicely despite having passed a couple of grenades recently. I decided I just might get to like the little robot. Jack obviously felt the same. And he'd chosen this moment to bond.

I couldn't fault his timing. Tabitha had begun to herd the kids toward the Wheezer. The rest of us raced after, leaving him free to demonstrate his affection for the newest member of the family. I caught it all in a single over-the-shoulder glance.

She might've had a chance if he'd barked. But he'd remembered their last encounter and decided to approach with wolflike stealth.

Under no orders to do otherwise, Astral sat down in the crackling brown grass and proceeded to groom the gray dust off her exterior, becoming so immersed in the job that he took her completely by surprise. His jump brought him over the top of her, giving him position to lick her right between the ears before he gently cuffed her with a big front paw. Despite the fact that he was careful, his boot sent her spinning. His this-rocks! grin, an expression I've yet to see on another dog, dropped off his muzzle when Astral flipped sideways, snarled in a metallic, my-gears-have-stuck sort of way . . .

And her head blew off.

It hurtled straight toward Bergman. Vayl dove for him, barely shoving him clear before it rocketed into the side of the building, ricocheted into the fence, and bounced onto the lawn like a renegade croquet ball.

"Holy sh—!" I stopped myself just in time to spare the kids, who'd turned to witness the carnage.

"Cool!" said Laal. "It's a robot!"

"And it blew up!" yelled Pajo. He tugged on his mother's skirt. "Do it again! Do it again!"

Moment of stunned silence while we watched Astral's legs jerk and Vayl made a coughing-up-chicken-bones noise that only I knew was his version of barely repressed mirth. I didn't dare look at him for fear I'd start laughing, and then Bergman, standing beside Vayl, holding on to the crown of his hat with both hands, would never forgive me.

I checked Jack to make sure his yelp had purely been one of surprise. He seemed to know he'd done something bad, because his tail remained between his legs even after I'd reassured him he was okay.

I picked up the body, which stayed stiff as one of those lifelike planters with the hole drilled in the belly for a bunch of geraniums. I risked a glance at Bergman. I couldn't tell if the deep furrow between his eyes meant he was holding back tears or he wanted to kick some kittybot-killing ass.

Always long on wisdom, Vayl decided to move away from Bergman so he wouldn't notice the shaking of my boss's shoulders. He walked toward the Wheezer, and had almost made it to the car when he stopped and said, "The head is over here."

We joined him, only some of us to gawk. Astral's head lay on the ground. While smoke still spiraled from the ears and clear fluid leaked from the neck, I didn't see much in the way of dangling parts.

Jack gave it a sniff and slumped into his I've-been-bad position, lying with his tail tucked under his butt, blinking soulfully up at us as if to apologize for our inconvenience.

"Look at him," I said. "He feels terrible."

"Aww." Laal and Pajo knelt by Jack and began rubbing him down, telling him it was okay. Tabitha kept glancing from them to the car and rocking from one foot to the other like she really wanted to make a break for it now that the coast was clear, but she knew it would be rude to run while her rescuers were mourning.

I said, "I'm sorry, Miles. Jack was just playing. He didn't mean to hurt her." I retrieved Astral's head, silently thanking Raoul's boss that her eyelids had shut.

"I'm really sorry, Miles," I repeated. Should I try to stick the head back on the body? Would some kind of internal magnet at least pull it back together for the burial? Such wishful thinking. "He was just trying to make friends."

When my dog started to get up I gave him my don't-even-go-there glare and he sank back down, dropping his head to his paws. Laal and Pajo began the scratchfest all over again. I said, "I'll cover the damages, of course." Though, considering what it must've cost to put Astral together, by the time I'd even halved the payment we'd probably both have forgotten about my debt, along with each other's names and where we'd left our teeth the night before.

"I don't understand," said Bergman, shaking his head. "Jack must've triggered her self-destruct mechanism. But how? I mean, he didn't even try to bite her." He came to stand in front of me, took a pen out of the collection he always kept in his pocket, and started poking around the neck.

"Uh, Bergman?" I said, catching the look on Tabitha's face. "That's kinda gross."

"It's just a machine," he said impatiently.

"But it looks like a cat. That you're doing a primitive autopsy on." I cleared my throat to get his attention, which I then turned toward the kids. Who were riveted.

"Oh. Sorry." He frowned at the remains. "This is a mess."

"You can fix it," Vayl said.

"Are you sure?" he asked.

He nodded. "It is what you do, and you are superb at your job."

Bergman considered Astral's innards with new interest as Tabitha rechecked her watch. "Shouldn't we be going? That door can't hold forever. And Ruvin will be so worried."

Both true. But watching her futz with her dress and hair, I sensed ulterior motives. Still, we jumped straight into the Wheezer, which now felt like one of those maximum-capacity clothes dryers.

I started the car and said, "Whoever has their foot in the back of my head better not have stepped in anything disgusting recently."

The offender moved the shoe and I beat it back to the rental house before anything else exploded, fired on us, or (God forbid) needed a ride.

Chapter Fifteen

The family reunion began just as you'd expect. Ruvin drove up in that glorious Jeep expecting to spend a few miserable hours driving us around while he pretended not to be freaked about his family. Tabitha and the boys ran out of the house. He'd just walked around to the front of the Patriot when he saw them. The surprise and relief sent him staggering back into the bull bar.

Hugs. Tears. More hugs and kisses. Then Tabitha grabbed Ruvin by the hand and said to me, "Look after the boys for a few, will you?" and dragged him inside.

Uh. What just happened?

I stared at Laal and Pajo, who gazed right back at me. When I looked to Vayl for ideas, he shrugged. Bergman remained just as silent, his attention still focused on Astral's repair job.

I said, "I have a niece."

What, are you trying to impress them with your babysitting qualifications?

"Where did Mummy and Daddy go?" asked Pajo, his lower lip beginning to tremble.

I looked desperately at my teammates. "Does anyone have candy?"

Vayl knelt down beside the boys, his demeanor so nonthreatening that a bystander wouldn't have been surprised to hear he made his living breeding and selling bunnies. "You know parents," he said. "They just need to have a talk and then they will be right back. I wonder, while we wait for them, should we go into the backyard and play a game? Hide-and-seek might be fun. I believe I saw several places boys your size could tuck into the last time I was there."

My jaw dropped. I'd been certain Vayl had forgotten how to play games somewhere near the turn of the nineteenth century. And he didn't actually participate in the hiding or the seeking. But he did laugh out loud when Jack gave the game away by running straight to Laal and Pajo's spots before Bergman and I could even get started. They didn't seem to mind, because when he stuck his nose in their faces, they giggled too.

This is your window into Vayl's past. Look carefully. It may never open again, Granny May told me. *This is what got lost when his boys died. And who knows? Maybe this is what he's searching for just as much as the actual reincarnated souls of Hanzi and Badu. A chance to pull a little bit of himself from the jaws of the predator he's become.*

Hard to fault that, especially when I remembered who I'd been before Matt had died. If I could retrieve the part of me that *hoped,* would I?

I realized the inside of my arm had begun to hurt. When I focused on it, I found I'd been scratching at it long enough to raise welts. A couple of them were even bleeding lightly. *This is my life now. Rashing out due to an untimely possession. And if I don't do something about it soon—*

Give yourself to me, Brude whispered, his voice itself like a lesion, searing bits of my brain as it crackled past them. *Fulfill the prophecy. Become my queen and together we will rule the Thin.*

The Thin? I asked. *Or all of hell?*

Soon there will be no difference.

Get out of my head, you parasite.

Or you will do what? Run to Lucifer and tattle? Even a woman with your courage knows better than to put herself near the Great Taker. No, there are only two ways to loosen my grip on you, lass. And I would suggest you pick the first. Because the second sees you in hell.

I wanted to respond with something clever. But all I could think of was, *I'll see* you *in hell*, which was kinda what he wanted. So I stayed silent and wished Granny May could pull in a couple of reinforcements. Anything to push the ancient king away from the front of my mind.

Her image appeared behind my eyes, just like I remembered her when we were dressed for church. She stood at the top of her steps, wearing a dark blue pantsuit and sensible brown slip-ons. Her bag matched the shoes. I knew it contained a few bucks for the offering as well as coloring supplies for us kids and a crossword book for her. She liked to say that she heard the Lord clearest when the reverend was droning and she couldn't for the life of her figure out eighteen across.

She said, *I know of another one who can help. But you're not going to like it.*

I'm past the point of picky. Bring her on.

Gran moved aside, revealing Teen Me. From the amount of eyeshadow and blush she was toting, and considering she was hanging out with Gran, I put her age at right about fourteen.

I started to chuckle. Even more so when I sensed Brude's spurt of fear at the realization that he was about to be set upon by an angry freshman who was old enough to play dirty and young enough not to give a crap how much it hurt.

Chapter Sixteen

Less than ten minutes later Ruvin and Tabitha appeared on the patio looking . . . mussed.

What the hell?

The backyard, recently the site of such a lively game of tag that we were still out of breath, transformed itself again as the boys squealed and ran to their parents, who stood beside the sliding-glass doors.

The rest of us joined them on the patio, each choosing a chair to fall into while the family enjoyed a second reunion. Vayl's expression masked itself sometime during Ruvin, Laal, and Pajo's bout of ecstatic hugs and kisses, watched somewhat indifferently by Tabitha. I wondered if she was jealous of their closeness.

Vayl seemed to have questions too, because I detected a hint of steel in his undertone as he said, "Tabitha, I know you must be anxious to get your sons even farther from the warren. But we need to ask you a few questions before you go."

She reared back her head. *She's gonna tell him where to shove it,* I thought. *And not because of the delay it'll cause either.* Something about the jut of her chin and the set of her shoulders told me she thought any form of cooperation spelled weakness. And at her size, she didn't think that was something she could afford.

"My husband said you people were filmmakers."

Ruvin put his arm around her waist and rubbed. His touch, like his expression, was enthusiastic. "What I said was that they told me they'd come from Hollywood to scout movie locations. Now, I know studio executives aren't normally capable of doing what they did. But these people are special, Tabitha." He jerked his head toward Vayl. "They have Gerard Butler on their side! Remember him in *The Transporter*? He's like a superhero!"

Oh. My. God. I cleared my throat. "Um, Ruvin? I believe you're thinking of Jason Stratham."

Tabitha had an even better point. She jabbed a finger at me and Vayl. "They had weapons."

"We're American. Pretty much everybody goes armed there," I lied, figuring my country's reputation would back me up. It did. She took a moment to watch Laal leap on Jack, his little hands disappearing into the malamute's thick fur as he patted him on the back. Pajo preferred bigger prey. He ran to Vayl, jumped onto his lap, and wiggled himself into the crook of my *sverhamin*'s arm so he could gaze happily at the rest of his family.

Tabitha sighed. "What do you need to know?" she asked.

When Vayl looked up from Pajo's grinning face, his eyes had lightened to gold with brown highlights. He blinked, the line between his eyes appearing briefly as he tried to refocus. He said, "We were just curious if the Ufranites told you why you were taken." He glanced at Ruvin. "Stories are a weakness of ours. You never know what will make a good movie."

Tabitha shook her head, her thick hair barely shifting as she said, "They never said anything about that to me directly. But I heard our jailer talking to the woman who brought our food. She said this would show the shaman the true price of betrayal."

"What do you think she meant by that?" asked Bergman.

"I have no idea. It almost sounded like kidnapping us was a punishment for the shaman. But we're seinji. We don't even know any Ufranites."

"Did you ever see the shaman?" asked Vayl.

Another head shake. "I demanded to see him. But the guard said a word I didn't understand, and then he said, 'As long as your husband is cooperating, you'll be fine.'"

"What was the word you didn't understand?" I asked her.

"Ylmi." She raised her chin, as if daring me to fight. About what though? I decided she must be a real bitch to receptionists and fast-food workers. Then I realized.

Ylmi was the word in the dead guard's amulet. Dammit, Cole, how long does it take to assemble a demon-bashing armory? We need your translating skills now!

Miles adjusted his ball cap while he traded a significant look with Vayl. So they'd both remembered the word too.

"What happened then?" I asked.

The sides of her mouth turned down. "I asked him what would happen if I didn't cooperate. He laughed and said it didn't matter. That Ufranite young would be feasting on my husband while he screamed for death by tomorrow afternoon."

While the conscious part of me saw Laal pause in his Jack-petting to get a reassuring nod from his dad while Pajo tucked his head into Vayl's chest, my inner librarian said, *You have less than twenty-four hours to complete this mission. If you don't succeed, people are going to die. You might blame it on an evil, no-faced gnome. But you know it will be partly your fault.* She jotted the info on an index card and filed it neatly in a drawer the length of a tractor trailer.

Where have you been? I demanded. *Granny May could've used backup when Brude was doing his mental manipulations before, you know.*

She sniffed and shut the drawer. *I've been organizing.*

That's no help!

She raised a slender eyebrow at me and tucked a stray curl into her French twist. *You'd be surprised. For instance, right now I'm compiling a list of every item you've ever heard, read, or learned about the Thin. If Brude wants to create a new hell based there, maybe something you know can alter his plans. That might send him spinning out of your head. Alternatively, knowing more about his species might help. You have no innate knowledge, so I suggest a session with Astral or, perhaps, Raoul.*

You know, for a brainiac, you're not half bad. Just don't let Brude know what you're up to.

Robert, that.

Um, it's Roger.

Oh. Sorry.

Well, it looks as if you are marshaling your forces. Brude strode to the forefront of my mind, grabbing me so firmly by the intellect that I froze in place. *It will not work, my Jasmine. You must understand, I am here for you. And also for what you can do for me.*

What do you mean?

I already told you I never do anything for a single reason. So I slipped into your mind, which is—he looked around and licked his lips—*nearly as delectable as your body. Because I promised to make you my queen, did I not? But you never asked why. Why you?*

He wants to transform the Thin into a chaotic realm and destroy hell, my librarian reminded me.

Granny May rose from her front porch rocker. *But he'll never do that without a massive army to fight Lucifer's hordes.*

Where's he gonna get that many lost souls? wondered Teen Me as she sat on the ledge, dangling one leg over while she leafed through one of Granny May's comic books.

"From me," I whispered.

Bergman had leaned across the table, his hands inches from mine like he thought I might need to be pulled from the brink of something anytime now. "What are you saying?" he asked.

I couldn't look at him. My eyes, glued to the covered barbecue, only saw my inner visions. Vayl stirred in his seat, gently lifting Pajo from his lap. "May I suggest that you take your parents inside?" he told the little boy. "Perhaps Jack will accompany you as well. Then you and Laal can play with him while Mum and Dad decide what to do next."

Murmurs of agreement from the parents. The *shoosh-snick* of sliding-glass doors opening and closing. I forced the words through a throat so suddenly parched it felt like it was lined with sandpaper. "Brude knows who I am. He believes if he can subvert my missions, he can cause just the kind of death toll he needs to build up his forces. And what better way to do that than from inside my head?" I felt my lips cracking. Next would come the blood. I turned to Vayl. "I have to withdraw from this assignment. I need to take a leave of absence."

"Absolutely not," he said. "You and I are a formidable team. If they separate us—they win."

"But . . . Vayl . . . the son of a bitch is in my *mind*. He can make me—do things. What if—"

Vayl leaned forward. Not much. Just the fraction it took to capture my attention. Something about the intensity in his bright blue eyes demanded that I listen, not just to his words, but to the things he couldn't say. Because Brude would overhear. "We will beat him. That is what you and I do, my *pretera*. We win. Together."

His touch, just a whisper of fingertips grazing my thigh, spelled out a sign we used for face-to-face attacks. I was so distracted by the zap of awareness his fingers raised, followed by an unbearable need to scratch, that I nearly missed the message. *You go in loud and annoying. I will slide in under the radar to make the kill.*

What the hell is that supposed to mean?

He caught me in his gaze, stared at me hard like I should be able to read his mind. *Geez, Cassandra, I wish you were here right this second so I could slap your hand on his and get a freaking clue!*

He whispered, "Trust me."

Aw, shit.

Chapter Seventeen

We joined Ruvin in the living room. He shook everyone's hand with a grip so firm I know my fingers tingled afterward. "We just can't thank you enough for all you've done for us. You Hollywood types are so gifted! I wish I had half the talent!" He nodded toward the bedroom. "Tabitha thought it would be better for the boys if we talked privately."

We'd all had enough of sitting. We wanted to run off in twelve different directions. Find the Rocenz. Continue discrediting the shaman. Destroy the larvae carriers. Demon-proof the house. But it seemed rude to tower over the little man, so we all sat. Vayl and I took the couch. Bergman sank into a chair. Jack lay at my feet, watching Miles tinker with Astral. He'd gotten her head reconnected, which Jack must've deduced was a good thing, because he kept flopping his tail against the floor hopefully.

Ruvin stood beside Miles, his eyes occasionally cutting to the intricate operation-in-progress as he spoke. "Again, I can't thank you enough for getting my family out of the shit. And, um, sorry about the quick exit before. To be honest, we're on something of a schedule. We are seinji, and it's just our luck that this is the week of the year when she's most likely to conceive . . ." His ears went bright red as he grinned down at his feet.

Collective "Ahhh" of understanding from our group as we realized why Tabitha had chosen an oooh-baby dress for a Wednesday evening when her hubby wasn't even supposed to get home until the pubs had long been closed. It also explained why she'd kept checking her watch and pacing. Seinji find it tough to bear children, which is why their physicians are among the top experts in the field of infertility. They combine cutting-edge science with some of the most off-the-wall rites in the world. Common practices included hanging upside down from a tree limb for three hours after sex and writing suggestive fan letters to the cast members of *Willow*. And if anyone questioned their approach, all they had to do was pull out the studies that proved their birthrate had risen by thirty percent in the past twenty years.

"So, ah, we need to get rolling," said Ruvin. "If Tabitha doesn't have a bowl of Yabbie Chowder within the next two hours we're doomed."

"You know the gnomes are going to try to get her back," I said.

He bit his lip and nodded. "We're going to her aunt's house in Christchurch, New Zealand. The gnomes don't live on the South Island, you know."

I did. They'd been driven out by bigger, badder beasts called attry-os nearly a century before and had never returned. But if I knew, so did Brude. I flashed a warning glance at Vayl. Which he smoothly ignored.

He said, "That is a wise choice. May we offer you our car for the journey? You can just leave it at the airport and we will pick it up later."

Ruvin grinned, leaping forward to grasp Vayl's hand and pump it up and down. "You're ripper, you are! I'm sure I can never thank you enough! But if there's anything I can do now . . ."

Bergman was the one who said, "I'm pretty sure we'll think of something."

Ruvin kept smiling. But at the same time his bottom lip had started quivering.

Uh-oh. I tried to back up, but the couch didn't have an emergency exit. So I had to watch helplessly along with Bergman and Vayl while Ruvin sobbed into his handkerchief.

"Sorry," he said. "It's just all finally crashed down on me. Do you have any idea how hard it was to pretend I wasn't shit-a-brick when that gorilla shoved me against the Patriot? And the worry was just eating my guts out." He wiped his eyes and blew his nose with a honking blast that made some night bird outside return the call.

Bergman nodded sympathetically. "We know exactly what you mean. Well, most of us," he qualified. "Probably not Jeremy."

We all looked at the vampire, who'd been the only one smart enough to get out of the line of fire during Ruvin's breakdown. He'd parked himself by the fireplace, leaning one arm against the mantel, obviously ignorant as to what a fantastic picture he made. He shrugged. "Every living thing feels fear at one time or another."

"Exactly my point," Bergman said.

"What do you mean by that?" asked Ruvin, his stress taking a backseat to this new distraction.

Vayl sat on the coffee table beside my propped feet. He played with the heel of my boot, a gesture I found oddly erotic, as he admitted, "I am actually Vampere. These people are part of my Trust, and we all work for the CIA. We have come to your country to eliminate the man who threatened you today as well as anyone who has agreed to act as his backup."

He paused. I could feel his power build and then drop. Whatever he said next, evidently he wanted Ruvin to decide for himself what to do about it. "We need you to stay in Australia. The Ufranites have chosen you as their hatchling feast, and at this late date I fear that if we force them to choose another, we will not be able to provide that family with the same sort of protection as we have you and yours. Do you understand?"

Ruvin looked down at his clasped hands. "You're saying if I go to Christchurch with Tabitha and the boys, probably somebody else's wife and kids will end up in the warren's boiling pot."

Vayl nodded. "I believe they will be like you in another respect as well. In fact, you can almost count on the Ufranites capturing another seinji family."

Ruvin bit his lip. "Why us?" he asked, his tone as bewildered as that of a child trying to make sense out of undeserved punishment.

Vayl took a knee in front of Ruvin, like the little man had the power to knight him. "The Ufranites are fanatical when it comes to purity of bloodline. And, as your historians are well aware, many generations ago gnomes intermarried with feragoblins and the Japanese sect of tryynets, thus creating the line from which you descend."

"So gnomes think we seinji are . . . impure?"

"They look upon you as an even lower form of life than their *kimf*. But do not worry over their willingness to harm seinji. We will guarantee your family's safety."

I stuck my fingers in my ears and wiggled them. Vayl had never cared before about the consequences of bringing civilians into our assignments. Cole was the perfect example. I'd argued against asking for his cooperation when he was still a private investigator, and look what happened to him. Poor schmuck had been lured into the good-versus-evil swamp with the rest of us.

I opened my mouth to say, "Don't do it, Ruvin. This way only leads to potential beatings and situations that require you to flirt with women who remind you of the computer geek from *Jurassic Park*."

But Vayl had asked for my trust, so I shut my yap. If he had a plan, fine. If not, maybe I could call on my head-girls to partially deafen Brude while we devised a better strategy.

Ruvin had listened closely to Vayl's entire presentation. In the end he said, "My wife's more the brains of the family. I should talk to her about this."

Vayl bowed his head slightly. "Of course. But you must not tell her who we are. Only that you feel leaving would endanger another innocent family."

Ruvin nodded glumly and trudged out of the room, his shoulders so bowed his neck looked three feet long.

I said, "That went well."

"He's freaked," said Bergman. "Can anyone blame him?"

"Will he play his part, though?" I wondered.

Vayl came to sit next to me. "I believe so."

"I don't know, Vayl. What's to keep the gnomes from taking another family anyway? With Tabitha and the boys safely away, they have no leverage on Ruvin."

Watching Bergman tinker with Astral he said, "I have an idea that will keep them on the same course."

The front door flying open made Bergman drop his miniwrench. I shot off the couch, Grief already halfway out of its holster as Vayl rose, raising his cane like the sword it hid was already unsheathed.

We all relaxed as Cole and Raoul rolled in, packing such an arsenal with them that they clanked when they walked. Deep in conversation, they didn't notice us at first.

"That works for you?" Raoul was asking.

"Women love it," Cole said reassuringly. "I'm telling you, dude, try it. You can't go wrong."

Raoul shook his head. "You don't know Nia. She—" He stopped as he realized they had an audience.

"Oh, hey!" Cole said. "We thought you guys would still be scoping out the schoolhouse. Did you miss us?"

I grabbed a belt off his shoulder that held a succession of small silver canisters and, as he nodded his thanks, said, "Actually, yes. We could've used you during the prison break." As his eyebrows shot up I added, "Don't tell me you've already corrupted my Spirit Guide. He's one of the good guys, you know."

Cole dumped a load of sheathed swords onto the floor and

swung a strangely flexible shield down off his shoulder before saying, "Raoul and I have a deal. Which is none of your business." He nodded reassuringly to the Eldhayr as Raoul gave him a warning look. "Although I have to say my odds of petting a kangaroo have spiked because of it. Now, tell us about the big escape. Did Bergman get himself arrested again?"

"I've never been arrested!" Bergman proclaimed, jumping to his feet like he meant to grab a sign and picket Cole in protest. Our sharpshooter's response was to fall onto the couch right in the spot I'd vacated. Vayl and I both moved aside as he dropped his head onto a beige throw pillow.

"Where's Cassandra? After we save her from demonkind, I think she should make us cake. And not that wheat-flour health-nut stuff she sells in her store, either. Sinfully delicious chocolate fudge cake with icing an inch thick. And sprinkles. I like me some sprinkles. Was she the one they arrested? But you said prison break."

"Cole!" I resisted slapping him. Just.

He sat up. "What?"

"We rescued Ruvin's family. And Cassandra's . . ." I looked at Vayl for some help.

"She is looking after some business," he said. "I will fill you in later." When Cole's eyes darted to mine before he looked back at Vayl and nodded, I realized the two of them might be keeping even more secrets from me. Because of the Domytr in my head. I wanted to clutch my hair and scream, except I had a feeling Brude would get a kick out of that.

Cole was saying, "You rescued Ruvin's family? Really? Already?" He thought for a second. "Without me?"

I snapped, "I was just saying it would've been nice—"

"Why do I suddenly feel like the guy the professional shopper brings along to carry her bags?" Cole nudged the pile of weapons with his toe. Watched Raoul add a miniature catapult and a box that, I assumed, contained ammo.

"What do you—"

"What am I here for? All I've done so far is buy Vayl a fabulous airport funeral procession, and help Raoul strip his armory of every weapon that could possibly injure a demon."

Vayl cracked his cane against the side of the table, which for him was about the most extreme demonstration of frustration he'd ever allow himself. "Beyond your theatrics, which I am sure these people find endlessly entertaining, we are depending on you to hold up your end when we return to check out the Odeam people."

Cole visibly swallowed as he remembered that, depending on the results of our search, he might be taking part in a mini-massacre. Didn't matter that the men would be facing certain death anyway. That we'd be replacing horrific, writhing agony with a quick, relatively painless exit. He'd never done a multiple before. And I could see he'd only begun to consider how that might work on his head, not to mention the softer, more spiritual organs. After a second, he nodded. "Okay."

"Plus, we need your translating skills," I added. I pulled out the Ufranite guard's stashed art and gave the paper to Cole. "Give this a look and let us know what you think."

While Cole studied the picture, Raoul began to hand out the weapons. He said, "If we knew these demons' identities, we could finely focus our attacks. But without pertinent details like parentage and proclivities, we had to go with the old standards. So we've brought one two-edged blade for each of you." He gave Bergman a sheathed sword, adding, "Try not to cut your own head off," as the weight of the weapon nearly caused Miles to drop it.

"Can't I have a bow or something?" Bergman asked. "It seems like we'd all live a lot longer if we fought these things from a distance." He turned the sheath in his hands, pulled the sword halfway out and shoved it back with a clang. "The farther back the better."

Raoul pointed to the canister belt Cole had carried in. "Those will do most of our long-range fighting for us."

"What are they?" I asked as he laid the belt down on the shield.

"Lima beans."

Silence.

I said, "Uh. What's the point? Beyond the fact that they suck."

"They were grown on holy land, by the Monks of Acquaro, to be specific. As soon as the beans hit hellspawn they'll burn into them like hydrochloric acid."

Bergman had begun to nod about halfway through. "So while regular explosives won't do the kind of injury we're looking for on this plane, if we blow up the cans . . ."

"Exactly," Raoul replied. "A direct hit should cause intense pain and even permanent damage. That's if we catch them anywhere around here. The idea, however, is to lure the demons into a plane where these cans can kill."

"Which is why Raoul's got his spies working to let us know exactly when we can expect another visit," Cole put in. "So far they say we're safe. Cassandra's stalker is having a tough time finding allies." He flashed me a grin. "Something about that badass bitch she's hanging with who took out the Magistrate not so long ago." He nodded at Vayl. "They're not too psyched about going against you either. What's the deal about you carving up a faorzig so badly he's still afraid to leave his den?"

Vayl shrugged. "That was a long time ago. And he deserved it."

I hid my surprise. Vayl had never told me he'd vanquished one of the hellspawn that's often confused for a vampire. Though it would've been appropriate given that my mom had been married to one before she met my dad.

As Raoul gave me a blade that felt like it had been designed by a guy who adored underfed redheads and I returned his own sword, he said, "Since the closest door between planes is just on the other side of your fence, we need to set up our—"

He stopped as he heard the click of a regular door opening. Ruvin led his family down the hall and into the living room. The boys took one look at the weaponry on the floor and in our hands, exclaimed, "You beaut!" and began asking questions one after the other.

LAAL: "Are those swords real?"
PAJO: "Are you going to cut people's heads off?"
LAAL: "Can I hold one?"
PAJO: "Are you going to cut people's arms and legs off?"
LAAL: "What's in the cans?"
PAJO: "What about their knees? People can live without their knees ya know. My grampa had his replaced."

Tabitha shushed them both. "They're all just movie props," she said. And even when Laal stared up at her doubtfully she trucked on. "I told you, these people are from Hollywood and they're filming a movie, which we have been a part of all this time."

"Where were the cameras?" demanded Laal. "And the microphones?"

"All hidden," she said. "They wanted it to be more like a reality show, which was why they didn't give us scripts either."

Seriously? You're lying through your teeth and somehow you think that's going to hurt your kids less than the crap they've just been through? What a crock! I suddenly realized that was what had made my relationship with Albert so strained. Who wants to cuddle with a dad who's not only gone half your life, but a lot of times won't even tell you where he's headed? It wasn't enough that he was a Marine. Or that later he'd worked for the CIA. Lies by omission are still lies. The worst kind, in fact, because they never give you the chance to challenge them.

Ironic that you are so good at weaving them, is it not, my queen?

Shut up, asshole.

While I stewed, Vayl introduced Ruvin and his family to Cole and Raoul. When I began to pay attention again he was in the middle of setting up an escort.

"—concerned that they should reach the airport safely," he was saying. "Perhaps one or two of us should ride with them."

When nobody spoke up right away, he pointed to Bergman. "What do you say, Miles? It would remove you from Ground Zero, so to speak."

While Bergman debated, Tabitha said, "I won't hear of it. You people have gone above and beyond what anyone should do for complete strangers. We can make our way from here."

Ruvin looked at her doubtfully, but something in the set of her chin must've convinced him because he said, "The wife's right. You've done more than your share. Now it's our turn."

Chapter Eighteen

Vayl went quiet after Laal and Pajo left. He didn't seem to notice my struggle to shove Brude out of every stray thought. He ignored Bergman's announcement that Astral was almost finished. Just brooded and helped Raoul, Cole, and I bring the patio furniture around front onto the driveway.

We were setting the last chairs in place when Miles said, "That's the last adjustment." He set Astral down onto the table and slowly drew his arm back. When she didn't topple onto her side he sighed with relief.

"Great!" I glanced at the living room window to make sure our cat killer was safely out of range. Jack stood inside with his nose pressed against the glass, trying to see past the shrubbery to figure out if he was in trouble or if we were just keeping him safe from passing cars and incoming demons. "Is she, uh, screwed on tight?" I asked.

"I think so." He set her on the table just in time to keep his sword belt from falling down around his knees. As he hitched it up he said, "I've put her through all her tests and she's functioning at acceptable levels in every aspect."

Cole gracefully flipped his sword out of the way just before dropping into a chair. "That's great news, kitty!" he said, talking directly to the robot like she was a real, live pet. "Now you're a Sensitive like me and Jaz. Can you say Lazarus?"

"Hello!" said Astral.

"Watch out!" Cole grabbed the arms of his chair and jumped his feet from the front to the back so he ended up crouching, holding it in front of him like a lion tamer facing down a particularly scary customer. He wasn't the only quick reactor. When I looked down I realized I'd pulled Grief without even thinking. And Vayl had dropped the temperature in our vicinity at least ten degrees. Only Bergman and Raoul seemed relatively calm. Maybe Raoul didn't know Astral wasn't supposed to talk like Long John Silver's parrot. And Bergman just kept shaking his head.

He said, "Astral, what's going on? Your voice-recognition program hasn't been initiated."

Astral said, "Hello!"

Raoul said, "How interesting. Her mouth's making just the right movements."

Bergman said, "Astral, shut down voice program until further notice."

Astral's ears started twitching. Two seconds later they began emitting the worst music I'd ever heard in my life. Again. "It's the gnome band!" I said as Raoul slammed his hands over his ears.

Vayl's eyebrows crooked. "Bergman, make it stop."

Miles reached for the cat, nearly lost his belt again, and compromised by unsheathing the sword. While he lightened his load, the rest of us watched his invention.

She didn't seem to be melting down. It was more like she'd piped the music in for her own enjoyment. Her tail began to twitch with the downbeat. Then she began to circle the tabletop, pausing every few steps to have some sort of all-body seizure.

Cole chuckled. "She's dancing!"

"It's not funny!" said Miles. "Astral, shut down your voice program."

The music stopped and she sat down. After a moment Vayl began to speak. We all turned to him. But his lips weren't moving.

"So is that how you want it, my *pretera*?" I turned back to Astral, realizing she was playing back another moment she'd recorded. Vayl, his voice low and suggestive, getting ready to bare all for me.

Holy shit!

I reached for her, ready to pop her head again myself, but Bergman was too fast. He dumped the sword on the table and swiped her off of it.

"I'll fix her, I promise!" he said, his voice high enough to qualify as a squeal.

"Don't you dare!" Cole was laughing so hard he'd dropped the chair. Even Raoul was having a hard time keeping a straight face.

"Perhaps if you could encourage her to play a form of music we could all bear?" Vayl suggested. Something in his voice caused me to spin around. Yup, no mistaking that glitter in his eyes.

"I am not amused," I growled.

He leaned in so only I could hear. "That is only because you did not get to see the end of the show. I promise you, it will be worth the wait."

Eeep! I forgot my embarrassment in the sudden rush of anticipation.

"Okay, Bergman," I said. "Astral's off the hook if you can get something reasonable to come out of her mouth within the next three minutes. If not, I'm stuffing her in an Express Pak and FedExing her to Zimbabwe."

Bergman nodded gratefully. Slinging the shield he carried over his shoulder, he pulled a set of miniature tools out of his shirt pocket and yanked his chair as close to the table as his scarecrow frame would allow. I sighed.

On the positive side, Cassandra was relatively safe, hiding deep beneath the Space Complex's guest quarters. Only, knowing her, she wouldn't be content just curling up in an abandoned storage cave. Nope, she'd probably had half a dozen visions and acted on every one, making herself twice as many friends (and probably a few enemies) in the process.

On top of worrying about her, the whole job-satisfaction rating had plummeted as well. Because lately it seemed like all we did was clean up after, around, and before ourselves. In fact, my muscles had already begun to ache from the heavy lifting we'd done in anticipation of the next few minutes. Because preparing for a demon attack is like getting ready for a party without the happy thoughts. Or the sneaky snacking.

The most important part was preparing for the portal crossing. They'd know about the door, of course, all *others* did. Weird to think they'd always been there, that I must've walked past hundreds of them without even realizing. Because I'd only begun to see them after a powerful creature named Asha Vasta had boosted my Sensitivity by brushing my cheeks with his tears. I still didn't know much about them though. It took Raoul to explain that the fence boards might buckle when the lima bean cans exploded. An acceptable loss. But that didn't mean the play sets on the other side had to be destroyed too. So we'd moved them out of blast range. The kids' indoor toys had already survived flying bodies. We figured asking the outdoor stuff to withstand shrapnel was going too far.

Since we'd lucked into a seminatural setting with the line of trees that separated the property from the hills, we capitalized on it. After rubbing mud on the cans to take the shine off, we made piles of brush to disguise them on either side of the door. They looked natural, like a dumping site where the owners had thrown the sticks out of their yard so they could mow. Raoul took the majority of the cans into the plane where we meant to lure the demons and Bergman rigged an ingenious trigger system for both sets. The one on the outside went off at a code word. The one on the inside exploded when you stepped inside the door. So anyone who went in from our group would have to jump and roll.

Raoul picked Bergman and Cole for that job, since he said they had the juiciest souls.

(At this point Cole got Bergman to do a bump and grind with him while Cole sang, "We are juiceee!")

He stopped singing when Raoul threw them both a set of full-body armor. It was a lot like the kind I'd worn in my battle with the Magistrate. Clung like a leotard. Protected like Kevlar. It would keep everything but their faces and hands safe from flying debris. It also made them look like blueberries.

"Jaz needs some!" Cole had protested.

"I only have two," Raoul said. "Besides, Vayl has them covered." He turned and raised his eyebrows at my boss. Was that a twinkle in his eye when he said, "Right, Vayl?"

It must've been, because Vayl stirred uncomfortably before he replied, "Our protection is in place."

I wanted to ask him what he meant by that, but the don't-go-there sign was flashing on his forehead, and I was still having too much fun razzing Cole and Bergman about their blueman suits.

So we went back to discussing our options, since the whole setup wouldn't work unless it didn't look like a trap in the first place. In the end we decided to summon our enemies. Show them one hand. Slap them with the other.

Vayl and Raoul took seats at the head and foot of the table. When they were in position, I sat to Vayl's left. I pulled up my right sleeve, unstrapped the syringe of holy water I usually kept tucked there, and laid it on the table in front of me. Cole, already parked beside Bergman, had been watching my preparations. Now he raised his eyebrows as Astral began doing a remarkably good cover of "Survivalism" by Nine Inch Nails.

Miles bobbed his head and kept the beat against his thighs until he realized we were all staring. "What?"

I began quoting lyrics. "I got my propaganda I got revision-ism . . . All a part of this great nation?"

He shook one of his fingers at me. "You know better than to trust your government. Or any government for that matter. Which is the best reason yet why you should dump the CIA and throw in with me. They've already gone crooked on you once."

When I started to protest, he added fingers until his whole hand was raised. "Don't try to tell me Senator Bozcowski was some kind of blip. He was a rotten apple in a crate of wormy fruit. And he nearly got you killed back in Miami, not to mention what he had planned for the rest of the country! They're all on the take. Which is why I'll work *with* them, but not *for* them."

Cole leaned forward. "I think you need to wipe your mouth there, Bergie. You're frothing at the corners."

"None of you can tell me I'm wrong!" Bergman insisted, though he did press his sleeve against his mouth.

"Of course we can," Vayl said, the absolute stillness of his posture a peaceful counterpoint to Bergman's seat-wriggling passion. "The very extremity of your position makes it questionable."

"Plus, you've forgotten the most important point," I said.

"What's that?" Bergman asked.

"Those government pukes you're so afraid of are our employees. And if they piss enough of us off, we'll fire them."

"It's not that easy!"

"Sure it is. Happens all the time. You're just mad about a lot more things than the rest of us."

"What if something terrible goes down? What if the entire cabinet gets infested with demons and starts some sort of coup?"

I leaned forward. "Just watch what we do next, and you should have some idea how much patience we'd have with an executive office full of possessed administrators."

At a nod from Vayl, Cole pulled his sword and cocked it over one shoulder like a ball bat. Raoul and I both had belts, his at his waist, mine at my back. We also drew.

Seeing all the metal put Bergman back in his seat. "I get your point," he said.

Vayl rolled his cane between his fingers as if it helped him think. He said, "Then shall we move on?"

We nodded.

Cole began. "Kyphas, drop everything and come flying."

"Kyphas, do not delay, we require your presence, your visage, your favor," said Vayl. He took the syringe off the table.

"Kyphas, rise quickly to our circle," I said as I pulled Raoul's blade across my forearm and let the blood drip on the ground between my feet.

"Blood to the hellspawn," I murmured.

"Nema," chorused Cole, Vayl, and Bergman.

We all spat over our left knees.

As we knew it would, the thrice-naming brought a feeling of electricity into the air that raised the hairs on our arms and made the backs of our necks itch. We rose together. Bergman and Cole strained to see into the night. Not a problem for the rest of us. Vayl and Raoul had natural abilities. Mine had come at a price I often questioned.

But it was almost worth it all to be able to see my blood and our separate puddles of spit merge and flow to a spot in the middle of the yard, like the driveway had tipped sideways, forcing all the liquid into the parched grass. The puddle expanded to the size of a manhole cover and Kyphas shot out of it. She landed badly, flopping onto the lawn like a beached dolphin.

Vayl threw the syringe into the middle of the summoning circle, shattering it. The holy water it contained boiled instantly, barring the gateway. But even our vampire wasn't fast enough to prevent a few of Kyphas's allies from flying through first.

"Slyein!" I yelled as I recognized the unlined faces of hell's scum. The kid killers.

In life they'd been adults. Moms and dads, truck drivers and CEOs, fanatics who didn't give a crap who died in the blast. In death they'd been doomed to the bodies they'd destroyed. Eternal youth screaming for the chance to grow up. Dream on. Fulfill.

The rage they brought to battle made them even harder to fight than their aerial capability, which could be awkward given the bloody rips they'd torn in their own wings. Self-mutilation. One of the sure signs that the creature you were fighting wasn't hellborn. Only the originals weren't subject to torture. Which made them harder to injure and, ultimately, destroy.

Still, we'd be lucky to survive the onslaught of the three monsters who'd followed Kyphas through the gateway before Vayl closed it. A girl with spiked black hair and eyes rimmed in purple, a blond boy whose reddened teeth showed he'd just been feasting on raw flesh, and a toddler with white curls and long black lashes who might've been a girl, except he wore a blue jumper with the words "I'm a good boy," stitched across the front.

"No," muttered Miles. "Can't be." He swiped his sword off the table. "Slyein?" His voice crept higher while he stalked toward Kyphas, who was halfway to her feet and already reaching for her hat. "You dare to bring those fuckers here?"

"Miles, no!" I yelled. "You need to *run!*"

We all *do! Look, see? Raoul's trying to lure them toward the trap. Follow him! No, you—this wasn't the plan and you know it!*

Ignoring me, he swung at Kyphas, who easily avoided his attack since he'd telegraphed it half an hour earlier.

I snapped, "Astral, protect Bergman!" fully realizing it might be an empty command. But my hands were full with the female slyein. With Vayl fighting the male and Cole trying to deal with the toddler, that left Raoul to save the crazed genius. And he'd only just realized nobody had followed him to the corner of the house.

As he rushed back to us, I slashed at the female's wing, forcing her to abandon her first run at me. That gave me a second to check on Miles. Kyphas's hat, which had done its boomerang trick, was just about to hit him. He turned aside, clearly forgetting that his shield still hung over his shoulder. The boomerang thumped against it, causing him to stagger backward, but doing no major damage.

Astral leaped into the air, snagging the boomerang between her teeth before it could return to its owner's outstretched hand. At the same time, George Thorogood and the Destroyers began rocking "Bad to the Bone" out the sides of her mouth. Talk about multitasking! Those metal alloy jaws clamped down and refused to let go, even when George kept insisting he was "b-b-b-b-b-bad," and her weight wasn't enough to stop the spin of the weapon.

Together Astral and the boomerang slammed into Kyphas, making her screech as something snapped in her forearm. But even that crash wasn't enough to stop their momentum. They spun into her chest, knocking the wind from her, and then bounced up into her face, bloodying her nose before flying off into the night like a demented whirlybird with kitty paws for landing gear.

Even Bergman recognized an advantage in a fight. While he pressed forward, slashing at Kyphas like she was an impassable jungle path and he wielded a machete, I ducked a dive-bomb designed to take off the top of my head.

I shoved my sword into the slyein's side. "'Hear, O Israel,'" I whispered as the creature who'd once murdered a teenage girl shrieked and yanked itself off my blade, "'The LORD our God is one LORD.'" *Don't kill it*, I reminded myself. *Even though you want to. Even if you can.*

Bergman's satisfied grunt followed by Kyphas's moan told me he'd struck at least one blow for the good guys. He bellowed, "'And thou shalt love the LORD thy God with all thine heart, and with all thy soul, and with all thy might!'"

Beside me Vayl allowed his foe to slash into his forearm so he could gain the position he needed to strike. Scripture would probably singe his tongue if he quoted it, even the verses specifically designed to damage demons. Still he nodded sharply as Cole said,

"'And these words, which I command thee this day, shall be in thine heart:'

"'And thou shalt teach them diligently unto thy children,' you son of a bitch." Sorrow twisted his face as he dodged the slyein's grasping claws, its dripping fangs, and punched it so hard in the jaw you could hear the surgeons discussing how many wires they'd need to repair it from three days away.

"Aah!" Bergman's cry of surprise brought me running. Kyphas had managed to disarm him and, despite heavy bleeding in her midsection, lift him over her head.

"Jaz!" Raoul yelled. "Behind you!"

I saw him begin his swing at Kyphas. Then I hit the ground, rolled and kicked as the slyein tried to tackle me. It missed its original mark, but slashed at my leg as it flew past. I only knew I'd been hit because the blood spattering the air like thrown paint couldn't have belonged to anyone else.

Glad I wouldn't have to deal with the pain until the adrenaline wore off, I leaped to my feet as the slyein spun away, momentarily stunned, its chest covered in blood, spitting something even blacker from the previous wound I'd given it.

I'd lost my sword in the fall, so I went for my bolo. In the time it took me to draw, Kyphas took Raoul's blow square in the back. She arched, crying out in rage as she threw Bergman straight down to the ground. Hard. Blood spurted from his mouth.

I screamed, no longer rational enough to form the words to tell her what damage I'd cause if she'd ruptured anything he couldn't live without. My throw, powerful and accurate, buried the bolo in her groin. She dropped with an agonized shriek.

"Move!" Vayl bellowed, the urgency in his tone returning my reason.

Together Raoul and I reached for Bergman's arms. "Can you run?" I asked.

"Yeah, I thig tho." He stuck a finger inside his mouth as we helped him up. It came out bright red. "That bith made me bite my tug!"

Relief made me grin. Tongues heal fast. Bergman would be fine—if we could get to the flaming plane portal before anybody else decided to pull another WWE move on him.

"Cole! Come on!" I yelled.

"Right behind you!"

The smallest slyein disagreed. It wrapped its wings around Cole's head, blinding him as it sunk its teeth in, tore out tufts of hair. He flailed at it, trying to hit what he could no longer see.

I left Bergman to Raoul, ran up behind Cole, and buried my fist in the slyein's kidneys.

This thing is not a toddler. It killed somebody's baby, I reminded myself sternly as its cries filled the air, so much like an injured infant's that involuntary tears filled my eyes. *Goddamn, I don't care. My job sucks today!*

It dropped away from Cole and together we ran across the dying lawn. We passed Vayl and his demon as my *sverhamin* delivered a brutal blow. The slyein dropped to the ground, moaning, one of its wings completely severed.

I wanted to reach out for my *sverhamin*. If I could just take his hand, I knew somehow nothing could defeat him. But he held his sword in one, his scabbard in the other. And my original foe, urged on by Kyphas's demands, had come after him.

Which was exactly what we wanted.

But luring hell's warriors into a trap is tough to survive. I glanced over my shoulder as we rounded the corner of the house, Cole to my right, Bergman and Raoul at our heels, Vayl bringing up the rear. I knew that thirty feet ahead of us the plane portal burned like a rock band's gateway. And we were the groupies, about to be hammered by security if we weren't gnarly enough to dodge their attack.

But the point wasn't to evade. Not yet, anyway. Which was why

Vayl was letting the female get in some major hits. By the time we'd reached the spot where the house ended and the fence began, she'd raked his shirt to ribbons and left his chest looking like something the butcher lets his trainees hack on, the other two slyein had joined her.

Fifteen steps to the portal and they hounded us all the way. We gave back only enough to make them think they were on the verge of a big win. Even Kyphas had come along, lured by the triumphant screams of the slyein every time a slash hit home. She'd folded up one of the chairs and was using it as a walker, holding it in front of her to help with balance as she stepped. She hadn't pulled my bolo from her leg, though maybe she should've. The way the handle wiggled every time she moved couldn't have felt pleasant.

Raoul had begun to chant under his breath. The portal shimmered and started to clear. I could see an endless plain littered with the shattered trunks of trees and the carcasses of dead animals. The slyein squealed at the sight.

Kyphas said, "The Great Taker must be pleased. Look where he's sending us after this deed is done!"

"Jasmine!" yelled Raoul.

"I'm ready!"

His chant changed. Within seconds the destination changed to a meadow covered in newly mown grass at the edge of which sparkled a large lake. As soon as the new picture appeared he leaped through. Cole and Bergman quickly followed. All three of the slyein chased them in. Two of them flew. But Vayl's original foe was forced to run. It tripped Bergman's trap. The explosion, held inside the portal by its own power, still looked spectacular. A lima-bean storm flavored with the blood of our foes.

At the same time Vayl wrapped his arms around me, his own blood instantly soaking into my shirt. Holding me more tightly than he ever had before, he leaped into the air as I yelled the trigger words Bergman had given me for the second explosion. "For Cassandra!"

We flipped backward, whether because Vayl wanted us to or because the blast twisted us in the air I could never determine. In those brief moments I strained to watch Kyphas, poised in front of the doorway, the chair held out in front of her like a plastic-woven shield. I wanted a camera to lock in her expression for future generations. I'd have called it two parts what-the-hell mixed with a generous dollop of how-dare-you and just a pinch of oh-shit-I'm-screwed! Then the second set of bombs blew out their pile-o-sticks camouflage with a sound like automatic-weapons fire, splatting her arms, back, and legs with holy veggies. Damn, did she ever scream.

She was still yowling when we landed behind the doorway, protected from stray shrapnel by a pit so deep when I stood up I could barely see over the rim.

"When did you dig this?" I asked, glad he'd at least thought to line it with dead leaves.

"I began it after we found your rash."

"Oh?" He crossed his arms. I did too. "Why did you dig a hole behind the portal, Vayl?"

"I supposed it was the last place you would look."

"You didn't want me to see?" He shook his head. "No wonder you kept sending me off to make other preparations for the fight. But why?" I demanded.

He shrugged. Jumped out and pulled me after him. I knew he didn't want to answer. But he was my *sverhamin*. So . . . "I dig holes when I am . . . frustrated."

Oh . . . Oh! So all that teasing he does makes him half crazy too. Or maybe three-fourths, because this muther is, like, big enough to bury a tractor in! "What happened the last time you dug a hole like this?" I asked curiously.

"I struck oil."

I was still trying to figure out how deep he must've drilled when we walked back around to where Kyphas lay. She was trying to pull herself to the door, sputtering ragged words that wouldn't change it until Raoul released his hold. As if she could've crawled more than a couple of inches with half her muscles melted off.

I crouched down beside her. Grabbed her by the chin so she'd stop screaming long enough to focus. "I wish all those souls you'd stolen over the centuries could see you now. Maybe they wouldn't have been so quick to cave. Which, by the way, is kinda what your back looks like. What do you say we make a deal?"

CHAPTER Nineteen

Kyphas lay on her belly in the room at the end of the hall, on the bed Cassandra would've slept in if she'd been around. Nobody had much wanted to help her get there, so Cole finally stepped forward as the only one of us who thought he could touch her without losing control and causing further damage. I hadn't missed the flash of pity in his eyes when he'd caught a glimpse of her wounds either. Surely we didn't need to have a talk? I mean, okay, he loved women. Almost all of them, without exception, could fluff that down-filled pillow he called a heart. But this bitch wanted to dip Cassandra's soul in shit and set it on fire. Forever.

We stood around the demon, trying to ignore the fact that frilly pink curtains hung from the two windows and a herd of ponies with excessively long manes and tails stared at us from the white shelves that had been built between them. Harder to glance away from was the toy chest beside the bed, so full of entertaining items the lid wouldn't even close. Which meant the little girl who'd stayed in this room had left her baby doll hanging halfway out, like a prisoner who hasn't dug the hole quite wide enough to fit her hips.

I moved my attention to Raoul, whose short brown crew cut had taken on a greenish tinge due to the fallout from the explosion. He, Cole, and Bergman had all huddled behind shields, which, along with the armor, had kept them safe from debris. But the goop had gone high, like a tennis ball lobbed over the head of the opponent, and splatted right over the top of them.

According to Cole it had decimated the slyein. But it had marked our guys as well, and they all needed about three days in the shower before they'd stop finding residue in their ear wax. Bergman had taken the glopping worst, and begun yelling at the other two to get it off of him almost before the last heap fell. Something about being pasted in lima bean/slyein remains had turned a key in his brain, sending him into a frenzy of disrobing and skin-scraping. When he came out of the portal he was down to his ball cap and briefs, heading straight for the bathroom.

"I hope you don't mind," he said as he jogged toward the front door. "I have to. You know. I can't stand . . ." The door slammed over his last words, tilting slightly because Vayl had only halfway fixed it.

We followed him into the house, slow both because of Cole's burden and because we really didn't want a closer look at Miles's Fruit of the Looms.

He was still in the shower.

"I wonder what Bergman isn't telling us," I said as I watched Cole pull a strand of ick from his hair and throw it in the wastebasket. I glanced at Raoul.

"Why are you looking at me?" he asked.

"Well, you know, you are . . ." I jerked my thumb toward the ceiling a couple of times.

"An experienced skydiver?"

"Now you're just being a pain in the ass."

Raoul shook his head. "I don't know any more about him than you people do. Probably considerably less."

"His best friend was murdered when they were children," moaned Kyphas.

We all stared, shocked that she'd known and we hadn't. She

turned to gaze up at us with her good eye, her smile devastatingly beautiful as she said, "The man tried to kidnap them both, but Miles ran. A therapist would probably say that he hasn't stopped running since. But I'm no shrink. I'm just the bitch who brought that man back into Bergman's life. Ah, the promises I made Miles. He could've shoved that freak under the wheels of a train. Thrown him off a roof. Strangled him so slowly . . ." She held up her blackened hand, her palm facing up. "His soul was sitting right here. I had him. If only he'd been a little less brilliant, a little more gullible. I guess I shouldn't have waited until he'd grown up. He'd become too suspicious by then, even of his clients." She laughed regretfully, but it quickly turned into a cough.

I strode forward and grabbed her by what was left of her shirt. Her moan of pain made me smile with satisfaction.

"Jaz!" yelled Cole. "What are you doing?"

"I'm dragging her back to the door. Taking her through so I can finish her off."

"But she might be the key to your freedom!"

"Don't care. Bergman can't—"

Vayl put his hand over mine. Held my eyes with his, which had gone the blue of storm-tossed waves. "Miles is a grown man. He can bear this, and he will, because he knows what it means to you. Give him that option. Besides, you can always kill her later if she does not cooperate."

I released the shirt, let Kyphas flop back to the bed, happy when she moaned again because at least I'd hurt her doubly in Miles's cause. When I began to speak to her, Vayl raised a finger. "Perhaps, considering the circumstances, I should be the one to negotiate?"

My first reaction? *Fuck, no! Nobody speaks for me!* But then I saw the message in his eyes.

Trust me.

I stared down at the stained beige carpet, fighting the urge to hit something. It wouldn't make what I had to do any easier, but the pain in my knuckles would be something I could understand. I loved partnering with Vayl. I'd laid my life in his hands multiple times and he'd never once dropped it. Why, now, was it so hard to lend him my edge?

Because I'm possessed. Because he knows it; knows Brude and what he must be up to. Therefore he's playing some kind of game with me. Manipulating me. And I have to play along. Let myself be played, for the greater good. And now I have to burn every one of those thoughts from my mind before I become the king's stooge. But after that, am I still just the vampire's fool?

I looked up at him. Felt the love he'd raised in me tear at the walls of my heart. In the past week it had healed hundreds of old wounds, introduced as many new delights, made me feel sweet and new and alive again. But where love lights up a dark place, it also burns. Now I knew all the ways I promised myself I'd never be vulnerable again were unshielded, and another direct hit to those soft places might just destroy me.

I couldn't say, *I'm scared.* Who, me? Badass, shit-kickin' Jaz Parks? What would he think? What would any of them think?

That you're human? Granny May suggested.

That you've read too many Stephen King novels? said the librarian.

Teen Me raised her hand. *Maybe they won't care. Maybe they're scared too.*

Bimbo-on-a-barstool snorted and leaned over to steal an olive from an open jar on the other side of the counter. *Your problem is you think too much. Do what you need to do and then go get laid. Gawd.*

While I was glad to see another member of my mental crew had made the long trek back from la-la land, now was no time to celebrate. Because I'd hesitated too long. A line had appeared between Vayl's brows.

Brude chuckled from a throne he'd built out of sticks and stones.

He's going to turn away from you. He is going to desert you, just like Albert. Remember how Daddy always left just when you needed him most? And, of course, Matt . . .

I felt myself start to shake.

"Jasmine?" Vayl said. "Do you need to use my belt buckle again?" He started to undo the leather strap at his waist, the concern in his eyes so sincere I nearly wept. Except I was laughing out loud. A ravishingly sexy vampire who's spent the past seven days making you hoarse with cries of ecstasy, who is just as worried that your rash is making you miserable, is not one who is going to crush your heart like a ripe grape.

"No, I'm, well, maybe later. But right now it's bearable. Go ahead, talk to Kyphas. I trust you."

He nodded and turned back to the demon. Nobody in the room but me knew about the bolt of heat that flared from Cirilai, flaming through my body, making Brude retreat the way he had when Vayl and I had first come together. I leaned against the wall, gazed down at the rubies glittering on my finger, and thought, *Take that, you Scots son of a bitch!*

Teen Me grinned. *You swear a lot.*

I slanted her a look, wishing I could send her somewhere safe. Knowing the ultimate stupidity of that desire when it was clear only Evie had emerged from those years somewhat intact. Still I said, *I kill a lot too. It doesn't mean either of them are good for you.*

Chapter Twenty

Vayl sat in a child's chair beside Kyphas's bed. You've gotta be some kinda stud to pull that off without looking ridiculous. He managed easily. The rest of us stood in a semicircle behind him. Except for the animals. I didn't want Jack near the soul stealer, and since the fence had weathered the blast after all, I'd let him loose in the backyard. Astral, who'd become way too unpredictable to take part in the delicate task at hand, was zoning out to some old Doors tunes in Bergman's room.

Vayl didn't lean in to make it easier for Kyphas to see him, and since she was lying on her stomach she had to strain if she wanted to meet his eyes. Which was astonishingly often for a demon whose back half looked like it had been mauled by a starving bear.

Vayl said, "You have heard of the Rocenz."

"Not at all," Kyphas said, her answer slightly muffled by her pillow.

"We left you alive for a reason. Perhaps you would like to cooperate long enough to hear it?"

She sighed. "So what if I have?"

"It is lost. It is demon made."

"And?"

"That means the most likely creature to find it again will be a demon."

"I don't see how this benefits me."

"If you help us find the Rocenz and use it to carve King Brude's name on the gates of hell, you may have his soul in place of Cassandra's." As she began to laugh, and then cough, he raised his hand. She stopped immediately. "He is Lucifer's Domytr. Your stock would skyrocket at such a catch. We can also give you three souls now serving in the U.S. Senate."

"Politicians are Antyrfee's territory." Did she sound envious? Why not? Antyrfee must be rolling in souls.

"But you would have the inside track," Vayl said. "We *know* them. You could probably snare all three within a week."

Kyphas looked up at Vayl, though the pain caused her to wince. "Antyrfee's never turned that many around so fast." She paused. "What do you have against these three?"

"They tried to suspend Jasmine after our last mission. Friends of mine talked them out of that decision"—by that he meant that his old Trust buddies Admes and Niall had dangled the Oversight Committee members from their roofs by their heels—"but politicians ooze more slime than slugs. I expect them to wriggle out of the deal sooner rather than later. I have researched this particular group. They possess no redeeming qualities. They are exactly your type. And think what status their souls would gain you among your peers."

"You'd be popular," said Cole.

"I'd settle for accepted. Do you know how long . . . *looong*, they've been making fun of me over this Cassandra issue?"

"It is a four-for-one offer with us aiding you. What do you say?"

She sighed. Went quiet for so long I thought she'd nodded off. "I'll draw up a contract," she finally mumbled.

Vayl reached over his shoulder to Raoul, who handed him a scrolled sheet of ivory paper. "We already have."

In our business you learn to appreciate the lulls. Now that we had Kyphas under contract we didn't need to worry about demon ambushes anymore. It should've been a somewhat relaxing time, waiting for Ruvin and Cassandra to return while we watched the clock tick off the minutes until we had to leave for the next phase of our original assignment.

Bergman had finally scrubbed himself to a shade of pink that satisfied his sense of outrage. He'd retreated to the room across from Kyphas's that he was sharing with Cole, closing the door so firmly we got the message as if he'd yelled it. *Don't mess with me. I'm still pissed.*

Cole and Raoul took turns showering and guarding Cassandra's demon while Vayl and I sat in the dining room, tending each other's wounds. Mine needed stitches. Vayl's would've put me in intensive care. But by the time I'd cleaned all the blood off only two of the deepest needed bandages.

"I like it that you can survive shit like this," I said. I taped some gauze over the second slash on his chest and sat back in my chair.

"It is one of my favorite, ah, as you say, perks of being Vampere." He rested an arm on the table, tapping his fingers as he watched me through half-closed lids.

"What?"

Slow release of breath, like the hiss of steam from a volcanic vent. "I sit here, half dressed and triumphant from battle, waiting for you to share my usual enthusiasm. And you . . . do not respond." Invitation in the silk of his voice. And behind that, pain. As if I'd rejected him outright.

If I hadn't felt so exhausted I might've jumped and run. Because Brude's wasn't the only voice telling me, *This will never last. You suck at relationships. The only man who understood you, who could put up with your crap, is dead. And you don't have the energy to try again. It's too hard to be half of a couple. Too scary. Get out before—*

I lunged forward, wrapped my hands around Vayl's back and kissed him so hard that I could still feel the tingle ten minutes later. When I finally came up for air I said, "I feel like hell. I'm still schlubbing around in blood-soaked clothes, itching like a kindergartner with chicken pox, and so worried about Bergman I'm considering sending him home. But no matter what happens, I will always want you."

His smile, slow and wicked, let me know I'd said at least one thing right. "A shower for you, then, and a new layer of lotion."

"Sounds like a plan." I crawled off his lap, where I seemed to have landed sometime during our mini-makeout session. "Uh, I was wondering."

He reached for his shirt, held it up, shook his head regretfully, and tossed it into the corner trash can. "Yes?"

"What did you think of Bergman's offer?"

His eyes, when they rested on me, turned a warm amber as he said, "If you would be happier working with him, so be it."

I backed up a step. He might as well have suggested we move in together. "Just like that?"

Rising so deliberately that I could see the muscles bunch and relax in his shoulders and chest, he took my hand and lifted it to his lips. Every finger got a light caress. Then he kissed Cirilai solemnly before looking up into my eyes, his own telling me things only my heart could understand. "We are *sverhamin* and *avhar* now. That means we walk in our own Trust. Together."

"For how long?"

His brow arched. "Who asks me this? The child of divorce? The bereft fiancé? The world-weary assassin?"

"How long, Vayl?"

He pressed my hands against the hard expanse of his chest. "Do you feel my heart?"

"Yes." It beat so slowly that only a power we humans acknowledged as *other* could move it at all.

"When it stops, I will still come for you. When I am reduced to my essence, it will not be complete until it has melded with yours. I will *never* leave you."

I sighed. "Cool."

"But now I have to prove myself," Vayl replied.

I shrugged. "People exchange marriage vows all the time. Ten years later half of them end up divorced."

He nodded. "But then you must give me the chance. That means no more throwing Cirilai in my face, and no more running from us."

"I wasn't—" I stopped at his don't-shit-me expression. "Okay, I might've been *thinking* about running. But I didn't actually throw on the shoes."

"It is a start."

"Thank you. And as a gesture of goodwill, let me offer you first crack at the shower now that Raoul and Cole are done."

"I would, but I am afraid my old-fashioned sensibilities would be mortally wounded if I were to avail myself of the facilities before the lady."

"What did you just say?"

"Go ahead. You are filthier."

"Oh. Okay."

Twenty minutes later I understood why dogs shook themselves after baths. Because it felt *good* to be clean! So good you wanted to just, *bbbggghhh*. I changed into a pair of hunter-green jeans and a velvety red scoop-neck top. Unfortunately my boots had given their all protecting my legular regions in my last battle. Which meant I had to resort to backup footwear—a pair of black cross-trainers, the laces of which Jack had chewed and partially digested before deciding he didn't like them after all.

Cole and Raoul looked up from a somewhat heated discussion as I joined them in the living room. Since they'd commandeered the couch, I pulled a chair over to the side, where I could see out the sliding-glass doors to check on the dog every once in a while. I leaned back and crossed my legs in front of me.

Cole immediately began to laugh. "What happened to your shoes?"

After observing my deformed, slightly shredded laces I decided to change the subject. "I'll tell you if you explain that shirt."

He looked down at his tee, which depicted a Neanderthal dragging his club across a rocky plain. In the distance a bunch of prehistoric emus were thumbing their wings at him. The caption read, I CAN'T WAIT FOR KFC.

He said, "It was all I had that was clean. Now you."

Raoul said, "Jack got into your closet, didn't he? Don't they sell bones for dogs to chew on nowadays? And toys?"

"I felt sorry for him because he'd just gotten back from the vet, okay? I figured letting him gnaw on my shoelaces was the least I could do. He seemed so . . . depressed."

"I told you!" Cole exclaimed. "You never should've had him snipped!"

"It wasn't the surgery!" I snapped. "He met this schnauzer named Eetza while he was in there and they kind of got attached. You know how it goes."

"Ah. She broke his heart."

"I don't know. He just seemed to miss her. He kept going to the door and licking it. And now, with Astral's head blowing off in his face, I'll be lucky if I'm not barefoot by the time I get home." I tucked my feet under my chair. "Okay, now I'm getting bummed. Can we please talk about something else?"

Raoul and Cole exchanged secretive glances. I said, "Yeah, that. Whatever you were up to, I want in."

"You don't even know the details!" Cole protested.

"It's gotta be shady enough that you don't want to discuss it with me. But Raoul's dealing, so it can't be evil. And that's exactly what I need right now. Come on, you probably need a third."

"Only if Vayl's okay with it,"

"Okay with what?" asked Vayl. Who looked, well, the word "edible" came to mind as he stood at the end of the hallway, drying his hair with a fluffy white towel as he moved his eyes from Cole to Raoul to me. Would it be rude to turn my chair completely around and just gawk? I mean, he was kind of inviting stares by coming in all clean and damp, wearing those ass-grabbing jeans and nothing else. I scratched at my knees and wished for x-ray vision.

"Okay with what?" Vayl repeated, a little louder and a lot more sternly.

Raoul sat up, his camo jacket (of which he seemed to have an endless supply) nearly snapping to attention as he straightened. "I've agreed to help Cole find and pet a kangaroo. They like to feed at night. I don't think it will be too difficult."

Vayl made a noise. Eventually we decided it was laughter.

"You are going to get your face caved in," he told Cole. "And because of that, one of us should probably go along to make sure Pete gets the full report on your demise. Since I have no desire to wander the countryside, I will stay with Bergman and guard Kyphas. If that is all right with you?" he asked me, his eyebrows raised.

I sighed, moving my nails up to my thighs. "I could use some exercise." What I didn't add was, *since I can't jump your bones, and I really wanna wail on Kyphas, and Bergman's problem is driving me slightly batso.*

He nodded. "So be it."

Which was how Jack and I found ourselves trailing two men who'd totally flipped their lids: the former ranger who thought he'd been transported to Candyland if the enthusiasm in his bated whispers were any clue; and the doof who hadn't learned his lesson after a bout of camel-tipping in Iran.

"It's dark," I whispered.

"It's after eleven," Cole whispered back.

"We don't even have flashlights. How are we supposed to find kangaroos in the dark without flashlights?"

"You and I are both wearing Bergman's night-vision lenses and Raoul can probably see better with his eyes closed. Besides, they'll be by water. Or food. Or both. Didn't you ever watch *Kangaroo Jack*?"

"Yeah. But I saw *Crocodile Dundee* too. Don't you think they'll be worried about becoming a midnight snack if they loiter by the river at night?"

"We're following a freaking Eldhayr! We'll find them!" he hissed. "What is your problem?"

"You mean besides the possession, worrying about Bergman and Cassandra, and saving the space program so her vision won't haul off and kick us in the ass?"

"Yeah!"

"My butt itches," I admitted.

"Well, deal with it! I'm sure not going to watch!"

So I did, and thought about how low I'd sunk. Scratching my ass like a beer-swilling, pot-bellied La-Z-lounger as I slunk through the foothills west of Wirdilling. Although, once I'd relieved the worst of my irritation, I realized the hills looked pretty nifty given the shades of gold and burgundy my contacts added to them, like a bowl full of mint ice cream scoops topped by waves of sugar-coated cinnamon sticks.

Even without our Miles-vision we'd have had an easy walk. At least at first. The hills had been grazed so close they traveled like a putting green. Yeah, we encountered some rocks and a few dips and folds. But compared to some of the bush I'd hacked through, this was pudding. Of course, I knew a devastating fire had done most of the clearing for us several years before. And as we climbed, we began to see its remains in the charred trunks of the pine trees that had once dotted the landscape.

Jack whuffed. Not a bark, but definitely a *pay attention* noise that stopped us. We stood silent, peering into the night. Then Raoul raised an arm, pointing to a copse of grass trees. They stood about sixty paces from us, looking eerily like a group of fingers tipped with frothy green rings. Behind one thick-trunked speci-men, standing absolutely still and staring right back at us, was a large kangaroo.

I kept watching. Yeah, now I could see more. Probably fifteen in this group, including four or five pouch-free joeys. Most of them were too busy eating to have noticed the small sound Jack had made.

Teen Me squealed. *Sew kewl!* I rolled my eyes. But I did have to agree. Because, holy crap, were they *large*!

When the first roo began to graze again, Raoul crept forward, motioning for us to follow. I moved my hand around toward my back. My jacket creaked and Raoul jerked his head toward me. Parallel reaction from Cole. I shrugged, dropping my hand, trying to ignore the growing prickles that felt like my rash had erected tents and dug a fire pit.

Raoul motioned first to himself, then to me.

What?

He made the motion again.

No! Have you seen how big these hoppers are? I thought we were going after, you know, little ones!

Again with the motion, this time insistent and combined with a jab from Cole's elbow. I sighed and nodded. I'd play up to a certain point, but no way was I going to get up close and personal with a creature whose feet looked like they were made specifically to crush my spine!

Raoul and I split, taking opposite tracks around to the back of the herd. Cole began to move forward. I gathered the plan was for him to try the pettage on his own. But if it didn't work, Raoul and I were supposed to spook the roos into hopping toward him, in which case he'd have multiple shots at success.

I finally found a spot I liked where I could observe the landscape from between the split fingers of a grass tree. Jack sat beside me, his ears twitching as he followed the action. Which was progressing, but slowly. Cole now crouched within reach of a five-foot female that seemed completely occupied with her meal. At least he'd picked one that was too young for motherhood. Maybe, without that protect-the-baby imperative riding her, she wouldn't try to cave his skull in when he touched her. Maybe she'd just squeal and run.

He stretched out his hand. His fingers were so close to her shoulder you couldn't have slipped a bar of soap between them when the female startled, veered away, and ran. The whole mob caught her mood and suddenly they were on the move.

Raoul leaped up from his hiding place, yelling, "Ha! Move! Hop! That's it!" Pause. "Jasmine, they're coming toward you!"

But it wasn't organized like a cow stampede. Fifteen kangaroos had chosen fifteen different directions out of that copse, and I was only guarding one exit.

A big male hopped at me, looking surprised and somewhat pissed. An expression I found eerily familiar. But that was no help, and I couldn't imagine how me yelling like a cowboy with his nuts in a wringer was going to turn the animal around. In fact, I kinda thought I was going to get pummeled. So I drew Grief and took a shot. Relax, I made sure it hit the ground.

Actually a couple of the roos did too. The sound must've scared them so much that they lost their footing. But they found it again and decided, as a group, that it should lead them away from me. At least three of them agreed that meant they should hop toward Cole. But this wasn't a leisurely stroll. This was run-for-your-life-dammit! They pounded toward him, covering six feet at a stretch. And he just stood there, grinning.

"Move, you fool!" I yelled.

"Good thinking!" he shouted back, wheeling around so he could pace the group for the fraction of a second it would take to claim his prize.

I watched him reach for a male the size of a giraffe. And then another roo veered into him, sending him rolling like a skater who's just missed his board.

Raoul and I ran up to him together, but before either of us could reach him he'd bounced back to his feet. "Did you see that? Was that not the most awesome moment ever? Tell me you saw that!"

"Yeah, yeah. You do know you're lucky to be alive, right?" I asked.

Cole dusted off his jeans, which had developed holes in both knees. "What's your point?"

"I . . ." I looked at Raoul, who was wearing the same this-kicks-ass expression on his face that I saw on Cole's. "I'm just saying, you missed."

"I know. That means we've got the whole thing to do over again." Cole held up his fist and Raoul, who was apparently a close observer of modern gestures, gave it an enthusiastic bump with his own. Which was why I dropped the protest.

I don't get guys half the time. But—I smiled to myself as we turned back for the house—*they can be awful damn fun.*

Chapter Twenty-One

When we got back to the house, the Wheezer was parked in the drive beside Ruvin's Jeep. Cole raced to the front door and threw it open. Vayl and Ruvin, who'd been sitting on the couch, talking quietly, jerked their heads toward him.

"Cassandra! You'll never guess . . . Oh yeah." By the time we'd crowded in behind him he'd decided his high-tops needed a polish and was rubbing one on the back of his pants leg. He glanced back at us. "I, uh"—he stuck his finger in his ear, wiggled it a few times.—"I need to pee." He nodded to Ruvin as he strode from the room.

I looked up at Raoul. "What was that all about?" I asked.

"Maybe he's worried."

"Cassandra can take care of herself." I didn't buy a word of it and I'd just said it.

I swallowed my concern, told myself Cassandra wasn't back yet because the exits were probably guarded, which meant we'd have to go get her as soon as we finished the mission. But that otherwise she was probably just fine. Really. Then I settled on the chair next to Raoul's. Jack, reacting to the mood, dropped to his belly and laid his chin on my shoe. He began to chew at my laces.

Bergman left his post in the hallway to come hover behind

us. I'd never seen him so grim. Which would've been enough to concern me. But I could almost see the gears turning as he stared toward Kyphas's room.

"Where's Astral?" I asked.

"She's watching the demon," Bergman said. My eyebrows lifted. "She may be . . . different now. But she still works." He cleared his throat. "Unlike my bug," he added, half under his breath.

I said, "Just because we haven't heard from the Odeam team doesn't mean your bug's failed. It could be—" I stopped, mostly because he wasn't listening. His eyes hadn't budged from the demon's doorway. Judging by the gleam in them, he was imagining some complex, devious revenge. Hopefully it would require an invention that would keep him out of trouble until we'd found the Rocenz and sent Kyphas out of range.

When we were settled Vayl said, "Ruvin's wife was retaken at the airport. Fortunately she was able to distract her kidnappers long enough for Laal and Pajo to escape to the plane, which is well on its way to New Zealand by now."

Ruvin dropped his face into his hands.

"What the f—?"

Vayl stopped me with a look. "We should be able to free her as before, but now we must wait until after we have accomplished our mission."

"This isn't right!" I said. I shoved my hands into my hair and pulled, but it didn't stop Brude from giggling like a first-grader who's just been visited by Santa Claus. With Tabitha back in gnome clutches the chances for a high body count—and thus an increase to his army's numbers—had just multiplied. Because Ruvin would do anything the Ufranites said now. Which meant when the larvae hatched, he'd be there waiting, a walking breakfast buffet, instead of following our plan, saving his hide and NASA's goodies as well.

As Brude danced around his throne room, which was quickly gaining form and color, Granny May murmured, *No, Jazzy, something about this isn't right at all.*

I peered through my curls at Vayl and Raoul. They should be dangling at the end of their collective patience as well. Instead they sat staring at Ruvin, silent and . . . comfortable. Shouldn't they be pacing? Or at least pissed?

I looked over my shoulder. Cole had finished his business and come out to stand beside Bergman. They were always quick to point out Vayl's questionable decisions. And this was a doozy. So where was the criticism?

Ruvin's shoulders were shaking, so I guessed he was crying.

But Vayl. Well, he was a master at hiding his thoughts, so who knew? Another thread of doubt drifted through my mind. I caught it before Brude could get a whiff.

Huddle!

My girls gathered on Granny May's front porch.

I'm questioning this scenario. But I know Vayl wants me to believe everything he's showing me. In fact, I think it's vital that I do, or else Brude will suspect and then we're probably all deeply screwed. So when I have a stray thought that might raise Brude's suspicions, you four have to distract him. I'm counting on you especially. I nodded to Teen Me. *In fact, I've been thinking . . . there's a place in my head where we might be able to lock him away.* I swallowed dryly as I remembered it. *You know the one I mean.*

Tears sprang to her eyes as I reminded her. *What do I have to do?* she asked.

Get in his face when I start to have doubts about what's real and what's for his benefit. Then, when the time is right, I'll give you the signal. You're going to have to open the door. You'll have to shove him in.

But . . . I'm trying so hard to avoid it. For me it's only a few years in my future.

As soon as you close the door you can lock it. He'll be stuck in there with the memories. And hopefully we'll never have to open it again.

The parts of my mind that had survived Brude's onslaught nodded grimly. When he noticed them talking and demanded to know what they were doing, Teen Me stomped down the porch steps, strode right up to him, shoved her chin practically into his sternum, and screamed, "You are such a prick!" Then she burst into tears and ran into Granny May's house.

Brude held out his hands, baffled by her outburst. *What did I do?* he asked.

I shrugged. *I guess your charm doesn't work on the virginal ladies.*

My Inner Bimbo spoke up, leaving the huddle to collapse into a wicker chair as she said, *Hell, it doesn't even work on the horny ones.*

Brude stalked off, Granny May's uproarious cackle poking him in the back as he went.

Now that Ruvin had returned, we couldn't put off the next phase of our mission any longer. Luckily it didn't require a full crew, just Vayl, Cole, Jack, and I. Which left Bergman, Ruvin, and the talking cat to guard Kyphas. Not a comforting combination. So we'd convinced Raoul to stick around until we returned. At which point we promised him he could get on with the rest of his evening.

Armed with every weapon I'd packed, including a blood-test kit designed for involuntary donors, I drove Ruvin's Patriot through the cold, trash-littered streets of Wirdilling. The fact that he'd allowed me behind the wheel of his dream machine showed how much this latest development had crushed Ruvin. Determined to make it right for him, Vayl sat silent at my side, his cane lying across his lap like a second seat belt. Cole took up the entire backseat, looking a lot more relaxed than the jumping muscle in his cheek let on. As he checked the sites of his Parker-Hale he said, "You know, I studied the pictures Bergman took of the primary school pretty thoroughly, but I didn't see much in the way of sniper cover."

"Some big eucalyptus trees are growing by the back corner along with a few pines," I replied. "You should be able to find a comfortable spot there."

"So the whole Odeam team is inside the building?"

"That is where Ruvin dropped them off," said Vayl. "They have no reason to leave until the appointed time. In fact, I suspect the Ufranites are stationed beneath them to make sure they do not wander off."

Cole nodded to the kit in my hand. "How confident are we in that tester?"

"The results are ninety-nine percent accurate," Vayl said. "Within thirty minutes after we take the team's samples, we will know which members—besides the vice president—are carriers."

I nodded. "Then phase two of the plan kicks in."

"If necessary," Vayl added. "Perhaps he will be the only traitor after all. In which case our mission will be finished before we leave NASA's guesthouse tonight."

"You're sounding awfully optimistic. What's the deal?"

Vayl was studying me with those gemlike eyes of his. "You are scratching less," he murmured. "It is only a matter of time, my Jasmine." A slow smile lifted his lips, which hadn't touched mine in so long I suddenly felt like a downhill racer. I needed Chap Stick for the dryness and cracking. And a long night by a cozy fire to warm all the spots that had begun to chill in his absence.

I said, "Oh. Yeah. Well." Why did my mind always spin and stutter when what I wanted most was to whisper all my deepest feelings into that perfectly curved ear of his right before the nibbling began? I sighed.

"You guys make me want to gouge out my eardrums. Seriously," Cole said. We'd almost reached the primary school by now. Approaching it from the back this time, I found a small neglected corner dominated by delicate-leaved sugar gums, thorny acacia, and a mass of vines twisting around the fence. I parked there, knowing it provided perfect cover for three people who intended to kill a man before the night had ended.

Chapter Twenty-Two

Though it might've been well lit while functioning as a school yard, the outer edge of our target's quarters now hid in deep shadows. The only working fixtures perched above the doors, both the one with the intricate lock we'd decided to avoid, and the basement illusion.

"Are you ready?" asked Vayl as Cole and I stood at the top of the steps. Cole finished screwing on his silencer, exchanged a look with me, and we both nodded.

Inside my head Brude shouted, *I will not allow this!*

"My brain-buster is threatening us," I murmured.

Vayl unsheathed his sword. "Then it is time. Cole and Jasmine, trade positions. *Now!*"

Like a switch flipping behind my eyeballs, the clarity of the moment sharpened to almost painful brightness. The speed of each movement, while outwardly phenomenal, still registered in my mind like I was playing it in slow-motion so it could be cataloged for future reference.

Cole slipped the harness of his weapon over his head and shoved the Parker-Hale into my hands along with his ammo belt.

At the same time I passed the blood-test kit into his.

Vayl spun and plunged through the fake doorway. Cole sped

after him while I sprinted to the fence, hauling the rifle's strap over my head as I moved. Once again my track training kicked in, allowing me to get a foot onto the fence, which gave me a boost into the lower branches of the nearest pine before Brude could roar, *What is happening?*

None of your damn business, I thought as I scaled the tree, needles and sap both leaving their mark before I was high enough to switch to a sugar gum that had grown in tandem with the pine.

Sweet silence greeted my final push to a sturdy crook where I could brace my hips while standing on the lowest branch. I unslung the rifle and checked my scope. Yeah, I had unobstructed views of all the windows and doors on this side of the school.

I disengaged the safety and chambered a round. I didn't have time to doubt Vayl's strategy. He had to figure one of the reasons the gnomes wanted easy access to their carrier(s) was to protect him/them. So he also had to bet their magic plant door would be alarmed once the carrier(s) took residence. But Vayl also knew Brude was a threat. So he'd decided to go in fast and dirty.

Maybe I won't have anything to do, I thought. *Maybe the riot we caused in the warren has already turned the guards against their shaman and the whole scheme has washed away like an eroded riverbank.* I only had thirty seconds to believe that angle, because after that the first head appeared, sticking out of the fake concrete passageway like a target at a county fair duck shoot. My shot hit it in the ear and it dropped instantly, half in and half out of the door. The same was true for my next three targets. Then somebody smartened up and quit sending the grunts into the line of fire.

During the breaks I snuck peeks at the action through the windows.

Vayl and Cole had separated. Cole's job, which would've been mine, was to anesthetize the team members whose affiliation we couldn't place and pull a blood sample. It would be a quick, simple procedure. Two plugs up the nose that released fast-acting sleepy gas. Then set the head of a device that resembled a staple gun against a major vein, hold it for three seconds while it lifted the vein to the top of the skin, and pull the trigger. Instant suckage followed by wound closure so quick most victims never realized they'd been punctured. The blood would be automatically stored in a compartment in the handle and a new vial moved into place for the next sample. The only downfall? You've gotta keep good track of who you're testing if you haven't marked the vials. So Cole would be murmuring descriptions into his transmitter as he went. That way Bergman, who was preparing to run the tests back at base, would have no doubt whose results belonged to whom.

A small light came on in the room closest to the main door. Cole had opened the test-kit lid, which came with its own built-in beam. "Black-haired dude with goofy mustache and a unibrow," he whispered. "I think it's the software engineer, Johnson."

"Got it," Bergman replied from over half a mile away. Have I mentioned lately how much I love his gadgets?

A shadow crossing past the windows in the room nearest the front of the building let me know Vayl had set to work. I couldn't see much through the gauzy white curtains. But thanks to Bergman, I could hear. So I glanced around the playground to make sure the gnomes hadn't made use of a different escape hatch, and listened close.

> Vayl: "You will speak to me in a reasonable tone of voice. You will not scream or call out. Do you understand?"
> Gnome-puppet (no doubt influenced by Vayl's hypnotic suggestions): "Yes."
> Vayl: "What is your name and title?"
> Gnome-puppet: "My name is Dade Barnes. I'm the vice president of Odeam Security Software."
> Vayl: "Do you understand what you carry within your blood?"
> Dade: "Of course. It's no big deal. Like an infection you get over

once they administer the shot. And now I'll be able to keep my house. My wife and kids."

VAYL: "Dade, there is no shot. You have been duped."

DADE: "Heh."

VAYL: "Who else carries the larvae?"

DADE: "Just me. They call me the godpleaser. I'm like a saint to the gnomes." *I can almost hear him grinning. He loves the adulation. I sense that he regularly got his ass kicked in high school.*

VAYL: "You have betrayed your country. You are about to cause millions of dollars of damage. You may be responsible for the deaths of thousands of human beings if—"

DADE: "You think I give a shit? What's my country ever done for me? What's my fellow man ever done for me?"

VAYL: "Ah, so your status within your company, the house, wife, and children. Those would all have been attainable in any other country by a social misfit whose parents regularly demonstrate for the nation's destruction?"

DADE: "How did you know about my—"

VAYL: "Answer the question."

DADE: "Highly unlikely."

VAYL: "And your fellow man? Are you saying you and yours have never benefited from advances in medicine such as antibiotics, cancer prevention and treatment, or even simple headache remedies? What about electricity? Clean water? Or perhaps we should discuss the woman who found your daughter wandering alone in Target and escorted her to the front, where her mother was waiting, before some monster could make off with her."

DADE: "Are you some kind of psychic?"

VAYL: "No. I am Vampere. And I have come to kill you."

DADE (his voice shaking now): "Y-you don't have to do that. I won't go into to the Space Complex tomorrow. Or ever."

VAYL: "No, of course not. But you will die. The larvae erupting will cause you a most excruciating and bloody death. You will not be a hero, nor will your widow be rich. But you can redeem yourself today. If you do not know who else on your team has been turned, at least tell me who turned you."

DADE (sniffling): "It was the shaman."

VAYL: "Where would a gnome shaman get such a large amount of money as you no doubt required?"

DADE (sniffling harder): "I don't know. I never even met her. After the first call it was all just Internet contacts and money wires."

VAYL: "Her? The shaman is female?"

DADE: "Psh, yeah. Are you sure it's going to hurt?"

VAYL: "Have you ever had a blister?"

DADE: "Yes."

VAYL: "This is like being encased in blisters that explode from the bone outward. You will die screaming."

DADE: "Aaaah, God."

VAYL: "I believe your god respects his children's choices. You made the choice, Dade. As a result your country has been forced to make another. Come with me."

DADE (quick intake of breath as Vayl's power lifted. I could feel it, even from outside, the icy-cold tendrils of a Wraith's touch, freezing the traitor into lethargy even as the smooth undertone in his voice insisted on cooperation.)

Distraction, as gnomes began to emerge, not from their faked door, but from bolt-holes in the back corners of the lot. I picked them off. Two from one. Four from the other. Pause to switch clips. Bam, bam, bam. Another set of head shots that left Ufran with yet more dead to process.

Stop shooting, you foul wench! Brude screamed, striking me with such a headache I was momentarily blinded.

"Help me out, ladies," I whispered, squeezing my eyes shut, hoping the tears that rose would clear them.

Teen Me launched herself at the chieftain, her first bitch released before she'd even screeched to a halt within millimeters of his rage-blotched face. *What is your major malfunction?* she demanded. *All this yelling just makes you look like a big, fat bigot! Admit it! The real reason you're half crazed is because Jaz won't kneel down and kiss your feet!*

Hogwash! She is to be my queen. How much higher can a man raise a woman?

Gimme a fucking break! You're not going to let her make any decisions when New Hell opens its doors. She's just supposed to keep her mouth shut and make you look good, right?

I already have a plan in place. I have no need for—

Yeah, I hear you. I also saw what you did the second she disagreed with you. Tried to hit her, didn't you?

I may have raised my hand. Even a dog must know who is master.

You son of a bitch! Guys like you are why women across the world are afraid to go home at night!

Once I was sure she really had him hooked, I moved my full attention to the playground and let the roaring and screaming become background noise.

Nothing moved at any of the exits. But Vayl and Cole had finished. Now was the key time. I saw the bodies that had piled up at the main door pulled back into the tunnel. No one else appeared. I needed to concentrate. Not wonder why Brude wanted to save gnomes when more dead should mean more soldiers for his army. I'd have to figure that out later.

"I think Ufranites are waiting to jump you as soon as you clear the building," I whispered.

"We are nearly ready," said Vayl.

Somebody stepped out of the basement door. Or seemed to. I trained my scope on the guy. He wasn't moving right. And his head tilted at a strange angle. Which was when I realized he'd been dangled from a sturdy metal coat rack by the back of his jacket.

Dade Barnes rolled his head up so he could blink at the light above the door. He smiled, mouthed the word, "Pretty," then dropped his head to stare at the round, red object that had rolled out of the wall to his left. He frowned as spikes shot from the ball's center. One of them emitted a plume of smoke, jumping the ball a foot into the air, where it spun in increasingly blurry circles until all I could see was a fiery sphere that began to spark like a metal-packed microwave. Moments later it exploded, tearing into Dade's body so viciously that huge chunks of him simply disappeared in the aftermath.

I kept my scope trained on the door as Vayl and Cole appeared through the smoke, running so fast I knew my boss must have a hold of Cole's wrist. They sprinted for the Jeep as I took out the first curious guard to show his head. I heard the pop of Cole's silenced Beretta as he helped clear their path. Another couple of shots from each of us and the Jeep's engine roared to life. Seconds later it had pulled around to the side of the building, within feet of my tree.

Cole jumped out, covering me as I shimmied down, jumping the last few feet. Moments later we'd screeched away, leaving behind us the scent of Febreze and a pile of bodies it would take the rest of the night to bury.

Chapter Twenty-Three

We parked the Jeep behind the house and took Cole's blood samples to Bergman, who'd set up his mobile lab on the kitchen table. So much for a family-style breakfast in the morning.

In fact, I thought as I watched Bergman retrieve the vials, some of which probably held larvae, *forget breakfast altogether.*

The guys didn't seem to have a problem with it though. Vayl leaned against the counter, sipping his favorite beverage from a coffee cup while Cole scoped out the contents of the fridge. "Does Cherry Coke count as fruit?" he asked me.

"Only if you're in college." I closed the drawer I was searching through and opened up another. Surely some food gadget inventor out there had created something that would double as a back scratcher!

Aha! Potato masher! Let's see what Jack thinks.

I ran the rounded tines through his fur a couple of times. When his tail slapped against the floor I decided to call it a thumbs-up and tried it on myself.

Huh. Not bad. Wish it was a little more pointy, but overall—

Raoul stomped into the kitchen, pointed at Cole, and said, "You like women. Go deal with that wounded monster before I drag her into another plane and chop off her head!"

Raising his eyebrows at me, Cole grabbed the Cherry Coke, a bowl of chocolate pudding, a large spoon from the wall rack mounted above the stove, and took off to see what all the fuss was about.

"It's time I left. I have better things to do," Raoul told me.

"Like what?"

He paused. Shook his head angrily. "All right, I don't. But Cole gave me the location of his train set and this is the perfect time to retrieve it."

"You should get Nia to help you set it up." I hid a grin as he tried to laser burn me with his glare. "I'm serious! Chicks dig being included in hobby stuff."

"That's not what Cole said."

"Do you want to charm her temporarily or wrap her up for good? Of all the humans in the house right now, I'm the only one who's been engaged." I gave a mental nod to the dull heartache that accompanied my words. Once it had been a pain so searing I would've had to run to the bathroom and shake until it passed. Maybe time had been kind after all.

After giving my comment some thought, Raoul said, "All right. I'll invite her over. But I'm going to use some of Cole's moves," he warned me. "They're really very good."

"I have no doubt about that. I just don't get how a handsome guy like you doesn't have some of his own."

Raoul glanced at Vayl, who'd abandoned his drink to help Bergman with a portion of his test that required three hands. Though he knew it wouldn't make much difference where my *sverhamin* was concerned, Raoul lowered his voice.

"I've never been very comfortable around girls," he admitted. "I think it's the lipstick. It makes them look so . . . unattainable."

"Ah. So you can talk to me because I don't usually wear lipstick?"

He shrugged. "Saving your life broke *that* ice."

"Too bad you didn't have any sisters. That would've . . ." I stopped. Raoul had gone still and white, his reaction so close to those of many of my former victims that I looked over my shoulder to see if Kyphas had miraculously recovered, slipped past our guard, and buried a knife in his side.

"My sister died when we were small," he said.

I understood instantly. During our last mission, when I'd called Raoul out over his crappy attitude toward Vayl, his colleague, Colonel John, had let slip that my Spirit Guide's history involved a nasty confrontation with vampires. This must be part of what he'd been hinting at.

"That must've been awful for you," I said. And then, because I could tell he didn't want to talk about it anymore, "You know how sorry I am, right? But just because you didn't develop mad communication skills in your childhood doesn't mean you can't do some shaping now. Just take it slow at first. Maybe pretend Nia doesn't wear lipstick."

"She doesn't."

"No?"

"She wears gloss."

"Oh. Shiny."

"Like the sun on steel."

"Okay, well, don't look at her lips, or her eyes, which are probably just as devastating, am I right?" He nodded miserably. "Look at her nostrils."

"What?"

"Have an entire conversation with the cilia inside her nose holes. If that doesn't ground you, I don't know what will."

Raoul chuckled. "Between your advice and Cole's, this may just work out."

I badly wanted to ask what "this" consisted of, since they only inhabited physical bodies a small percentage of the time. But I found Raoul and I hadn't developed our relationship to the bump-ugly point yet. And, come to think of it, I hoped it never would.

Jack and I showed him to the front door. "You can keep the weapons we brought until your deal with Kyphas is done. I can't tell you how she'll try to turn on you, only that eventually she will."

I nodded, returning his somber look to let him know how seriously I took him. "Thanks. For everything."

He knelt, gave Jack a swift rub on the head, then leaned forward and whispered something in his ear. After which Jack backed up a few steps, sat down, and nodded. *What the hell?*

Raoul smiled up at me, and for a second I saw through the body he wore to the being he'd become. His beauty made me close my eyes.

When I opened them again he said, "You did right to keep this dog." And then he left.

Jack and I stared at each other. "What are you two hatching?" I asked him. He just licked his nose. Then he trotted to the kitchen to hover over his empty food bowl.

"What, have you got a tapeworm? You just ate like, an hour ago!" Pathetic eyes, blinking soulfully, followed by a sloppy drink that clearly didn't satisfy. "Okay, I'll get you a snack," I said. "But I don't see how you can eat at a time like this."

I went to my room, followed by the hungry mutt, who seemed to think I needed an escort to remind me of the importance of my current mission. Deciding Jack needed some exercise, I detoured past Kyphas's room on my way. Raoul had moved an adult-sized chair beside her bed, on which Cole currently lounged. He'd made himself comfortable by putting his feet up beside hers.

She was laughing.

We'd all removed our party lines, but I didn't need cutting-edge technology to overhear the convo.

"Naw, none of my brothers are nearly as charming as me," Cole was saying with his usual utter lack of humility. "I think the only reason Trig and Pait are married is because their wives have no judgment when it comes to character. They actually think I'm a solid citizen."

Kyphas giggled. I shoved my hand in my pocket. The hilt of my knife fit smoothly into my palm.

"Jasmine?" Vayl came up from behind me, hooked my elbow, and led me to our room, waiting until Jack had followed us in before closing the door. "Why am I sensing barely restrained violence from you?" he whispered.

I jerked my head back toward the demon. "She's a menace. We should've taken care of her along with the rest of them."

"You know we chose the wiser course."

"She's going to try to steal souls the whole time she's with us!"

"She is a demon. We cannot prevent that because she cannot sign a contract that contradicts her nature."

"But—"

Vayl stepped in closer, rubbing his fingertips from my shoulders to elbows as he spoke. "Enough, my *pretera*. Worry about matters you can influence."

"Like?"

"Why you began scratching like a flea-infested mongrel in the first place. After all, it did not occur at the first bite."

I dropped my fingernails from my rash-covered arms. "Oh, I'm pretty sure I know what the problem is."

Vayl's eyebrows inched upward. "And?"

"He wasn't calling the shots then. Now he's making a play for all the control centers in my brain. And the rash shows you how successful he's been so far. I do think I know how to put him in a place where he can't reach me anymore. But . . ."

When he realized how hard it was becoming for me to explain, Vayl sat on the bed. He pulled a box of treats from my trunk and gave Jack a couple to crunch on while I pulled myself together.

Finally I sank down beside him. I ran a hand down his thigh, watching my fingers trace the hard outlines of his muscles. Ignoring an itch behind my knee, I reached toward him with my other hand, sliding it across the flatness of his belly. His breath caught as I swung my leg over his, sat on his lap facing him, and took his face between my hands. "Help me," I whispered.

He clasped his hands around my back and pulled me so close it felt like we must be melding in some way. "I am here," he murmured into my ear.

Are you ready? I asked Teen Me.

She stood at a door so tall it seemed to touch the mountains of my mind. At least a dozen locks secured it. She looked fearfully over her shoulder, but Brude had retreated, as he always did when Vayl touched me. Her small nod allowed me to lean back, to look Vayl in the eyes.

"You've read my file." His chin inched downward, the most extreme nod I'd ever seen him pull off. I looked away, feeling the locks give, remembering the terror you only get the first time death stares you in the face—and laughs. I sucked air and forced out the words. "My first kill wasn't the vulture of that vamp nest in Atlanta."

His hands tightened, helping my spine straighten. "No?"

"I was seventeen. Evie was sixteen. She was dating a senior named Bret Ridden. We all liked him at first. He was smart. On the Math Team. He'd built his own computer. He was seeded first on the school's tennis team. And he had plans, you know? College. A solid career in finance. I think Evie saw all that potential stability after a lifetime of shifting roots and . . . she fell. Plus, he wasn't bad looking."

Vayl rubbed my back gently enough that he didn't even start an itch. "I take it the romance fizzled."

I began playing with the buttons of his shirt. "He turned out to be a control freak. And when Evie didn't dress or act like he wanted, he pushed her around. Literally."

I stopped, dug my hands into Vayl's chest as Teen Me began her work. Chills hit my soul as I heard the locks crack. Fast. Way too fast. I didn't feel ready. But I had to be.

Vayl's hands fell away. When I looked down, I saw they'd clenched into fists. His voice was almost a growl when he asked, "When did you first discover the abuse?"

I shrugged, like the memory might slide off my shoulders, make the burden somehow easier to bear. "She came home with a black eye. She made some lame excuse that Mom bought. Albert might have questioned her closer, but he was out of the country." I swallowed. "Dave and I knew better. We forced her to admit that he'd hit her because she'd stopped to talk to a guy from Chemistry class about the lab experiment they had to do that afternoon. Bret said she was flirting. And, hell, maybe she was. But, knowing Evie, probably not. Anyway, he got irate, they argued, and he punched her."

"But she stayed with him." Vayl sounded tired. How many versions of this story had he heard during the long course of his life? I stared into his eyes, wondering what lay behind those troubled indigo depths.

"Yeah. We begged her to dump him. But she said he'd cried afterward and promised never to hurt her again."

"They always do."

"It did take him a while." I went on. "Maybe two months later she came into our room after a date." I dropped my forehead onto Vayl's shoulder. "She looked like hell," I murmured. "They'd had another fight. She'd ordered something at the restaurant that she hadn't ended up liking, so she didn't eat much. And he was pissed that she was wasting his hard-earned money by leaving a full plate. Then he was mad because she'd insisted on paying for her share. In the parking lot he brought up the Chem lab guy again and as soon as they got into his car he started hitting her. She cracked her head against the window before she could finally get out. A couple of her friends were in the same restaurant, so she ran in and got them to bring her home."

"Did she break it off then?" The snap was back in his voice. Angry at him for dishing it out. At her for taking it. I'd felt exactly the same.

"Yeah. That was when the death threats started. We got the cops involved, but the state we were living in had crappy harassment laws at the time. And Evie was so scared. He'd stare at her from the other end of the hallway at school, and when nobody was looking he'd slide his hand across his throat. He left a dead squirrel in her gym locker. It just went on and on, until she was half crazy from fear."

"What did your mother do?"

"She didn't want to take any of it seriously, but Granny May kept nagging her, so she finally decided to move us in with Gran until Dad got transferred again. We tried to keep it quiet, but news gets around. And Bret found out. The Friday before we were supposed to move, Stella had to work. She left Dave, Evie, and I at home to finish up with the packing. Then Dave got a call. One of his buddies had been in a bad car wreck and they were all gathering at the hospital to support him. So he left."

"Was his friend really hurt?" As if he knew. I stared into those old eyes, saw the rage, and knew it wasn't just for Evie.

"No. But by the time he figured it out, Bret had already broken into the house. I'd gone into Stella's bedroom for more boxes when I heard a weird sound from our room. A thump, like somebody had fallen. I don't know why I didn't yell at Evie about it. Maybe just the fact that we'd been so freaked for so long. Or maybe because she'd suddenly stopped singing along with Christina Aguilera." She still went white whenever "Genie in a Bottle" came on the radio.

His hands had moved back to my hips. They pushed at me, like he wanted to stop the replay, because he knew how much it hurt. But he also knew it had to be done. So he asked, "What did you do?"

"I put the boxes down. Looked around Stella's room for a weapon. Which was when I saw Albert's gun cabinet. I grabbed the key from where he kept it in his desk drawer and pulled out his Winchester." I paused, licked my lips. "I was scared shitless, Vayl. My heart was pumping so fast I was afraid I'd pass out before I found out I'd just been imagining things. My hands shook as I loaded the rifle from the box he also kept in the cabinet. I was terrified the sounds I made echoed through the house like a bell. I was afraid my imaginary intruder was real, and that he'd walk in before I was ready. Mostly I feared I was too late. That Evie was lying in our room, bleeding to death while I tried to remember everything Albert had taught me about shooting."

I began to shake and Vayl pulled me close. I breathed in his scent, trying to calm myself as Teen Me yanked the doors wide open with a shrill screech that made my head ache.

As Brude's attention riveted on a vulnerability he might be able to exploit, Vayl said, "Stop. You should not—"

"No. I have to finish." I licked my lips, unable to prevent myself from falling back into that time, looking out at the familiar scene through the fear-glazed eyes of the teenager who'd joined the crew inside my head.

I crept through the living room, listening so hard I was surprised I didn't hear the neighbor's TV blaring. A choking sound. An angry whisper, way too low to come from a girl's throat. As soon as I knew Evie was alive and in trouble, I stopped feeling altogether. I brought the rifle up to my shoulder. Moved to the edge of the door. He'd left it open. Maybe he figured to find both of us in there. I heard another thump.

"Where is she?" he hissed. Evie whimpered, a sound that cut into my heart like a surgeon's scalpel. The sounds put them in the corner diagonal to the door. In my mind I saw them standing next to the closet under the poster of Ricky Martin that Evie blew a kiss to on the mornings she was in a really good mood.

Next to them would be a waist-high bookcase Granny May had given us that had been packed with Evie's books before she'd boxed them. Then her bed. It still had a canopy, which might block my shot if I got my angles wrong. My bed stood across the room, directly opposite the door. We kept our stereo and speakers on a narrow table along the wall next to it. The floor was cluttered with book bags, piles of clothes, and Evie's purse collection.

I stopped. If the lead-up had been hard, this would be excruciating. But Brude had taken the bait. I could sense him looming, making Teen Me clutch at the door handles like a big wind might come and blow her away if she didn't hold on tight enough.

"Finish it," Vayl said, gripping me like he thought I might fall.

I cleared my throat.

I stepped into the room. It only took a second to work out what had happened. He'd caught her while she was unloading the closet for the next round of packing. Shoved her face-first into the wall so hard some of the paint had flaked onto the floor. Used the butcher knife in his hand to shred the back of her shirt, leaving a couple of bloody lines where he'd gotten too eager.

He stood with his back to me, but his face was turned to snarl into hers so he caught my move peripherally. And I knew. I had to act before he could think. Before either of us could, really. I fell into drill-sergeant mode instinctively. Because it had always gotten immediate compliance for my dad.

I screamed at my sister first, "Evie! Nuts!"

Her heel flew up, striking Bret in the groin. Not a solid shot, but still hard enough to make him grab at himself with the hand that had been pinning her.

"Duck!" I bellowed, using the tone Albert saved for only those dire moments when he thought we were about to pull some ultimately stupid stunt like running into traffic or jumping off a bridge. She dropped, screaming as she went because Bret had caught her by the hair.

"You fucking bitches!" he rasped. "I'll slice you both into tiny little piec—"

His knife hand punched toward Evie's back. But I took the half second I needed to aim. And when I fired, all I felt was the kick of the gun butt against my shoulder. I watched blankly as Bret's skull shattered and parts of his brain sprayed across the closet door and the floor, Evie's clothes, and Evie herself.

Without looking at him, she scrambled away, screaming so loud my ears started to pound. I pointed the rifle to the floor so I wouldn't accidentally shoot my sister, just like Albert had taught me to do.

And that was when I started to cry. I'd made somebody stop breathing. Forever. Even after the police came, after the newspaper stories and the inquest, where people I'd never seen or met before cleared me, I cried myself to sleep. Not because I was a killer. But because something so horrible and final, something only God should have charge of, had felt so right. I had come face-to-face with my inner monster. And she fit me like a second skin.

"And now?" Vayl asked, running his hands up to my shoulder blades. "Have your feelings changed?"

I looked at the window, like the world on the other side of the faded brown curtains might be different if I could give him the answer I wanted to.

"Some," I said. "I know in my head that what I do is vital to my country. And I've saved the lives of thousands, if not millions, of people who run to the grocery and Wal-Mart and football practice, blissfully unaware that I've just offed the scumbag who wanted to turn their kids into nuclear waste. But . . ."

"Yes?"

I winced. Made myself meet his gaze. "I know something is broken in me. Not so bad that I can't see what side I should be fighting on. Or where I need to draw the line. But enough that I'll never be right. I'll never"—I drew in a breath—"be normal."

The doors in my head swung wide. Brude swept in, howling with glee. All he saw were the walls, covered in scars, some of them so new the blood was still drying on the floor beneath them. All he felt was the dull, unrelenting ache of hopelessness beating out a rhythm that sounded horribly close to the words, "Loser, loser, loser," repeated with the conviction of an eyewitness.

I grabbed Vayl's shoulders, dug my fingers in, and willed the tears away. *Now.* I gave him my fiercest look. *Help me, Vayl.*

For a moment he didn't move. A spike of terror drove itself into the back of my neck. *You said I could trust you! Don't let me down, dammit!*

Then he yanked me against his chest and in one swift move, rolled me onto my back. His lips met mine with a force that blew the doors closed on Brude. Every touch, every stroke, the winding of our tongues and bodies set another lock into place.

Between caresses he said, "Someone as remarkable as you should never reach for normal. I know the word appeals to you, but the existence would bore you into committing real mischief. If you change, I swear to lock you in my castle until you return to your usual strange ways." *He has a castle!* shouted Teen Me, who immediately discovered a huge wooden bar that she slid into place just at the point where Brude's relentless door pounding wouldn't even bother me in my sleep.

I sighed. Relieved. Strung-out. And increasingly excited by Vayl's wandering hands and lips. Which was when my stomach began to itch. I tried to scratch, but he pulled my hand away, raised the hem of my shirt so he could see the double-heart belly ring he'd given me surrounded by blotchy redness.

"I was right. It is improving," he said. "But not enough for me to put you into further misery."

"But I *want* to be miserable!" I protested as he rolled off me and propped himself up on an elbow. I sat up. "Wait. That didn't sound right."

"Jasmine, you are rubbing your leg against the side of my boot. And I am certain at least half of the writhing you were doing was to set your back against the comforter just to relieve the itching there."

"Ah. Uh."

He reached over and kissed me on the forehead. "When you have recovered, I promise to make up for every moment we have missed. And then some."

I smiled. How lovely to have snagged a dude who kept his promises. Once I would've said there wasn't more than one in the world. Now I knew there were at least two. And I had fallen for both of them.

Chapter Twenty-Four

I wanted to spend more time celebrating. Let Vayl know what he'd really done for me in this tiny bedroom whose bare white walls seemed to sparkle with silver-pink now that I knew Brude was trapped. But maybe I should wait. Yeah. Make extra sure I had control back before I started the festivities.

So I let Vayl return to the living room to check on Ruvin without saying a word about our success. And then, the moment I stepped into the hall, it dropped to the bottom of my priority list. Because, despite Vayl's reassurances that Cole knew how to take care of himself, when I heard his chuckle thread around Kyphas's laughter, I lost it. Just a little.

I called for Astral. "Snoop time," I whispered to her as I knelt between the doors to my bedroom and the bathroom. "I want you to spy on Cole and Kyphas. But don't you dare start singing. In fact, don't talk at all. Don't even record any audio." There, that should cover all the bases. Besides, it seemed a little too invasive. "And above all, don't get caught!"

Astral slipped into Kyphas's room and began streaming video, mostly of Cole sitting by her bed, talking, sharing spoonfuls of pudding, smiling with his usual übercharm. He looked so comfortable! Didn't he know demons had no net of values to prevent them from stealing the souls of great guys like him? When he helped her turn over, because her back had already healed that much, I nearly growled.

That's it. The next time Raoul threatens to behead her, I'm handing him an axe.

I joined Vayl and Ruvin in the living room, but the waiting around we were forced to do didn't improve my mood. We discovered that late-night television in Australia consists of crappy old movies or infomercials that none of us wanted to veg out to. With nothing to distract us, we took turns throwing a tennis ball down the hallway so Jack could race after it. How he managed not to smash into the wall I never could decide, but he always retrieved it without causing any damage.

In the kitchen, Bergman had finished centrifuging the blood. But the next part of the test would still take a while and Ruvin had started checking his watch.

"Are you sure this plan will work?" he asked Vayl for the third time. "The Odeam team did say they wanted me to pick them up at two a.m. That only gives you fifteen minutes to identify the rest of the infested."

"It will be fine," he said with a confidence I would've had to fake.

"Why are they leaving so early?" I asked.

He shrugged. "When they first called to book a ride from the airport, Dade explained that they were just supposed to stop over at the guesthouse for a nap, to sort of rejuve after the flight. And then he wanted me to drive them to the Complex early, he said so they wouldn't be tying up everyone's computers during the busiest time of the workday."

"Makes sense," I told Vayl. "But that means if Bergman doesn't get the tests done on time—"

"We will not know who is infected and who is clean."

"Maybe they'll find the body and call the cops. That'll delay this whole deal by at least a day."

"We both know the gnomes have probably cleaned up that entire mess by now."

"But we can't let them get into the Space Complex."

We both turned toward the kitchen and said, "Hurry up, Bergman!"

"You can't rush these things!" he called back. "That's how you get false positives. And vice versa!"

Which was why two a.m. found Vayl, Jack, Astral, and I in the Wheezer, following Ruvin and his clients in the Jeep, none of us any wiser as to who in the team, if any of them, had drunk the larvae-laced lemonade.

Since we'd decided to leave Cole back at the house to nurse/babysit (guard) Kyphas, we'd given Ruvin his party line doodads. He tried to do the chatty, but nobody's ever up for light conversation at two in the morning. Especially not two software engineers, a marketing manager, and the mistress of a missing vice president. And, well, Ruvin wasn't all that gifted anyway. So only once did they have anything to say. And that was when they got into the Jeep.

"G'day, mates! Do we have a sleepyhead, then? I only count five of you and I'm sure I brought six from the airport."

"Our team leader left a note saying he had a family emergency," one of them replied shortly. "I'm surprised you're not the one who drove him to the airport."

"Oh, no, Mr. uh . . ."

"Johnson."

"No sir, Mr. Johnson, that wasn't me. I'm so sorry to hear . . . well, if there's anything I can do . . ."

"Just get us to work before Tykes starts whining about his arm again."

"It hurts!" came another voice, higher than the first and laced with pain. "I have a mark. Did one of you punch me when you were trying to wake me up?"

Chorus of denials, although I thought I heard a third voice, which must've belonged to the marketing guy, Pit, mutter, "I'd like to take a swing at you."

Then Tykes said, "Look, Bindy's asleep already. It's a miracle that bimbo got dressed as out of it as she was before. Does she take sleeping pills?"

"Dunno," said Johnson. "But she's gotta be on something, because she wasn't even upset when she heard Dade took off." Geez, had Cole given her a double dose of knock-out nose stuffing? I waited for more info, but that was the last any of them said.

I fell far enough back that they couldn't have seen my headlights even on the straight sections of roadway. Sometime in the next five minutes the nail we'd driven into Ruvin's back tire would release enough air to flatten it. Hopefully by then Bergman would have the results. Otherwise we'd have to move on to plan B. Which involved holding everyone at gunpoint until we knew for sure who to plug.

Vayl's phone rang. *Bergman, you are such a great—*

"Hello, Martha," Vayl said.

"Why is our secretary calling you?" I whispered. "It's the Oversight Committee, isn't it? They've found some sort of loophole and they're—"

Vayl made a swift, cutting gesture with his hand. One he'd never used on me before. When his fingers clenched into a fist I knew the news was bad.

"When?" he asked.

While he waited, I tried not to dredge up all the possible nuggets o' nasty she might be feeding him. Problem was, in our business, that was all we ever dealt with. So nightmare visions kept slapping the backs of my eyeballs. Floraidh Halsey wasn't as decrepit as we'd thought when we'd left Inverness. She'd recruited a new coven and declared war on the CIA. Or worse, another zombie king had risen in Tehran, one too powerful even for our friend Asha Vasta to combat. Or—

"All right. Yes, I understand." Vayl closed the phone. "Pull over."
I didn't protest. He knew the risk we were taking with such
a delay. Which meant I really didn't want to be driving when he
dropped the bomb. I eased the Wheezer onto the narrow shoulder,
even remembering to activate the hazard lights before turning to
face him. "What is it?"

"Pete is dead."

Chapter Twenty-Five

I sat so still, staring out onto the hood where I'd last seen Pete's image that I could've been a corpse. Like Pete was now. Lying somewhere, inanimate. Nothing left to lift his hand, brush it across those two proud hairs on his head. No spark to light his eyes when he talked about his wife and kid.

Who's going to bitch at me when I throw a dent into the fender now? I'll be totally out of control! I'll be like a one-woman Demolition Derby!

Vayl said, "Jasmine. Are you listening?"

"Um."

"He was murdered in his office. Slashed across the throat with something duller than a knife. Theories abound, but Martha believes it was a claw. His computer was stolen. His files ransacked. Whoever did it now has access to every field agent's identity and current location. Everyone is being called in. Officially, the department will be shut down until a full investigation can be completed." His voice went arid. "Which, according to Oversight Committee estimates, will take at least six months."

"I just reorganized all those files. Remember? While my collarbone was healing. God, was Pete pissed."

"Jasmine?"

The concern in Vayl's voice woke me up just enough to show me what to do. "Everyone I care about dies. You see that, right? Matt and Jessie, my crew. Granny May and Gramps Lew. I don't know if my mom counts, but Pete does. You have to go."

"What?"

I shot out my door, ran around to his side, and yanked his open, ignoring Jack's attempt to poke his head outside. "If you stay with me, you're going to go poof. Like a big cloud of steam coming out of a locomotive, and all that'll be left is your cane, and bits of really expensive cloth, and some ash, which I'll have to scoop up and put in some kind of container that I'll be able to carry around with me the rest of my life. Not an urn, because the lids pop off at the worst possible moments. Maybe a Rubbermaid container. Tell me you don't want that! Tell me you don't want to ride around in a plastic box like a piece of leftover turkey!"

I said the last part into the lapel of Vayl's jacket, because he'd come out of the Wheezer sometime during my rant and toward the end had pulled me into a bone-squeaking hug. "And I was afraid you would not react at all," he said softly. "But perhaps you could agree this is somewhat extreme?"

"How?"

"I am Vampere. People have been trying to murder me for centuries. And you see how successful they have been?"

"Even an idiot can get lucky," I muttered.

"Which is why I have you. Now, do you truly want to abandon the subject of our conversation?"

I said, "I can't talk about h-him right now. After?"

He inclined his head. "Then let this be of some consolation. Before Martha disconnected she gave me a code phrase."

"Yeah?"

"She said, *Owls are not the only night-hunters.*"

"But . . . that means . . ."

He shrugged. "Martha must never have been a secretary, because now she is the acting head of our department. Also in code, she directed me to complete our mission and to report back only to her."

I shook my head. "It's too much."

"So let us save Ruvin's life and, in so doing, rescue NASA from these zealots, as Pete requested in the first place."

Is this what Cassandra meant? Have we failed already and Pete is the first of many to die as a result?

Pete! You dumb son of a bitch! Why did you let them do it?

He assumed he was safe, Granny May said sadly.

I hunched my shoulders. *Why don't they ever know better?*

Chapter Twenty-Six

The Wheezer was damn near choking by the time we caught up to Ruvin's Jeep. Since the party line's reach maxed out at around two miles, we hadn't heard the conversation when the tire went flat. But there the vehicle stood, parked by the side of the road just as we'd planned.

"Where's the jack?" While my dog panted in my ear to let me know he hadn't gone far I added, "And the spare? Ruvin should've been faking some repairs while he waited for us."

"In fact, where is Ruvin?" Vayl asked as we pulled in behind the Jeep. The tinted back windows revealed nothing of what might be going on inside. "Do you feel anything?" he asked.

We could both pick up on extreme human emotions, but when I shook my head I could tell he agreed. Either everybody inside was grooving to some great new jazz tune, or it was empty.

I drew Grief anyway. "Jack, stay. And don't scare the robokitty. Astral, you stay too. We may need you later. With your head attached."

"Okey dokey, pokey!" she said. Vayl raised his eyebrows at me as I shrugged. Personality change was one thing, but this cheerful bullshit was wearing thin quick. Deciding it would be okay if Jack gave Astral another nasty surprise, I approached the Jeep's driver side, keeping step with Vayl, who'd taken the opposite.

"Ready?" he asked softly.

I reached forward. Wrapped my hand around the back door handle. Raised my gun and nodded once.

"Now."

We jerked the doors open, Vayl's sweep of frigid powers preceding my shout of, "Don't move!" I jumped back as a body flopped out the door, torso first, its hips and legs remaining inside. It was Dade's mistress. Or what was left of her. "Shit!"

I moved back into position, training Grief on every possible point of attack. All I saw was a second body, slumped over the feet of the first, still bleeding onto Ruvin's upholstery. They were both full of bullet wounds and missing their heads, so we couldn't tell who the second body belonged to until Vayl slipped off its wedding ring. *Lyssa & Max forever* had been engraved on the inside.

"I believe that is the marketing executive," he said.

"Which means Ruvin and the software engineers are missing."

We did a quick perimeter check. No more bodies. No sign of a struggle.

"Why?" I murmured. "You just change the tire and keep moving. It's not that big of a deal."

"Do you suppose Ruvin told them about us?"

"Possibly." It didn't feel right though. "Maybe . . . I don't know, maybe Brude had something to do with this. He's got resources other than me. And the shaman might be able to reach into the beyond. Maybe they connected somehow. Maybe he let the information slip before I got a handle on him."

Vayl sent me a piercing look. "Are you saying you have control now?"

I hesitated. Aw, what the hell. I hadn't heard a peep from him, and my whole crew of mental misfits had returned. "Yeah. As much as I can with him stuck in my brain. I know my thoughts are my own. He can't move me. And he can't snoop into my conversations anymore."

Vayl stepped toward me. For a second I thought he looked taller. Then I realized the relief had been so immense that I'd actually seen it release him. He grasped my shoulders, stared deep into my eyes, like he needed more assurance.

"Yes," he murmured. "Finally. I knew you could do it."

"*We* did it. Together."

Realization widened his eyes. "Ahh. I only wish . . ." He rubbed his thumb across my bottom lip, leaving a trail of tingles that multiplied so rapidly I had to grab his elbows to hold myself steady. He went on. "But we have just begun this night's work."

Dammit! We need another vacation! To Mars!

"True," I said, sighing. Vayl's phone rang again and we stared at it with dread. But this time the source was expected. Vayl spoke into it for a total of ten seconds and then hung up.

"That was just Bergman confirming what we already suspected. The software engineers, Johnson and Tykes, are both carrying gnome larvae for the Ufranites."

"Okay. So our targets are clear."

"And now I can clarify our other plans as well. You see, the flat tire idea was never real. We only developed it because we were sure Brude would find a way to leak it." Vayl's voice had loosened in his relief, become fuller as if every revelation released a strangler from his throat.

"Oh. So. Where are they?"

"They are on foot, just as we wished it." He paused. Grimaced so deeply the sides of his lips actually turned down. "We should have been here sooner to chase them into the ambush we had set up, but the news about Pete . . ." He paused. We both drew a breath before he went on. "Ruvin's chatter leads us to believe we should still be able to turn events to our advantage."

"What ambush are you talking about? And how are you hearing Ruvin but I'm not?"

Vayl chose to answer the second question. "Ruvin is carrying a bug, so we can listen in on his conversation."

"On another frequency," I said bitterly.

Vayl said, "Tap your earpiece three times."

I followed his instructions, realizing I was aping the move Cole had made when we'd arrived back at the house after the failed kangaroo petting mission, when he'd been so eager to talk to Cassandra. Suddenly I could hear Ruvin, panting, saying, "Are you sure I can't talk you out of this? Aw!" And the sound of his feet scrabbling to keep himself upright after an obvious shove.

Vayl said, "You must understand, our misdirections have only been because of Brude. Because we could not work out how to fool him without excluding you as well. And . . ."

"What?"

"You are not going to like this."

"So say it fast."

"Come, let us walk while we talk." We started up the hill to the west of the car. In a low voice so as not to spook those we pursued Vayl said, "We have proof that the Ufranites are not acting alone. They are, in fact, being funded by a group who wants to keep the moon free from human interference. At first it bewildered us how such vastly different *others* could meet. But Cassandra's investigations have yielded a trove of information."

"I like that," said Cassandra. "It makes me sound like the kind of pirate who would never hurt anyone."

I stuck my finger in my ear. "Cassandra! Are you okay?"

"I'm fine."

"But you didn't just hunker down like I told you to."

"How could I? When you handed me the drawing from the

dead guard, I Saw that some of the gnomes were disgusted with the shaman and I knew that could be our route to discrediting him. After Cole translated '*ylmi*' to mean 'tainted' I realized the gnomes with the crowns were actually Ufranites with stars on their heads. Pure gnomish. And the sign of the Resistance is the star tattoo, just like the one we saw on the guard. So I began searching for others like him. I had so many visions I began to feel like I was walking in a dream. But I found them. They're only a handful, but they recently discovered the truth. That the shaman is a female, born without a tail or a blue nose."

"Do you know who she is?"

"Not yet. They're taking me to her quarters now. As soon as I touch her belongings, I'll know."

"What about this partnership?"

"That was what I'd sensed earlier with Ethan Mreck's death. Werewolves. The Ufranites are working with the Valencian Weres, who will come out of this deal wielding vast powers among all moon-changers if they can prevent humans from further exploring, or worse, settling on their most sacred site."

"I don't get where Brude fits in though. Or how the Ufranites and the Weres partnered up to start with."

"I think he might be the middleman. The guards say the shaman took a pilgrimage that catalyzed her rise to power, because that's where she heard the voice of Ufran. Guess where she went?"

"Dunno."

"Scotland. Just south of Inverness, to be exact."

"No way."

I could almost hear Cassandra's head bobbing. "According to the shaman, Ufran wears his hair in long black braids. And his chest is covered with tattoos."

"Oh. Shit."

* * *

Vayl and I didn't have time to hash everything out. But he'd probably already reached the conclusions I was rapidly catching up to. If Brude had cooked up this deal years ago, then his infiltration of my psyche had a lot more to do with my current mission than my future afterlife. The bastard must've been shaping this scheme for ages. He'd just been waiting for the perfect patsy to ride to the finish line. And boy was I ever ideal. I wanted to put my hands to my head and shake it till his teeth rattled.

No! yelled Teen Me. *What if that breaks the locks?*

Fine, I won't. But if he ever makes it to solid again, I'm carving another tattoo on that jerkoff. And it's going hilt deep.

Ruvin's voice interrupted my internal bitchfest. "Here's the trail I told you about." He was panting. Fearful. On the edge of tears. He must've thought our no-show meant we'd deserted him.

He said, "Watch your step; it's curvy. But it'll lead us to that *rock shelter* I told you about. The Ufranites and the aborigines both worship there." Information he wanted us to have, not the Odeam team. But they didn't know that.

The voice I'd come to know as "Johnson" said, "That's common knowledge, dumbass, otherwise we wouldn't be following you."

A grunt from Ruvin. I wished they wouldn't keep pushing him. It was already getting tough to control my temper. And the last thing this country needed was another bushfire.

Vayl and I followed their trail, a series of signposts ranging from crushed grass to white scars where the bark had been brushed off the remains of fire-blackened pines.

"Explain this," I whispered, mostly to calm myself down. "How is it better for them to walk than to drive on a spare? And you still haven't answered my ambush question. Is Cole up there? Or have you called in even more reinforcements?" The thought chilled me. My people I could trust not to blab about my current condition. Strangers—never.

"No, we have not requested extra help. Yes, Cole is in position higher up the hill. Ruvin and the Odeam team are walking because the Jeep's spare is back at the rental house."

"Okay. But why not stay on the road?"

"Ruvin produced a map that he told them the original carrier had given him in case of emergency. It proves that the Ufranites have a tunnel leading directly from the rock shelter to the Space Complex, so they will still be able to get inside and hatch the larvae without interference. By the way, remind me to praise Bergman for his quick work in drawing that up. It looks remarkably authentic."

As I made the ascent, moving carefully past rocks that would gleefully snap an ankle if I stepped wrong, I said, "This should be a pretty quick hit, then. As long as we haven't been followed."

Which was when I heard it. A scrabbling among the rocks. Not claws, like you might expect to hear from a foraging wombat or opossum. No, that was definitely the click of a heel.

"Call Astral," whispered Vayl.

"Why? She's stuck in the Wheezer."

"No, she is not."

He must've left its door cracked. Which means Jack's loose too. Shit! Okay, worry later. I whispered, "Here, kitty. Make it fast, and give me video on your way to my location."

Astral's view appeared in front of me. She'd leaped out of the car and come racing up the hill. I couldn't tell where Jack's curious nose had taken him, but I did see her pass a series of armed Ufranites. They were moving slowly, creeping along so the night noises, mostly crickets and the occasional hooting owl, covered their advance.

"I count ten gnomes at our backs," I whispered. I drew Grief as I looked ahead. Could they be trying to herd us into another crowd waiting up the tree-dotted hill? Probably not if Cole was already there. Which meant they just wanted us to move too far from the road to consider escaping by car.

Vayl paused, checking the trail, considering our options. He tapped his ear. "Are you both in position?" he asked.

When Vayl nodded at a conversation I couldn't hear, I said, "You didn't tell me about a second sniper up here. Which means you're still hiding stuff from me. And while I understand why, I'm about to risk my life without knowing the whole picture. Which is pissing me off."

"Will you ever fully trust me?"

"I have no idea. I'm trying, but people close to me have been jerking me around my whole life. It's hard to put your next breath in another person's hands after that."

"But I am not another person," he said. "I am your *sverhamin.*"

The first of the gnomes had almost reached Grief's range. Which meant I'd be a clear target for his weapon as well. I sighed. "What do you want me to do?"

"Kiss me."

My supervisor had just been killed. My dog was missing. A radical fringe group of gnomes had partnered with a bunch of Weres to destroy one of my country's most precious resources. And suddenly that was all I wanted to do. I rose on tiptoe, felt him lean down and wrap his arms around me. Our lips met, a mix of despair and promise in their tender touch. What an odd time to feel *home.*

Vayl moved his caress down to my neck. "You must survive this," he murmured against my throat. "Promise me you will live on." Like I was crushed inside, where even surgeons couldn't reach.

"I promise," I said. Because we both needed me to, though I didn't understand the source of his request until he kissed me again, and I felt his fangs pierce my bottom lip.

Cold shot through me, an icicle rocket threatening to rip off the top of my head. I screamed into his mouth as frost rimmed my teeth and tongue. The skin on my face and hands tightened painfully. My entire body felt like it had been buried in a snow bank. I jerked away, too cold even to shiver. I stared down at my arms. They were covered in ice.

"What have you done to me?" I demanded. It took a while to get the words out. My mouth didn't want to work anymore.

He stared intently, his expression an odd mixture of triumph and dread. "I have lent you this, my greatest power, because I could not warn you that Cassandra had Seen this attack, embroiled as it had been in all her other visions of the shaman, the Weres, and Brude. If you had donned a bulletproof vest for this leg of our mission, we assumed Brude would have soon become suspicious and warned the shaman. So I have armored you." He stopped, swallowed. "Are you all right?"

I tried to shake my head. But it didn't want to turn. So cold, right to my core, as if he'd pumped liquid nitrogen directly into my bloodstream. I could feel everything falling, failing. I wanted to shriek, but my mouth had frozen shut.

"Jasmine?" Cassandra could've been a mile beneath my feet, crouching behind an Ufranite sun generator, but her voice sounded close and urgent as she said, "Listen to me. Vayl only attempted this because of my vision. You can survive, but you must summon up that rage, the one that burns so hot in you that it catches your surroundings on fire when you release it."

I can't! It'll ash part of my soul!

Though it wasn't one of her skills, it seemed like she could read my mind when she added, "The ice will keep it contained, Jaz. I Saw this. Call out your fury. Let it warm you."

I reached for the anger that always seemed to simmer right beneath my civilized surface. And found it, churning like liquid iron around a massive anvil engraved with the names of everyone

I'd ever lost. The newest, PETE, shone like silver next to the others, which had aged to dull pewter.

Suddenly all the voices in my head, the ones who'd stayed and those that had just returned, screamed, *Pete's dead! Matt's dead! Jessie's dead! They're never coming back, and I'm possessed, and my mother's hell-self tried to kill me less than two weeks ago and everybody I know has been Lying To Me! FUUUUUUCK!*

I opened my eyes, not even realizing I'd closed them until I saw Vayl's face hovering over mine, eyes wide, jaw tight with suppressed panic. I blinked. Nodded. *I'm okay.* The ice still encased me, but now it felt less like a freezer pop body bag and more like mega-stiff coveralls.

"They are coming," he said. "We must lead them up this hill to the path."

"Why?"

"Cole and Kyphas are waiting among the trees, perhaps fifty yards up."

"*Kyphas?* So that whole sickbed thing . . ."

Vayl's lips tightened. "It was largely an act to mislead Brude. I made a separate deal with her, when you—and he—could not hear. She has agreed to fight with us."

"Because it's in her best interests to!"

"She has also vowed to do no violence to any within our Trust."

"Trust. That word bites on so many levels," I muttered as we struggled up the slope, both of us now armored in such thick coatings of ice that when the first shots hit us we barely noticed them. In fact, some of them actually sounded pleasant, like Jack barking, that's how wishful my thinking had become.

"Faster," Vayl urged.

I grunted to let him know I was moving as quick as my creaking outer skin would allow. But when I felt the impact of a gnome slug slam into my back, I paused. Did a slow-motion spin. Raised

Grief and commanded my finger to pull the trigger. The extra three seconds it took helped my aim. The guard crumpled, a hole in the socket where his eye had once been.

I glanced at my gun and felt glad I'd been holding it when Vayl had covered me. Because its grip had frozen to my palm, and if I hadn't had my finger inside the trigger guard when the icing had gone down, I'd be cruising the woods for a club right now.

I backed up, took out another pursuer who was so sure of his future success that he'd stepped out from behind a grass tree to shoot. His buddy, sitting in the lower branches of the tree next door, dropped to the ground to check on him. I took him out, as well as another guard who was moving toward us from the same small hide.

"Come, Jasmine, run!"

Turning back, I forced my legs into a slow lope, my inner fire warming my muscles as the adrenaline boosts from all the shards flying off my body boosted me to even greater speed. Vayl led me straight uphill to a spot where a gravel path crossed ours. We turned sharply right to follow it. The trail would've been a cinch in any other conditions. Rising gently upward toward the skirts of Mount Eliza, its width allowed us to jog shoulder to shoulder. In places planked bridges gave us easy access to the opposite sides of shallow gullies. To our right, the trees grew closer together, giving us better cover than we'd had since beginning the chase. To our left large rocks had begun to take the place of trees, jutting from the side of the hill like giant, fleshy mushrooms.

"Do you see the bend in the path ahead of us?" Vayl asked.

"Yeah."

"That is our goal."

I'd turned to shoot again when I heard the sound of gunfire coming from behind us. We'd passed Cole. I'd seen the flash from his muzzle. Heard the death-scream of a pursuer. Swift movement from Astral's feed caught my eye. Kyphas, flinging her boomerang, laughed with delight as she watched it crush the throat of a careless Ufranite before it flipped back into her hand.

I may now owe my life to a demon. This sucks!

I pushed forward, making the bend just in time to dodge a shot that cracked into the rock behind my left shoulder. I'd escaped a bad blow. Plus the shadow trotting at my feet assured me Astral had come through the firefight unharmed. But I had no time to celebrate. Something punched me in the chest, taking me to my butt. I looked down. The ice had shattered, leaving a hole the size of a pool ball.

Astral sat beside me, her head cocked. "Hello!" she said.

I said, "Shit! They're ahead of us, Vayl!"

We rolled into the brush, taking shelter behind a pile of nearly leafless branches. Vayl slammed his hand against the trunk of a nearby tree. The ice encasing it shattered, giving him the flexibility he needed to access his sword.

Astral leaped onto my lap, lost her grip, and skidded down my legs like a ski jumper. She hopped clear when she reached my ankles, sat at my feet and stared at me reproachfully.

"See what you get for behaving like a cat?" I told her. "R2-D2 never would've pulled such an embarrassing stunt."

She turned her back to me, licking little frozen shards off one pitch-black paw. Every time she opened her mouth I could hear Foreigner singing, "You're as cold as ice."

"Smartass," I muttered. I squeezed my eyes shut. When I opened them again, I saw what hadn't been clear before. Movement under a bridge that lay the length of a football field ahead of us. Which put us within range of their weapons. But we'd have to get a damn sight closer before we could strike with ours.

They were a group of chasers who'd circled around and set themselves up under the bridge's wood-planked shelter. The path continued beyond them, and I studied it with a sense of urgency so deep it made me twitch. We had to get past these goons fast, before Ruvin became infant formula. But how? Trees continued beyond their position along our side of the hill, so we could approach from that direction. But we wouldn't have them pinned. Because it looked like a gap in the rocks by the bridge led to another trail.

"What do you think?" I whispered. "Charge them?"

"How many do you count?" Vayl asked.

"Astral, go get me video of those gnomes."

Though she stalked off like I'd told her cats would never be superior to dogs, her pictures came back quick and clear.

I took inventory. "Eight."

"All right, then. How is your armor holding up?"

Covering the hole, I said, "Terrific."

With the exception of letting the Ufranites ahead of us slip their net, Cole and Kyphas were dealing with the ones behind pretty well. But they could only hold them off for so long. Cole would be running low on ammo soon. And Kyphas, despite her heritage, was still only one versus an organized unit. We needed to move this group of troll wannabes out of our way.

Then I heard it again. Barking. Definitely my canine pal, whose Chewbacca-like vocalizations currently let us all know he'd discovered the best game ever.

I could die any second and my mutt is playing. This is so typical. Maybe when I finally croak I should just have my coffin painted like a checkerboard and install a keg in the funeral home's foyer. That way all my "friends" can party at the visitation.

What I couldn't place was the second sound joining Jack's ruffs. Hard to describe. Like a dense thumping, as if the earth was a drum and hands the size of houses were playing it. I could feel the beating, thrumming up through my legs. And then branches started to snap. Bushes rattled. Grass trees whooshed. Here and there a gnome screamed independent of Cole's gunshots.

Kyphas yelled, "Watch out! They're everywhere!"

Cole nearly deafened me with his shout. "Jaz! Your dog's panicked a whole mob of kangaroos! They're pounding up the hill like it's a trampoline! Only they're going, like, three hundred different directions! I never saw such chaos! Aw, man, that one just trampled a guy!"

"Are you in a safe place?" I whispered as I peered around the corner.

Cole said, "Yeah, but I'm not sure about Kyphas." Was that worry in his tone? And if so, could it be bribed out of him? I was betting he'd promise anything for a lifetime supply of bubble gum.

More screams now, which drew the first two guards out of hiding. I cocked Grief and got ready to run. Vayl made a motion. *Wait.*

They crept into the opening opposite the trees, one waving for the next to follow. Finally all eight had moved out from under the bridge, the hems of their pants dark from wading the shallow water of the creek it spanned.

Vayl made four quick gestures, pointing himself in the direction of the trees and me toward their escape route. I felt his powers rise again, a cold wind at the back of my neck that sent my pulse pounding as I moved forward. Luckily the gravel on this part of the path had been ground into the dirt by countless hikers who'd never dreamed that one night two assassins would be stalking up the same walkway, leaving a string of bodies behind them, planning even more destruction ahead.

I set my back to the rock wall, glancing behind me to make sure Cole and Kyphas hadn't missed any stragglers. Motion. I raised Grief, my finger solid on the trigger. A kangaroo burst out of the trees, paused half a second to recalibrate, spun toward me, and leaped past.

I lifted Grief's barrel. Laid my head back. *Shit!*

But then, unmistakable, the sound of running feet. I took

aim. "Jaz! I'm coming toward you. Don't *shoot* me, all right?" Cole had barely gotten his request out before he appeared, his hair flying as he skidded to a halt.

I dropped my arms. Squinted up at the Big Guy. *Really? Are You trying to give me a heart attack, or do close calls give you the giggles?* No reply. Typical. Probably the next time my Maker spoke to me, he'd be in full lecture mode and I . . . well, I'd be altogether dead.

CHAPTER TWENTY-SEVEN

I leaned hard into the massive rock formation behind me. Something about it made me feel oddly calm. It had only been commanding this location for hundreds of thousands of years. If it could survive that long, I could damn well make it through the next few minutes.

Cole tapped me on the shoulder.

"Quiet," I directed. "We're going after another group." I set off, prepared to shoot anything that looked remotely like a gnome.

Cole fell in behind me. "Okay, but can I just say Jack is having the time of his life down there? Did you tell him you wanted a kangaroo for your birthday? Because I think he's bringing you a present."

"My birthday isn't for four more days. And Jack doesn't strike me as an early giver. But I'm planning to reward him for his excellent timing anyway."

"Good. Because they saved our asses."

"Speaking of asses, where's Kyphas?"

"Finishing off the few that didn't get mangled."

More like leaning over the mostly dead, making deals they'll eternally regret. Shaking off the image I said, "What a stellar addition to our crew. Now, can you shut up for three seconds while we take out these guards?"

"Okay. We'll talk about how I got to pet one of the big boys later. It was really beautiful. Like giving a governor a wedgie while he does his adultery confession next to his stunned but supportive wife."

"How is that beautiful?"

"Things are satisfying in different ways, Jaz. You just gotta go with me on this one. I feel like I got away with something major."

"Great. Now shut the hell up."

He clamped his lips together and pulled an imaginary zipper across them. Rolling my eyes, I stepped forward, moving quickly now that I knew Vayl must be in position. When I reached the bridge I slid around the corner.

"Vayl?" I asked.

"I am under the bridge."

His approach would take him low, through the nameless creek. Mine was a three-foot ledge, possibly man-made, that hugged the rock face as it threaded deeper into the heart of the hill.

"You continue on the main path," I whispered to Cole. "Scouting only. Report back as soon as you find something. Astral, you're with Cole. Follow his orders until I tell you otherwise."

"Be careful," Cole said, patting my back. I realized I shouldn't have felt his palm against my left shoulder just as he said, "You're flaking pretty badly in places."

Too freaking true.

I stepped forward as he slunk away, robokitty a shadow at his feet.

Within minutes we found the gnomes in a gorge that was blocked at the far end by an old rockfall that had taken several trees with it. Water flowed over the boulders to the creek below, raising a mist, making footing treacherous.

The Ufranites had found excellent cover. They should've stayed behind it. But like many newly initiated to violence, they overestimated their abilities and attacked first. The lead gnome's shot slammed into my right leg, spun me back into the wall. Since

I was slicker than the rocks supporting me, I lost my footing before I could even attempt to regain my balance. I took another shot as I fell. A shout of pain let me know I'd hit one before I landed on my hip, teetered on the lip of the ledge, and then rolled off. Ice flew like shattering glass as I swept down the slope, banging into an outcropping before landing at the bottom in a foot of water.

I stared up, estimated that I'd fallen at least a story, and began my inspection. Yup, I'd be bruised worse than a sloppy stuntman, but nothing seemed to be broken. Except the armor, which had taken a helluva pounding. A slick coating still covered my head, arms and legs, but it was cracked so badly I didn't think it would protect against anything more intense than a friendly tap. My theory gained weight when I felt water trickle through the gaps, soaking my jeans.

"Shit!" I crawled onto the creek bank.

"Jasmine, are you all right?" Vayl crouched over me, shielding me from the steady onslaught of killer steel.

I looked up at him, kneeling like a warrior praying before battle, supremely confident behind his icy coating. And wanted to punch him.

"Your goddamn armor put me on my ass!"

"I hardly think—"

"Stop protecting me, okay? It's going to get me killed!"

I rolled to one side, squeezed off three shots, hitting three guards who'd chosen that moment to rush us. Their buddies, who'd peeked above cover to catch the show, ducked when I continued to pull the trigger. Pausing to reload, I noticed that Vayl had disappeared.

I caught sight of him a few seconds later, moving like a mountain goat among obstacles that would've broken another man's legs. "Walking icebergs shouldn't be that graceful." I didn't realize I'd muttered the words out loud until Vayl replied.

"Would you prefer it if I went sprawling?" he asked, his tone as cold as his coating.

"No! I just don't want anyone else saving my life, that's all."

"That is the most ignorant comment I have ever heard you make."

Oh, he sounds mad, said Teen Me, biting her nails. *Maybe you'd better back off. What if he breaks up with you?*

My Inner Bimbo finished off her Jack and Coke and yelled for another. *There's more where he came from.*

Um, not really. But he just refuses to see the big picture! Every time someone pulls me back from the brink I end up farther down the road to Freaksville. Right now, if I was in a game show audience and the host said, "Would all the humans please stand up?" I wouldn't know what to do!

Luckily the Ufranites didn't give a crap what I was. Which forced me to swing my mind back to the job. I took another shot, watched my target drop as Vayl's sword swung and the chill of his powers filled the air. Realizing our opponents were out of Grief's range, I crawled forward, sliding across the ground like a sled on snow.

Another swing, the gargling protest of a dying foe. Then Vayl dropped behind a rock the size of a mattress. A grunt. The clash of metal on metal. One last whooshing report from a gnomish gun. And then nothing.

"Vayl?"

No reply.

"Vayl?" Nothing.

Naw. No, no, no! I creaked to my feet and scrambled to the spot where I'd seen him last, hopping from tree trunk to stone step without a single thought as to how I was going to get out of this dead end if I broke a bone.

I found him kneeling over one of the bodies, searching its pockets.

"What the hell are you looking for?"

"I am searching for clues as to the shaman's identity or location."

"Why didn't you say anything?" I demanded. "You scared the crap out of me!"

He looked up. "And if I had been in mortal danger just now? If I could have died as you can? What would you have done to save me?"

"I . . ." I clamped my mouth shut.

"Jasmine?"

"Still trying to put me through my lessons, are you?" I asked bitterly.

"I have a great deal to share and you are, usually, a quick study. So, yes. I want you to understand the lengths to which I would go in order to assure your continued existence."

"You sound like a damn Vulcan. You know, from *Star Trek*? So freaking smooth and logical with all your emotions locked down like death row prisoners."

He raised an eyebrow. As if he knew how much that single move would irritate me. "Perhaps this conversation would be better saved until we have no audience?"

"What, you mean we should tune the others out? Like you've done to me for the past few days?"

"You are the one who got yourself possessed. I am simply trying to complete this mission successfully with you, though clearly I would have been smarter to ship you back to Cleveland the moment I learned that your situation compromised every move we attempt."

"I didn't get myself possessed! I saved my life, and Raoul's, by biting that monster! And now he's in me, like a poison, and all you've done is cut me off like I'm already dead!"

Not fair, I knew. No way could we pull this off with Brude undermining us, which he'd do every chance he got because clearly the gnomes and the Weres had promised to help him bulk up his army. But I'd taken care of that problem myself. Me. Without any help, dammit! Just like I could do everything else!

Vayl came at me so fast I didn't even have time to jerk away. His hands gripped me, the ice instantly melting beneath his touch. His eyes, black as the pit I felt yawning beneath me, speared mine.

"I did what I had to in order to make this mission work. Tell me you would not have done the same! And then promise me you will never die!"

Silence. And then, quiet but clear, the singsong voice of Cole ringing in our ears, "Jazzy's a pain in the a-ass. So glad she gave me a pa-ass!"

Vayl snorted.

I chuckled. Then I said, "I'm sorry. It's Pete." I closed my eyes against the burn of unshed tears. Forced myself to roll on. "And the ice thing." I glared up at him. "I get your point, okay? But you *bit* me, dammit! You know what that means. Nobody saves me without consequences. And it seems like the part of me that pays is my humanity. I can't . . . Jesus, Vayl, how much more can I afford to lose? I mean . . ."

I couldn't go on. He didn't make me. He crushed me to his chest, the clash of our armor sounding like a gunshot in the gorge. What didn't break off began to melt, the ice running so quickly to water that I could feel his muscles straining to press against my breasts.

Cold, slick ice on my hands. On his back. Both of us practically writhing beneath it, burning to touch one another in ways we were still just discovering.

Knowing we could be overheard, I kept my pleas silent. Begging him with my eyes to *do* something.

Suddenly his fingertips were on my face. He'd dropped his sword. Entwined his hand in my wet hair.

I felt material under my hands. The abused denim of his jeans, splitting as he adjusted his stance, giving me room to slide my fingers around to the back of his thighs and up—to more ice.

I tore at it, ignoring my broken fingernails, my bleeding knuckles as it came away in sheets. I nodded. *Yes, yes!* Pressed into him as our lips met, warm and lush as an afternoon in the rainforest.

A great weight left my back. I heard the crack of ice breaking on the ground beside us and then Vayl's hands, tearing away the remains of my coat. Sliding underneath the shirt it had protected.

More cracking as our remaining armor heated and fell away.

I felt his lips again, this time feathering against my neck. Teeth nipping. The soft, wetness of his tongue. Everything sensed but unseen between us seemed to whirl around our bodies, creating a storm so electric and powerful that I felt the hairs at the back of my neck stand on end.

We both knew what was missing. The swift pain of fangs, piercing, sucking, raising me so high on tiptoe that my precarious balance would force me to shove my fingers into his sopping curls, to press so hard against his body that I couldn't imagine us as separate beings. Already we wanted it so badly we could hardly resist. What would it be like a month, a year down the line?

Vayl raised his head. "Duty," he said hoarsely.

"Yeah."

He threw his head back and swallowed, licking his lips like he'd just chugged a can of Coke and needed a minute to clear the acid aftertaste of what had been a predominantly bitchin' drink. When he looked at me again his eyes had softened to amber.

"Are you ready?"

Instead of answering his question the way I wanted to, I checked my Astral-feed. It showed a dark path similar to the one we'd come in on. And then, a flicker of light. "They've found something," I said.

He grabbed me and kissed me, quickly, deeply, before whispering into my ungadgeted ear, "Never mind the bustier. I want you in wet, tattered clothes. Imagining peeling them off of you, and the hot, soapy shower to follow, is suddenly driving me mad."

"Do I need to get you a shovel?"

His eyes widened. That choked sound that passed for laughter gurgled out of his throat. He nodded slowly. "Perhaps."

I allowed myself a moment of pure delight despite the mass of emotions that still clawed at me. Even though I'd regained control of my mind, I'd lost Pete forever. Who knew what would happen after the department reopened? And what the hell was I becoming?

Heavy sigh. *Oh well, everybody's got their shit to deal with. At least I have Vayl at the same time.*

Chapter Twenty-Eight

With Vayl's hand wrapped securely around mine, I ran up the trail beside him, the wind of our sprint making droplets of moisture fly from my hair. Cole met us at a spot where the trail rose abruptly, the steepness of its ascent made user friendly by a set of wooden stairs.

"I figured you'd seen what I saw, but I was coming back to get you just in case," he whispered as we huddled beside the first step.

"I can't make out much," I told him. "Astral is just inching forward, so she must be pretty sure they'll catch her if she moves any faster."

Cole responded to Vayl's puzzled look. "Ruvin and the software guys aren't inside the rock shelter like we thought they would be. They're on top of it."

"How did they get up there?" asked Vayl.

"Not sure. I didn't see a ladder and the boulders are too smooth to make it a quick climb even if you know what you're doing."

"Another illusionary door?" I suggested.

Vayl squeezed my hand. "Brilliant. Let us find it."

We ran up the stairs, the breeze of our movement chilling me as it plastered my wet clothes to my body. I put my discomfort aside as we came to another wooden bridge that spanned a shallow ravine and led us to the shelter, a simple arrangement of one massive boulder leaning on another that left a triangular space clear underneath for wanderers who needed shelter from the rain. On top of this monolith our quarry had lit a fire. The angle didn't allow me to pick out any faces other than Ruvin's.

"I'm not hearing anything from his bug. Are you on a different frequency again?" I asked.

"No," said Cole. "Do you think it could've fallen off while they were shoving him around?"

"Search for a door," Vayl ordered.

Cole slipped inside the white fence that kept tourists from touching the ancient paintings I could see adorning the bottom of the bigger boulder. He began combing the outer edges of it as I moved to go inside the shelter.

"Are you sure you want to do that?" Vayl asked. When I raised my eyebrows at him he added tactfully, "I realize it probably would not bother you much that tons of rock were hovering over your head, waiting for just the right earth tremor to shake it to the ground. But if I went in you would not have to be disturbed at all."

I waved him off. "Naw, I feel great!" And I ducked inside, realizing I did feel awesome. Better than I should considering my circumstances.

It's Vayl's bite, said Teen Me. She'd found herself a beanbag chair and thrown it on Granny May's front porch, where she'd also, somehow, installed an Xbox 360. *You've got a megahigh going on.*

I am not high, I snapped. *I've never done drugs in my life.*

Okay, fine, she agreed without looking away from the flatscreen she'd bolted to the porch rail. *What would you compare it to?*

I pressed my lips together, only now feeling the soreness from where Vayl's fangs had sunk in. I felt oddly uncomfortable discussing the aftereffects of tremendous sex with my adolescent self. But I did have that same grin-and-click-your-heels feeling that the world was singing a special tune only I could hear. Even though I'd experienced similar reactions after Vayl's two previous bites, I still wasn't prepared to relax and go with the flow. Because later on I'd crashed. The first time, pretty hard. The second had been shorter, but just as debilitating. I needed to wrap up this case before my body demanded a milk shake and hammock time.

So, while I hummed that soaring song under my breath, I ducked into the shelter and conducted a quick search that netted nothing.

Maybe it's on the other side. I went through, noting that the path, however far it meandered beyond the shelter, eventually came around to the back of it. And right up next to the formation, nearly buried behind a pile of dead branches, was a Jaz-sized boulder whose face looked like granite but felt like Silly Putty.

I went back for the guys. "Found it," I whispered, motioning for them to follow me.

"I'll go first," Cole volunteered. "After all, if I'd picked a better spot to snipe from, Ruvin wouldn't be in this mess." Before we could argue he'd stuck his head through the door. And just as quickly pulled it out.

"Duck!"

He pushed me back, falling on top of me as a deep rumble from inside the boulder made me wonder if we were all about to be crushed. Vayl covered us both as a hail of pebbles shot from the door, followed by a spurt of dust and then a door-sealing rock lodged half in and half out of the opening.

We stared at it for five long seconds. I said, "I hear something."

"Another boulder?" Cole asked as the guys rolled to their feet. He looked up fearfully.

"No," said Vayl, lifting his eyes to the star-filled sky. "Something unnatural."

Chapter Twenty-Nine

Vayl was the first to leap on the door-blocking boulder, using it as a launching pad for his climb. While I waited for him to clear it so I could start up, Cole slung his rifle over his shoulder and said, "I'm going up the other side."

"This is stupid," I said. "They're just going to throw us off the second they see our hands reaching over the rim."

"Which is why I'm letting Vayl get a head start. Hopefully he'll keep them occupied until I can make it up."

"Wait a second," I said, grabbing Cole's sleeve before he could move away. "What about that weird noise?"

He cocked his head. "You know what it is, don't you?"

"No."

"Jack's tired of the kangaroo. Now he's found a herd of platypi and he's stampeding them right toward us."

"Platypi?"

"That clacking is their bills snapping together. They do that when they're enraged. You should go for higher ground, Jaz. They've been known to chew women's legs off."

"With beaks?"

"Well . . . it takes a while. And you kinda have to stand in one place—"

"When you two are quite done," came Vayl's voice over the party line. We looked up. He was already halfway to them. Above him, only visible because it had begun to sway, I saw the outline of a wire. The type that lodge owners connect to lifts so skiers can chug up the mountain from dawn to dusk.

"Son of a bitch!"

"What?" Cole shaded his eyes, like we were standing in the noonday sun instead of the blackness that blankets a mountain's apron at three in the morning.

"Vayl, they've got transportation. I'm thinking some kind of open-air, no, check that. I see it now. Sky car, black, roomy. It's coming in quick! And it's got passengers—I count five!"

Cole pointed into the air. He said, "Hey, Jaz! The car looks like a big nose!"

Go Ufran. We watched the air trolley descend to the boulder. A couple of Ufranites scrambled out to help the humans and one struggling Ruvin inside. "This is bad."

"Why?"

"Because suddenly I feel like I've been transported into an Austin Powers movie, which means any second now the kittybot will probably turn on us and start shooting torpedoes out her tail. I wouldn't have objected if we'd been able to rescue Ruvin. Had the Odeam guys called our bluff and brought in their 'A' team? Or had Ruvin given up on us and decided to save his wife the only way he knew how? Either way we were pretty—"

I gasped as the sky car hummed away and, at the same time, Vayl launched himself from the boulder, barely managing to grab hold of the axle for the maintenance wheels that jutted beneath the nose like blackened teeth. The car rocked at his impact, causing Ufranites to crowd the windows, but nobody saw him raise his legs to slide them over the second axle.

"Vayl!" I called. "Are you okay?"

"Fine! I believe I can reverse the car's course from here. If my calculations are correct, it should fly back to its source. Since the warren is under Wirdilling's primary school, this car must be stored somewhere in the same town. Meet us there!"

"What if you're wrong?" asked Cole.

"I cannot be," Vayl replied. "We have no time to spare."

"Let's get our asses back to the Wheezer. That means you too, Astral." I turned to run back down the path, whistling for Jack as Cole called Kyphas on his phone and asked her to join us.

"Jaz isn't going to wait long," he told her after a pause.

"Put her on speaker," I snapped.

He pushed the required button.

"—not quite finished here," Kyphas was saying.

"If you're not down the hill when I start that car, I'm leaving you!" I said flatly. "We've got to get back to town before everything blows up in Vayl's face!"

"You sure can pick the rental cars."

I ground my teeth together and glared at the demon in my backseat. "Shut up," I said.

Kyphas peered at me over the top of Jack's furry head. "I was just—"

"I could happily kill somebody right now. And since you're immortal in this realm, I'm gonna be real tempted to take a few stabs at you if you don't—just—chill!"

For the hundredth time I ignored her smirk and glanced in the rearview mirror. My eyes skipped past Astral, who'd taken her regular window seat. She had an even better view of Cole as he leaned over the Wheezer's trunk, pushing the car along the road that would eventually end in front of Crindertab's. Of course, by the time we reached the restaurant, Ruvin would be little more than a skeleton, picked clean by infant gnomes who'd already have caused irreparable damage to NASA's connection to the cosmos. And we'd never want to eat again. Not to mention the fact that Cole would be too tired to lift his weapon, and Vayl would probably be dead.

"Jasmine?"

I touched the reciever in my ear. "Cassandra! Are you back yet?"

"No, I . . . was hoping for one last vision. Do you need help?"

"I'm going to when I get back to Wirdilling. Can you shake out a few Resistance gnomes for me?"

"I'll see what I can do."

Kyphas opened her yap. "I was just going to say that I thought you people were better organized. I would've thought twice if I'd known I was tying myself to a bunch of hack—ow!" She stared down at the syringe waving from her arm and at my thumb, hovering over the plunger.

"I did warn you." My thumb jerked.

"Okay! I'm sorry! Take it out!" I resheathed my supply of holy water while she rubbed at the spot. "It hurts! Did you squirt some?"

I shrugged. "Could be. It's pretty sensitive. Not your ordinary prescription-fill. Bergman designed it for me."

"Tell me about Bergman," Kyphas invited.

I glared at her. "You blew your chance. If you try to take his soul again, if you hurt him, if you even bump into him hard, I will kill you."

"Ooh, I'm so scared."

I held her eyes. "I didn't say how long I was going to take to do it."

Kyphas lost her yen for conversation after that and decided to spend her time gazing out the passenger window.

I didn't realize Cole had stopped pushing until the Wheezer came to a stop in the middle of the road. I looked back. "Pop the trunk," he instructed.

I did as he asked and got out. Which was when I heard it. The roar of an oncoming vehicle. Cole grabbed a couple of flares, fired them up, and set them in a line behind the Wheezer. Just in case the driver coming up on us at what sounded like light speed didn't get the message in time, I pulled the animals out of the car and took them a few steps past the shoulder. I was hoping Kyphas would stay inside. I'd get a kick out of a good demon-smooshing right now. But she emerged, making sure Cole got a load of her long legs before she moved to his side.

As soon as he smiled at her I marched over and dumped Astral into her arms. "This is an extremely valuable tool. Don't let it get broken." Jack panted loudly in agreement.

She shook her head in confusion "I don't—"

"Over there with the priceless robot," I said, waving her to the shoulder. Once she'd left earshot I grabbed Cole's arm and jerked him down so he could hear me better. "Stop being nice to the evil demon."

"She seems okay," he said.

"So did John Wilkes Booth. Then he killed the one guy who could've hammered away a big chunk of the bullshit prejudice that black Americans still have to piss with today."

"I think she's got some good in her," he insisted.

"I think she's got big boobs, and in your mind that's the same thing."

Cole grinned. "You could be right. Although you know what else I was thinking?" As I shook my head he lit a third flare and waved it around. "I can write my name in the air with this!"

Jack also thought it was cool. He kept biting at the dropping sparks, though he was at least smart enough not to go for the whole banana.

"What are you gonna do when you singe your tongue?" I asked my dog. When he let it hang out of his mouth I said, "That might work. But don't expect any pity when you can't eat anything but gravy for the next month."

Jack grinned and wagged his tail, like he knew I'd never let it go that far.

Cole set the last flare in place and we waited. Lights appeared in the distance, played hide-and-seek for a while, and then came barreling down on us so fast that we evacuated the road.

But the driver stopped in time. With only a minimum of tire-screeching, she rolled her lemon-drop yellow Hyundai Accent to a stop an arm's length from the first flare. By the time we'd reached her door, all three of her passengers had bailed, two guys and another girl, all of them giggling and staggering like they'd been partying since dawn.

"Oh goody," Cole murmured. "We are saved."

I snorted as I watched the driver try to herd her horde back into the vehicle.

"Hello," said Cole, pasting on his I'm-unforgettable smile. "I'm Thor Longfellow and this is Lucille Robinson. We're from Holly—"

"G'day, mate!" the driver sang. "Would you help me gather up this mob before they trot off into the never-never?"

She asked so cheerfully despite the relative impossibility of the task, her black ponytail dancing along with the request, that he immediately said, "Oh, uh, sure!"

The other girl, a double-chinned brunette wearing jeans so tight you could see the cottage cheese below her butt cheeks rippling through them, friendlied up to Cole right away. So he had no trouble escorting her back to the car.

"Kyphas!" I called. "Get the big guy!" Leaving Astral to study her reflection in the Wheezer's hubcaps, Kyphas went after the dude whose scars were either a sign that he kept running his face into people's fists or that he thoroughly enjoyed his rugby. I tagged the smaller one.

"You are one luscious lady," he told me, his breath reeking of cheap beer as he dropped an arm around my shoulders.

"And you are going to puke like a school full of flu-bitten kids. But hopefully not until your friend's gotten you home. What's your name?"

"Lance."

"Lance-a-lot-o'-fun!" called out his buddy.

"That's Rory," Lance said. "He cannot hold his liquor. But he is a ripper, Rory is. Rory's a ripper!" Lance announced loudly.

"Clearly. And the girls?" I pointed to the driver, who, Lance informed me in what he probably thought was a bedroom voice, was Dachelle.

"We're just friends," he said, trying to wink and succeeding only in squinching his face together like a constipated old man. "Me and Gabbie are also only just friends," he went on, nodding at Cole's newest fan. "We're all friends here!" he shouted. Then he gave me a one-armed hug. "Can we be friends?"

"Well, that depends."

"On what?"

"On whether or not Dachelle can give me and my colleagues a ride to Wirdilling. Fast."

Chapter Thirty

I don't know what it is about college kids. Maybe tuition also buys them the knowhow to squeeze large numbers of people into small spaces such as telephone booths and imported vehicles. Whatever the case, we all managed to find a tiny bit of butt room inside the Hyundai. Dachelle drove, while Gabbie shared the front with Cole and Jack, both of whom spent most of the ride hanging out the window, which provided some relief to their fellow sardines. That left Kyphas, Rory, Lance, and me to rub hips, thighs, and damn near everything else in our effort to catch up to the escaping Ufranites. Among us, only Astral seemed comfortable, lying in the back window like an Egyptian statue. Luckily she'd obeyed my demand to stay silent. So far.

Since Kyphas kept adjusting her position on Rory's knees without raising even a moan, I thought he'd passed out until he reared his head back, snorted, centered his eyes on me, and asked, "So what're you doing at Wirdilling?"

"We work for a movie company called Shoot-Yeah Productions. Our boss sent us out to scout locations for some night scenes, but we have to get back to town quick because he's lined up a bunch of auditions that we're supposed to tape."

"At 3:30 in the morning?" asked Dachelle.

"We're still working on American time," Cole drawled.

I rolled my eyes. If everyone but Dachelle hadn't been so wasted they'd never have swallowed such a line of crap. But the designated driver had her hands so full trying to make her friend behave she had no room left in her bullshit net for our load.

She yelled, "Gabbie! Quit rubbing Thor's leg! I'm sure he doesn't want a quickie with a drunken Biology major."

"Who would?" asked Rory. Lance giggled.

"You blokes are flaming jerks!" Gabbie declared.

Mostly to prevent myself from punching the defenseless bastards I said, "Dachelle, I'll give you and your friends each fifty bucks if you get us to Wirdilling in five minutes."

"Hang on, mates!" Dachelle called. "I've had my eye on a pair of shoes at Mathers for the past three weeks and now I've finally got the chance to snatch 'em!" She floored it, sending Lance and Cole sliding into the window frames. Cole caught himself but Lance banged his head, which turned out to be the last straw. He passed out with his forehead against the window, which meant every time Dachelle took a sharp curve we could hear his skull bang against the side of the car.

Twelve minutes later we crawled out of the Hyundai and waved goodbye to Dachelle and friends. Lance kept rubbing his head and grimacing, but the rest grinned happily as they sped away since I'd decided to pay them for getting us there in one piece. Even though the timing sucked, I was sure nobody could've pulled us in faster.

While Jack strained to reach a fire hydrant at the street corner and Astral rolled around on the asphalt like a kitten, Cole, Kyphas, and I stood in the middle of Wirdilling Drive, staring at the dusty storefronts and empty alleyways, trying to figure out where the flying nose could've landed.

"Maybe he couldn't reverse the sky car," said Kyphas. "Maybe it stopped near the Space Complex and right now they're all—"

"They're here," I said flatly.

"How can you be sure?" she asked. "What if it was never here to start with? What if they stored it miles away in some deserted canyon? That's what I would do."

"It's here." I sounded a lot more confident than I felt. Because if Vayl had been close, I should've been able to sense him. I couldn't. But he'd told us to meet him here, so this was where we were going to be.

"Why isn't Vayl talking to us?" asked Cole.

Because he's miles and miles away? "Because they'll overhear him if he says anything. Which reminds me. Bergman? We're standing in front of Crindertab's. It's about to get pretty hot downtown. Now that you're done with all the lab work, we could use your help here."

"Oh. Sure. I'll be right there." He coughed to hide how his last word tried to climb right out of his throat.

I said, "Let's find that sky car."

"How?" asked Kyphas. "The cables are practically invisible."

"So were their doors at first, but now we've discovered three of them." I didn't tell her my sudden surge of confidence was probably based on the rush I still felt that began at the clotting bite on my lip and ended at my tingling toes.

"Are you sure the drop is even in town?" asked Bergman, sounding slightly out of breath.

"Yeah, I think it's here," I said. "They'd want easy access to it, and the car was coming from this direction. I know our analysts never picked up on it, but maybe the Ufranites only use it at night. Much less chance of being seen at three a.m. Especially if your shaman has thrown a camo spell on it."

Cassandra spoke up. "Jasmine, can you hear me?"

I crouched down and touched the road like she was standing right underneath me. "Is everything okay? You sound [tearful] different."

"I'm fine. You can't even imagine . . . Jasmine, the most wonderful thing has happened! I heard—no, let me tell you to your face. It'll be soon because I'm nearly done here. Remember I said we were sneaking into the shaman's quarters? You'll never guess what I found there."

"Tell me."

"Tabitha's dress."

"*Ruvin's* Tabitha?"

"She's the shaman."

I wanted to ask Cassandra if she was sure, but she was a freaking Seer. Of course she knew! Now Ruvin's sacrifice to the larvae made perfect sense. Wives killed off their husbands, and vice versa, all the time. But why? Did Tabitha-Shaman really believe Ufran needed his privacy? Or did she have ulterior motives even her people, from whom she'd hidden her real identity, didn't understand?

"That's . . . you've gone above and beyond," I told her. "Now do something even more important and get yourself out safe. If anything happened to you, Dave would never forgive me. And I kinda like it that he's finally speaking to me again."

"In that case I'll be seeing you very soon," said Cassandra. I could hear the smile in her voice. "In the meantime, why don't you ask Astral about the sky-car dilemma? Or rather, her *Enkyklios?*"

I turned to the cat, who was currently dragging her hindquarters through the dirt between the sidewalk and the road and singing, "Oh, get down, turn around, go to town, boot scootin' boogie."

"Astral, you whacked robot, you are not Brooks or Dunn! Get over here!"

"What happened to her?" asked our psychic.

"You know what? I'm just gonna let you touch her and See the whole moment in surround Sight. You bringing reinforcements?"

"As many as I can manage." Which would probably be, what, seven?

"Cool, I'll talk to you soon."

"Be safe."

"Probably safer than you."

She chuckled as Astral trotted to my side and said, "Hello!"

"What do you know about the Ufranites' sky cars?" I asked her.

After the usual I'm-searching ear wobble, a deeper voice came from her moving mouth, one more suited to a broad-shouldered, potbellied history professor. "The vehicles in question were built during the early twentieth century and improved upon after the devastating nose-to-nose crash of 1945. Though somewhat ponderous and slow-moving, they are built to move twelve to fifteen gnomes from one to another of ten points in the ACT."

"Yadda, yadda, yadda," I griped. "Where's the station?"

"The main access point is inside the old water tower," Astral said, like I should've figured that out hours ago.

Holy crap! That's right beside the damn post office!

"Bergman, you know where that is?" I asked.

"Yeah."

"Meet us there."

"Hey! You'll never guess who I just saw dancing around in the playground of the old primary school."

"Miles, this is no time for—"

"Tabitha!"

I paused for a beat to trade a significant look with Cole and make sure Jack was still trotting at the end of his leash. "Bring her."

Small yelp. "Who, me?"

"Time to prove yourself. If you want to be my future partner, she'd better be dangling off the end of your fist the next time I see you."

CHAPTER THIRTY-ONE

I n Australia, land of fire and drought, sharks and surfers, water is damn near worshipped. If nobody's built a shrine anywhere they probably should, because I'm pretty sure people would come and kneel, take a drink and then, like humans all over the globe, make a wish and throw coins in to seal the deal. If somebody did decide to erect a monument, maybe it would resemble the old wooden tower that had once provided sustenance to Wirdilling. Though a new metal one had been erected within sight of the original, it seemed almost sacrilegious that true Aussies had let the old girl go to waste. Which might've been why the gnomes had latched on to her.

Outside she looked like your typical nineteenth-century aboveground town well. Except the section created to hold the juice was square, built on a platform that jutted out slightly farther than the container to give maintenance workers room to walk the perimeter. Nine sturdy posts held the tower a good thirty feet aboveground, their crosspieces stained an even darker brown than the rest of the structure, as if to emphasize the fact that they provided stability *and* helped ensure that the pressure stayed nice and high. We knew the place hid something marvelous simply from the fact that it was humming like a power station when we approached it.

"What now?" asked Cole.

I said, "Kyphas and I investigate. You get into position and wait."

"For what?"

"I'm pretty sure you'll know when it happens." I looked down at Jack. Who, while multitalented in doggy terms, hadn't yet mastered pole climbing. I handed the leash to Cole. "You guys grab some high ground."

Cole nodded quickly and, grinning down at my dog, said, "Come on, dude. Let's hit the roofs. You can be my reloader."

"Be careful, Cole," said Kyphas.

His smile went crooked as he met her gaze, which was so damn sincere I nearly bought it. I pulled a Vayl, standing stock still, internalizing the eye rolling and grimacing that wanted to crease my face as he replied, "No need to worry about me, beautiful. I was born under a lucky star."

Oh, gag, did he really say that?

"Besides," he added, without missing a beat, "I've got angels watching over me. Right, Jaz?" His eyes swept to mine, their sparkle so bright they could've lit fireworks.

"Close enough," I said, coughing to hide the laughter as Kyphas put a hand to her stomach and made an I-may-vomit face.

He wheeled around, taking Jack for a quick trot down the block and around the corner, where he was sure to find a handy fire escape. Kyphas watched him all the way.

When she muttered something under her breath I asked, "What was that?"

"Nothing."

Astral spoke up. "Kyphas just said, 'That one, he is so *likeable*!' Her tone is somewhat irritated, which does not compute with the wording."

"Shut up, cat!" Kyphas snapped.

"I am not programmed for your orders."

I said, "Have you noticed what a great ass he's got too?" Cole, listening in on the party line, chuckled with delight.

"Are you joking? Every time he turns around my fingers begin to ache!"

I stepped in front of her, nose to nose, to make sure we had pure communication. But I didn't have to say a word.

She held up her hands. "I know, I know. Nothing in heaven or hell will stand between you and my slow, screaming death if I harm any one of your babes." She flipped back her shining hair. "Already you bore me. So are we climbing this tower or—"

"Yeah. You first."

Flash of suspicion. But she went up, stiff in the legs and back, like she half expected me to stab her on the way up. As if I'd reduce my meager forces at such a key point. But I still enjoyed making her uneasy.

I looked down at the kittybot. "This is where you take a break, Astral. Hang out here until Bergman shows up and then do what he says until I need you again, okay?"

"Hello!"

"You are so fried."

I followed Kyphas up to the platform. Though we searched like a couple of treasure hunters, we discovered no Ufranite doors. Which meant we'd have to be patient. Surely Vayl would find a way to contact us soon.

I motioned for Kyphas to post herself at the south end of the tower while I took the opposite.

"I'm in position," Cole whispered. "Your dog's peeing on the roof vent. I think that means you own Crindertab's now."

I nodded to let him know I'd heard. Wondered how Bergman was doing and decided no news was good news.

So hard to sit and wait. I touched Cirilai, wishing it would signal me, frustrated that it and my vamp-sense were my only connections to Vayl.

Or are they? The only reason I didn't ignore Teen Me, who was straightening her hair in the empty hope that she could make it look like Jennifer Aniston's, was that too many other people already had.

What do you mean? I asked her.

He's a vampire, she told me, like I was some kind of dufus for having to have the obvious pointed out to me.

I nearly said, *So?* But I took a second to think beforehand. The first time he'd taken my blood he'd formed a bond with me that had enabled him to sense my strongest emotions. After the second time, my Spirit Eye had opened wide enough for me to track the Vampere. And now? What had happened to us with this exchange, Eldhayr blood for Vampere power?

No clue, I thought as I crouched against the railing. But that took too much energy, so I hit my butt. Because I was suddenly so tired. The after-bite crash had come. If I'd had to raise Grief in that moment I'd have said, "To hell with it," and hoped for an asteroid impact to do my work for me.

We waited for an eternity. Stars came to life and died in the time I sat there trying to decide if I was already too old for this gig. I began to think I could sense the earth revolving while I remained in one place, like a chess piece that could only be moved by the hand of the universe. Then I realized I was dizzy.

Vayl, where are you? Reach me, dammit!

I closed my eyes, but that only made the vertigo worse. Instead I focused on the fat-headed nails that held the walls of the water tower together. They blurred into a rust-colored mass, like the bricks on a fog-shrouded building. And then I realized I was standing. Not in Wirdilling, Australia, at nearly four in the morning. But in London under a full moon, long before garbage trucks and sewage plants, if the stench gave any clue.

I began to walk, each step bringing my situation more sharply into focus. I had never been so strong. I felt like I could single-handedly tear the bridge I currently strolled upon from its very moorings. And part of me wanted to. It yammered inside of me like a mad dog straining at the end of its chain. Because my boys would never draw breath again.

Oh, fuck.

I glanced into the water. Saw a tall, broad-shouldered man whose shoulder-length curls were held secure by a band at the back of his neck. He wore a long black coat buttoned over a red waistcoat and black breeches. His white stockings were stained with mud, his black buckled shoes needed to be resoled. But I could never mistake those high cheekbones, slanted brows, and fierce, kaleidoscope eyes.

I'm Vayl. Or he's me. How—?

I stopped, raised my nose to the foul night air and scented something that did not belong, even here on these careless streets. Werewolf!

I ran, still new enough to the power that I exulted in the speed I could gain and maintain. Within moments I had reached the abandoned building where the wolf hunted. Pulling my dagger from the sheath at my waist, I crept after it, the freezing river that now fed each of my humors rising quickly to a flood. It took all of my will not to release it upon the city itself, like a rain of razor-sharp ice. But I had freed the deluge once before. Some actions should never be repeated.

I found it upstairs. A shiver ran up my spine at the sound of its claws raking across the grime-laden floor as it battered its shoulder against the bedroom door. Its final blow caused a rupture that made the wood crack like the shots that had taken my sons. I jerked as if hit, my mind tearing as it tried to evade memories too fresh to bury. But I could never turn from their faces, their dark lashes brushing their cheeks as if they had simply stopped beside the road to take a nap before coming home to supper.

A scream jerked me from my nightmare and pulled me into hers. I leaped through the doorway to find the wolf crouching, grinning at the child as his distorted features and dripping fangs caused her to writhe with fear.

I know those eyes! Where have I seen that Were's face?

"Trespasser!" I cried, speaking the only word I had heard from other lips since my travels began.

The wolf spun. His scent hit me fully, causing my gorge to rise. It smelled as if his last meal had been dead for quite some time before he had indulged. He growled as he came for me, his yellow eyes intent on my throat.

I let my arms hang limp, as if his charge had petrified me. At the last moment I spun aside, burying the dagger deep into his chest. Now he screamed, more from rage than pain, since my weapon contained no silver. He staggered into the wall and turned for another charge, but could not find me. I hovered above him, hanging from the ceiling, my hands and feet anchored to the boards that had been uncovered when chunks of plaster had fallen during the building's decay.

Having lost sight of his latest quarry, the wolf stalked toward the child, his low-bellied rumble raising the hairs on the back of my neck. The moment he walked beneath me I dropped, landing prone on his back like a trainer of wild horses. But this beast would never be tamed. And so, as he rolled and snapped, clawing at me over his shoulders, I buried my fangs in his neck.

His blood tasted foul, and I did not sup. Only summoned the cold fury that rode me every waking moment and pushed it into the wound I had made. It felt . . . delicious. I found I could not stop. I wanted him to choke on my sorrow. To die again and again since I, damned father that I was, could not. I shoved the ice of my undeath into him until his eyes bulged and his ears cracked.

"Is he dead?"

Such a small voice. And miraculously steady for what she had just seen. I raised my head. "Perhaps. Werewolves are notoriously difficult to kill, however, so you must run home."

She looked around at the filthy, curtainless room with its corner full of papers and four distinct marks where a bed had once stood. "I am home."

"How old are you?"

"Eleven."

I dug into my pocket and gave her a pouch containing all the money I had left in the world. "Go find another home. One that is clear of both dirt and monsters."

She looked at me with wide blue eyes. "Will you come with me?"

"I . . . cannot. My time for homes is past."

She nodded, as if she understood how the warm blood pumping through her body tempted me even now. After she left I turned back to the wolf. Silver I did not have, but I thought I knew another way to finish him. Ah, if only he did not smell so damned—

"Jaz!"

I jerked my head, banging it against the tower so hard my ears rang. I looked down. Bergman stood at its base, his hand gripping the arm of Ruvin's wife.

I signaled to Cole and Kyphas that I was heading down. As I climbed I told myself firmly, *No. That's all. Just, no. I'm not going nuts today. Okay, so now I can relive Vayl's past. That's fine. Some people are skilled fishermen. You don't see them hurling themselves off water towers just because they know which lures to pick for the big tournament. I've just gotta figure out why I had that particular vision. The girl looked familiar, but I think she's just reminding me of some young actress. So it's the Were, right? I'm sure I've seen those yellow eyes somewhere before. Yeah, and those raggedy ass ears too. Vayl didn't end up killing it after all. It survived. And now . . .*

I reached the bottom rung. Felt the ground, solid beneath my feet. And grinned. Because I knew, strange as it sounded, that the wolf was Roldan, Sol of the Valencian Weres.

Which means he's been alive a long damn time! Judging by Vayl's clothes, that gig couldn't have gone down any later than 1770. And I've never heard of a Were living longer than a hundred and fifty years. So what the hell's gotten into him? Or should I say who?

Maybe Miles's little buddy could tell me. I glanced at Astral, who sat quietly, whir/purring like she'd never spoken a word in her short, bizarre robolife. "Make sure you record this for the *Enkyklios*," I murmured to her. "Somebody might find it helpful in the future." I'd never have known she heard me, except she glued her attention to Tabitha and never let her eyes waver from the shaman once during our entire conversation.

I said, "Tabitha, why aren't you with your sons?"

"I . . . was looking for Ruvin," she answered. "He's turned off his phone. And that's not like him. I was afraid . . ." She trailed off, maybe seeing the doubt in my eyes. I'd believe a lot of emotions from Tabitha. Fear wasn't one of them.

"What an interesting outfit you chose to wear for your hunt," I told her, reaching out to rub the feathered collar of her knee-length tunic between my fingers. Beneath it she wore loose pants made from an animal she might have tanned herself they looked so primitive. The seams were sewn on the outside with a dark brown strip of leather strung every few inches with red and blue beads. Emu feathers hung from metal rings clamped into the pants at knee level.

Tabitha looked down at herself. "This is, ah, a traditional seinji pantsuit designed to hasten the conception process," she said.

"Bullshit."

Her eyes bugged. "I beg your pardon?"

"You know, something's been bothering me from the start. I couldn't put my finger on it because it seemed almost normal to me. And then I realized, that's because I grew up with a bitch for a mother."

Her eyes darted to mine. "I have no idea what you're talking about."

"No, I don't guess you would. They never do. But, take my word for this, good moms never leave a dangerous situation ahead of their sons. During the rescue, you charged out of the warren first, with them running behind you trying to keep up. And back at the house, they should've run to you for comfort. Instead they came to Ruvin and us. You know why? Because they've figured out, at some level, that you don't give a crap about them."

"You are out of line—"

"But here's where I get a little fuzzy. Why, if you're so disinterested in Laal and Pajo, are you so eager to have another baby?"

"I don't think they're actually hers," said Bergman. "Remember their bone structure? How even and symmetrical their faces were? But Tabitha and Ruvin have long foreheads and chins. I think—"

"They're adopted, all right?" Tabitha snapped. "They're not even . . ." She started to say something, stopped, began again. "I just want a child of my own flesh. What's so wrong with that?"

"Plenty, if you're treating the other two like crap." I wanted to shake her. I jerked my head at Miles. He still had a good grip; maybe he'd get the message. "I don't know why you're getting so wound up in this DNA bullshit. It doesn't make for a happier family, believe me. I can point you to thousands of couples who'd give everything they own to raise a child that didn't share their biology. So what's your problem?"

"*Ilda fra priladr neld!*" she growled.

Cole's voice rose, excited, in my ear. "Jaz, she's starting to curse you. Don't let her finish it."

I nodded. I could feel the stirrings of power as well.

"What did you just say?" I asked.

"*Echreada Ufran pilrat sritarnem, de aflor drmep sehike!*" she replied, almost smug, not realizing I had a translator listening in.

I grabbed the nearest handy piece of clothing, which happened to be Miles's baseball cap, and slapped her with it. The rudeness of my interruption clipped her curse short, shocking her into silence. But not for long.

"How dare you strike me?" she cried. "I am Ufran's chosen, the shaman of my people!"

"Tell me about that. How does a woman without a tail or a single spot of blue on her nose rise to the highest place of honor among her people?"

"Ufran spoke to me," she said simply. "He told me to return to the warren and take my rightful place. He said I deserved everything that had been denied me all the years my mother hid my identity and my deformity."

"Where were you when Ufran gave you this message?" I asked.

"Ruvin and I were in Scotland adopting Laal."

"And I suppose you traveled to Valencia, at Ufran's bidding, soon after?"

Her jaw dropped. "How did you know?"

I shook my head. "Did you arrange your own kidnapping?"

"How else was I supposed to get Ruvin's cooperation?"

"You're willing to sacrifice your husband for some insane scheme that's only going to get your people killed?"

"If that is what Ufran commands."

"Wow. You're a bigger dumbass than I thought."

The whole time we'd been talking, Cole had been making strange noises in my ear. Like he was holding back a bad cough. Now he lost it. Peals of laughter rocked my eardrums. I said, "Cole! What the hell?"

"Jaz! Look at Bergman!"

I raised my eyes. For a moment my lips sealed themselves and I feared Brude had retaken my brain. Then I realized the shock had simply paralyzed me for the seconds it took to process the fact that our genius consultant, the most practical, logical person I knew, had gotten a perm. And dyed his hair blond.

"Aw, shit, Miles."

Bergman's shoulders slumped. "Cole gets all the girls. I thought, you know." He grabbed one of his curls and tugged. "Maybe I could have just one."

"But he's never going to let any of us live this down."

"Damn straight!" Cole hooted. "I've got the luv-do. Next thing you know Vayl will be stepping into the beauty shop for a little Cole-over."

"See what I mean?"

Tabitha cleared her throat. "I like it."

Even Astral sounded extra interested as she purred, "Hello!"

Chapter Thirty-Two

While Miles smiled shyly at his new admirers, I shoved the Braves hat back on his head. "Get a grip, dude. Literally. Keep this murdering piece of trash waiting in the street until I call for you. And whatever you do, don't let her talk. Got it?"

He nodded.

"Astral's got your back. Don't hesitate to sic her on Tabitha if she gets out of line. I'm going back up." I shook my head at the idiocy of some people.

Cole's chuckles echoed through my head as I, once again, scaled Wirdilling's old water tower. "I'm gonna make up a song about the Cole-do," said my sniper, his ego ballooning so drastically I was surprised he didn't float right off the roof. "What do you think about this one, Jack? We'll rap it until we get some music down. *Wild man, wild hair, waving in the breeze, like a whip-crack, lip-smack, gimme some squeeze.*"

Despite the fact that I could hear Jack's enthusiastic *woo-woo* in the background, I snapped, "Keep your day job. In fact, tell me you're actually doing your day job."

"Chill, wouldja? I'm looking through my scope like I have been since I took position." Short pause. "C'mon. Admit you like my hair."

"I'd like it better if your head wasn't so full of—" I stopped, my hand on the platform. "I felt something," I whispered as it began to thrum. "Get ready."

I pulled myself up and took my original position just in time to see the sky car flying toward us from the direction of the trail.

"How did we beat them here?" Cole wondered.

"Vayl must've figured a way to slow them down," I replied. "Kyphas! You got that hat of yours moded out?"

"I am readier than you are!" she said.

Grimacing, I pulled Grief and prepped it to fire as we moved to the north side of the tower, Kyphas on the post office corner, me on the Crindertab's side. Now we could make out bodies, large and small, all of them moving inside the swaying vehicle. Vayl still rode the undercarriage, the outline of his body reminding me of a huge spider waiting to pounce.

"What are they doing here?" Tabitha screamed. "They're supposed to be at the Space Complex!"

She began to chant, more gnomish that I didn't understand and Cole didn't have time to interpret. But I could feel something stir inside the tower. "Shut her up, Bergman!"

"I'm trying! Ow! Stop biting me!"

"Watcha doing up there, mate?"

I took a second to glance down. A couple had strolled into the street. The girl I recognized as Polly, our waitress from Crindertab's. She held a baby-blue robe closed across her chest, like she didn't trust the belt to do the job. The guy she'd brought along wore a T-shirt, boxers, black socks, and ankle boots.

"We're practicing a scene from the movie!" I said. "You'll have to clear the street. We can't risk—"

"I told ya, Lymon!" Polly said excitedly. "Didn't I say we should keep an eye on these blokes? Never know when the cameras will roll. Do you need extras?" she asked.

"Incoming!" Cole yelled.

The tower began to shake hard enough that I had to brace myself against the wall. A crack appeared about ten feet above my head and worked its way to the top.

"Bloody hell!" I heard Lymon say. "Those are amazing effects!"

"Ow! Dammit!" Bergman yelled. "Jaz! Tabitha's going for my nads! Astral's chasing her own tail, and my mother taught me never to hit a girl!"

Fuck!

"Let her go, Miles!" I ordered. "And get those civilians under cover! Now!"

The crack widened. I realized the only original wood was the material we'd been able to touch. The rest was gnome grown. And because people never noticed what they passed every day, rarely even looked up, no one had realized.

I clicked on the safety and stowed Grief in its holster. "I'm going in!" I said. The crack was now the width of my shoulders. But even if I jumped I wouldn't be able to get a hand on the edge.

"Do you need a lift?" I'd run to Kyphas's side of the tower, where she stood tossing her boomerang up and down so casually you'd have thought we were about to have a distance-throwing competition.

"Yeah."

Giving me her I-know-more-than-you-do smile, she leaned over and cupped her hands. Which was when I hopped onto her shoulders and sprang onto the roof.

"Hey!" Her protest, backlit by Cole's chuckle, was quickly lost in the wave of sound that washed into the tower as the sky car arrived right after me.

Chapter Thirty-Three

My hands sank through a foot of plant material until they found a solid support. Knowing a two-by-four when I felt one, I grabbed hold and flipped the rest of my body around to join my hands inside the tower. My collarbone twanged as I asked it to contort more than it had since I'd broken it weeks before. But it held, giving my legs a chance to find the stud that angled up to meet the one I held. I worked my way to the floor of the tower just in time to look over and see Kyphas land on the balls of her feet beside me.

She grinned. "I'm better than you are."

"Go ahead," I told her, giving her Lucille's winning smile. "Keep thinking that." *It's just going to make kicking your ass that much more satisfying in the end.*

A frown marred her perfect brow as the sky car came to a rumbling halt inside the cube, its temporary door already growing closed as the passengers waited for the stairs to roll to their door. Except no grunts were running around the massive wooden hangar pushing trolleys full of suitcases or waving orange-tipped dildo lookalikes to direct everybody else where to go.

I watched the car sway above the floor's center, its cable glinting in the lights that had begun to glow the moment the roof shut.

They'd been strung like Christmas twinklers along the frame of the building proper. The planted sections of tower had their own set of support beams that had folded back to admit the car and then returned to center. I reminded myself to give Bergman a tour if we all survived this.

"Cole! We're going to need you here as soon as—" I whispered. I heard a pop. "What the hell?"

"Don't worry. Just a gum-bubble breaking. I'm on my way. Where should I leave Jack?"

"There will be no dumping of my dog. You figure out how to haul his ass up here or you don't come."

"Weakling," Kyphas sneered.

"Spinster."

She tossed her boomerang in the air and glared.

Vayl dropped to the floor, rolling to soften the impact. I saw fang flash as he ran, blending into the shadows even better than those of us who were standing perfectly still.

"I believe the Space Complex is safe for now," he said as he joined us. "But we must free Ruvin immediately. Johnson has begun to show signs of illness."

That meant the larvae could arrive at any time!

"How are we supposed to get to him? I don't see any stairs," I said. Before Vayl could suggest a plan, the gnomes began to climb out the sky car's door. Working with remarkable cooperation, holding on to one another from wrists to ankles, they formed a living ladder that reached the floor. Johnson and Tykes came next, stepping on heads and fingertips, occasionally slipping. The gnomes moaned as Tykes made his way down because his waist alone had more rolls than a school cafeteria. He fell the last five feet.

The two gnomes left in the sky car came to the door, holding a struggling Ruvin between them. It looked like they intended to drop him. Apparently larvae didn't care if the midwife's flesh was full of broken bones, only that it still lived.

"Go!" said Vayl just as a shirtless Cole burst through the plant roof carrying Jack next to his chest in a homemade, sleeve-fluttering sling.

Kyphas flung her boomerang toward Ruvin's guards. She hit the one on the right so hard that his nose imploded and blood sprayed out the door as if somebody had turned on a hose full of cherry Kool-Aid. I saw him stagger backward just as I slammed into the gnome ladder. The two nearest the bottom dropped to the floor.

I sprang up, grabbing the lowest hanging guard by his fancy pants and hoping he believed in belts as much as he felt that broken ankles should be discussed but never experienced. He wriggled and kicked, but didn't think of loosening his grip until I'd latched on to the next gnome in line.

Later Vayl confessed he was so concerned about me falling and breaking another bone that he nearly let Cole and Kyphas do the rest of the work. They did make a disturbingly fluid team. While Kyphas immobilized an Ufranite on the floor, Cole stripped off the shirt sling and let Jack run, giving himself full access to the Parker-Hale he'd packed on his back. His first shot took out the second sky car guard, but not before he'd given Ruvin a hard push.

Vayl sped forward to catch the seinji. Who was a dense little man. The impact sent them both through the tower's floor.

I began to pick gnomes off the ladder. Already breathing heavily from the exertion of climbing, holding, hanging, and fighting, they couldn't seem to function when I punched them in the diaphragm. One after another they dropped, falling prey either to their awkward landings, or Cole and Kyphas's attentions. Finally I was in.

I took a quick look around. Plush seats on either end. Poles in the middle with handholds on the sides. *Where the hell are the controls?* I felt along the smooth backrests and footkicks. Then

I tore the cushions off. Under the second one I found a set of indentations in the seat, beside which had been written words in a language I didn't understand. But above them, for the illiterate or slow-on-the-uptake, color pictures of the various destinations at which one might expect to arrive if she thumbed one of those hollows. I jammed my finger into the one next to a pristine white beach. The sky car lurched.

I looked out. Saw Kyphas grab Johnson by the collar and begin to whisper to him. He shook his head. She bit a gaping hole in his ear. He screamed, but his hands didn't go to the new wound. They were at his chest. Ripping his shirt open so he could watch his skin split.

"Kyphas!" I yelled. "Kill him now!"

She smiled, pretending not to hear as he fell to the floor, convulsing, blood staining his thighs and shoulders as the larvae began to emerge. A single loud shot. Cole, at least, had heard my order.

"Watch for larvae!" I called as a new section of roof began to retract and the sky car turned, performing an automatic cable change that hardly even made it sway. He nodded, saw one inching toward a downed guard and stomped. Jack had found another, taken a bite and pronounced it yummy. Holy crap, what kind of food would that mutt ever snub? While my dog ran around the room, snapping up snacks, I watched the distance between the sky car and the roof narrow. If I timed it just right I'd be able to jump back onto the tower supports. If not, I'd plummet to my death.

"Jaz!" Cole called.

I looked back. He cracked a stirring guard in the back of the head with the butt of his rifle. "What?"

"We're missing one!"

"Gnome?"

"No! Carrier! I think Tykes went out the hole in the floor!"

No big deal. Probably. I mean, Vayl had gone first with Ruvin. No doubt they had him surrounded.

"You going to be okay?" I asked, not looking back. It was almost time for my jump.

"As long as Jack doesn't puke right away I think we're good. Meetcha on the other side!"

I slid to the edge of the sky car's door. And jumped.

Chapter Thirty-Four

The sky car lurched just as I left it, throwing me sideways so that I hit the tower's maintenance platform rolling. I scrabbled for a hold, my fingernails digging in so deeply that splinters flew. But I was moving too fast to stop my spin. I fell over the side, reaching for any kind of hold that could slow my momentum. My hand punched into empty air, my fingers flailed. Then my forearm hit a support beam and I locked my elbow around it, grabbing my wrist with my opposite hand to complete the circle just in time to stop my descent.

"Jesus!" I screamed as the wood dug into my joint, making me wonder briefly if my muscles and tendons were going to rip free, forcing me to go hook hunting before my next mission. They held.

I dangled there for a second, my knees banging into the tower's supports, trying not to blubber from the pain and relief. Then I found a foothold and began a more controlled descent, wishing I had time to rub the sore spot. Or at least pout a little.

That's it, Pete, you and I are going to— I stopped. Pete had died. Murdered in his own office. And I would never get to mentally bitch-slap him again. I took a deep breath.

Later, I promise. I will cry for you until my lungs bleed. And after that I'll find your killer. That's another promise, my friend. But for now, surely you'd want me to do this.

I hoped so. But even if my late boss would've preferred me to fall into a useless heap of snot bubbles I'd have kept climbing. Because that was the only way I knew to survive.

Vayl and Ruvin weren't hanging out under the tower. Okay, then. Maybe my *sverhamin* was slamming Tykes into Crindertab's porch-side wall while Ruvin clapped his hands in delight. Which wouldn't last long once he heard about Tabitha.

Maybe we can get one of the Resistance gnomes to tell him.

I'd taken a couple of steps toward the restaurant when I heard the command.

"Stop where you are, Lucille." I turned toward Wirdilling Drive. Where Tabitha stood holding a little girl in her arms. It was Alice, the barefoot wonder from Crindertab's, looking sleepy and somewhat confused as she realized her mum was nowhere nearby. She began to struggle, but Tabitha had a firm grip. Behind her stood the last living carrier, Tykes, looking pale and nauseous. Kneeling before her—*aww no!*—Ruvin and Vayl.

"Do you see what I have done?" she exulted as I slowly walked toward her. "I have sent your leader to his knees. And all it took was the life of a little child." Her wrist moved slightly and I saw the steak knife she held, probably stolen from a drawer of the house from which she'd nabbed the girl while her mom and Lymon were distracted.

I should've told Bergman to kill her when he had the chance. Not that he'd have been capable. But then I wouldn't have this searing guilt.

"Not much can down a man of his caliber," Tabitha said, smirking down at Vayl. "But when I saw him talking with Laal and Pajo, I knew I'd found his vulnerability."

The rage that erupted inside my head actually surprised me. Oh, I'd felt levels of anger that would shrivel most souls. But this—it felt so big that I wouldn't have been shocked to find it billowing behind me like a giant storm cloud. That she'd dare to try such a move on any honorable man would've made me want to cut her throat. But that she had taken *my* man and tried to make him grovel, as if that proud head could ever be bowed. I ground my teeth and wished that I could burn her where she stood. Yeah, despite the consequences, I might have if she hadn't been holding a tearful toddler.

I looked at the little girl. And felt something I hadn't in Crindertab's, when I'd been distracted by karaoke and greasy fries. A small stirring from a tiny body that had, I'd wager, already died once in this life. I stopped by the side of the road. And smiled.

"You're going to be all right," I told little Alice. "When this is all over Cole and I will take you up to the mountains, where it's cold and snowy. If you're like us, which I'm sure you are, you won't even get chilled."

I dropped my eyes to Vayl's. As soon as his flashed from black to red, I knew he understood. I felt his power snap, eager to roar out of him. But there was still Ruvin to consider. The seinji knelt, blank-faced, brokenhearted, shaking his head every few seconds as wave after wave of truth crashed over him. So even if Tabitha's hostage was a Sensitive, which would give her near immunity to Vayl's attacks, Ruvin might not survive the blizzard my *sverhamin* wanted to bury his wife in. We'd have to make this one surgical.

Tykes began to convulse. "Wha—what's happening?" he asked.

"You're about to die," I told him. "Slowly. Painfully. It's going to be a closed-casket funeral."

He shook his head as Tabitha kicked Ruvin in the back. "Get up!" she said. "As soon as the larvae have begun feasting on you I'll carry them to the Space Complex myself."

"How're you going to do that?" I asked. "It's a long walk from here and your sky car's on its way to a clambake."

"I'm not just proficient at stealing babies," Tabitha said, shaking Alice in her arms. She jerked her head backward, directing my attention to an old pickup truck so covered with dust it looked more pink than red. She'd parked it in the alley between the doctor's office and the hardware store, so all I could see was the tailgate and the dented chrome where she'd cornered too fast and slid into the side of the building.

Tykes screamed as the skin of his face began to bulge.

I raised an eyebrow at Vayl. He lifted his chin. As we poised to attack, a voice behind Tabitha said, "Hello."

Astral came trotting around her feet to stand at mine.

Alice squealed, "Kitty!" and reached down for her, dropping her weight so fast that Tabitha couldn't keep her balanced. She clutched at the single leg that remained in her grasp while dropping the blade to prevent an accidental stabbing.

Vayl whirled, grasping Tabitha's knife hand so quickly that his movements blurred. We heard a crack. A scream. And then Vayl was on her. And not even Ufran could stop the forces he speared through her body.

"Ruvin! Run!" I yelled, lunging for the kid just as Astral roared—like the MGM lion! Ruvin started, fell, scrabbled toward the road's shoulder.

Alice didn't even squeak as I pulled her out of Tabitha's stiffening arms, she was so busy giggling at the funny kitty. Who'd crouched in the road, her tail lashing the asphalt like she meant to spring on her prey at any moment. I didn't know what she thought she could do to Tykes, who was flat on his back, bleeding so heavily his clothes looked more like field bandages than office attire. But she looked serious.

I gave the kid to Ruvin. "Get her away," I told him. "Don't let her see. Anything." He nodded and hustled her into the shadows.

"Miles," I snapped. "Can you hear me?"

"Yeah."

"Tell Polly and Lymon their kid's okay and we'll bring her in a minute."

"Uh-oh. Polly just went to check on her—" Blood-curdling scream. Polly hadn't been kidding about the lung capacity. She could do the victim in a slasher movie any day. "I'll tell them."

"And stay away, dude. The larvae are hatching and I don't want them to catch your scent."

"Jaz!" It was Cole. "What do you need?"

"For you and Kyphas to control those Ufranites until we figure this out!" I replied.

Vayl rose, dropping Tabitha to the road, a blank-eyed shaman-doll whose icy blue skin had finally given her nose the hue she'd always wanted. She wasn't dead. No, not quite. We couldn't afford to make a martyr of her. But she was going to take a while to thaw.

"Anything?" I asked him. He had a nifty way of absconding with others' powers. So I was hoping . . .

He shook his head. "She possesses nothing innate. It is all contained within the feathers and leathers she wears. She simply acts as a conduit."

I drew Grief and walked up to Tykes. His face, stretched in a silent scream of pain, might've been covered in tears. But you couldn't see them for the blood.

"No larvae yet," I said.

Vayl came to stand beside me. "They do say every birth is different."

Tykes moaned. "Kill me. Please."

So easy to pull the trigger. Usually they're begging me not to. I'd like to say it's a little harder then. But . . . no. Maybe I'm like an alcoholic who knows she's offing brain cells but doesn't care because she can't see them dying. Only mine are in my soul. Hey, as long as I avoid any sort of introspection for the next sixty years, I should be fine.

"I'll be happy to," I told Tykes. "But first how about you tell me what the bad guys really want? How do we stop this from happening again?"

"I don't know, okay? My boss just told—" The sound choked off as Tykes's neck began to bulge.

I said, "Vayl? I don't think this dude's all that fat after all. I think—" The upper half of his body exploded with a sound that I'll never forget. Skin ripping. Bones cracking. Joints popping. Blood gushing out in a larval-clogged spray.

I closed my eyes in time, but it doesn't do much good when your face is dripping with gore, and dozens of man-eaters the size of garden slugs are chomping their way into your brain stem.

"Jasmine!"

I couldn't reply. Didn't dare open my mouth in case one of them slid in.

Don't panic! Don't panic!

I dropped Grief and grabbed at my nose, the stings on my upper lip telling me they had my airway nearly covered. I ripped a handful away and took a deep breath. I wanted to scream. *God!* Cry. Stamp my feet and hyperventilate. But if I let go, even just a little bit, I'd die. Eaten alive by infant gnomes.

I felt Vayl's hands on me. Tearing larvae and skin. Pulling out hair along with the nasties. He yanked off my shirt and I moaned. So many of them feeding at my legs and belly. But more trying to get at my neck, my ears, and I only had two hands.

Vayl came at me again, and then I felt warm liquid. What? Didn't know. Didn't care. Where it hit the larvae dropped. And it left behind a soothing tingle. I finally cleared my eyes. Yeah, my face was okay. I felt my head, my neck. All good.

I risked a look at Vayl. He'd stepped back. Okay, so he hadn't miraculously discovered that Crindertab's coffee killed gnome larvae. What—I looked down. At Astral. Who was spraying me. Out of her butt. Like a tomcat.

At her paws lay the larvae, twitching.

"What?" croaked Tabitha.

I kept running my fingers through my hair, over every part of my body. I didn't feel anything. Could I really be free?

"Bergman? Why didn't you tell me you'd invented a larval spray for Astral to carry? It's knocked them out!"

Cole piped up. "I can see them through my scope," he said. "I think they're stoned!"

"How did she pass the spray?" Bergman asked.

"Ass projectile!" Cole hooted. "Took those larvae down like beer on slugs!"

"But it's not nearly that potent!" Bergman insisted. "Just a mist that's supposed to neutralize her scent in case the target has dogs!"

"What's in it?"

"A few chemicals I'd rather not talk about. The base is salt water."

Tabitha's screech didn't last long, but it came straight from the heart.

Chapter Thirty-Five

Vayl and I raised Tabitha upright. She tottered slightly, but finally stood in place, like a life-sized collectible with a steel rod shoved up her back to make sure she didn't slouch to one side and ruin her pretty costume. At her feet lay Tykes's remains, his torso a mass of blood and pulp, made even more obscene by the perfect intactness of both his legs, encased in tightly creased gray trousers lightly spattered with red. They reminded me of the wooden figures old towns set up to commemorate historic events. Except they usually keep their mannequins out of the streets.

I leaned in, holding the tails of the shirt Vayl had lent me back so they wouldn't touch her and somehow become contaminated. "How come you're so ticked about the salt water, shammy?"

She was so angry her hair shook as she said, "That's what the nursemaids cocoon the larvae in, you interfering piece of shit!"

"Tut-tut. We can't have the leader of a major religious movement like yours swearing in public, now, can we?" I asked.

Vayl said, "So are you saying the salt water triggered the larvae into beginning their next developmental phase?"

Tabitha sneered at me. "You like your lovers dumb, don't you?"

No thought. Just a windup followed by one hellacious slap that snapped her head sideways. I said, "He's too much of a gentleman to seek revenge for what you tried to do to him before. But I was raised by a woman who's now doing time—in hell. I suggest you remember that before you insult him again."

Cole hissed, "Heads up! The Ufranites are coming!"

"Cassandra brought our reinforcements?" I asked.

"If you count the whole warren."

"No kidding?"

"I'm watching them through my scope. Cassandra's riding on a cushioned stool in the middle of the crowd. I'm not sure what that means, but considering all the adoring looks she's getting, we may have to buy her a tiara for Christmas."

Vayl adjusted Tabitha's stance so her back was fully turned to the oncoming crowd. They came quietly, their approach made all the more threatening by the total absence of background murmur that let us know they'd come with an agenda.

He waited until they could overhear our conversation. Then he said loudly, "Go ahead, Lucille. I will allow you to execute Tabitha since her larvae nearly killed you just now."

I retrieved Grief. Made sure the shaman watched me chamber a round before I said, "You got any last words? Or are you okay with going down in history as the cult leader who was willing to sacrifice her flock's children so Ufran could run around in his boxers all day?"

Tabitha laughed. "You believed that nonsense? You're as much a patsy as the rest of those bow-legged cretins."

I said, "You mean you didn't want to kill off the kiddies?"

"Of course! That was the point! When Ufran spoke to me, he told me what I needed to do in order to have my own child. He said that I should sacrifice the gnomes' children, an entire hatching. And he told me how. The longer the plan evolved the more beautiful it became. First it was just Australia's bunch that would tear into Canberra Deep Space Complex's connections. Then I convinced the Ufranites in Madrid and California to join in. But the closer the time came, the more jittery they got. Only my partnership with the werewolves, and their generous donations to each church involved, have kept our plans on track."

"What about your people? Don't you think some of them will want your head on a platter when they learn how you've betrayed them?"

"Why would they? I've earned them enough money to buy new sun generators for the entire colony. They'll be able to grow crops without worry for the next twenty years."

"And all it took was the death of everyone's larvae." Okay, they weren't all dead. But I was going for dramatic effect, okay?

"Who cares? I am the shaman! And now I'll have a child of my own."

"I don't think so."

She'd recovered enough by now to nod. Even her skin had pinked up. "Ufran promised me!"

"That's just it. He didn't."

She laughed. And stopped when she saw neither of us were joining in.

I went on, "The guy you saw was a Domytr named King Brude. He was just posing as a god to get you to do his dirty work."

Denial in those darting eyes. The lips, however, trembled slightly as she said, "I don't believe you."

"He has a tattoo on his stomach shaped like a scythe. There's one on his left shoulder that reminds me of a sea turtle and a lawn chair doing the horizontal mambo."

"H-how did you know?"

"Like I said, Tabitha, you don't talk to gods."

"But I do," said Cassandra. The Ufranites had lowered her to the ground. She stood among them, wearing a heavy, shapeless robe and a green woven hat that added at least eight inches to her height. Still she managed to look like a beauty queen. How fair is that?

Vayl spun Tabitha around, and when she saw Cassandra standing safe among all her followers I heard her gag.

"As I was leaving the shaman's quarters, I laid my hand on the traditional headdress. And Ufran came to me," Cassandra said softly. The light in her eyes was new. Otherworldly. "He had tried to speak to me before, but I have not acted as an oracle in so long that I missed his message the first time."

"How could that be?" snapped Tabitha. "He always spoke loud and clear to me."

"You were talking to Lucifer's bounty hunter," I told her.

Cassandra nodded. "Ufran speaks in a gentle, quiet voice. Because he is not a god who would want his people to sacrifice their young for any reason."

"Yeah!" came the roar from the crowd.

"Nor does he want them entering life having cannibalized another creature. Dead flesh works just as effectively for them and is much more humane." Cassandra threw a package of hamburger into the street. The nearest larvae wriggled slowly toward it. As soon as they encountered plastic they burrowed right through and into the meat.

"I would beware of who I agree to partner with as well," Vayl said. "The Valencian Weres may talk respectfully, but their loyalties lie completely with their Sol and his pack."

Loud murmurs of agreement from the Ufranites. But underneath, a new sound. One so faint I would've missed it if I hadn't been standing almost on top of it. I looked down. Tykes's trousers had ripped at the seams. Because his legs had doubled in size.

"Vayl! Cassandra! Run!" I blew outta there so fast I'd reached Tabitha's getaway truck and jumped into the bed before I heard the fleshy splat of exploding tissue. Even from my vantage point I could see blood and larvae fly into the air.

And then Tabitha began to scream.

Chapter Thirty-Six

I stood in the rental house shower, technically goop-free as of five minutes ago but still feeling polluted. Brude. Even if we were able to find the Rocenz and scrape him outta my brain, would I ever consider myself clean again?

Plus, we'd heard from Martha. Only our mission had succeeded. NASA had taken hard knocks in California and Madrid, from which it wouldn't soon recover. So Roldan's stock had just doubled, making the Valencian Weres the newest, worst threat to national security. Bad news for the good guys. Especially considering Cassandra's vision. More than ever before I worried for the safety of my team. In light of Pete and Ethan's deaths, I'd pleaded with them all to go home. Let Vayl and I tackle the next leg of this quest alone, especially since it wouldn't be an Agency-sanctioned mission. Only Cassandra had agreed to fly back to the States, and I still thought the main reason was because Dave had called to let her know he was about to come home for a couple of months. At least she was taking Jack along. Now I wouldn't have to worry about him becoming possessed too.

A knock at the door. "Occupied!" It opened anyway. "What the hell?"

Vayl said, "I have sent the others into Canberra to secure

transportation for us to Sydney and, from there, to Marrakesh. They will be, how do you say, crashing at a hotel in the city afterward."

I leaned against the wall. So tired. What was that saying? Yeah, I guess I could sleep when I was dead. "Okay. Wait, you sent what others?" I strained to hear. Was that a coat dropping to the floor?

"All of them."

"It takes four people to book plane tickets?"

"No. But it takes one person to watch Cole and another to monitor Kyphas; therefore, I sent the lot."

Yup, that sounded like a belt buckle. "Where's Jack?"

"In the backyard."

"And Astral?"

"Locked in Bergman's room with orders not to slide beneath the crack."

"Wow. You got rid of everybody."

I tried to ignore the Inner Bimbo, who was chuckling and noting that elimination was kinda his job. The librarian was also waving for my attention. She wanted to tidy up the piles of unshelved experiences. Tabitha's demise. Ruvin's quiet exit. Cassandra's Ufran-trance, during which she chose the new shaman. The call we'd made to Martha after. The tears we'd shed for Pete before agreeing to lay low until she could set up new deep cover offices. We hadn't told her about the plan to find the Rocenz, or that we'd need to travel to Morocco to do it. Just let her know we'd do our best to be back for the funeral. But I wanted to leave all of that until the hot water ran cold. I figured I had ten minutes left. That was all I wanted. Ten minutes of—

"May I join you?" Silky request that sounded more like an invitation from the other side of the shower curtain.

"Yeah."

I just stared at him for a while after he'd stepped into the tub.

Already he'd taught me the pleasure of patience. Anticipation. I watched the water droplets trickle down his shoulders, nestle in the hair of his chest, emphasize the muscles of his thighs.

"You look amazing. If I were an artist, I would totally paint you."

The sides of his lips quirked. "Perhaps I should purchase you a set of brushes."

"But I can't—"

"Ahhh, surely you could think of other uses for them?"

He pulled me into his arms, his hands, his skin warm against mine, his lips and tongue all working to remind me that crap was always lying around in a steaming pile. But I could sidestep it if I wanted. Get wet and soapy with a gorgeous vampire and remind myself why life could be good. If I decided it should be.

Acknowledgments

Gotta thank the hubby and kids, you know? Not because they'll give me the silent treatment if I don't (they're talkers, the lot of them), but because they are the coolest people on earth. I can say that. I know them best.

Deep appreciation to Christina Tanuadji of Temptation the Romance bookstore in Perth, Western Australia, and April Barton, also of Australia. Both ladies helped me immensely with details of scenery and language that, I think, helped make *Bite Marks* a much better story. Bethan David, ranger at Tidbinbilla Nature Reserve, and Jean-Pierre Issaverdis, manager, Marketing and Business, at Tidbinbilla, also provided vital information regarding the behavior of kangaroos and the lay of the land for part of the book's climactic scene. Thank you both so much for your help!

My groovy agent, Laurie McLean, deserves a round of applause (wahoo!) as do my editor, Devi Pillai, and the rest of my übercool Orbit team: Alex Lencicki, Katherine Molina, Jennifer Flax, and Penina Lopez. (I'd thank Tim Holman too, but since he's technically my boss it seems a little too much like kissing up. Can I just say that he may seem like a mild-mannered Brit by day, but I've heard that by night he transforms into a crime-fighting superhero? Rumor also has it that he can fly. I'm just saying.) Special thanks, as well, to Orbit's genius art department for cranking out the go-jus covers! If you liked this one, just wait until you see what's coming next! And thanks also to my manuscript readers, Katie Rardin and Hope Dennis—you ladies rock!

Canberra Deep Space Communication Complex does exist, and to the sci-types who work there . . . I hope you're not offended that I suggested you don't have a marvelously intricate alarm system set up to counter an attack by fanatical gnomes. That would just be silly.

And no, I haven't forgotten you, my reader. Of course I'm glad you're here! So, yeah, thanks for hanging out with me and Jaz.

extras

orbit

meet the author

Cindy Pringle

JENNIFER RARDIN began writing at the age of twelve, mostly poems to amuse her classmates and short stories featuring her best friends as the heroines. She lives in an old farmhouse in Illinois with her husband and two children. Find out more about Jennifer Rardin at www.JenniferRardin.com.

introducing

If you enjoyed **BITE MARKS,**
look out for

BITTEN IN TWO

Book 7 of the Jaz Parks series

by Jennifer Rardin

Holy crap, do you smell that?" I asked. I leaned away from the square, sun-bleached building and spat, but the creeping stench of death and rot had already made it down my throat.

Cole didn't answer, just nodded and pulled the collar of his new gray T-shirt up over his nose. Vayl and I had presented it to him as we'd waited to board the endless flight from Australia to Morocco. He'd worn it over a fresh white tee every day since, making this the third night in a row I'd read the sharp red letters on the front that said, THE OTHER GUY GOT THE GIRL. On the back, a black widow perched on her web with her mate's leg dangling out of her mouth while her rejected lover observed it all from under a striped beach umbrella as he sipped a fly-tai. The caption read: DAMN, THAT WAS CLOSE!

"Promise me you'll wash that tomorrow," I whispered as I peered down the narrow cobblestone street. Nothing moved to stir the layer of grime on the windowsills of the red ochre buildings that lined it, their adjoining walls melding like coffin lids. Every door remained shut, locking poverty and misery inside, but each displayed its own unique inlaid design that shoved even this neglected neighborhood into the category of Ancient Beauty. I had bigger distractions than the work of long-dead artisans, however. *Where'd you sneak off to, asshole?*

"Washing seems like a waste of time," Cole mumbled, his voice muffled by one hundred percent cotton. "I'm just going to wear it again because, you know, it's only the best shirt ever. I'm not saying you look like a spider, but if you were to cannibalize Vayl, I'm pretty sure that's exactly the picture the tabloids would end up printing."

"Holy crap, Cole, just throw some suds on the thing!" To soften the blow I added, "Make it my birthday present."

"Tomorrow's your birthday?"

"Nope."

"Tonight?"

I nodded. *And here I stand under the rickety metal awning of a building so old I can practically hear the ghosts screaming from behind these stucco walls. I should be lolling on some beach with my half-naked lover—make him all naked; I don't have time to waste on foreplay. But no. I'm stalking a vampire through the back alleys of freaking Marrakesh, sniffing what has to be the city's cesspool, with a guy who has apparently invested in a company that only sells red high-tops.*

Moving quicker than I'd have given him credit for, Cole pulled me in for a hug that made me glad I'd left Grief back at the riad. Otherwise I'd have spent the rest of the night running around with the imprint of my modified Walther PPK outlined on my left boob.

"Happy birthday!" he said. "You're twenty-six on May twenty-sixth. How cool is that? Especially since I didn't miss it. I thought it was earlier this month."

"Why?"

"That's what your file—uh, I mean—"

"You read my file?" I balled his shirt into my fist, forcing his collar past his nose to reveal his gaping mouth. The scent of cherry-flavored bubble gum wafted past, giving my churning stomach a break. Then it was gone and my nose hairs recurled.

"Vayl read it too," Cole reminded me.

"That doesn't make it okay!"

Cole plucked his shirt out of my hand and repositioned it as he asked, "Why don't you want anyone to know the real date you were born?"

"Because I hate surprise parties. And I'm not interested in shar-ing my best secrets with snoops like you." I tapped the thin plas-tic receiver sitting inside my ear, just above the lobe, activating my connection to: "Bergman? He's slipped our tail. Have you got a read on him?"

"Gimme a sec, someone's at the door."

Our technical consultant's clear reply confirmed my suspi-cion that we were still within two miles of him and the Riad Almoravid, where we'd set up temporary headquarters. We'd only left the town square, which locals called the Djemaa el Fna, twenty minutes before. And since the fountain in our riad's courtyard could probably shoot a few sprinkles onto the square's crowds of merchants, performers, and shoppers on a windy day, I'd figured we were within the limits of Bergman's communica-tions gizmo, which Cole had named the party line. Nice to be right about that, at least.

Now, instead of using his own transmitter, Cole leaned forward and spoke into the glamorous brown mole I'd stuck just to the left of my upper lip. "Bergman, today is Jaz's birthday. We need cake!"

"Ignore him, Miles. Just find—" I stopped when the swearing began.

Cole nodded wisely. "See what happens when people hang around you? Poor Miles probably didn't even know what those words meant before you lived with him."

"Nobody should be blamed for the language they teach their roommates in college."

"Your potty-mouth is gonna get you in trouble someday." Cole turned his head, like Bergman was skulking in the shadows next to us. "Right dude?"

Bergman growled, "Goddammit, that girl's back! I thought maids only worked in the morning!" We heard the door open. "I have plenty of towels—"

"Hello, Mr. Bergman, sir." It was the chirpy voice of the riad's go-to gal, who'd barely conquered her teens, but oozed the confidence of a woman twice her age. Though Riad Almoravid belonged to a Frenchman named Franck Landry, our girl did it all, from laundry to breakfast. She said, "I finished the book you loaned me. May I borrow another?"

"I'm kind of busy here, Shada. Besides, shouldn't you be home by now? Your family—"

"My father is happy that I have made many American friends. He likes me to learn new things. What is all that electronics about?" Though Shada had the long dark hair and natural beauty of a native Moroccan, she spoke with a British accent, which made me wonder where she'd gone to school. If I knew, I'd call up the headmaster and let him know that her English teacher had aced second language instruction, but the curriculum hadn't taught Shada crap about minding her own business.

"We're doing a study on climate change," Bergman muttered. "Stay right here. I'll go get the book."

Shada called after him, "Should you not be at one of the poles? I read that much information can be gleaned from the ice—"

"Climate's everywhere," Bergman replied irritably. "Plus we're close to the Western Sahara. What better place to monitor heat increases than a desert?" For once Shada had no answer. Bergman said, "Here's another book I bought for the plane trip over here. Now if you'll excuse me, I have work—"

"Did you read it? Shall we discuss it when I am finished?"

"I read them all. It was a long flight."

"Oh, wonderful!" I heard the patter of clapping hands. "I would like to ask you about the story I just finished, okay? I have many questions, such as why any sane man would believe that a bear could talk—"

"Okay, we'll do that. But later. Because I have to work now. The weather waits for no one."

"All right then, I will see you tomorrow!" I barely heard the last bit, because it came after the door had clicked shut.

"What a pain in the ass," Bergman muttered. "She's like a helpful infection. You want to get rid of her, but she's so *nice*. I'll bet her face hurts at the end of the day from smiling so much."

"Do you want me to take care of her for you?" asked Cole.

"No!" Realizing he'd jumped in too fast and way too loud, Bergman added quickly, "Have you seen her brother meet her for the walk home? He's bigger than a dump truck. Make a move on her and he'll crush you like an old metal garbage can."

"Sounds like you've thought this through," said Cole, grinning at me as he drew a heart in the air with his forefingers.

"Uh," Bergman cleared his throat. . . . "Don't we have more important things to worry about?"

I sighed. "Muchly, so get busy, will ya?"

I imagined him checking his satellite maps and hacked surveillance video, not to mention the tracker he'd attached to our target's right boot heel. While we waited for his pronouncement, Cole reached behind his back and pulled a tranquilizer gun out from under the light jacket he wore. It was a lean, black weapon that blended so perfectly with his jeans that it disappeared when he dropped his hands to his sides.

"That looks . . . lethal." *Could be, too, if we got the dosage wrong. Which we didn't, because I double-checked it myself. Maybe we won't need it, though. Maybe he'll cooperate.* I cleared my throat. "Was it stuck in your belt?" I asked.

"Yeah. But don't worry, the safety was on." He lifted the barrel slightly. "Hey, imagine what would've happened if I'd shot myself in the butt. My cheeks would've been numb for a week!"

I took off down the sidewalk. I kept to the shadows, avoiding puddles of brown liquid that I knew weren't water because according to Franck Landry, who'd been ecstatic to rent all five of his riad's rooms to us, it hadn't rained in the past two weeks.

Cole jogged after me. "Jaz, where are you going? We don't even know—"

"I'd rather walk aimlessly than discuss your ass, all right?"

"Yeah, but this isn't just my ass. This is my *numb* ass. Do you think my legs would stop working too?"

I was getting ready to grab the gun and perform an experiment that would satisfy both his curiosity and my irritation when Bergman said, "Got him. Two blocks northeast of you. He's not moving."

We turned the corner, moving so quickly we nearly plowed into two men who'd just exited a diamond-painted door. Just before it closed I saw a lantern hanging above a mirror at the end of a tiled hall with four arches along its length leading off into darkness. Cole mumbled an apology in French and pulled me around the men, who wore light shirts, long pants, and baseball hats, all of which were blotched with mustard-colored stains. And damn, did they stink! They must work at the dump we'd been smelling.

One of the men, a black-mustached thirtysomething with a scar under his left eye, spoke to Cole, who replied sharply, his hand tightening on my arm. Already I was used to natives offering to guide us anywhere we wanted to go, but these guys didn't have the look of dirham-hungry street hustlers. I looked up at Cole. His face had gone blank, a bad sign in a guy who assassinates his country's enemies for a living.

The .38 strapped to my right leg weighed a little heavier, as did the knife in my pocket, reminding me of my offensive options. But I didn't want to spill blood knowing a vamp was prowling nearby. "What do they want?" I asked.

"The dude with the scar is demanding a toll for the use of his road, and extra payment for nearly running him and his friend over."

"What's his name?"

Cole asked, and while the man replied I checked out his companion. He was maybe fifteen, a brown-eyed boy with lashes so long they looked fake. He couldn't even meet my eyes.

Cole said, "His name is Yousef. The kid's name is Kamal."

"Tell Yousef I'll pay."

"What?"

"Tell him."

Cole began to talk. I swished forward, making sure my skirt swirled around my knees as I moved. I looked up at Yousef like he was the cutest teddy bear I'd ever hoped to squeeze. Even though he couldn't understand the words, I figured he'd get the tone as I reached down the V-neck of my dress with my left hand and said, "Just gimme a second, okay? I keep my money in here so I don't have to worry about pickpockets. I understand they can be something of a problem in Marrakesh. Am I right?"

By now I'd come within an arm's length of the reeking man, who was staring at my hand like he wished it were his. He never saw the base of my right palm shoot up. Just grunted with shock as it jammed into his jaw and knocked his head backward. He staggered. Cole aimed the tranq gun at Kamal to make sure he stayed peaceful as I followed Yousef down the sidewalk, throwing a side kick that landed on his chest with the thump of a bongo drum. He landed flat on his back in the street.

I watched him struggle to breathe as I said, "We go where we please, you son of a bitch."

Cole translated. To my surprise Yousef smiled. I looked over my shoulder at Kamal. He was staring around nervously, making me think he didn't savor a conversation with any authorities that might show up to investigate the noise. But he didn't seem worried about Yousef. Maybe girls hit him a lot.

"Feel better?" Cole asked me.

I backed off Yousef before the bully's blech could stick. "Yeah. Let's go."

We headed down the street, keeping our eyes and Cole's gun on the little gang until we reached the end of the block and turned north. Yousef called after us.

"Unbelievable," said Cole as he shook his head.

"What did he say?" I asked.

"He wants to know if he can see you again. He says his uncle's friend owns a good restaurant above the Djemaa el Fna."

"You're shitting me."

"No." Cole's wild blond hair danced at the suggestion. "I think he liked what you did to him. In fact, I think he liked you."